J.D. Pennington

THE OTHELLO CLUB

DATURA

*"But jealous souls will not be answered so.
They are not ever jealous for the cause,
But jealous for they're jealous. It is a monster
begot upon itself, born on itself."*
— WILLIAM SHAKESPEARE, *OTHELLO*

DATURA BOOKS
An imprint of Watkins Media Ltd

Unit 11, Shepperton House
89-93 Shepperton Road
London N1 3DF
UK

daturabooks.com
Strangers in a divorce support group

A Datura Books paperback original, 2025

Copyright © J.D. Pennington 2025

Edited by Dan Hanks and Dan Coxon
Cover by Sarah O'Flaherty
Set in Meridien

All rights reserved. J.D. Pennington asserts the moral right to be identified as the author of this work. A catalogue record for this book is available from the British Library.

This novel is entirely a work of fiction. Names, characters, places, and incidents are the products of the author's imagination or are used fictitiously. Any resemblance to actual events, locales, organizations or persons, living or dead, is entirely coincidental.

Sales of this book without a front cover may be unauthorized. If this book is coverless, it may have been reported to the publisher as "unsold and destroyed" and neither the author nor the publisher may have received payment for it.

Datura Books and the Datura Books icon are registered trademarks of Watkins Media Ltd.

ISBN 978 1 91741 512 5
Ebook ISBN 978 1 91741 513 2

Printed and bound in the United Kingdom by CPI Group (UK) Ltd, Croydon CR0 4YY

The manufacturer's authorised representative in the EU for product safety is eucomply OÜ – Pärnu mnt 139b-14, 11317 Tallinn, Estonia, hello@eucompliancepartner.com; www.eucompliancepartner.com

9 8 7 6 5 4 3 2 1

For Mum and Dad. Miss you Dad.

Not forgetting Louise, obviously! My map, my compass, and my North Star.

1

EMILY
2 May

Nobody was supposed to get hurt. She drew a line. No violence. They all swore agreement. But one of them has broken their covenant and redrawn that line in blood.

Emily perches on a leather armchair, one of six arranged in a ritualistic circle, attempting to recalibrate her spiralling thoughts. Dulled to the drone of Malcolm, their group therapist, she studies the faces of her five accomplices. For signs of culpability, or contrition, but realising with terrifying lucidity how little she knows about them. If divorce taught her anything, it's that you can't trust anyone. Even the people you love. Especially the people you love. Let alone perfect strangers like these.

Fear billows through her, carrying with it a fresh wave of nausea. She fights the urge to vomit. Or rather, dry heave, the contents of her stomach already disgorged following the shock of that heinous news headline. After scouring the details online, Emily swore never to return to this toxic cabal. Every instinct screaming to take flight. To call the police and end this aberrant madness. Yet here she is, compelled to uncover the malefactor among them. The only thing she is sure of is that one of them is guilty of this atrocity.

Or, it occurs to Emily, perhaps they all are.

2
ROSA
25 May

"Love is brutal…" I crane forward, resting my elbows on the interview table. "Believe me, I know. In fifteen years as a detective, I've witnessed every act of cruelty possible. But nothing compares to the savagery of crimes committed in the name of love. Especially when its pathology turns to hate."

I select one of the crime scene photographs fanned across the table and dangle it in the suspect's face like a macabre tarot reading. Her emerald gaze remains fixed on mine. Emily Hunter is a girlish thirty-three. At five foot eleven, she looms over me by four inches. She could have just breezed off a catwalk, save for her broad swimmer's shoulders.

"Why won't you look at the photographs, Emily?" I keep my tone agreeable, to relax the suspect, and reveal more pretext.

"Why do you think?" Cool as Kasparov, Emily exposes none.

"Guilt?"

"Not in the way you're implying, Inspector. I am not responsible for that."

"Who do you think is responsible, Emily?" DS Sean Nicholls breaks the spell.

I'd almost forgotten my balding colleague was there. If

not for the smell of cedar wood oil from his moustache, perched above his mollifying smile.

Emily turns her tractor-beam on him. "I've told you everything I know, Detective Nicholls."

Unlike the suspect, I can read Nicholls like a trashy airport novel. He's like a mesmerised teenager interviewing a starlet for the school newsletter.

"Need I remind you, innocent people are dead, Emily, brutally murdered."

Emily's jaw muscles tighten. A signifier of anger. Triggered by something I said. *Brutally murdered*? No, *innocent* was the inciting word.

"You don't consider them innocent, do you, Emily?"

"Are any of us?"

"You think they got what they deserved, don't you, Emily?"

"Of course not."

"How did it make you feel when they got what was coming to them?"

"Are you a detective or psychiatrist?"

"A good detective is a little of both."

"You know what they say about a Jack of all trades?"

I mask my vexation with a smile. From her background check, I know Emily is a fellow psychology graduate, receiving a first from Cambridge. As opposed to my two-one from the University of London. For the first time in a long while, I feel outclassed.

"We don't have time to play games, Miss Hunter." I abandon the first-name familiarity, prodding a percussive finger at the lurid photographs. "You won't look at the evidence, Emily, because you are responsible."

Emily's harlequin eyes dart from the grotesque images,

betraying the first glimmer of emotion. "I had nothing to do with that."

"So you say, Emily." I lean closer, scenting blood. "But even according to your questionable version of events, you still share the burden of responsibility."

"Nobody was supposed to get hurt." A fissure creeps into Emily's voice.

"Yet they did, didn't they, Emily. And I'd say 'hurt' is an incredibly benign way of describing murder." I can feel the balance of power restoring.

Emily steers her gaze to the bloody gallery, her lithe shoulders quivering beneath the police station paper jumpsuit.

"Why don't you tell us what really happened, Emily?"

Emily traps a sob with her hand. "It all just... spun out of control."

"When did it spin out of control, Emily?"

A tear glides down Emily's sharp cheekbone, falling onto the glossy print of a charred corpse stretched on a steel dissection table. Burnt beyond recognition of sex, or age, it stares back at her from scorched eye sockets, ivory teeth glinting from a gaping rictus trapped in a silent scream.

Emily takes a breath, summoning the words. "Where do I begin?"

3

EMILY
Eighteen months earlier

Emily thrust a wad of notes at the cab driver and stumbled into the dingy streetlight, staggering up the steps to the Chelsea maisonette. Deafened to the driver's protests of overpayment, she prodded the doorbell so hard her nail snapped. Another detail lost to her emotional oblivion. Like the sweatpants and T-shirt she threw on in her stupor, her heedlessness of the subzero temperature, or that it was past midnight. Time had no meaning anymore, nor gravity, or love, or loyalty, or trust, or any concept Emily valued. All that mattered was seeing the only person who could mitigate her misery. Her best friend and business partner, Charlotte.

The light snapped on inside, before a voice at the intercom crackled, "Who is it?"

Emily recognised the voice of Bryony, Charlotte's younger sister. "It's Emily." She shivered in the muted pause, the cold hitting her. "Bryony, open the fucking door." The door buzzed open, and Emily barged inside the communal hallway.

"Emily?" Bryony's porcine face peered over the chrome banister at the top of the stairs, mumbling about it being late as Emily charged up the staircase. "Emily, is something wrong?"

Emily scoffed at the understatement. "I've had better nights." She lumbered past Charlotte's sister, guarding the apartment doorway, into the open-plan maisonette. "Where's Lottie?"

"Upstairs, asleep. I'll get her." Bryony tightened her robe around her ample girth.

"Sorry for barging in like this… I just need Charlotte." Emily collapsed on Charlotte's couch, as Bryony waddled up the glass and steel staircase, embedded with LED lights.

Emily peered at the enormous mirror above the fireplace, jarred by her own reflection. The baggy sweatpants, hair scraped back in a ponytail, no makeup, eyes red and puffy from crying. She averted her gaze to the glossy white kitchen, strewn with takeaway cartons, ice cream tubs and wine bottles. Bloody good idea, she thought, launching to her feet.

From the fridge, Emily grasped an opened chardonnay, twisted the cork with her teeth and gulped it from the bottle.

"Em, what's up?" Charlotte descended the stairs, tying the sash on her silk robe around her Monroe curves.

"Dan is having an affair," Emily said.

Charlotte's eyes narrowed, like she'd heard this tune many times before. "Em, we talked about this."

"No, you don't understand, Lottie. His trip to New York is a total fucking lie."

"How do you know that?" Consternation battled Charlotte's Botox.

"He left his fucking passport."

Charlotte shut her eyes. "OK, Em, that doesn't look good, but it's not empirical proof either."

"What would be? Lipstick marks on his cock?" Emily took another swig, wine dribbling down her chin.

"Would you like a glass for that?" Charlotte took a clean wine glass from the dishwasher.

"I'm good with the bottle."

Charlotte poured herself a glass of water and corralled Emily to the sofa. "Come on, let's sit you down before you fall down. How did you find his passport, anyway?"

She sounded a little judgemental to Emily. "I was planning a holiday... God, I feel so fucking stupid now!" She pinched the tears from her eyes. "Back to the Amalfi coast, you know, where Dan proposed. I thought we could renew our vows in Ravello, at that beautiful church I told you about..."

Charlotte squeezed her hand. "Oh, Em, that's a lovely idea."

"I thought so too, until checking my passport was up to date, and there, right beside mine in the fucking drawer, was Dan's. Through all the hushed phone calls, the texts, changing his password, he accused me of being paranoid."

"It's OK, Em." Charlotte placed her glass on the coffee table, spread her arms and cradled Emily. "I know it looks bad right now, but in the morning, when you've had some sleep, you'll see things differently." She brushed the hair from her friend's face. "Look Em, I have known Dan as long as you, and he just isn't the cheating type – and I should know, I've had my share of them."

"What about the credit card bills? The flowers. The hotel suite... The Savoy, of all places..." Emily choked on the words.

"I'll bet the flowers were for his mum, and the hotel is probably something for work."

"Like what? He's a fucking travel blogger now? He said he was in New York that day too, seeing his agent."

"Some of his clients are hoteliers, aren't they?"

"Yes, but why would he stay there without me? And not even mention it?"

"Look, Em." Charlotte glanced at her watch. "You know I love you, and I mean this in the best possible way... with everything that's gone on the last year with you guys, the IVF and everything, maybe he needed a break. It's probably a ruse to go on a weekend bender with Chris. You know what those two are like, overgrown children growing old."

Charlotte's words permeated with Emily. Dan's best friend, Chris, despite his seven-figure banking salary, long-suffering wife and three kids, had never grown out of his student hedonism. Since Cambridge, he and Dan were prone to disappear on laddish crusades.

"Sometimes we all need to hit the pause button. Maybe Dan is pushing his, and actually, Em, I think you should do that, too."

"From Dan?" Emily sat up, horrified.

"No. From work. Take a few weeks off. You haven't been yourself in a while."

"I know." Emily's head sagged. "I'm sorry."

Charlotte lifted Emily's chin with a manicured finger. "Hey, you have nothing to apologise for. You've been through a lot, and no one knows that more than me, Em. You are the strongest person I know, but right now, you need to look after yourself. We can manage, you know."

"I know." A weight lifted from Emily's shoulders. "I thought the same thing, which was the reason for the holiday..." She closed her eyes, the recollection jabbing her.

"Em, if you overanalyse everything, you see things that aren't there."

"You sound like Dan. That I'm imagining it."

"If enough people tell you something…" Charlotte let her words hang, rising to her feet, confiscating the chardonnay bottle. "How about a coffee?"

"OK." Emily nodded, too tired to argue.

"You could stay over, but Bryony is in the guest room." Charlotte popped a capsule in the Nespresso machine. "Speaking of which, you think you've got man trouble. This will make you laugh…"

Emily wasn't listening, still festering on the plausibility of Charlotte's explanation. "Do you really think he's with Chris?"

"Definitely." Charlotte tore into a bag of demerara sugar.

Emily yanked her phone from her sweatpants. "Let's find out."

Charlotte returned with Emily's coffee, her eyes wide with alarm. "Em, who are you calling? Chris?"

"No, Dan." Emily clamped the phone to her ear. A ringtone chirped from the sofa, muffled but emphatic. Emily and Charlotte's gaze steered to the melody emanating from the velvet cushions. Emily reached between them, withdrawing an iPhone, generic, except for her name and number flashing across the screen.

Dan's phone.

Emily's eyes shot at Charlotte like darts. Her best friend stared back, struggling to fabricate an explanation, but even the queen of PR spin had no defence. Fifteen years of friendship, gone at the sound of a ringtone. Emily glared at Charlotte, her expression morphing from prey to predator.

"Where… is… he?"

"Em, we didn't…"

"Where is he?" Emily's eyes snapped upwards, following the LED lights embedded in the staircase.

"Em…"

Emily was already bounding up the stairs. At the top, she charged along the landing, bursting through the closed door to Charlotte's bedroom. Mortified, Dan covered his reclined nudity with the duvet, as though his sudden modesty might somehow moderate the shame. "Emily, God, I didn't…"

The blood rushing in Emily's ears muted his apologies, her mind scrambling to process the sordid array of betrayal. A sweating, half-empty bottle of champagne on the bedside table, two glasses, one filled with orange juice. Clothes, discarded in lust, strewn across the floor. Lingerie Emily recognised, that she helped Charlotte pick out. Another excruciating detail she would recall for the rest of her life.

The stench of sex hit her. Sweat, secretion, and Charlotte's favourite perfume. Emily's own beloved scent suddenly made her gag. Hand clamped over her mouth, she lurched to the ensuite, the contents of her stomach splashing into the toilet bowl. The remnants of the meal she had eaten earlier, while planning her and Dan's holiday – a fresh start. Emily longed for that blissful ignorance, rather than the irreconcilable new reality lurking next door. She wiped her mouth with toilet roll, climbed to her feet and staggered into the unthinkable.

On his feet, Dan yanked up his briefs so hard the fabric tore. Charlotte loomed in the doorway, a more composed, recognisable version of herself.

Emily shook her head. "What have you done?" A question aimed at either of them.

"Emily, I'm sorry." Dan hopped on one leg, sliding a foot into his skinny jeans.

"You said it was me. That I was paranoid."

"I know, I'm sorry. I didn't want to hurt you."

"Fucking epic fail."

"We were trying to protect you, Em," Charlotte said.

"You shut the fuck up. You are dead to me."

"We're in love." Charlotte smiled. A defiant curl, she'd been dying to reveal.

Emily's anger turned into concentrated fury. She lunged, gripping Charlotte's throat, slamming her breathless into the steel balustrade on the landing.

As Dan leapt to intervene, his ankles twisted in his jeans, toppling him face first onto the mahogany floor with a sickening thud.

Charlotte's face turned purple, her eyes bulging as Emily's grip tightened. Seconds from asphyxiation, Emily could feel the hyoid bone straining in her grasp. Another second and...

Bryony yanked Emily's head backwards, tugging her ponytail. Emily smashed her elbow into Bryony's cheekbone, catapulting her onto the hardwood floor. Charlotte gasped for air, but Emily wasn't done, and she tightened her grip.

"Emily, stop." Dan's voice was nasal from the blood pouring from his broken nose, as he wrestled to free himself from his twisted jeans. "Emily, for Christ's sake, she's pregnant."

Emily uncoiled her fingers. Charlotte collapsed to her knees, choking and wheezing.

"Please, Emily, she's pregnant." His feet unhooked from his jeans, Dan crawled over to Charlotte, shielding her in his arms.

"No, no, she can't be," Emily pleaded, knowing it to be true, staggering backwards as pieces of the puzzle formed in her mind. The orange juice in the champagne flute, and Charlotte's recent aversion to alcohol. Her bouts of sickness, attributed to her latest detox diet. Whatever duplicity Emily had imagined these past months, nothing could have prepared her for this.

"Dan, call the police," Charlotte screamed.

"Charlotte, please?" he asked.

"She tried to fucking kill me. I'm pregnant, for fuck's sake. I want her arrested."

Emily was already gone, careening on wobbly legs, past Bryony, crumpled on the landing. She teetered down the stairs, numbed by the shock, the full impact of her agony not hitting her yet.

Yet.

4

EMILY
Two months ago

Emily grinds another cigarette into the slushy cobbles, irked her boots are tide-marked. A poor choice of footwear for the weather and the occasion. She expels a frosty sigh, feeling overdressed. The client meeting scheduled earlier at Soho House blew her out. Hardly surprising given the West End is a tundra, though a cancellation call would have been polite. But, with her fire-sale reputation, who would take PR advice from someone who can't protect their own maligned image?

Emily checks her watch again. Two minutes to seven. Despite her disdain for lateness, for this appointment, she would joyfully make an exception. She stares at the inscription on the brass plate beside the black door: Divorce Support Centre. A drink in the Nag's Head pub next door suddenly seems a more attractive proposition. But right now, so would a pint of bleach. On a freezing night like this, she could help at the homeless shelter, doing something useful. *What am I doing here?* she wonders. Her sister's constant nagging, that's what. Plus, Sara has paid up front for the sessions, so now she can add guilt to her anguish. Emily watches a well-dressed couple strolling towards the Royal Opera House. Once Dan had surprised her at the office, wearing his tuxedo, carrying her gown, shoes and tickets to *Madam Butterfly*. As the rush of pain and anger manifests, Emily realises she can't go on like this. Sara is right, she needs help. But first, Dutch courage. She rouses herself, crunching across the snowy cobbles into the pub.

As she savours the salutary burn of the vodka, Emily has the uneasy feeling of being watched. Across the bar, a man looks away, giving her the opportunity to survey him back. Handsome, he has sharp cheekbones, full lips, an athletic torso filling a tailored grey suit, and crucially, as shorter guys exaggerate Emily's height, tall. Six one at a guess. The mandatory beard, of course. But given the homogeneous grooming trend, you would have more chance of finding a unicorn than a clean-shaven man. Even Dan has grown one, she recalls, having succumbed to another masochistic visit to his Instagram.

Conscious of her stare, or perhaps having roused the courage, he meets her gaze with irises so dark brown, they spill into his pupils. Opaque and undecipherable, like a shark. He smiles, lightening the severity, raising the dregs of his Guinness in a toast. Cute smile, but no match for Dan's. The yardstick she flagellates herself with. *Enough prevaricating.* Emily slaps her empty glass on the bar, flashing a farewell smile at the cute guy, and steals herself to the door. *Here goes absolutely fucking nothing.*

5

CALUM

As the black door buzzes open, Calum wipes Guinness from his upper lip, and climbs the gloomy staircase to the first floor. Rather than calming his nerves, the booze has only fuelled his scepticism. A workmate recommended this place after his wife ran off. Martin was a mess throughout his divorce, worse than himself, so there must be some merit to this endeavour, Calum hopes. At the top of the staircase, he halts before a smoked glass door with gold lettering. Divorce Support Centre. He was apprehensive even before his online "discovery session" last week. But the anonymity of a Zoom call is one thing; spilling your guts to a group of strangers is another level.

Calum closes his eyes, takes a breath, and finds his centre. "Once more unto the breach." He swings the door open and steps into a white reception area adorned with cut flowers and Zen-like paintings of trees and flora. Central heating engulfs him after the chill outside. Calum slithers from his topcoat and scarf, and shuffles to the glossy desk, where a florid receptionist marshals her bubbly facade.

"Do you have an appointment?"

"Yes. I'm Calum Greyson. I'm here for the divorce group counselling."

As she drums carmine fingertips on the keyboard, her

smile inverts. "Oh, I'm afraid your session has already begun."

"Sorry, my tube was late. Is that a problem?" he asks, praying it is.

"Malcolm is strict about not disturbing a session once it has begun, but as it's your first time, hopefully it will be alright. Room 2B, just along the hall."

Hopefully? Calum thinks, twisting the chrome door handle to room 2B. As he peers around the door, an accusatory silence meets him from an eclectic group seated in a circle of equally assorted chairs.

Malcolm Lindsay twists to the interruption like a dowager disturbed from holding court. Calum recognises him from his online introductory session, although he appeared more amenable then. Malcolm peers down his scarlet-framed spectacles. The only colourful concession to his monochrome ensemble. With his slicked-back hair, greying at the temples, black turtleneck, trousers and brogues, he conveys the air of an architect.

"Sorry. Problem on the tube." Calum winces inwardly at the trite fallback of every tardy Londoner.

"Sit." Malcolm nods to the incriminating vacancy of an acid-lemon armchair.

Calum feels chastised, like his wayward Labrador, Prince. Misappropriated in the divorce by his ex-wife, Bex, along with everything else he held dear. He hangs his coat on a laden rack and performs the walk of shame to his appropriately coloured seat, feeling like a lemon himself.

He casts an apologetic smile across the attendees. First to a well put-together brunette, who blanks him. From his ex-wife's exorbitant tastes, Calum knows money when he sees it. From her handbag, shoes and bling, she is wearing it, largesse.

Her stick-up-her-arse posture and haughty indifference seal the impression. Though her lack of expression looks courtesy of Botox and world-class plastic surgery. Which makes her age tricky to calculate, between mid-thirties and fifty.

Beside her is a razor-thin guy, wearing a Covid mask. *Maybe he's vulnerable*, Calum thinks. His fashion sense certainly is, wearing a baggy purple Currys uniform shirt, enveloping him like a clown suit. Late twenties, about six feet, but so rangy he appears taller. He fidgets with his black-gloved hands. A mop of lank hair falls in bangs over John Lennon glasses. The bottle-top lenses magnifying his glassy, dark-ringed eyes, determinedly avoiding eye contact.

In contrast, the hulking guy next to him is all about eye gaze, appraising Calum with an ice-blue glare. With his buzz cut, and black beard streaked white like ermine, Calum feels like he's in a staring contest with the Devil. He looks about fifty. No taller than the Currys-shirt guy, but twice the width, his tattooed, muscled arms crossed over a straining black polo shirt. Calum is no stranger to the gym, working out his aggression in the last year. But this guy looks like he lives there, and his demeanour couldn't be more truculent if he had "fuck off" tattooed on his forehead.

Happy to accommodate, Calum averts his gaze to the agreeable smile of a woman with a neon pink bob. Late thirties, with her inch-thick makeup and ruddy flesh bulging out of a magenta cami top, she looks ready for a Magaluf singles bar.

Seated beside her, Calum recognises the statuesque girl from the pub. Before he can register his surprise, she gives him a mock admonishing head shake. At least, he hopes she is joking.

"We have a policy, not to enter a session once it has

begun. In the future, I would ask everyone to please respect that." Malcolm glares at Calum, then at Calum's colluder.

Calum grins, impersonating her reproachful head shake, which she reciprocates with a conspiratorial smile. Under the favourable pub lights, the pint of Guinness and Jameson's chaser, she looked stunning. In the sobering glare of the ceiling spotlights, intoxicatingly so. There is a beguiling Pre-Raphaelite quality about her beauty, ethereal, yet formidable. Calum isn't in the market for a new relationship, and after the daily Promethean heart-ripping recently, he doubts he ever will. Besides, his pummelled *amour propre* aside, he suspects she is out of his league, and it puzzles him how someone like her could wind up here. A thought simultaneously comforting and disquieting.

"For the benefit of our late arrival, I will start again. My name is Malcolm Lindsay. I am an accredited divorce coach, qualified psychotherapist, acclaimed author, and formerly a criminal lawyer practising for twenty years. After a great personal struggle, breaking up with my partner, I wanted to help others through the heartache and trauma of separation and divorce. So, I retrained and set up the centre. In five years, the programme has helped hundreds of clients navigate the challenges of divorce to happiness and empowerment." Malcolm pauses, as if expecting a round of applause.

"Without doubt, the death of a loved one is the greatest loss, but the grief of a painful separation can be a close second. The emotional response is very similar, but in some ways can feel worse. Relationship grief isn't given the emotional support of bereavement, where friends and family offer comfort and sympathy. Despite dealing with losing of your partner, they are ever present – during the legal wrangling of divorce, and if you have children, tied into joint parental responsibilities."

Tell me about it, Calum thinks.

"If unresolved, relationship grief can develop into complicated or pathological grief, which has similarities to PSTD, causing increased anxiety, insomnia, difficulties focusing and uncontrollable anger."

All the above, Calum checks off.

"But let me assure you, there is light at the end of this darkness." Malcolm speaks with a flurry of gesticulating hands. "With my ten-step programme, I will show you the coping strategies to re-establish your emotional equilibrium, so you can move on and rebuild the life you want."

As Malcolm's soliloquy continues, Calum's attention drifts to a familiar print on the wall behind him. Hieronymus Bosch's *The Garden of Earthly Delights*. The same print hangs in his study. Or rather, hung, he recalls. It now decorates the kitchen wall of his barren one-bedroom flat. Bex hated it, but then, she would. The painting narrates the perils of temptation, culminating in the eternal torments of Hell. The Law of Contrapasso. For every sinner's crime, there must be an equal and fitting punishment. It seems a curious accompaniment alongside the sedative pictures of flowers adorning on the walls, but an apt metaphor for divorce, Calum concedes, given the nine circles of Hell he endured from his own earthly devils – Bex, and her new husband, Matt. The flashy prick. Calum tunes back in to Malcolm's monologue, in full swing and building, he hopes, to a conclusion.

"Our meetings provide a positive and non-judgemental environment. Where from each other's experiences you will realise you are not alone and gain perspective on your own situation. Before we start, I must inform you our sessions together are digitally video recorded, though I can assure you they are completely confidential." Finally finished, Malcolm waves at the tea and coffee urns resting on a counter. "Please help yourself to refreshments before we begin."

At first, awaiting communal endorsement, nobody moves, until the woman from the pub rises to her considerable height. Calum watches her long strides to the counter, pouring herself a coffee with milk. The Botox brunette is next, selecting a bottle of Evian. The pink-haired woman has tea with milk and three sugar sachets. The thin, nervy guy remains seated, momentarily removing his face mask to swig from his own two-litre bottle of Coke. The big guy stays put also, his glacial eyes doing his imbibing. A coffee wouldn't go amiss, Calum thinks. But after the Guinness, his bladder is as taut as a snare drum, and Malcolm surely wouldn't appreciate another leave of absence.

With everyone returned to their seats, Malcolm balances a leather notebook on his knee. "We will begin with a brief introduction from each of you. Who you are, what stage in the separation or divorce process you are at, and what you hope to achieve from our sessions together." Consternation sweeps the circle like nuns ensnared in a game of spin the bottle. Malcolm pops the lid off a gold fountain pen and nods in Calum's direction. "Calum, why don't you start?"

Typical, Calum thinks, straining to his feet. A one-in-six chance, and he craps out again.

"There is no need to stand, Calum. This isn't an AA meeting."

Nervous laughter ripples around the group, as Calum sits back down, feeling his face reddening.

"It's natural to be nervous during your first session, Calum. Just try to remember you are among friends."

Calum glances at his detached cohorts. With friends like these? "I'm Calum. I work in recruitment, in the city. And I've been... was... married for eight years. I have a six-year-old daughter, Bella, who is the only thing that has kept me going this last year... sorry." Calum judders to a halt, spooked by his emotion. With a deep breath, his glossy eyes fix on the Bosch print above Malcolm's head. The first panel of the triptych. The garden of Eden, a utopia, before everything turned to shit.

"Take your time, Calum. You're doing well."

This is even tougher than Calum imagined, and once again, he wishes he'd stayed in the pub. When the shitstorm hit from Bex's affair and the shock of her leaving, all he did was talk about it. Until he'd sucked the marrow of sympathy from his friends, colleagues and family. Now, among these strangers, it's the last thing he wants to talk about.

"My decree absolute came through three months ago." Calum ups his tempo to get through it. "In which, my money-grubbing succubus of a wife – sorry... ex-wife – has already remarried the flashy city-boy prick she was screwing behind my back."

"And what is your primary goal, Calum?" Malcolm asks in his buttery therapist voice.

"What I want..." Conscious of his fists digging into his thighs, Calum unclenches his fingers. "...is to get past this feeling of being angry all the time. Especially when I see my daughter."

"Thank you for sharing that, Calum."

Embarrassed, Calum nods, wiping his tears. His conspirator smiles supportively.

"I'm Rachel." The upscale brunette has the type of cut-glass accent nowadays only imitated in period dramas. "I am a property developer, entrepreneur and film producer. I have a daughter, Florence, aged thirteen. And for the last eighteen months, I have endured the divorce from hell. Courtesy of my narcissistic shit of a husband, traumatising mine and my daughter's lives. With no visible sign of an end, unless I agree to his ridiculous financial demands, which, while I still have breath in my body, I never will." Rachel brushes a speck of lint from her cashmere sweater and leans back in her chair like she is done.

"What do you want to achieve here, Rachel?"

Irritation struggles to register across her Botox features. "It is not a question of want, rather one of need. The reason for which I informed you during our initial *private* consultation."

"This process only works if we express our emotions and situations candidly, both to each other and to ourselves. Please, Rachel, tell us why you are here."

"I am here because of a condition of my suspended sentence."

"What did you do?" the pink-haired woman asks with an Irish lilt.

Rachel's reproachful stare bounces off the Irish woman, so thick-skinned, or merely impatient for her tidbit. It isn't just her curiosity that is piqued; the rest of the group, Calum included, listen intently.

"Harassment," Rachel says, swapping chagrin with defiance. "It was a few phone calls. Blown out of proportion and exploited by Jack, my husband. Who, among other ignominious pursuits, is a divorce lawyer."

"Fucking lawyers! Vultures, the lot of them," the big guy says, with a Glaswegian timbre so deep, he sounds like an echo from a crypt. "No offence, pal." He nods to Malcolm for slandering his former occupation.

"None taken." Malcolm's smile can't mask his irritation. "With the similarity to your own personal motivation, why don't you go next, Steve?"

Steve's expression stiffens, the veins in his temple protruding. Calum notices a thin ivory scar from his temple to his hairline, adding to his sinister countenance.

"I'm Steve Fallon. I served in the British Army for twenty-one years, and the Metropolitan Police for thirteen. I've been married for twenty-three years and have twin daughters, Molly and Daisy, aged thirteen."

"And what part of the separation process are you in, Steve?"

Steve's jaw tightens under his beard. He crosses his arms tighter, distorting the Celtic ink. Curled around his powerful right bicep, set across a dagger pierced bleeding heart, is the word *Dìoghaltas*. On his left, impaled in the claws and beak of an eagle: *Ceartas*. Calum makes a mental note to Google them after the session.

"It's not my separation," Steve says, "it was the wife's idea. She's got some stuff to sort out. Time apart kind of thing. There's no talk of divorce."

"How long have you been separated?" Malcolm scribbles in his notebook, further antagonising Steve.

"Nine months."

"After such a long separation, divorce is a distinct possibility, isn't it, Steve?"

Steve shakes his head. "Not me and Sue. She's done this before, see. Years ago, when I was on a tour in Afghanistan... military wives, you know... they get... lonely."

"Your wife had an affair previously?"

Steve's iceberg eyes narrow to slits. Soldier's eyes. Killer's eyes. "It was a long time ago. I... we, got through it then, and we'll get through this now."

"Avoidance and denial are common coping strategies for dealing with relationship breakdowns. Especially in men. But unless you accept the reality of permanent separation and divorce, you cannot move on with your life. We can't skip emotional stages, Steve. We must confront them, as painful as they might be."

"I'm not avoiding anything, pal. I just know my wife, right?"

"Tell us why you are here, Steve?"

"Because a judge in his infinite senility thought it would be conducive to my freedom." Steve winks at Rachel. "Like yourself."

"For harassment?" the woman from the pub asks, vocalising Calum's curiosity.

Steve shakes his head. "Went to have a wee word with my wife's..." He pauses, scrolling his lexicon for the right word. "...fella. My fists ended up doing the talking."

Calum glances at Steve's mallet fists, feeling sorry for the recipient.

"Maybe I should have just ended the fucker."

"And now you would be in prison, Steve, deprived of the rest of your life, too," Malcom says.

Steve shrugs. "People's actions come with consequences. Or they should."

"If there is one thing that will thwart a person's ability to move on, it is their inability to reconcile their anger and resentment they feel for their ex."

"So we just bend over and take it up the arse, while they just walk away scot-free?" Steve asks.

Malcolm takes a breath before answering. "I know anger is a powerful distraction from dealing with your emotions right now. And jealousy is one of the most intense feelings arising from a difficult breakup. You feel outraged by your hurt, so you want to hurt your exes in return. A natural reaction, but..." He takes off his glasses for gravitas. "...harbouring those feelings will lead you along a path you do not want to go down, and the further you travel along it, the more you will lose yourself." Malcom replaces his glasses. "Just like Shakespeare's Othello. If you let that toxic voice pervade your reason – that insidious, whispering Iago residing in all of us – you will become the villain of your own story." With an avuncular smile, he waves a hand to the ruddy-faced Irish woman. "Ciara, your turn?"

"I'm Ciara Devaney. I'm from Cork, but I've lived in London now for, well, more years than I'd care to remember. Came over after I graduated from Dublin University, with Jim, my husband, or STBE." Ciara glances around for recognition, finding only bemused expressions. "Soon-to-be-Ex. Anyway so, we met at uni, where I was studying environmental health, and Jim was at Griffith College doing photography, but I don't think it was called that then. We were married for twelve years, and we've got two lovely kids: Stephanie, eleven, and Patrick, nine. Well, mostly lovely. Steph can be a bit, you know... she's hitting that teenage stage a bit early like... misses her da, and she's taking it out on me. As if it's my all fault, you know–"

"If we can stick to the abridged version for now, please, Ciara," Malcolm says to Calum's relief. "Can you tell us what stage you are at in your separation?"

"Aye, sorry, I can go on a bit you know." Ciara splutters a smoker's laugh, a waft of tobacco on her breath. "Just tell me to shut up."

Sage advice, Calum thinks.

"Anyhow, everything was grand, happy families like, you know, until Jim ran off with some fucking bimbo model he met on a photoshoot. Half his fucking age, she is, the fucking skinny slag. Is that a fucking cliche or what? Not a thought in his head for me and the kids, either. The only thinking going on was in the front of his fucking Levi's. I should have seen it coming, though. Suddenly he's going to the gym, giving up smoking and drinking, dressing like a teenager, and all that fucking vegan bollocks. He used to be a laugh and all. We used to have such a craic together–"

"Ciara, just the salient points, please."

"Aye, right so, well, we've been separated for a year now and the divorce has been dragging on for most of that."

"Why is the divorce proving so difficult, Ciara?"

"If I'm honest, I have been digging my heels in a bit, you know." Off Malcolm's raised eyebrows, she continues, "Why should I make it easy for him? So he can swan off with his wee slag of a girlfriend – the emphasis on girl. Half his fucking age, she is. Classic midlife crisis, but he thinks he's in love. Dickhead couldn't have got himself a fucking sports car, could he?"

Malcolm peers down his spectacles, curtailing Ciara's yarn.

"Anyway, so, we can't agree on the maintenance, a parenting plan, visitation agreement – well, fucking any of it, to be honest with you. We tried mediation, but that didn't help either. The mediator had to separate us at one point."

"Your coping strategy is all too common, Ciara. By sustaining the divorce, you are subconsciously maintaining your past relationship and preventing yourself from embracing your future."

"Yeah, well, the gobshite wants to sell the fucking house from under us. And I'll be bolloxed if I'm going to help him kick our kids out on the street so he can get a fancy love nest with that skinny tart. They're shacked up in his photography studio, so they are. Half his age she is, the fucking skinny slag."

"What is it you want to achieve from our sessions together, Ciara?"

Ciara sighs. "I need some help, to cope… you know… to move on."

Malcolm beams. "That is a very honest, positive attitude, Ciara. Try to keep mindful of that."

"Yeah, I don't want the fucker to think he's won."

Malcolm maintains his smile and turns to the skinny guy. "Talbot, your turn, please?"

"I prefer to be addressed as Doctor Yilmaz."

Doctor? Calum puzzles. *In a Currys electrical store uniform?*

"I like to create an environment of intimacy and honesty in our sessions together, so if we can address each other by first names please, Talbot?"

He pauses before his responses, as if analysing the transaction. "My name is Doctor Talbot Vilmaz, but you can all call me Tal."

We're honoured, Calum thinks, reaffirming his original weirdo first impression.

"If people are wondering, Tal has a doctorate in mathematics," Malcolm says.

"Actually, I have a DPhil in mathematics from Oxford. I was born in Ankara, Turkey, but came to live in London in nineteen-ninety-two, when I was two years, three months and fifteen days old. I was married to Simone, and I have a son, Lukas, who will be four on Saturday." Tal's eyes shine with pride. "I have purchased a very special present for him."

"How long were you and Simone married, Tal?"

"Four years, three hundred and fifty-four days."

Not that anyone is counting, Calum thinks.

"And you work with computers, Tal? At Currys." Malcolm nods at his uniform.

Tal's expression darkens, his gloved fingers pinching at his shirt. "This is only a temporary position. I was the top quantitative analyst at Carter and Hedges." Disappointed by the blank expressions, Tal impresses, "It is ranked sixth in the S&P Global Market intelligence report of the one hundred largest banks in the world."

"Can I ask why you left the bank, Tal?"

"I do not wish to discuss that. Change the topic."

"OK, Tal. How long have you been divorced?"

"Four months and sixteen days."

"And what do you hope to get out of this process, Tal?"

Tal's head droops, staring at his scuffed shoes.

"Why are you here, Tal?"

"Change the topic."

"You are here because your Cognitive Behavioural Therapist suggested it might help with your transactional development and reassimilation in your life with this transition. Isn't that right, Tal?"

"I do not wish to disclose that. Change the topic." His go-to refrain.

"Our success in this process, Tal, depends on your honesty, transparency and trust." Malcolm's eyes rake across the group. "You were all informed in your discovery session, there are no secrets between us."

"No secrets between us," Tal repeats like a parakeet.

His repetition catches everyone's look, Calum included.

"Tal has autism spectrum disorder," Malcolm says. "His

repetition or echolalia occurs when something is wrong, or he becomes stressed."

Tal frowns. "I don't like that term. The word *disorder* has negative connotations, and I have an IQ of a hundred and seventy-eight."

"What term would you prefer, Tal?"

"I prefer not to discuss it at all, but if you insist on labelling my condition, I have an extremely high-functioning form of autism called Asperger's syndrome." Tal lunges to his feet. "I need to use the facilities."

"Of course, Tal. In the hallway, second door on the right."

As Tal lurches to the door, Calum realises his chance to request a toilet break and rises to his feet.

"Now, last, but not least, can we hear from you, please, Emily?"

Intrigue quelling his need to pee, Calum folds himself back into the chair.

Emily stares at the dregs of her coffee cup. "I'm Emily. Not so long ago, I had a perfect husband, a successful business, a beautiful home, a beautiful life. Now, they are all gone."

"Past relationships appear perfect through the rose-tinted prism of retrospection, Emily. But it is important to see the negatives as well. When were you divorced?"

"A year ago, today. Which I suppose makes today my anniversary."

"After a long period of separation, Emily, why do you still wear your wedding band?"

From her own wedding ring, Emily flicks an inculpating glance around the circle. Across the shiny bands adorning the fingers of Tal, Steve, Ciara and Calum. Except Rachel, her sole digit not bejewelled. "Old habits, I suppose. Like most of us, I seem to have an issue with closure."

Calum's gaze falls to his platinum wedding ring, his own postmarital incongruity dawning on him.

"Is that why you are here, Emily, for closure?"

Emily tilts her head up, the light kindling her jade irises. "I just want my life back."

6

ROSA
25 May

"So, she's got form for violence." DCI Hughes slurps his Starbucks over my shoulder.

I can smell the caramel latte on his breath and see the purple capillaries of his whisky bloom. With his albino hair and a face like crumpled laundry, he looks ten years older than his fifty-three years. He peers over my shoulder at my computer screen with dead eyes, the spark long extinguished. "Not exactly, sir. The witnesses rescinded their statements."

Half of my unit circles behind us, watching the playback of the interview, the male half, as if it were an England World Cup final. Interviews with suspects as attractive as Emily Hunter are as rare as snow leopard sightings, but so are serial murder investigations. My personal mobile phone buzzes under a file on the desk. I lift the papers for a peek, frowning, seeing the caller is Bruce, my husband.

"You want to take that?"

"No, just a personal call." I slip the red-cased iPhone (distinguished from my homogenous black work phone) into my suit jacket. "I want to get back in there. Sean, can you dig out the original witness statements?"

"Nicholls has stepped out," Hughes says.

"Probably having a wank." I recognise the sardonic tone of DI Pat Kruger; his private school accent is as distinctive as his excessive cologne. Hubris for Men. In our line of work a sense of humour is a prerequisite, especially at Homicide and Serious Crime, but I'm not a fan of Kruger's fraternal brand of noughties comedy.

"Alright you lot, get back to work." Hughes glowers as the team disperses. "But it shows she has a propensity for violence."

"If you'd just caught your husband in bed with your best friend, then discovered she was having the child you never could, perhaps she showed restraint."

"Perhaps day is night, Hawkes, but even you can't disagree she has motive."

"I'm not contesting that, sir. All of them have motive. The oldest one there is."

7

TAL
15 March

In the staff room, Tal admires his son Lukas's birthday present. A fire-engine-red bicycle, propped against the vending machine. The polished chrome and factory fresh paintwork glistening under the strip lights. It cost more than a week's wages. An hour's pay in his old job at the bank, Tal laments, reattaching his Covid mask. His current position at Currys electrical store is fathoms beneath him. But after the divorce and his emotional breakdown, as the bank's psychologist had put it, he "lacks the coping mechanisms necessary for the high-pressured environment of merchant banking".

Twenty minutes later, the lactic acid in Tal's arm muscles burns, having carried Lukas's bike from the store on Oxford Street. To distract from his discomfort, Tal counts his steps. Six hundred and twenty-eight. He could have wheeled the bike, but that would have dirtied the tyres. Tal wants Lukas's birthday gift to be perfect. Six hundred and thirty-eight. He could flag a taxi, but with his restricted income, he can't justify such extravagance. Memories of his opulent position at the bank assail him, when indulgences like taxis, dining in Michelin restaurants and expensive gifts for Simone were routine. When she abandoned him, all Simone left him was crippling credit card debt and an emotional turmoil he hadn't experienced since his mother died when he was four years, three months and sixteen days old.

Twenty-six steps from his family's restaurant on Great Titchfield Street, Tal's insides cramp with anxiety. It has been precisely one year, three months and fourteen days since he has visited the family restaurant. Like not seeing a parent for a long while, it looks jarringly aged. The weather-beaten gilded window frames, filthy stained glass, torn canvas awning, and the golden sign – Yusef's Finest Turkish Cuisine – is blistered with peeling paint.

As Tal pushes the front doors open, the familiar smells of cumin, coriander and roasted lamb transport him to happier times. He recalls his mother greeting guests at the door, enchanting them with her smile, making them feel special. Like she always did Tal. The interior has fared no better, and the place looks deserted. Back in the day, journalists and celebrities packed the restaurant and bar. Their dusty photographs still adorn the walls in a ghostly memorial of glory days. Since his father, Yusef, retired two years ago, his eponymous empire fell into the apathetic hands of Tal's brother Mehmet – the eldest and favourite son.

To dispel his anguish, Tal uses a technique from his CBT therapist, focusing on the positive of seeing Lukas. He peers into the gloomy dining area, face igniting as he spots his son, surrounded by school friends, about to blow out the candles on his birthday cake. Tal's father, Yusef, looking as antiquated as his kingdom, watches as Lukas blows the flames out in one go. Pride swelling, Tal steers the bicycle between tables, until a waiter with bulbous eyes blocks his passage.

"Sir, you can't bring a bicycle here."

"It is a birthday present... for Lukas... I'm his father," Tal stutters through his mask. Over the waiter's shoulder, Tal watches the joyous milieu of Lukas's birthday party, until meeting Simone's glare.

She slams her wine glass on the table and jabs her elbow into the steroid-enhanced ribcage of her beau – Tal's moustached brother, Mehmet. "I don't fucking believe it." She launches to her feet, dispatching Mehmet's arm from her shoulder and spraying his beer bottle.

"What the fuck?" Mehmet asks, then seeing the cause of her fury, tussles after her like a psychotic bouncer.

"What the fuck are you doing here?" Simone asks.

"Not in here," Mehmet says. An inch shorter, but a hundred pounds heavier than his brother, he frogmarches Tal and the bike to the door.

As Tal strains to see Lukas, he glimpses his father's chagrin, ashamed of his forsaken son.

Hurled into the street, Tal and the bike clatter onto the pavement. With grazed hands, he pushes himself to his knees and fumbles for his glasses. Relieved they are intact, he replaces them and assesses the damaged bike. "Look what you've done..." Tal gasps, horrified, shaking his head. "No, no, no –"

"What the fuck are you doing here?" Simone shoves him back onto his knees. "You know you shouldn't be here."

"To give Lukas his birthday present." Tal struggles to his feet, lifting the bike like a fallen comrade.

"He's already got a bike," Mehmet says, "we got him one at Christmas, dickhead."

"We got him one at Christmas, dickhead," Tal repeats. "Dickhead, dickhead, dickhead."

"Shut up, you fucking freak!" Simone jabs a manicured

finger in his face. "How did you know about his party, eh? You've been hacking me again, haven't you?"

"What choice do I have? It's the only way I see Lukas."

With a baleful head shake, Simone trots back inside.

"Please? Let me see him." As Tal steers the bike after her, his neck snaps back, yanked by his parka hood. Mehmet's fist smashes Tal in the side of his head, felling him like a rotten tree, crunching on top of the bike. Delirious, he gropes for his glasses, finding both lenses shattered this time. He puts them on anyway, his vision a fragmented kaleidoscope.

Simone turns in the doorway. "I've told you before, you're not seeing Lukas until you pay proper maintenance, like the judge agreed."

"You know my financial circumstances have changed... I can't afford that on my salary."

"Well, get your old job back then, cuz that's the only way you're seeing Lukas again."

"Please. He is my son," Tal pleads through his face mask.

"Like fuck he is." Simone regrets the words as they leave her mouth.

Mehmet flashes her a look. Even with his impaired vision and myopia of nonverbal cues, Tal grasps the implication.

"Until you pay the full maintenance, I meant." Simone storms back inside the restaurant.

At the door, Mehmet turns back. "Do yourself a favour, bruv, and fuck off before you get properly hurt, yeah?"

Tal's fractured gaze falls upon Lukas's bike. The handlebars twisted like a broken neck; spokes mangled past repair, the fire-engine-red paint scratched to ruin. He lifts its mangled corpse and limps away, counting the steps of his retreat. But even numbers are cold comfort for him now.

8

CIARA

Ciara squats on her bedroom pouffe, where she has spent the last hour applying makeup, fake eyelashes, and straightening her now platinum hair. Satisfied with her efforts, she struggles to her feet and poses before a full-length mirror, slurping a glass of prosecco. Her third. Or is it fourth?

Most of her wardrobe is heaped on the bed, having tried it on, but Ciara is finally content with her selection. The blouse exaggerates her modest cleavage, billowing out at the hips and hiding her muffin top and arse, which has admittedly ballooned recently. The crow's feet and the laughter lines can't be helped, though she must admit the smoking hardly helps the ageing process. Fuck it, everyone is entitled to one vice. Or two, she concedes, draining her glass. As she reapplies lip gloss, Ciara focuses on the evening ahead and her date. Maybe this one will be alright? His Tinder photograph looked OK. A bit young, but what choice does she have? For a soon-to-be-divorced mother of two, on the arse end of her thirties, the dating scene is a lopsided playing field. Eligible men her own age want a younger model, leaving only fellas old enough to be her da, or guys in their twenties, whom, as Ciara discovered, aren't exactly relationship material. *What do they say about blondes having more fun?* she muses, preening her hair, giving herself another appraisal. She could pay a fortune for Botox and fillers, like that posh tart at the divorce group. What a waste of time that was. Other people's problems are so fucking depressing. She only agreed to go at the nagging of her thirteen (going on thirty) year-old daughter Steph, who with perfect timing comes crashing in.

"Have you heard of knocking?" Ciara says to deaf ears.

"Have you seen my red Vans, Mum? Dad will be here soon!"

"Alright, calm down! They'll be buried under your floordrobe in that pigsty you call a bedroom. And see if you can prise your brother's fingers from that PlayStation controller."

"It's an Xbox One."

"Whatever, get him off it."

With an eye roll, Steph halts her retreat. "You're going for it tonight, aren't you?"

"Thank you." Ciara grins at the mirror.

"That wasn't a compliment, Mum."

"Oi, lady, if you're living in my house, you'll show me a little respect."

"Fine, I'll live with Dad."

"Yeah, right, I'm sure that skinny tart will appreciate that."

"She has a name, you know."

"Don't I bloody know it. You never stop going on about her. You might show a bit more loyalty, you know, lady. Anyway, rather than winding me up, wouldn't your time be better spent looking for your trainers?"

With a huff, Steph departs. So much for solidarity. Ciara

reappraises her reflection, considering Steph might have a point, as the doorbell chimes.

"He's here!" Steph squeals on the landing.

"Shite." Ciara steals another look in the mirror, before colliding with Steph, barging past with her weekend bag, hammering down the stairs.

"Tie your shoelaces." Ciara carries Patrick's *Star Wars* rucksack in one hand, still gripping the empty prosecco glass in her other.

Ignorant as ever, Steph barrels down the stairs, wrestling with her nine-year-old brother, Patrick, to open the door.

"Daddy!" Patrick springs into Jim's arms.

"Hey Paddy lad." Jim bear-hugs his son, before placing Patrick on his feet, and stepping into Steph's embrace. "Hello Princess." He grins, kissing the top of her head.

The image sucks the air from Ciara's lungs, but she hides her pain with a smile. Jim's signature scent greets her as she descends the stairs, trying to appear graceful, yet aloof. Not easy in four-inch heels, and having to hurdle their ancient cat, a white Ragdoll, splayed at the foot of the stairs. Named after Jim, because of his bright blue eyes.

"Alright Ciara?" Jim flicks her a wink with his Paul Newman baby-blues.

"Grand. And yourself?"

"Can't complain." Roughly the same vintage as Ciara, somehow Jim improves with age. "You've gone blonde, tonight."

"Fancied a change." As she hands him Patrick's rucksack, Ciara's finger grazes Jim's, feeling the static heat of his touch.

"Don't we all."

"Don't I know it, too?"

"You off out?" Jim doesn't rise to the bait.

Ciara feigns nonchalance. "Oh, yeah. A date, you know."

"Good on ye."

So much for appealing to his jealousy. The fucker sounds genuinely happy for her.

"Starting as you mean to go on, I see." Jim nods at her empty flute.

Shite! She forgot the glass was still in her hand. "Just the one."

"Right." He cocks his head dubiously. "We'd better be off, or we'll miss the start."

Ciara fails to mask her fury with a smile. Issy, Jim's girlfriend, is making her debut in a West End musical. Not a big part, according to Steph, but it marks a transition in her career from modelling into acting.

"Tell Björk to break her leg," Ciara says. "And her fucking neck," she adds under her breath.

Jim's grin slips. "Kids, go wait in the car. I want a wee word with your ma."

Steph rolls her eyes knowingly, shepherding Patrick out the door.

"Don't I at least get a goodbye?" Ciara asks as the kids scamper to Jim's BMW in the driveway of their Croydon semi-detached.

"I'm warning you Ciara, this stops now."

"What?"

"Don't give me the innocent act. You damn well know what."

"Oh, come off it. A few comments on Instagram. That's why it's called social media."

"A few dozen, more like."

"Tell her to stop bragging about how fucking wonderful her life is with my fucking husband, then."

"I mean it Ciara, it all stops. The online stalking, the

pissed-up phone calls, and slagging Issy off to the kids. Like that snide crack just now. 'Break a fucking leg.' And Bjork, for feck's sake. At least use a contemporary reference."

"Bjork is Iceland's only memorable fucking export. And that's what you're supposed to say, isn't it? To thespians, or failed models transitioning into failed actors."

"You need fucking help, you know that?" Jim twirls his forefinger to his temple. "You've got fucking borderline personality disorder."

"Fuck off. Who Googled that shite? That skinny tart, no doubt."

"No." Jim shakes his head, his expression betraying the truth. "I looked it up myself, and you've got all the symptoms. You need help."

"I need help?" Ciara scoffs. "That's rich from someone having a midlife crisis and shagging a child."

"She's twenty-five, for Christ's sake. There's no talking to you when you're like this."

"Like what?"

"Pissed."

"Fuck off, I've had one."

"Yeah, one bottle. I mean it Ciara, one more call, or online troll, and I'm going to the cops."

"I don't know what you're on about. I wouldn't waste my time on that skinny tart."

"Don't you fucking dare call her that. You're not fit to speak her name."

"I'll call her whatever I want, and I'm worth ten of her."

"You weigh ten times more than her, you mean. Look at the state of you. You can dye your hair all the colours of the fucking rainbow, but you're still a fat, old, jealous cunt."

Ciara lunges her weight at the door, slamming it shut

behind him. "Bastard." She tugs her Benson & Hedges from her handbag on the coat rack. The tears she fought to contain come unabated now. As she lights her quivering cigarette, Ciara catches her reflection in the hallway mirror. Mascara bleeds into the gullies of her crow's feet like a sad clown. Even through the soft focus of tears, they hardly resemble laughter lines now.

"Bastard." She hurls the prosecco glass exploding into the mirror, splintering her visage into a jagged web of tiny fissures.

9

RACHEL

Rachel sits in vigil at the end of Florence's bed, plagued by the question of why her thirteen-year-old daughter cut herself with a disposable razor. Asleep, or rather sedated, Florence looks like the contented little girl of old, apart from her bandaged wrists, cleaned and dressed by Rachel's private physician.

They are minor cuts, no veins were severed, and there is no need for hospitalisation, Doctor Kaufman assured her. He did, however, advise Rachel to seek psychiatric help for Florence. *Perfect*, she thinks, *mother and daughter, both in therapy now*. Rachel's glamorised face is a mask of anguish and misery, as she stares out of the window of her eight-bedroom Holland Park mansion, aware the question she flagellates herself with is rhetorical. The cause of her daughter's distress is her estranged husband, Jack, and his constant lack of consideration, failing to pick up Florence three weekends in a row. The real question is what to do about Jack? Before Florence's cry for help progresses into something that antiseptic and gauze can't mend. After the doctor left, and having persuaded Olivia, Florence's nanny, to go ahead with her date as planned, Rachel needed a sedative herself.

Two Diazepam and three large gins later, she prods Jack's number into her phone.

"Your daughter is in bed, sedated thanks to you..." Rachel slurs into Jack's voice mail. "Whoever you are screwing, who you think is more important than your own daughter, you can continue doing, indefinitely. I don't want you in her life anymore. Stay away from us, Jack, or I swear on my father's grave, I will wipe you from the face of the Earth, you narcissistic piece of shit."

In the early hours, Rachel awakes on her sofa, groggy, her mouth dry as sawdust. As she's climbing the staircase to bed, she hears Jack's car crunching up the gravel driveway. Instantly sobering up, she descends the stairs, chastising herself for leaving the front gates open. In her addled state, she forgot to shut them, but Rachel hadn't expected him so soon. His Friday night binges used to carry on until Sunday morning, when Jack would return, hungover and fetid with remorse and the perfume of his bimbo du jour. Rachel scurries past the front door, through the kitchen into the utility room, to observe the bed of CCTV security screens. She can tell from his gait, swaggering from his Porsche, that Jack is high.

The first time she saw him at a mutual friend's wedding, Rachel considered Jack the most handsome, charming and erudite man she had ever met. With his adroit knowledge in their shared interests and tastes, it was as though fate had brought them together, but years later, in the heat of a row, Jack confessed to hiring a private detective to research her. He'd targeted her from the start, or rather, her money.

After ringing the bell and hammering his fists on the door, Jack's face looms into the CCTV camera above the front door.

Given his Kamikaze degeneracy, apart from his foppish blond hair greying at the temples, the hedonistic shit has barely aged.

The intercom crackles on. "Open the door, Rach. I want to see Flo."

After her ultimate indignity (Jack impregnating the nineteen-year-old daughter of her deceased father's friend), Rachel changed the locks and installed a top-of-the-range security system. Illegal, according to Jack, demanding right of access to the property. Fuck him. That's for her lawyers to deal with, and God knows she pays them enough. Even given her considerable solvency, the legal fees are staggering, and although Rachel knows that protracting the divorce settlement is self-sabotage, she would donate her entire fortune to her lawyers rather than Jack.

"Let me in, Rachel. I demand to see my daughter."

Rachel prods the intercom button, composing her tone through the speaker. "It's a little late for filial concern, Jack. Anyway, you can't see her, she is in bed, sedated, thanks to you."

"Like her hypocrite mother, I'll wager."

"Yes, congratulations for turning both of us to drugs. Which are prescribed, unlike that filth you put up your nose."

"Just open the fucking door, Rach."

"You won't be seeing her tonight, or anytime soon once I speak to my lawyers. Now get off my property."

"Half mine too, remember? Or it will be soon."

"Like hell it will. Get out of here, Jack, before I call the police."

"I wouldn't do that if you want to keep custody of Florence. Not to mention your liberty."

"Oh, save the hyperbole for your clients." Rachel masks the concern in her voice.

Jack presses his iPhone to the intercom and replays

Rachel's drunken message. "'I will wipe you from the face of the Earth, you narcissistic piece of shit.'"

Shit. Rachel castigates herself, suspecting what is coming.

"That constitutes a malicious communication, conveying a threat to cause distress or anxiety, and breaches the conditions of your suspended sentence for harassment."

"Is everything alright, Rachel?"

Rachel spins, relieved to see Olivia peering around the utility doorway. "Yes, thank you, Olivia. Everything is fine. Go back to bed."

With a mollifying smile, Florence's nanny retreats to her ground-floor room. Rachel watches her saunter back through the kitchen in her pyjama shorts. A recent addition to her employ, Olivia has been a godsend for Florence, but she could never have hired such an alluring temptation when her lecherous husband lived under the same roof.

"I make one phone call, Rach, and you'll get six months in prison," Jack's voice rattles through the intercom. "And they will award me primary custody of Florence. Is that what you want?"

"You'd use your own daughter as collateral for blackmail?"

"Oh, Rach, have I taught you nothing? What do I always tell my clients? Prepare for battle because divorce is war. And you, my love, just lost, so I suggest you surrender with dignity and sign the peace treaty."

Rachel clings to the marble counter for support.

"I'll be back in the morning to collect Florence, whereupon I will expect your signature on the consent order. Nighty-night, my love." The intercom crackles off.

Long after Jack's taillights have vanished, Rachel stares into the void of the security screen with a hatred as fierce as the love for her child.

10

CALUM
16 March

Calum savours the sunshine through the windshield, and the radiance of his nestling optimism. He usually dreads the biweekly drive through the Essex countryside, but this Saturday morning feels different. The counselling group felt like a step forward, taking back a modicum of control in his life. Plus, the added incentive, he thinks, of the beautiful Emily. As he steers along the snaking driveway to Bexingham Palace (his nickname for Bex's new home), Calum smiles. Hope, at last, of escaping this purgatory.

Even as he parks his Audi TT alongside Matt's new Lamborghini Diablo, Calum is determined to remain positive. He steps out of his car and strides towards the Palladian-style mansion, where his ex-wife awaits at the top of the limestone steps like she is posing for a cover shot of *Hello* magazine, in an outfit that costs more than his car.

"She not ready?" Calum asks, trying to sound upbeat.

"Still out riding," Bex says in a courtly accent as augmented as her breasts. "They'll be back soon."

'They' meaning his daughter and Matt, the flashy prick. Horseback riding on Saturday mornings normally includes Bex, Calum recalls, mounting the last step with a foreboding sense.

"Not riding today? You not feeling well or something?" he asks.

Bex shakes her salon-fresh blonde hair. "No. I wanted to speak to you in private. You'd better come in."

Never previously invited inside the inner sanctum of Bexingham Palace, Calum knows something is amiss. "Sounds ominous."

"Actually, it is good news." She leads him into a vast reception hall, her exorbitant heels clacking the marble tiles. In his imagination Calum pictured the interior as an ostentatious shrine to excess. Yet everywhere he looks is a galling reminder that money can buy anything, even good taste.

"I see Matt's got a new car." Calum tastes the bitterness in his mouth like bile. "For that kind of money, he could have had an actual penis enlargement."

"Trust me, he doesn't need one."

Calum masks the sting with a smile. "Funnily enough, trust isn't my first instinct with you, Bex."

"Don't fucking start, Calum, or Bella will stay here this weekend, OK?" Bex snaps, exposing her Essex accent.

"OK." Calum raises his hand like a white flag. "Just a joke. You used to like my jokes."

"People change." Bex strides onwards, the percussion of her stilettos echoing behind her.

No argument there, Calum concedes, his good mood inverting with every step. He follows her into a chateau-style kitchen, where a chocolate Labrador squints at him from his basket, barking as though Calum were the intruder he feels.

"Hey there, Prince, it's only Daddy."

Prince rises from his bed, registering his former master, and plods over. On his knees, Calum embraces the elderly hound, allowing him to lap at his face and mouth. Disgusted, Bex leans on her enormous marble island, playing with a gaudy pendant dangling between her breasts. Whilst conducting her affair with Matt, she had duped Calum that the thirty-grand gold and ruby encrusted "B" pendant was a performance-related gift from her work as an estate agent. "B" for betrayal, more like. Or bitch.

"He's started shitting in the house," Bex says, examining her beautified fingernails.

"Who, Matt?" Calum strokes the old dog's belly.

"Hilarious. Matt thinks putting him down is the humane thing to do."

"Yeah, the paragon of humanity. There's no fucking way he's killing my dog."

"You take him then."

"You know I'm not allowed pets in my flat."

"You'll have to sort something out either way."

"Alright, I'll take him tomorrow when I drop Bella… back." Calum curbs himself from saying *home*.

"Whatever," Bex huffs, ending the topic. "You want a latte?"

"OK." Calum fumes inwardly. *Not content with stealing my wife, and usurping my role as a father, now he wants to whack my dog.*

As Bex toils over a coffee machine, her top rides up, revealing a new tattoo on her lower back – scribed in calligraphy: FOREVER MATT.

Anger surging, Calum looks away in search of distraction but everywhere screams money. How can one individual gain this much wealth legally? Calum couldn't afford a down payment on this lifestyle if he worked to a hundred years old. It seems obscene, but then, city boys like Matt are used to taking more than their share. Playing with other people's money. Other people's lives. Other people's wives. This kitchen alone probably cost more than his pokey flat in the Docklands. Bex always wanted a place like this, and a gold band on her finger wouldn't bar her access. *Whatever it takes* would have been a more appropriate tramp stamp on her back. But how long would she stick around if Matt's fortunes were reversed?

"The suspense is killing me, Bex, what's this good news?"

"Matt has a new job offer." Bex beams, passing him his latte. "A huge promotion. Loads more money."

"That is wonderful news. You'll forgive me if I forgo the cartwheels."

"I knew you'd be like this."

"Like what?"

"Selfish and jealous."

"I'm selfish? You're having a laugh, aren't you?"

"Shut it, Calum. That's not the only good news."

"Let me guess. He's getting a new yacht. Or is it a private jet–"

"I'm pregnant."

The word hits Calum like a bullet.

"I thought you should hear it from me before Bella says something. She's excited about having a little brother or sister."

Calum stares through the window out to the landscaped grounds, that would make Versailles look like an allotment.

"Nothing to say?"

"What are you expecting, Bex, congratulations?"

"That would be nice, but there's more. Matt's old firm has offered him a job…"

"Like I said, what's it got to do with me?"

"It's in New York."

Fear pierces Calum's chest, but before he can protest, Bella ambles into the kitchen in muddy jodhpurs and riding boots.

"Daddy!" She hurtles into his arms.

Calum envelops her, before staring at her cherubic face. With her pale skin and mousy hair like her mother, Calum often wonders why his African genes lacked the prepotency of Bex's. But Bella's eyes, impenetrable onyx pools, are undeniably his. She is his, too, at least for now. Peripherally, Calum can see Bex nodding at Matt. Their signal that the dirty deed is done. He looms in the doorway in his riding attire, like a spray tanned Mr Darcy. Calum can feel his world spinning, his limbs leaden and yet weightless, as though gravity itself is departing him. He clings to his daughter, afraid if he lets go, he will be lost. No longer in purgatory but cast into hell.

11
STEVE

Steve always struggled to keep pace with his thirteen-year-old twins, Molly and Daisy, marauding Bluewater shopping mall. This Saturday was no exception, leaving him more depleted than any combat fitness test. Dinner at TGI Fridays and a trip to the cinema followed. Steve didn't watch the film – the latest superhero movie, an endless montage of wankers in spandex blowing shite up. In the benign projector light, he watched his girls, marvelling and lamenting how they were changing. When they were bairns, the twins insisted on dressing the same, matching hairstyles, even mimicking expressions and the cadence of each other's speech. It wasn't easy telling them apart. Recently, though, they have groomed their individual styles. Molly is all sportswear and expensive trainers, whilst Daisy sports a vampiric Goth look, pallid foundation and black fingernails. Steve isn't keen on either ensemble, but having lived in a household dominated by women, he knows when to pick his battles.

On the drive home, having fallen asleep on the back seat, the girls awake as the car pulls onto the driveway at their four-bedroom detached in a leafy suburb of Hertfordshire. Home.

Only, it isn't Steve's home anymore. It isn't his car either, or him rousing the twins in the back seat. Steve is a hundred yards away, parked across the street, observing through a powerful telescopic lens as his wife's lover, Nick, shepherds his daughters inside his house, with his wife.

Steve rests the camera on the passenger seat, wondering what they have reduced him to – spying on his own family. Eighteen months ago, he was working specialist operations in counterterrorism. Now he's a lowly private investigator. Since he doesn't require a licence to practise as a PI, and with his criminal record, it's the only work Steve's skill set suits, legally. Insurance fraud, mostly, and matrimonial investigations, catching cheating spouses.

His stomach tightens, reminded of what awaits him in the glove compartment, where it has remained unopened for over a week.

"Just get it done." He pulls out a large manila envelope, tears it open, and draws the document out as far as the top line.

ACKNOWLEDGEMENT OF SERVICE OF PETITION FOR DIVORCE.

All he can read before ripping it to shreds. Steve starts the car and takes a last look his old house.

"Night, night, sleep tight. For now."

12

EMILY

Curry spits and belches in an industrial-sized saucepan like an aromatic geyser. Emily stares into the pot, pondering how her Saturday nights have come to this. She began volunteering at the homeless shelter kitchen a few months after the split with Dan. It gave her a distraction, at first, but then she began identifying with the emotional outcasts and refugees fleeing the wreckage of their lives. In Soho, off an alleyway on Greek Street, the shelter is a hundred and fifty metres away from Emily's old office on Wardour Street. She knows this, as it's fifty metres clear of the restraining order Charlotte imposed following her assault charges. The charges were later rescinded, in exchange for Emily's discounted shares in the company, and the house in Chiswick, where Charlotte and Dan now live. Her home, the thought stabs her. Her life.

"Fuck!" Emily snaps back to the acrid smell of burning. "The rice."

She switches off the flame and scoops a ladle into the gloppy rice. Only burned at the bottom of the pan, it's salvageable. More so than her career, she laments. Not to mention her social life. Most of her friends were shared with either Charlotte or Dan, and like her former clients,

Charlotte waged a campaign of disparagement to cleanse Emily from their friendship circle.

Emily dispenses the steaming curry into serving trays as gentle giant Frank, the shelter's manager, saunters in. With his pot belly straining at his Ramones T-shirt and his silver ponytail, Frank resembles a retired wrestler rather than a chartered accountant.

"As much as we appreciate you sacrificing your Saturday night, Em, shouldn't you be out on a date with some lucky chap?"

"Only with you, Frank." Emily blows a lock of hair from her face and slips on oven gloves.

"If only I was twenty years younger."

"Oh, what's a couple of decades?" Emily hefts the metal tray of rice, carrying it towards the doors. "But you're telling Angela."

"Ha! I'd end up in one of these serving trays." Frank falls in behind her with a tray of boiling curry. "But speaking of admirers…" His tone drops an octave, suddenly cautionary. "You've got a visitor at reception."

Dan? she thinks, expectancy coursing through her like an electrical current. As she backs through the double doors and turns into the canteen, her hopes plummet.

A tall guy, muscles packed into a brand-new suit, springs to his feet, flashing a bouquet of red roses and a row of yellowed teeth. Despite his sartorial makeover, Emily recognises Dwayne Campbell.

"You want me to get rid?" Frank asks, eyeing Dwayne warily.

"No, it's fine. I know how to handle him."

"I'm sure you could charm the Devil into your bidding, Em. But be careful with that one."

Emily inserts the tray of rice into the hot plate, slips off her oven gloves and ducks under the counter.

"Alright, Em?" Dwayne says with a husky Liverpudlian accent, embracing Emily in an awkward hug.

His cheap aftershave stings Emily's nostrils, but it is preferable to the aroma of their usual clientele.

"These are for you." A Tesco £10.99 price tag is visible on the wrapping as he presents the bouquet. "Shit. Forgot the price tag."

"It's a lovely thought. You hungry?" Emily gestures towards the hot plates.

"No ta. I've tasted your cooking before, remember?"

"Cheeky Scouse sod. Come on, I've got five minutes before we open, let's sneak a cigarette outside." Emily ushers him past the eclectic assortment of colourful dining tables, through a fire door and outside into a brick courtyard.

Emily first encountered Dwayne on a wintry night on the streets, when she and Frank were dispensing food parcels and sleeping bags, finding him half-dead with pneumonia and trench-foot. Emily slept in the A&E waiting room whilst doctors struggled to save his infected feet from amputation. When Dwayne was discharged, minus a toe, she checked him into a rehab clinic affiliated to the charity, and upon his release, secured him accommodation at the shelter and a job interview as a night cleaner at Billingsgate market. Now Dwayne is clear of his addictions, and his former occupation as a cat-burglar.

Emily pulls a crumpled pack of Marlboro Golds from her apron, offering them to Dwayne.

"Nah, gave them up with the spliffs. Off the lot now." He flashes a nicotine grin. "High on life now, me."

"Good for you."

"Nah." Dwayne shakes his head, his tone slipping gears, serious. "It's all down to you, Em."

As she lights a cigarette, Emily shakes her head. "No, Dwayne, you deserve all the credit."

"I don't know about that, but I hope you'll let me show my gratitude."

"Seeing what you've achieved is thanks enough."

"Would you… I mean… like to go out with me for dinner, like?"

"You mean on a date?" Emily tries not to sound defensive.

"I heard you and your fella split up. I thought you might enjoy a bit of cheering up, like."

"Oh, Dwayne, that's sweet of you, but… I'm not ready for that yet." The truth of her words hit Emily, making her voice crack. "I'm just not ready."

"Hey…" Dwayne reaches out a hand, touching hers. "Don't cry, Em, love. I came here to thank you, not make you upset."

Emily nods, wiping tears with her apron.

"That dickhead husband of yours must have done a number on you?"

"Just a little."

"Do you want me to sort him out?"

Emily laughs, but realises he is deadly serious. "That won't be necessary, but it's good to know someone is in my corner."

"Always, Em, whatever you need. I'm here for you."

Sensing the romantic overture returning, Emily grinds her cigarette into an overflowing ashtray and rubs her hands with antibacterial gel. "I'd better get back to it."

Back inside, a dishevelled queue forms at the hot plates, Frank and Angela dolloping rice and curry onto their plates.

Emily tugs a face mask from her apron pocket, putting it on, and leads Dwayne through the foyer, jostling past the shambling procession of the hungry and bone weary.

At the heavy security doors, Dwayne passes her a folded slip of paper. "My mobile number if you change your mind. Or if you ever, like, need me… for anything."

With a diplomatic smile, Emily slips it into the pocket of her apron. "Thank you, Dwayne. It is lovely to see you… doing so well."

"You too, Em." With a salute, Dwayne shuffles out.

As the door closes behind him, Emily berates herself for wishing her visitor was Dan. It couldn't have been him, anyway, she realises, having clicked on Charlotte's Instagram post yesterday. The usual boastful selfies of Charlotte, Dan and the baby, this time at Gatwick Airport. Emily blocks the thought of where they might have flown, when her phone vibrates in her jeans pocket. Another bulletin on Charlotte's Instagram. Unable to resist her masochistic fascination, Emily clicks on the post and hearing the piano chords of "Clair de Lune" she wishes she hadn't. Charlotte has indeed added to her story. Not the usual fisheye lens, blurry selfies, but professional photographs of Charlotte and Dan's wedding, on the Duomo steps in Ravello. The same Italian church where Emily had planned to renew their wedding vows.

13

ROSA
25 May

"That's why you went back to the group?" I ask her across the interview table.

"Yes. I was desperate."

"Desperate for what, Emily?"

Emily considers the question. "Help, getting on with my life."

"Or help to execute your plan for revenge?"

"No!" Tears glisten her eyelashes like dewy cobwebs. "But if I'd never seen that Instagram post, this would never have happened. At least, I wouldn't have been part of it."

"That's what we are trying to establish, Emily." DS Nicholls slides her a box of tissues. "What part you played in all this."

"Only an unwitting part." Emily wipes her eyes with a tissue, her grateful glance eliciting a smile from Nicholls. "I have nothing to hide."

"Everyone has something to hide, Emily," I say.

"I hardly need reminding of that."

I search Emily's face for transmitters of disingenuous sadness. Suspects faking tears often remain farcically dry eyed, but that is not the case here. Her furrowed brow and tension in the glabellar muscles, between the eyes, isn't difficult to manufacture, but Emily's vibrating chin is a signifier of genuine emotion. Or a talent for faking it.

"When was revenge first mentioned?"

"The following week, after the session, someone suggested going for a drink, so we went to the pub." Emily's voice cracks. "If only I'd never gone back…"

I lean back in my chair (as far as I can with it screwed into the floor) and employ the best weapon in the interrogator's arsenal, the pause technique: keeping eye contact, remaining silent after a question, lulling the suspect to fill it.

Emily doesn't oblige, wiping her glossy eyes with a fresh tissue, waiting for me to break the silence.

"Have you heard the adage, Emily? 'Before you embark on a journey of revenge, dig two graves.'"

Her chartreuse gaze meets mine. "If only it was just the two."

14

EMILY
21 March

"She robbed your fucking wedding venue, too?" Ciara snorts a plume of cigarette smoke, her cheeks incandescent with rage, or alcohol. Under the glow of an infrared pub heater, it's hard to distinguish.

Emily nods, lightheaded from the cigarette and four large vodka tonics.

"How come you didn't get married in Ravello in the first place?"

"I planned to, but mine and Dan's careers were at a crucial stage, so we settled on Chiswick Town Hall registry office. The money we saved went towards building Dan's painting studio in the garden. I always thought we would go back one day..." She takes a breath, composing herself.

"Why can't you have kids?" Ciara asks, as casually as enquiring about the weather.

"A severe case of endometriosis, which makes my uterus a hostile environment for the egg, sperm and embryos. The holy trinity of infertility."

"Fuck me. Of all our shitty stories, you win hands down, Emily."

"Lucky me."

Ciara jettisons a smoke wreath towards the Divorce

Support Centre offices above. "Bit of an odd bunch though, that lot, eh?"

"It's an eclectic mix, for sure, but I suppose the impact of divorce is universal."

"Universally shite." Ciara flicks her butt onto the cobbles. "Come on, it's my round."

At the bar, after ordering the drinks, Ciara vanishes, leaving Emily to pay and carry the tray of drinks through the crowded pub to the group, ensconced in a booth at the back.

Rachel, having returned from calling her daughter's nanny (for the third time), quails at the taste of her drink. "This isn't Hendrick's."

"Sorry, they ran out. Only had Gordon's, I'm afraid."

"Oh well, desperate times."

"Snooty cow," Ciara whispers to Emily.

Collecting his Guinness, Calum gives Emily an appreciative tilt of his chin.

"Gave up my army career for Sue…" Steve snags his glass from Emily's tray. "Thanks, doll."

Emily balks at the chauvinism, passing Tal his vodka and Coke, which he accepts with a gloved hand and no eye contact.

"Tell me about it." Calum nods in eager agreement. "I was a teacher when I met Bex, never happier, too. But there's no money in teaching, and that didn't fit Bex's aspirational vision."

"The one true love of my life." Steve raises his glass in a toast. "Faithful to the last."

"Your wife?" Tal asks.

"No, you numpty," Steve bellows laughing. "The army."

"You resigned your commission from the military so you could monitor your wife," Tal says, wiping the rim of his glass with a baby wipe.

"No, pal, to spend more time with her, and so we could start a family."

"I take it your wife ended this relationship with her previous lover?" Emily asks.

Through Steve's beard, she can see his jaw muscles tighten. "Like I said, it was a long time ago."

"Once a cheat, always a cheat," Rachel says.

"Aye, but hindsight never won a war, did it?" Steve drains his scotch, in a veritable speed-drinking game with Ciara, who has already emptied her prosecco glass.

"What does everyone think of our emotional guru, Malcolm?" Rachel asks. "Anyone feeling their identity redefined yet?"

"Yeah, he's a little didactic." Calum wipes Guinness from his lip. "But a friend of mine swore by him after his divorce."

"Crock of shite if you ask me. Talking about your troubles won't make them disappear. Whose round is it, anyway?"

"Why would you even come to counselling if you're so cynical?"

"Believe you me, sweetheart, I wouldn't if I didn't have to."

"The conditions of your sentence?" Rachel asks.

"Aye."

"Was it worth it?" Tal's eyes bulge with intrigue. "Assaulting your wife's lover?"

"It would have been if I hadn't been caught. Forgot all my training though, eh."

"What do you mean?" Calum leans forward, his interest piqued.

"Never let emotion cloud your judgement on an operation."

"When you were in the military..." Tal's words are slurring now. "How many people did you kill?"

"Can't tell you that, pal, or I'd have to slot you, too."

Tal's eyes widen with alarm.

"You dafty." Steve laughs. "I'm pulling your leg."

Tal looks disorientated, not getting it.

"I'm joking with you." Steve slaps his shoulder and raises his glass. "I propose a toast." Out of ceremony, the others raise theirs. "To our lying, cheating, bastard exes."

Laughter peals and glasses clink. Except Emily, finding it in poor taste.

"I lost count of the times Jack cheated on me," Rachel says.

"Your husband had a lot of love affairs?" Tal asks.

"Affairs, yes, but nothing Jack does has anything to do with love. Except for himself, that is. Every time they employed a pretty intake at his firm, it was like a personal crusade to screw her."

"Sounds like a sex addict," Ciara says.

"Among his many other dependencies. You name it – group sex, bondage, autoerotic asphyxiation – there is no level of depravity Jack hasn't plumbed."

"I thought your husband is a practising lawyer?" Tal asks.

"The biggest degenerates of them all, darling."

"Amen to that." Steve raises his glass.

"Of all Jack's vices, and they are legion, beautiful women are his Achilles' penis. Model types, you know – tall and leggy, but with tits. I'm sure he would adore you, Emily."

"If he prefers tall, beautiful women, why was he attracted to you?" Tal asks, po-faced.

"I love this kid," Steve cackles, slapping the oblivious Tal on the shoulder. "No filters."

He's not the only one, Emily thinks.

Rachel strains a smile. "Two things govern Jack: his cock and his wallet. I fell into the latter category."

"Why did you put up with it?" Emily asks.

"Who knows?" Rachel sighs. "My mother used to say, a husband is like a tight shoe. Even though it's constricting, a wife must wear it and suffer. Though it sounds better in Yiddish."

"You don't believe that?"

"No, of course not. I suppose I kept believing his false promises, and apart from him being an exceptional liar, I loved him. The shit. The only time he displayed remorse was when he was accused of sexual harassment. Not that Jack was concerned about my feelings, of course, he was afraid it would ruin his chances of making partner."

"What happened? Did he lose his job?" Calum asks.

Rachel shakes her head. "Jack is far too slippery to let anything impede his ambition. A private detective he employed at the firm dug up some smut on the poor girl. She'd dabbled with an escort service to help pay for her university fees."

"Blackmail," Steve growls.

"Sweetened with two hundred grand of my money, to assure her discretion."

"A sale of indulgence." From their perplexed expressions, Calum explains, "It's what the rich used to pay the Church to absolve their sins."

"It washed Jack's sins away like a pilgrim at Lourdes. The girl retracted the accusation, resigned from the firm, and his golden boy status was restored. If only they knew."

"Aye, if only…" Steve's brow furrows in thought, his jagged scar whitening.

"That's what you do for a living now, isn't it, private investigation?" Ciara asks. "Sounds exciting."

"Only on TV. What is it you do again, Ciara, love?"

"I'm an Environmental Health Officer for Westminster council. Yeah, I know, the epitome of excitement and glamour." She peers into her empty glass.

"So, you could close Tal's brother's restaurant down?" Emily asks in jest, trying to rescue the sinking mood.

"Sure, I suppose."

Steve's eyes narrow. "Aye, that'd teach the fuckers a wee lesson."

"Teach the fuckers a wee lesson," Tal echoes, his echolalia no longer garnering the others' surprise.

"If the premises aren't compliant with safety or hygiene standards… Jesus, would you listen to me? I'm fucking boring myself."

"No, that's interesting."

"Trust me, it's the polar fucking opposite." As the last orders bell rings, Ciara springs to her feet as if it were a starter pistol. "I'll get them in. Emily, would you give us a hand?"

Wedged into the bar, whilst Ciara screams their order to the barman, Emily realises it has been a long time since she's socialised like this. Not since… She shakes the thought, focusing on their previous topic. "Could you really close Tal's brother's restaurant?"

"Yeah. Like I said, if he was breaching food hygiene standards. Why'd you ask?"

"Just curious."

"Thirty-eight fifty," the barman shouts.

Emily turns to Ciara, who has once again performed her Houdini act. With an eye roll, Emily hands over her debit card. At least Ciara deigned to carry the tray of drinks this time.

As Emily returns to her seat, the mood has spiralled into melancholy, as Calum informs the group of his daughter's imminent departure across the Atlantic.

Steve's outrage is palpable. "How long is his contract in New York?"

"Two years."

"Fuck. That's not right, pal."

"Or legal," Tal nods. "They cannot take the child without your written consent."

"I know that. I spoke to my solicitor, but he reckons the process would be lengthy, not to mention expensive. I'd also require getting a mirror-order in the States, which would mean hiring another lawyer Stateside. I'm already strapped from the divorce… but it's not about the money. I'd sell everything I own if I could stop it, but my solicitor thinks they'd win anyway."

"It's only for two years." Emily offers a sympathetic smile. "And you can visit her in New York."

"Yeah…" Calum's head falls to his chest. "I just can't help feeling I'm going to lose her…"

"She'll always be your daughter." Emily places her hand on Calum's.

"It's not fucking right!" Steve hammers his fist into the table, which isn't as startling as the ferocity in his eyes. "You can't let them get away with that."

"There's nothing I can do."

"Not on your own, maybe." Steve rubs his beard. "But together we could. Right some of the wrongs our exes have done to us."

"What do you mean?" Emily already suspects his answer.

"I mean, payback."

"Revenge?" Rachel asks in a whisper.

"Aye, why not?" Steve's eyes sweep the pub.

"I'm sorry," Emily says, "what about Malcolm's big speech about letting go of anger and resentment?"

"Och, just words, fucking vowels and consonants spelling the same bullshit. That we lie down and play dead while our exes swan off with the spoils. Let me tell you something about anger. If it's directed in the right way, it can be a powerful weapon. When diplomacy fails, there is only one language some fuckers understand."

"You're not suggesting violence?" Emily asks, alarmed where this is going.

"Whoa, slow down, big guy," Calum says, "this sounds like a plot from a Hitchcock movie. You want us to kill each other's exes? Perfect alibis and all that?"

"Christ, you watch too much fucking Netflix. I'm not talking about violence, not in the physical sense at least."

"Pity." Ciara's expression is deadpan. From Emily's glare, she grins. "I'm fucking joking."

"I'm not joking." Steve's tone is laced with menace. "If we pool our resources, the six of us could cause some serious shite for that lot. No violence, we just fuck with their Instagram-perfect lives."

"How do you propose to do that?" Rachel asks.

"Infiltration, subversion and intimidation."

Emily frowns. "Your military parlance isn't assuaging my concerns."

"You've no need to fret, doll. We'd just give them some of their own medicine."

"An eye for an eye..." Calum says, clearly drinking the Kool-Aid. "A heart for a heart."

"Idioms aside, you're still talking about revenge," Emily says.

"Christ, tell the whole pub, why don't you?" Steve places a finger to his lips and lowers his voice. "But yeah, fucking right I am. I don't know about youse lot, but I'm done with taking the hits and fighting a war with nothing but blank rounds." Steve spreads his palm on the table, Musketeers style. His T-shirt rides up, revealing the word *Dìoghaltas* inked across the bleeding heart stretched on his massive bicep. The Gaelic word for vengeance. "Who's with me?"

"I am." Tal places his gloved hand on Steve's.

"Me too." Ciara slaps her hand down like a drunken gambler.

"And me." Rachel's bejewelled hand surprises Emily.

But not as much as Calum's joining the coalescence. "Fuck it. Count me in too."

Emily surges onto wobbly legs. "You are all insane, or pissed – probably both. And on that note, goodnight." She totters to the door, unused to the alcohol, struggling to fasten her coat.

"Emily, hold on." Calum catches her up at the door. "I'll walk with you to the tube."

Emily shakes her head, provoking her inebriation. "It's only a twenty-minute walk to my flat."

"At this time of night those streets are teeming with drunks and unsavoury characters."

Emily glances at their gloomy cohorts. "I'd rather take my chances out there."

"I could walk you home."

"Thanks, but I'll just flag a taxi."

"Then I'll wait with you."

"I think I'll be OK."

"Come on, I rarely get to be chivalrous these days."

Emily opens her mouth to shut him down, but her sister's advice echoes in her mind. "The only way you will get over him…" That, and the puppy dog vulnerability in Calum's brown eyes. "In that case, lead the way, Sir Knight."

"After you, Milady." Calum grins, holding the door open.

Emily steps outside, bracing for the rush of cold air. The orange glow of a taxi sign approaches along Floral Street. As she flaps her hand, the cab slows. "It appears your valiant services are no longer required."

"Seems to be a theme." Calum's smile tightens as the black cab draws alongside. "Tonight was… interesting."

"Yes, listening to drunken divorcees complain about their exes is like being trapped in a Dolly Parton song."

"I'm more of a Johnny Cash man myself." Calum opens the taxi door for her.

"Do you think he was serious?"

"Johnny Cash?" Calum cracks an impish grin.

"No. Steve, and his *Strangers on a Train* pitch?"

"Nah, just the booze talking."

"There was more to it than that," Emily says. "Something about him… scares me."

"I reckon he's more bark than bite. Bollocks, that reminds me, I need to walk Prince or he'll crap all over the flat."

"I'm assuming, and hoping, Prince is your dog?"

"He was, but along with everything else, Bex, my ex, won custody in the divorce. Now Matt, her new husband, wants to have him put down."

"No!"

"I know, right? No way I'd let that happen. But there's a no-pets clause in my building. You have no idea how hard it is smuggling an incontinent eighty-pound Labrador out for his evening walk."

"You're gonna need a bigger coat."

"Is one of you actually going somewhere?" the taxi driver asks impatiently.

"Sorry, yes, Bloomsbury Square please." Emily climbs into the back seat.

"Nice address." Calum arches an impressed eyebrow.

"It's only a one-bedroom. I'd have to knock through to next door to swing a cat in it."

"You should see the size of my place. A hobbit would consider it bijou. Still, I'll be evicted soon, anyway. Drowning Prince's barking with deafening drum and bass is probably counterintuitive."

"Good luck with that."

"See you next week?"

"We'll see."

As the cab peels into the traffic along Bow Street, through the haze of booze, Emily has an ominous sense of having booked passage on a doomed ship.

15

EMILY
25 March

Outside the Charlotte Street Hotel, Emily and her oldest client, Mia, part with kisses and promises of catching up. As Mia's taxi disappears into the traffic, Emily feels like her career is departing with it. Charlotte's campaign of disparagement on her professional reputation is worse than she feared. She considers hailing herself a cab, but having splurged on an extravagant and futile lunch, frugally decides to walk.

As she rounds the corner of Hanway Street onto Tottenham Court Road, Emily narrowly collides with a baby stroller. Inside the pram is a cherubic girl, with a smile so angelic, it extorts a smile from Emily's troubled features. "Isn't she adorable. What's her name?" Emily asks, glancing up at the father.

"Hello, Em," Dan says, as mortified by the encounter as his ex-wife. They remain paralysed, like actors in a play fumbling to remember their lines. "Ella... her name is Ella."

"I know." Of course Emily knows, with excruciating clarity. Not only has she endured Charlotte's crowing social media posts, but when Emily and Dan began trying for a baby, Ella had topped their list for girls' names. "It suits her."

"What the fuck are you doing here?" Charlotte races from

the chemist, hugging a pack of nappies. "You're breaching your restraining order."

"Lottie, for God's sake. It's just a coincidence," Dan says.

"Like fuck it is. Nothing with her is accidental." Charlotte's squealing pitch sets the baby off in stereo. As Dan reaches to comfort Ella, Charlotte fumbles with her handbag, tugging out her phone.

"It's OK, I'm going." Emily stumbles into the human traffic.

"Stay away from us, you psycho bitch."

Charlotte's words spiral after Emily staggering towards a taxi, unloading a family of Chinese tourists wearing face masks. She mumbles her address to the driver and slumps into the back seat, preparing for the inevitable tsunami of emotions. Yet as the cab merges into the afternoon traffic, Emily holds firm in the deluge, wading into the eye of the storm, channelling all its vengeful wrath.

Fuck. Her.

16

CALUM
28 March

"You're serious?" Calum asks, Guinness frosting his lip.

"Deadly." Emily's eyes corroborate her conviction.

"Count me in." Steve grins.

Like dominoes, a consensus follows from Ciara, Tal and Rachel. Finally, all heads turn to Calum, wiping his mouth with the back of his hand. "Seriously?"

"Let's have it, Pretty Boy, in or out?"

Calum pictures Bex and Matt's clandestine glance, after delivering the New York news. "OK, I'm in."

"Before we go on…" Emily locks eyes with Steve. "There won't be any violence, is that clear?"

"Fuck that for a laugh then, I'm out," Ciara snorts. From their startled expressions, adding, "I'm messing with you. Obviously, no violence."

"Do you all agree?" Emily asks, her eyes raking across the others.

With acquiescent nods from Calum, Tal and Rachel, Emily trains her glare on Steve.

"Define violence?"

"None of our actions can cause physical injury to anyone. Is that any clearer?"

"Lucid." Steve scans the bar for eavesdroppers,

before beckoning them in. "Before moving on to the operational stage, we need intelligence, and lots of it. All the information you can get on your exes and their new partners. Phone numbers, email addresses, passwords if you can get them. If not, relatives' birthdays, pets even, anniversaries, any significant security information to hack their digital defences. Be creative. I'm talking deep personal stuff. Medical conditions. Strengths and weaknesses. Hopes, dreams, fears, phobias, turn-ons, turnoffs, kinky shit, bad habits, vices. By the next time we meet at the group session, I want a dossier from each of you, outlining the ins and outs of your exes' arseholes."

Emily baulks, rolling her eyes at the crudity.

"I can assist gathering digital intelligence and capturing personal data," Tal says, capturing everybody's attention.

"Thanks pal, but I've already got a black hat I use regularly. It'll take a couple of weeks to set up but–"

"Thirty point five, two, five, eight degrees north, by forty-seven point seven degrees east."

Steve's eyes narrow to slits.

"What does that mean?" Calum asks, intrigued by Steve's muted astonishment.

"It is the GPS location you were rescued from in Basra, Iraq, by your regiment, in the twenty-second Special Air Service."

"How the fuck did you find that?" Steve hisses.

"I can hack any security system I want. MOD, GCHQ, MI5. You name it, I can infiltrate it." Tal grins, in his element. "Would you like me to tell you which pornography website you frequent?"

"No, pal, you've made your point."

"Fucking hell, you were in the SAS?" Calum asks in hushed reverence.

"That information is more than your life's worth. Understood?" Steve jabs his finger like a lethal weapon.

Calum nods, with the daunting sense that Steve means every word.

"So, what's the next step?" Emily asks.

Steve drains his scotch, his icy stare sweeping the pub. "Not here."

17

EMILY
7 April

Two Sundays later, Emily drives along a dirt track somewhere in rural Hertfordshire. Steve forbade the use of satellite navigation systems and mobile phones, and gave them written directions instead, puzzling Emily how anyone found anything before mobile phones. At last, she stumbles on her destination, steering her car onto a concrete driveway where several cars are parked outside a narrow, prefabricated building.

Buzzed through a security door, Emily steps into a long hallway. Following the stained carpet tiles, she peers into a kitchenette and a cluttered office. The headquarters of Steve's private investigation business, she presumes, and from the pillow and quilt on the lived-in leather couch, his home too.

"It might not look like much, but it suits me."

Startled, Emily turns to Steve. "No... it looks very... homely."

"Aye, well, it's perfect for our needs." Steve spins on his boot heel, leading her along the hallway. "Any trouble finding the place?"

"No." Emily's smile irons out the lie.

"Good." He waggles a finger. "I need those directions back."

"Sure." Emily fumbles in her handbag, passing him the crumpled A4 sheet.

Steve tears it into quarters and pushes open a Formica door. He waves her inside a spacious meeting room, where the gang sits around a white boardroom table. With the closed venetian blinds on the opposite wall, the blanching strip lighting above casts their faces in austere shadow. Emily reciprocates cursory nods from Rachel, Ciara and Tal, but no Calum. Maybe he's come to his senses, she thinks, curiously wistful at his absence.

An enormous whiteboard fills the wall space opposite the shuttered windows, not that there is much white evident. Covered with surveillance photographs, data printouts and flow diagrams, it looks like something from a police drama, or a serial killer's basement. The latter, Emily chooses not to dwell on.

"Bloody hell, you don't mess about."

"We're not here to mess about, Emily."

Emily resists rolling her eyes and sits on a plastic chair beside Ciara, now sporting a brunette bob, apparently changing her hair colour like a schizophrenic chameleon. Emily steers her gaze across the whiteboard, along the rogues gallery of their exes, until resting on images of Dan and Charlotte. Captured unawares in the driveway of her old house in Chiswick, at the organic coffee shop on the high street and outside her former offices on Wardour Street. A montage of their life, oblivious of the retribution awaiting them.

"There's coffee and biscuits in the kitchen," Steve says as if they were settling into a game of bridge.

"I'm fine." Emily smiles, peering at an ominous form jutting under a dust sheet.

"We're just waiting for Pretty Boy."

At the buzz of the security door, Emily feels a flutter of relief.

"Speak of the Devil." Steve jabs a finger at a door lock release button. "About time."

Calum peers around the door, ignoring Steve's glower, and saunters over to the whiteboard. "Wow, you don't waste any time."

Steve doesn't resist rolling his eyes. "Can't say the same for some. The directions." Steve clicks his fingers. "Give them here."

Calum slides the folded sheet onto the table, making Steve reach across for it, which he tears as though ripping Calum a new one.

"Hang on, he's in the wrong place." Calum points at a photograph of Rachel's husband. "That's Jack Noble. Bex's scumbag divorce lawyer."

"Small world." Rachel's Botox brow struggles to furrow.

"Fucking hell, he's not your lawyer too, is he?" Calum asks.

"Hardly. He is my husband."

"You're joking, right?"

"I can assure you, there is nothing about Jack that I find amusing."

Calum slides into a seat opposite Emily. "First kill all the lawyers." From their perplexed expressions, he adds, "It's a lawyer joke from *Henry VI*."

"Right, now you've deigned us with your arrival," Steve says, "let's get down to it."

"Yeah, sorry, I had to drop Bella off, and the traffic was a nightmare through Ongar."

"I'm not interested in excuses. If we are gonna do this, we do it my way. That includes arriving on time for operation briefings, and being where I say, when I say, got it?"

"Hang on, mate, I don't remember anyone voting you commander-in-chief."

"Twenty years served in the British Army, twelve of which in special forces and another twelve in the Metropolitan Police for Counter Terrorism Command. What are your qualifications, eh, Pretty Boy? A two-one from the University of Manchester in English, though I note on your CV it states you got a first."

Mortified, Calum opens his mouth in protest, but Steve is relentless.

"After your PGCE in Birmingham, you moved to the bright lights of London, where you found a job teaching English Literature in Stratford, until you met your ex-wife-to-be, Rebecca, AKA Bex, at Tower Records, buying a James Blunt CD – which, by the way, should have been a giant fucking red flag about her, right then and there."

"OK, that's enough–"

"Bex's father secured you your first position in the covert and high-octane world of espionage, also known as recruitment, in which you still endeavour. Or have I missed something?"

Chagrined, Calum shakes his head. "No."

"You're sure? Cuz I can I relay the details of your backpacking trip to Koh Samui?"

"No." Calum looks rattled. "You've made your point."

Steve's glare rakes the room, challenging anyone to make eye contact. Only Emily holds hers. "Aye, I've done background checks on all youse. So, unless anyone else thinks they're qualified to command this operation?" From the unanimous shaking heads, Steve takes his cue. "First off, I need your phones."

"No fucking way," Ciara says.

"You'll get them back. Tal is going to install an end-to-end encryption app, so if any of you are stupid enough to communicate via text and SMS messaging, at least it will be private and secure."

Emily draws her iPhone from her bag. The others follow suit, holding them up as Steve stalks around the table collecting each.

"Good, you were listening. All switched off." Steve places the phones on the table for Tal, who goes to work. "Better still, if you're on an op, leave your phone at home."

"If we can't use our phones on an... op..." Emily begins, disbelieving the James Bond vocabulary is already part of her vernacular, "how do we communicate with each other?"

From a leather sports bag, Steve slides an antiquated-looking cell phone across the table to Emily, then to each of them. "Burner phones. Untraceable. Use them only in an emergency, mind. Once they're finished, or compromised, dispose of them by smashing the phone and snapping the sim in half. Under no circumstances use your home or work landline, or your personal computers, to contact each other. We don't want any digital footprints leading back to us."

Rachel rolls her eyes. "I appreciate the need for discretion, but this seems a little excessive."

"With a suspended sentence hanging over your head, do you fancy six months in jail, Rachel?"

"Of course not."

Emily opens her mouth to speak, but Steve charges on. "The first sign of funny business, who are our exes going to be pointing the finger at, eh?"

"Us." Tal beams like a puffed-up prefect.

"Fucking right, they will. We do this my way, agreed?"

Concurring nods and murmurs ripple around the collective, except Emily. "But–"

"No buts, doll. Just in or out. There's the door if youse don't have the minerals."

Emily glances around the table. No one is moving. Least of all herself, she realises.

"OK then. Each of your burner phones has all our new contact numbers programmed in, under codenames. Tal is Cassio."

Rachel examines her phone, an archaic Nokia 130, as if it was dipped in shit. "What, may I ask, is my codename?"

"Emilia. Emily, you're Desdemona."

Recognition dawns on Emily.

"Ciara, you're Bianca."

"What's the relevance of these codenames?" Ciara asks.

"From the play." A smile curls Calum's lip. "Perfect."

Ciara looks bemused. "What fucking play?"

Emily glares at Steve. "Why would you choose characters from *Othello*?"

"It was just something that airy-fairy therapist, Malcolm, mentioned. Now, can we–"

"But my character, Desdemona, gets throttled at the end."

"Well, you can't be Emilia. It's too like your own name."

"Technically..." Tal interjects smugly, "Desdemona was suffocated with a pillow."

Calum frowns. "Who am I?"

"Roderigo," Steve sighs.

"No way. Roderigo is an imbecile, whose solitary role is to provide insight into Iago's agenda."

"It's just a fucking codename, man. Don't read anything into it."

"What's your codename then?"

"Othello."

"So, you've cast yourself as the hero?"

"He wasn't a hero," Emily interrupts. "He was a disturbed, manipulated puppet, who strangled... sorry, *suffocated* his innocent wife." She smiles at Tal, punctuating her sarcasm.

Oblivious of irony, Tal nods approvingly.

"Either way, he's the protagonist," Calum says, nettled. "And in that case, I'd rather be Iago."

"Alright then, Pretty Boy, you can be Iago. Happy now?"

"Who the fuck is Iago?" Ciara tuts. "Or am I the only one not a world authority on *Othello*? I fucking hated Shakespeare at school."

"Iago is the real villain, who revels in the pain and havoc he causes," Emily says.

Calum grins. "Better a villain than a patsy."

"Enough. Hero, villain, whatever your literary interpretation, it's just a fucking codename. Anyway, it was Tal's suggestion, not mine, and as codenames go, they're as good as any, right? Enough of this shite!"

"I have a question." Rachel raises her finger.

Steve's jaw tightens. "Aye?"

"Given our new endeavour, are we to continue our sessions at the divorce counselling?"

"Aye, we carry on as normal. Altered behavioural patterns are the red flags the police look for. Besides, some of us are legally obliged to finish the course."

"Police?" Emily asks. "There you go again with your casual implication of breaking the law."

"There's nothing implied about it, doll. Allow me to clarify. This operation requires us to break the law."

"No one gets hurt, though?"

"You've made your point, sweetheart. No violence. Are we agreed?"

"Yes, but never call me sweetheart, or doll, or babe, or love. I answer to Emily, or, I suppose, during an op, Desdemona. Is that agreed?"

Steve's wintery eyes lock on hers, but she holds firm. "Aye," he says, breaking the deadlock. "Before we get to the plan, I just want to mention costs."

"Here we go," Calum snorts. "I knew there was an angle."

"There's no angle. I have legitimate running costs, for expenses, associates' fees, payoffs and I'm not even charging for my hours."

"I will pay for all of it," Rachel announces, before Calum can speak. "Including your hourly rate."

"No, that's OK…"

"I insist. Just keep me updated on costs and invoice as you go."

"No, that won't work, there can't be a financial trail between us."

"Then I will instruct my accountant to set up a shell account offshore. Would that suffice?"

"So long as it can't be traced. I mean, without extreme difficulty. As Tal's talents have reminded me, you can trace anything."

Even beneath his Covid mask, Tal's boyish grin is evident.

"If my accountant can hide assets from Jack's parasitic forensic team, I'm sure he is capable."

"Fair enough." Steve strides to the curious shape under the dust sheet. "Now for the grand finale." Like an impresario, he tugs off the sheet, revealing a vast screen, eighty inches wide, mounted on the wall above a computer station. The screen splits into a dozen portals, like a shopping mall security system, each a voyeuristic tableau of their ex-partners' lives. Steve folds himself into a swivel chair at the desk, as the group approach with gasps and expletives.

"Jesus, is that what I think it is?" Calum asks, voicing Emily's thoughts.

Emily spies into her old house in Chiswick, where Dan feeds his daughter Ella baby food, on a highchair clamped to the kitchen table. *My kitchen table. Where is she?* Emily wonders, until Charlotte looms into view on the adjacent screen, peering into her office computer. *My office.*

"Wherever possible, we've hacked into the targets' existing CCTV camera systems. Otherwise, I've installed hidden cameras in their homes."

"How on earth did you manage that?" Rachel asks.

"What you don't know can't hurt you. And thanks to my boy Tal's exemplary skills, we've infiltrated the webcams on their work laptops and computers. Which explains the blank screens. They're only activated while they are switched on."

Of course, Charlotte is at work on a Sunday. Nothing, especially not the Sabbath, would impede her ambitions.

Calum steps closer. "Does it have sound?"

"Aye." Steve clicks a mouse, expanding the screen to one tableau.

From Calum's description, Emily recognises the palatial kitchen of "Bexingham Palace."

"How many roast potatoes do you want, babe?" Bex asks.

"Whatever, hon," Matt says, distractedly texting on his phone.

"Would you believe it?" Calum says, without humour. "She couldn't cook toast for me."

Steve clicks back to the multiple screens. "Youse all have passwords, so you can watch the live streams. Just remember to log out when you're done."

Emily shakes her head, too disturbed to speak. Voyeuristic prying of their exes on social media is one thing, but this intrusion seems a step too far. She looks at her cohorts for support, but finds no sentiment, or doubt, on their faces.

"The targets' mobile phones have also been accessed." Steve's fingertips flurry at the keyboard, and the interface from Matt's phone pops up on screen, showing his text discourse. An intricate back-and-forth detailing a financial trade.

"How the hell can you do that?" Calum asks.

Steve spreads his palms like a game-show host. "Over to you, Tal lad."

"Military-grade spyware I have been working on, which attacks security vulnerabilities on Android and iOS phones and installs spyware by calling the target," Tal explains as if it were elementary. "The recipient does not even have to answer the call, and once infiltrated we can activate the camera and microphone, intercept emails, messages and track their GPS location. Best of all, the installation is untraceable."

"That's not the best of all." Steve grins. "We can control their phones remotely."

"You mean, we can message from their phones, as if we're them?" Ciara asks.

"Aye." Steve clicks back to the multiple screens. "The lad's a bona-fide genius." He pats Tal's back. "You missed your vocation, pal. You'd make a fortune in data protection."

"Or cybercrime." Emily gazes at Dan playing with his daughter, her stomach plummeting. "This doesn't feel right."

"Right?" Steve looks staggered. "Right?"

"It doesn't seem... fair."

"Do you think they played fair?" Steve stabs a finger at a monitor.

His wife, Sue, is curled up on the couch in the muscled arms of her lover, Nick. Steve's twin girls are splayed at their feet on beanbags in the glow of the television.

"You think they accorded the rules of engagement with us?"

"No." Emily shuts her eyes.

"Look at them, laughing at us. But I promise you this. They won't be laughing soon."

"They will not be laughing soon," Tal parrots.

"I feel sick," Emily mutters.

"Aye, so do I. It turns my stomach to look at it. But we need optimum intel. If you don't have the guts, speak up, cuz after today there's no turning back until the operation is completed. Is that understood?"

Calum is first to nod his allegiance, then Tal, Ciara and Rachel. Their eyes fall upon Emily. She stares at the screen, watching Charlotte through her web camera at work. As her erstwhile friend types out an email, Emily realises Charlotte is sitting at her old desk. *My desk*. Charlotte always envied the view from Emily's office, and, as it transpired, her life as well.

"OK." Emily nods. "What's the plan?"

18

EMILY
8 April

Emily tries to recall her last job interview, long ago, before she and Charlotte set up the company. *My company.* She shakes the thought, pleased with her performance at securing the position with the law firm where Rachel's ex, Jack Noble, is on the cusp of becoming a partner. Through his recruitment firm, Calum proposed Emily for the vacancy as head of PR and marketing. A role which the human resources executive spent the past hour informing her will be pivotal to the firm's forthcoming merger with a monolithic North American outfit.

After agreeing the terms, Emily strides along the glass hallway towards the lifts. Turning the corner into the reception area, she stops dead.

At the elevators, Jack exchanges a farewell handshake with a matrimonial client. A grotesque Toby Jug of a man, bemoaning his gold-digging wife. Emily hangs back, listening.

"*Cherchez la femme,*" Jack says to his perplexed client. "It means, women are trouble."

"Too bloody right and all." The client waddles into the high-tech elevator.

"Such a pleasure." Jack's smile slips as his client steps from view.

"Hold the lift, please?" Emily hurries to the elevator.

Jack turns as Emily sweeps into the lift, his eyes poring over her approvingly.

Emily smiles, as the doors slide shut. *Cherchez la femme* indeed.

19

RACHEL
9 April

At a trendy gym in Bishopsgate, Rachel emerges from the changing room, neck to ankle in Lycra. After performing a few stretching exercises, she is already sweating like Pavarotti on a treadmill. Since the divorce, and her father's death, Rachel has let her once zealous exercise routine slide. Funny how certain habits are easy to break, whilst others appear to have Hulk-like indestructibility.

She glances at the clock – two minutes until her appointment with Steve's wife's new partner. Her eyes slide to her quarry, Nick Kamara, over by the exercise bikes, coaxing a client through the last burn of her workout. Rachel recognises him from Steve's surveillance photographs, but in the flesh, Nick is quite the specimen. Handsome and tall, with a body chiselled from granite, she can see the attraction. From their post-workout high fives and flirty tactility, so, it appears, can his present client. Rachel notes the white band of an absent wedding ring on his client's left hand. Safely in her locker perhaps, too precious to risk damaging in a workout? Or a more adulterine motive? If so, the subterfuge is irrelevant, as wedding rings are no deterrent for Nick.

Rachel ambles over to the exercise bikes. In the mirrored

wall, glimpsing her protruding flesh, she berates herself and pedals furiously.

"You must be Rachel, my three o'clock?" Nick asks, with an African patois.

"Yes," Rachel says between gasps.

"You're looking for some personal training?"

"Can't you tell?"

"You're looking pretty good to me." He tilts his head, giving her the once over like a used car. "A little tightening up, maybe?"

"Apparently, you're the man I need to get the job done."

"I think I'm up to the task." Nick chuckles. "But I have to warn you, I'm gonna push you pretty hard."

"The harder, the better," Rachel says flirtatiously, getting into the role.

"I can see that. You were giving it some just then. You'll put me out of a job."

Rachel almost feels sorry for him.

20

EMILY
11 April

Emily has worked tight deadlines before, but coordinating a restaurant relaunch whilst juggling her new PR job at the law firm has been a Herculean task. Earlier in the week, she'd called Tal's brother, Mehmet, posing as a publicity representative from the Turkish Chamber of Commerce and Industry, informing him Yusef's restaurant had been selected to represent Anatolian cuisine in the UK. Along with prominent members of the Turkish community, there would be substantial press coverage, as well as food critics and bloggers in attendance.

The catch, however, was that they only had days to prepare, as the original restaurant (Mehmet's local rival) dropped out for personal reasons. Despite the short notice, Mehmet snatched the opportunity, hiring decorators to spruce up the restaurant and even flew in an esteemed chef from Istanbul. No expense has been spared, and like the fabric on his wife Simone's new designer dress, Mehmet's finances are stretched to bursting.

After days of constant phone calls cajoling favours, Emily is bone-weary, her nerves taut as piano wire. And now, as the big night unravels, even her facial muscles are hurting from smiling at party guests. Particularly Tal's brother,

Mehmet, whose predatory eyes follow her arse like a cut-out painting from a *Scooby Doo* cartoon.

Still, so far, everything has gone perfectly. Anglo-Turkish socialites mingle with journalists and critics, guzzling champagne, caviar and sampling the exquisite taster menu. Laughter fills the packed restaurant, perfumed with the delectable scent of cumin, sumac and grilled meats. The atmosphere is intoxicating.

So far. Emily's chest tightens at the thought of what follows the last course.

Calum slips alongside her dressed as an Ottoman waiter, complete with a fake moustache, carrying a tray of humus and pita bread. "Would madam like to try the humus?" he asks with a bad Turkish accent.

"Nice touch with the moustache. Authentically louche."

"I rather like it. I'm thinking of growing one."

"Go with that. Apparently, the Village People are recruiting." Emily smiles as a food blogger dips his pita into the bowl of humus on Calum's tray.

"The countdown begins," Calum says as the blogger merges into the throng.

"Don't remind me."

"You OK?"

"I'm not entirely comfortable poisoning these people. I actually like one or two of them."

"Don't worry, Ciara said the symptoms will just be like mild food poisoning, so there'll be no come back to you. It's harmless, at least long term."

"And short term?"

"If you need the loo, go now, because when this stuff kicks in, there'll be a queue like Black Friday at Harrods." At Mehmet's commanding finger, Calum nods fealty. "Got to go. Just be ready to leave, before dessert." He slides into the crowd.

Emily watches as Mehmet, Simone and their hungry coterie fall on Calum's platter like ravenous seagulls. Mehmet's salacious gaze meets hers, his eyes sweeping over her. He wipes humus from his authentic but equally comical moustache and raises his glass. Emily strains another smile, her reservations abated. Bon appetite, douchebag.

21

CIARA
12 April

This was the most contentious part of the plan for Ciara, but following an expletive-riddled tantrum, a majority vote overruled her. Rachel was an executive producer for several movies, and one of her old contacts, Geoff Lancer, the producer of a hit television swords-and-sorcery show, owed her a favour. So, as Ciara sips prosecco, lolling on the couch, laptop on her knees, she watches with a large measure of cynicism.

"Jim, you will not believe it." Issy barrels into the photographic studio-turned-apartment, her keys still swinging in the steel-panelled front door.

"Oh aye, what's happened, love?" Jim asks, slumped on his couch, engrossed by an Ireland-England rugby match.

"Guess who called Ronda about me?" she asks, all Icelandic hard consonants and drawn-out vowels.

"Who's Ronda?" Jim turns up the volume with the TV remote.

"My agent." Issy flops on the couch, her ivory cheeks red from sprinting.

"Right, so."

"You'll never guess who called her, wanting me to audition?"

"Who's that then, love?" Jim's eyes remain affixed on the game.

"Geoff Lancer."

"Who?"

"The executive producer of *Swords of Destiny*. He wants me to audition for a part, a big part, Ronda reckons."

Jim's gaze snaps from the game. "Seriously?"

"They want me in on Monday at eight in the morning. They've already emailed me the script. I'm going to rehearse all weekend."

"That's great, love," Jim says, sounding the opposite.

"He must have seen the me in the play."

Doubtful, Ciara thinks, *it was bloody awful*.

"Or maybe he saw me on an ad campaign."

Again debatable, unless Geoff what's-his-name subscribes to the Next Direct online catalogue.

"Ronda said something about him loving my look for the part. I'd be playing an Ice Sorceress. How perfect is that?"

Jim nods, looking like it's inconveniently perfect.

"I'm getting that bottle of Bolly I got from Mamma." Issy darts to the kitchenette.

Jim switches the TV off and follows her.

Ciara taps the mouse pad, switching to the hidden kitchen camera and zooms in.

"No." Her platinum hair glows in the refrigerator light. "That might jinx it." Issy replaces the champagne and slams the fridge door.

Ciara grins, knowing Jim so well she can read his thoughts. If Issy makes it, how long is a moderately successful photographer, divorced father of two, pushing forty, going to last? Not bloody long, Ciara tallies, her cynicism evaporated, now considering Rachel's plan is genius.

"This is it, Jim, I know it is." She leaps into his arms, kissing his face off. "There is one potential issue." Issy stares at him with her irresistible ice-blue eyes. "The series has a lot of nudity." She unzips his chinos. "You wouldn't have a problem with that, would you, baby?" As she grasps Jim's flaccid manhood, Issy finds her answer.

Ciara spits her prosecco, laughing so hard.

22

EMILY
12 April

Through the looking glass, Emily watches on her laptop, via the camera Steve concealed in the boardroom of her old offices. Sat in her galley kitchen, she sips a glass of Barolo, savouring both it and the show.

Charlotte peers at the afternoon traffic on Wardour Street seven floors below. She turns back to the gaggle of twentysomethings gossiping about last night's film premiere event, and folds herself into her chair with a smug, faraway look.

Probably dreaming about her weekend plans, Emily assumes. She knows from Steve's reconnaissance, Dan's parents are minding baby Ella, and he and Charlotte are flying to Paris later. They are staying at the Hotel Plaza Athénée and have reservations at the three-Michelin-starred L'Arpège. At least, that was the plan.

Emily smiles.

On cue, Michael, head of social media, charges into the boardroom. "We've got a problem with Jake Simmons." Charlotte's celebrity chef client.

Prone to the dramatic, Michael's theatrical entrance has little impact. "Whatever self-destructive soup the idiot has fallen into now," she says, "I won't let him ruin my good mood, or my weekend, hauling him out of it." Registering the petrified expression of Pete, the IT guy, distant alarm bells appear to ring. "OK. What's he done now?"

"The sexual harassment, the drugs, the racism. It's all over social media," Michael says.

"How the fuck did it get out?" Charlotte bolts upright.

Michael steps back. "From us."

"What are you talking about?"

"There's been a data breach," Pete says, staring at his shoes. "Someone's hacked our server network."

The alarm bells in Charlotte's head must be ringing now, like Quasimodo after speedballing coke and heroin. Which, as it transpires, is another of the Jake Simmons revelations trending on social media. "Shut the system down, you fucking moron."

"We can't," Pete announces to his Converse. "The hacker has locked us out of the system."

"Fuck!" Charlotte slides back in her chair, good mood vanished, and with it any hope of their trip to Paris.

"Poor Charlotte." Emily grins. This is just the beginning.

23

CALUM
13 April

As his tyres crunch gravel on the driveway of Bexingham Palace (for once a satisfying sound) Calum congratulates himself on his impeccable timing. Bex and Matt crest the steps to the house like dismal spectres, witnessing his fleet of expensive cars being repossessed. After his insider trading arrest, authorities humiliatingly froze and seized Matt's assets.

Calum opens the back door of his Audi, and Prince lumbers out. "Come on, boy." As he strides towards his ex-wife, Calum resists the urge to click his heels together like Dick Van Dyke.

"What are you doing here? It's not your weekend." Bex's voice is hoarse, from crying and screaming at Matt.

"I brought Snuffles." Calum whips a fluffy pink unicorn from behind his back, waving it like a white flag. "Bella left it at mine. I was passing this way, so I thought I'd drop in. It's not an inconvenient time, is it?"

Bex opens her mouth to retort, but only a sigh escapes.

"While I'm here, I could take her for a ride. Get some ice cream or something. You know, with all this going on."

"Yeah, that would be good. I'll get her." Bex disappears into the house.

Calum skips up the steps to Matt, impotently watching

his Lamborghini be driven into a trailer. As Prince mounts the last step, he growls at him.

"That dog never liked me." Matt frowns.

"That's because he is a righteous judge of character." Calum stoops to stroke Prince's neck. "Aren't you, boy?"

"You're loving this, aren't you?"

Calum grins. He is, and has been all week, observing Bex's marriage dissolve into a ceaseless barrage of arguments, no doubt causing Matt to regret being granted bail. Who needs Netflix when you have Bexflix?

"I take it the American move is off?"

"Fuck off." Matt drags himself and his electronic ankle bracelet back into the house.

"'The evil deeds of the wicked ensnare them; the cords of their sins hold them fast,'" Calum says.

"Don't give me that sanctimonious shit, Calum. You're no angel." With a lugubrious head shake, Matt disappears inside.

Actually, a trip to the States isn't out of the question for Matt, all expenses paid by the US government. With his illegal trades spanning both sides of the Atlantic, federal prosecutors are appealing for Matt's extradition. Although the UK's own Financial Conduct Authority and the Serious Fraud Office aren't likely to hand over their biggest trophy case in over a decade. Matt was already on the FCA's radar, but insider trading is difficult to prosecute unless the defendant is stupid enough to leave a smoking gun. Fortunately, thanks to the evidence provided by a mysterious benefactor, Matt's case is like a smouldering Howitzer, directed point-blank at his head.

"Daddy." Bella bolts from the house into Calum's arms.

Finished strapping her into her child seat, Calum glances

up at the house, seeing Bex in the gothic arched window on the upper staircase, peering from behind a curtain, her face a scrim of grief. It reminds him of an image from his father's book collection, *Paradise Lost*, illustrated by William Blake, depicting a distraught and remorseful Eve castigated and banished from Eden. For some sins there can be no contrition or absolution. Only retribution and damnation.

24

EMILY
18 April

"I give them a month." Ciara's laugh turns into a paroxysm of coughing. With her scarlet bob, having dyed her hair yet again, she reminds Emily of the Chucky doll from the *Child's Play* movies.

"At the most. L'chaim!" Rachel clinks Ciara's glass, suddenly the best of friends.

In contrast, Emily feels detached from the jubilance of the group, gathered around their usual pub booth.

"Especially when Jim hears the series is being filmed in Canada. Fucking legend!"

"A six-month shoot, starting in a couple of weeks," Rachel says. "And the coup de grâce... Issy's new leading man is none other than Vince Kane – living adonis and pathological womaniser, who with Pavlovian predictability, invariably screws his leading lady."

Ciara snorts, prosecco dribbling down her chin.

"What's 'goodbye' in Icelandic, I wonder?" Steve asks.

"*Bless*," Tal says. "The Icelandic word for goodbye is *bless*."

"You're fucking kidding me? Well, in that case, bless the skinny wee slag. And bless us, too. To a perfect plan." Ciara raises her glass.

"No, credit where it's due. That part was all Rachel."

Steve seems uncharacteristically jovial. He has good reason. Rachel's accusations of sexual misconduct have led to Nick's suspension from the gym, and as result, Steve's wife has thrown her young lover out of the family home. "Who's laughing now?" He clinks Tal's glass. "Eh, Tal lad?"

"Who is laughing now?" Tal echoes stiffly, his mood similarly buoyant after Mehmet and Simone's reversal of fortune. Inundated with complaints of food poisoning, Ciara and her team of Environmental Health Officers closed the restaurant. In reality, ipecac syrup (a potent emetic) and magnesium citrate (a powerful laxative) caused the symptoms. Ciara swapped the samples taken from the kitchen, lacing them with salmonella. Consequentially, on top of the restaurant closure, Mehmet might yet face criminal prosecution. Either way, given the cataclysmic press and social media onslaught, his restaurant is toast.

"The success of that op is all down to Emily." Steve raises his whisky glass.

Emily feigns a smile. Only Calum, over at the bar, appears not to share the ebullience of their victory. Throughout the counselling session earlier, he seemed reticent and withdrawn. Malcolm focused on past relationships, and not only had Calum opted not to contribute, but he also sat in solemn silence throughout the session.

Emily slips through the Thursday night drinkers, squeezing in beside Calum at the bar. "Are you OK?"

"Yeah, apart from offering to help Ciara get the round in, and somehow ending up with the tab." He taps his debit card on the reader.

"She is rather slippery when it comes to the bill."

Calum's features brighten into a smile.

"You seem a little subdued tonight. Is everything alright?"

Calum's brow furrows. "To be honest, Emily, I'm a little concerned... about tomorrow night."

"You mean Operation Honey Trap?" she asks, imitating Steve's accent, but sounding like a camp Sean Connery. "You're not getting cold feet, are you?"

"No. It's just..." Calum takes a fortifying sip of his Guinness. "Are you sure you know what you're doing?"

"I took some acting classes at uni. I think I can pull it off."

"Karate classes might have been more useful."

"I've worked in PR for twelve years, and handling douchebags like Jack Noble is part of what I do, Calum." She draws out a paper napkin from a dispenser on the bar, and wipes Calum's Guinness moustache. "Besides, you and Steve will be close by, watching and listening."

"I thought Steve scared you?"

"Not when he's on our side. And so far, the plan has worked like a Swiss watch." Emily scoops up drinks.

"So far." Calum collects the remaining glasses.

"I'm sure it will be fine," Emily says, convincing herself as much as Calum. As they return to the table with the drinks, Emily catches Steve's leery eye, watching them.

25

EMILY
19 April

From the fifty-second floor of The Shard, Emily surveys the iridescent cosmos of London at night. The view, both exhilarating and unnerving, is a perfect reflection of her vertiginous emotions. Amid the Shangri-la Hotel Gong bar, she feels like a femme fatale from a noir thriller, dressed in a long black halter dress, a martini glass in hand – all she needs is a cigarette holder, and a pistol concealed in her garter. She has a subminiature camera and microphone hidden in her purse, but right now she would prefer the cigarette option. Emily would also rather Steve hadn't cut a hole in her clutch purse, from which the camera protrudes, but mostly she'd prefer to be somewhere else entirely. Calum's warning about Rachel's wayward ex-husband, Jack, lingers in her thoughts, combining with her anxiety over her upcoming performance.

It seems surreal – the movie-set backdrop, tech gadgets and the Bond girl costume – but she is here to play a role. The seductress. Earlier, dressing in the mirror of her luxurious hotel room, she fretted the dress was too alluring. The front split flashes thigh with every step, and braless, her breasts threaten to fall out at any moment. From the twisting necks and popping eyeballs, Emily keeps checking they haven't.

Still, you can't catch a mouse without cheese. Or, in Jack's case, a rat. Like the one laid for Jack, the evening is in effect one big honey trap. Ostensibly a party celebrating the law firm's twenty-fifth anniversary, its real aim is to cajole their potential American partners into consummating the takeover deal. Ironically, Emily has spent the evening swatting away the advances of their American associates, but has yet to speak to her intended target, Jack. She has observed him from afar, schmoozing the Americans, but he hasn't once glanced in her direction. Emily steers her gaze to the bar where Jack holds court with the senior partners and their Usonian brothers. Given his constant flirting all week at the office, Emily assumed she'd need Jack-repellent tonight, but maybe Rachel exaggerated her ex-husband's degeneracy.

Emily glances at her watch. Ten minutes to midnight. *Fuck it*, she thinks, draining her martini. *I didn't get dressed up for nothing*. As she approaches the bar, Jack has disappeared. Her eyes sweep the party, but he's nowhere to be seen.

Distracted from his conversation, an American partner leers at her, his alcohol-flushed face both cheery and cruel. "Is there a more tragic sight than a lady with an empty glass?"

I'm looking at it. Emily smiles.

"Can I refresh that for you?" He prods a tanned finger at her depleted martini glass.

"No, thank you. I think I'm done here." Emily strides away, ignoring his appeals, slipping through the throng of intoxicated lawyers towards the egress of the elevators.

26

CALUM

Two hundred and fifty metres below, on a side street behind Guy's Hospital, Calum hunches in the passenger seat of Steve's car. In their laying-up position, as Steve called it, watching Emily's clutch-cam on a laptop. Steve wears a navy suit and white shirt, whereas Calum is dressed head to toe in black. A sartorial choice he regrets, recalling when Steve picked him up earlier from his docklands flat. "Fuck me," Steve had said. "It's the fucking Milk Tray man. Why don't you just black up and have done with it? How naïve can you get?"

On the laptop screen, they watch as Emily stalks towards the exit.

"Shite," Steve growls. "She's heading to the lifts."

"Good." Calum exhales with audible relief.

"What are you talking about, man? She's gonna fuck up the plan."

"We shouldn't have put her in that situation, anyway."

"She's in a five-star hotel, surrounded by fucking lawyers."

"Yeah, I'm the naïve one?"

A figure blurs across the screen.

"Shut up." Steve thrusts his palm out, a relieved smile

spreading across his face. In contrast to the trepidation sweeping Calum's.

27

EMILY

In the sleek metallic elevator, Emily jabs the gold button for the forty-fourth floor and expels a sigh, not born of relief, but disappointment with herself. From her ruined clutch, she draws out the burner phone, texting an abort message.

"Not doing a Cinderella act, I hope?"

Startled, Emily fumbles the phone back into her purse and spins to the voice. Jack Noble saunters into the elevator wearing a silk-detailed suit and a fervent grin.

"Disappearing before all the midnight fun starts?" Like she hadn't got the joke.

"My glass slippers are killing me," Emily says, conscious of the lift doors swishing shut.

"I could give you a foot massage?"

I bet you could, Emily thinks, forcing a smile. Maybe Rachel wasn't exaggerating after all.

"You're on the forty-fourth floor?"

"How did you know?"

Jack nods at the illuminated elevator button.

"Oh yes, of course. Long day."

"What a coincidence. I'm on the same floor."

Yeah, right, she thinks, tilting her clutch purse and camera up at the target.

28

STEVE

"That-a-girl." Steve's eyes bore into the laptop screen.

"She's not a prize poodle competing at Crufts," Calum says. "This is dangerous shit."

Steve dismisses him with a head shake. "Come on, Em. You've got him on the hook, now reel the fucker in."

The camera bobs along, revealing plush carpet and an oak-panelled hallway, as Jack escorts Emily to her room, and beyond, if she pulls it off.

Steve claws at his beard, like he used to before a mission. It doesn't compare to the thrill of combat, but what does?

"I don't like this." Calum's features squirm with anxiety.

Amateurs, Steve rues, once again regretting Calum's inclusion on the op.

"I said we should have booked the next room."

"Good plan, Jason Bourne. And what if he clocked you, eh? He's your ex-missus's lawyer. He knows who you are, remember. Game over, that's what."

"But he doesn't know who you are."

"Aye, and that's how I intend to keep it. Quit your whining, I can't hear a fucking thing."

29

EMILY

Emily withdraws a gold key card from her clutch bag, careful not to expose the miniature camera inside. "This is my room," she says, teasing Jack with a smile.

"Aren't you going to invite me in?"

"It's a little late." Her key card ignites the green light, releasing the lock.

"Just for a moment. I'm curious to see the view from your room."

"Your room doesn't have a window?"

"It has a shockingly inferior vantage to your side. Besides, I would imagine any view including you would have an ocular edge."

"OK." Emily tilts her head in a yielding gesture and waves him inside. "But just for a moment."

As Jack takes in the city below, Emily positions her clutch bag on a side table, providing a widescreen view of the room.

"The Cheese-grater, the Scalpel, the Walkie Talkie, the Gherkin, not to mention the Freudian monolith upon which we stand – what is this postmodern obsession with erecting bigger phalluses?" Jack says, with a caffeinated tempo.

"Because the architects are all men." Emily slips her shoes off. "It's basically an expensive dick-measuring contest."

Jack splutters a dirty laugh, swaggering to the bottle of rosé sweating in an ice bucket on the counter. "Excellent, champagne. A sin to waste it." He tugs the bottle out, dripping on the carpet.

"Not for me, thanks. I've had enough."

"Nonsense. I promised I'd buy you a drink tonight." Jack twists the wire cage off the bottle.

"Yes, but we're in my room, so technically, that's my champagne."

"Actually, it's complementary of Chepstow, Brown and Lowe. As I'm about to be a partner, technically it's mine." The cork pops, frothing onto the carpet. Jack fills a glass, then pours a second.

"No, none for me. I'm knackered."

"I have a cure for that." From his jacket pocket, Jack dangles a baggie of white powder to the light.

Explains his sped-up cadence, Emily realises. "Oh no. No thanks."

"You don't mind if I have a cheeky line?" Jack tips the powder onto the counter and tugs a black American Express card from his wallet.

"Yes, I do mind. It's not appropriate, or legal," Emily says firmly, for the benefit of the camera.

"Chill out. You won't get into trouble." Jack chops two chunky lines and offers her a rolled-up twenty. "I'm your boss."

"I said no."

"Suit yourself." Jack snorts both lines, in extreme close-up on the camera.

Job done, Emily thinks. *Now to get him out of here.*

"Fuck! You don't know what you're missing." Jack's pupils eclipse his irises, focusing on hers with terrifying intent.

Out of her shoes, two inches shorter than him, for once, Emily feels disadvantaged by height, and trapped in a hotel room with a coked-up sexual predator. "You need to go."

"Relax." Jack slumps on the emperor-sized bed. "Come, sit." He pats the bed like a zealous dog trainer.

"No. I want you to leave. Now."

"Is it courteous to speak to your boss that way?" His lust is as palpable as Emily's dread, which only seems to feed the former. "I think someone needs a lesson in manners." Jack grins, but his eyes aren't smiling.

30

CALUM

Calum stares at the laptop screen, frozen with horror.

"Jackpot. Got you by the bollocks now, dickhead." Steve pounds his palm into the steering wheel.

Calum glares at him. "Can't you see how fucked up this is?" He tugs the burner phone from his black leather jacket and begins tapping a number.

Steve snatches his wrist. "Who the fuck are you calling?"

"Dominos for a pizza. Who d'you think? The police!"

"Are you mental? What are you going to tell them we're doing here, eh?"

"I don't know... I'll report a disturbance in the room."

Steve yanks the Nokia from Calum's grasp. "You're not jeopardising this operation. She's a big girl. Trust me, she can handle it."

Calum snaps his troubled gaze back to the screen.

Jack rolls off the bed and lumbers towards Emily. "You really want me to leave?" he asks with audible contempt.

"Yes, I do. Right fucking now."

With a shrug, Jack wipes his nostrils and swaggers towards the door. "You are making a very big career mistake."

"Like the other women's lives you have ruined. I'll take the risk, thanks."

"Thank Christ. He's leaving," Calum says. But his relief is short-lived, seeing Steve's expression clouding.

"Keep on walking, dickhead," Steve says, his icy stare fixed on the laptop.

As Emily reaches for the front door handle, Jack yanks her wrist.

"You fucking cock-tease." Jack wrenches her into his arms. "Dressed up like a cheap Russian hooker, shaking your tits at me all night."

"Get off me–"

Jack grabs her throat, squeezing her windpipe, trapping the sound. With his weight, he topples her onto the counter, knocking the camera tumbling to the carpet.

The camera view now only presents a low angle of the bed, but Emily and Jack's struggle is still audible.

"What the fuck is happening?" Calum asks, panicked.

"Shut up!" Steve turns up the volume, straining to hear through the laptop speaker.

"You know you fucking want it." Jack's voice is followed by the sound of torn fabric and the clink of a belt buckle being undone.

"No." Emily's cry is silenced as the laptop screen glitches to black.

Calum grips the car door handle, but Steve drags him back, jabbing a finger in his face.

"Stay here."

Before Calum can speak, Steve's door has slammed shut, and he is gone. Febrile with anxiety, Calum reaches for his phone, remembering Steve has it. "Shit." Calum stares at the blank screen, powerless and impotent. "Fuck this." He flings the passenger door open.

31

STEVE

Steve swerves through the Friday night revellers onto Saint Thomas Street, halting his run to a less conspicuous pace. Across the road, the illuminated monolith of The Shard looms into the indigo sky. At its concrete and steel base is the glass entrance to the Shangri-la Hotel, but Steve scans for the access point, past the two doormen at the front doors, focusing on the service entrance, fifty yards beyond. Discreetly pulling out his burner phone, he speed-dials a number, zigzagging through the traffic, crossing the road. "Casio, all eyes down."

At the service entrance, using the hotel employee identification badge (pickpocketed the previous day), Steve swipes the barcode on the security screen, and the door buzzes open. For days, Steve has studied the security guard drills and memorised architectural plans and schematics hacked by Tal, so he passes through the inner sanctum like a ghost. He emerges from a service door behind the reception desk and strides towards the bank of elevators when his burner phone vibrates in his breast pocket. Steve tears the pocket lining, tugging out his phone, and scans the screen.

DESDEMONA. Emily's codename.

"Desdemona?"

"Yes," Emily answers.

"Are you… alright?"

"I'll live."

"He didn't…?"

"No. I talked him out of it."

"Are you hurt?"

"I'm a little banged up, but I'll be OK. Can't say the same for your camera. It's broken."

"Broken how?" Steve eyes the guests mulling around.

"Broken, as in smashed into pieces, broken."

"Doesn't matter."

"Easy for you to say."

"It's all backed up on the laptop hard drive."

"You've got it on film?"

"Aye, in technicolour."

"Thank Christ for that." He can hear Emily exhaling with relief. "So, Operation Honey Trap was a success?"

"Aye, more like a bear trap, with his balls in it."

"What's left of them."

A smile spreads across Steve's face. "That's how you talked him out of it, eh?"

"I'll fill you in at the debrief."

"You not coming down?" Steve asks, perplexed.

"I don't have the energy. I'm going to sleep here tonight."

"Is that a good idea?"

"My door is locked and trust me, whatever rock Jack Noble has slunk under, he's not crawling out again tonight."

"Aye, well, so long as you're OK. You did good tonight, Em." Steve spots a commotion at the front entrance, where Calum is arguing with the doormen. "Shite, gotta go."

"What's wrong?" Emily asks.

"Your knight in shining armour, Iago, needs a wee bit of saving himself. Over and out."

Steve pockets his phone, morphing his demeanour and voice into an aristocratic lilt. "Stuart, my boy, I told you to wait for me in the car."

The doormen turn, perturbed by the posh beefcake squeezed into the suit. The incongruity clearly snags their instincts, but no one looks more blindsided than Calum.

"Apologies, gentlemen," Steve continues, parroting his former commanding officer's cut-glass accent. "Stuart is the best driver I've ever had, but he's a little slow on the uptake." He twirls a finger at his temple. "Nasty blow to the head. Isn't that right, Stuart?"

Calum nods, his mouth opening like a guppy fish.

"Come along, Stuart." Steve clamps Calum's arm before he can speak and frogmarches him through the doors.

As they march back along Great Maze Pond, Steve jams his fists in his pockets, so as not to use them on Calum.

"What's all that shit about? I haven't had a nasty blow to my head."

"It's still early. What fucking part of 'stay put' did you not understand?"

"What was I supposed to do? Just sit there?"

"Aye. You're supposed to do what I tell you. Rule one. Rule two: never let your personal feelings impede an operation."

"What personal feelings?"

"Och, come off it, Pretty Boy. Your head spins like *The Exorcist* every time she walks in the fucking room—" Steve halts in his tracks, seeing the passenger door of his car is wide open. He breaks into a sprint.

As Calum reaches the car, Steve is murderous. "Where's the fucking laptop?"

"It was on the front seat…" Realisation hits Calum. "Oh, shit."

"You left the door open, you fucking dick!" Steve slams Calum into the side of the car. "The recording was on the fucking hard drive."

"I'm sorry."

With whatever self-restraint he possesses, Steve releases his grip.

"What now?" Calum asks despondently. "He just gets away with it?"

Steve shakes his head. "No danger…" He stares up at The Shard's jagged blade puncturing the darkness. "He'll get what's coming to him."

32

EMILY

Emily examines her sore neck in the hotel room mirror, imprints on her throat already marbling into a contusion. Pain jabs at her lower back, where Jack shoved her into the counter. It might have been worse. Emily shudders at the thought. "Bastard."

As she peels off her ripped dress, Emily sees the teeth marks puncturing the skin above her left breast. She traces her fingers over the wound, the pain igniting her recall of Jack biting her:

"You know you fucking want it." Jack wrenched her halter dress, tearing fabric.

Emily's wrists burned, pinned to the marble counter held in his grip. She could feel Jack's hardness rubbing at her crotch, sour alcohol on his breath as she twisted away from his slobbering maw. The searing heat of his teeth sinking into her flesh. As he unbuckled his belt, Emily seized her chance. "No." Rage surging, she shoved him backwards with her free hand. Caught off balance, Jack didn't expect the ferocity of Emily's swimmer's shoulders, and her powerful thigh muscles, as her knee connected with his groin.

Jack doubled over, clutching his testicles, spraying vomit on the carpet. "You... bitch!" he said, between heaving.

Emily staggered over to the bedside table, regaining her breath.

"You'll be fucking sorry for that, I promise you." Jack spat the last of his yellow bile.

"Not as sorry as you, if you don't get the fuck out of here, right now." Emily grasped the bedside phone receiver, hit zero for reception and pressed speaker. "I need help!"

"OK, I'm going." Jack hobbled to his feet, wiping puke from his mouth with the back of his hand.

"What help do you require, madam?" a woman asked through the phone speaker.

"I'm fucking going, OK."

Jack yanked the door open, clutching his groin, scowling back at her as the door closed behind him.

"Sorry, false alarm." Emily hung up the phone, inhaling deep breaths and counted the seconds until her breathing regulated.

Emily shakes the memory. From the mini-bar drawer, she selects a miniature Belvedere and pours herself a glass. Jack's downfall now feels personal, and like the salutary warmth of the vodka, she savours the prospect of making him pay. The last of her adrenaline departing, Emily places the glass on the nightstand and collapses face first on the bed. She shuts her eyes, memories with it, and plummets into a fathomless sleep.

33

EMILY
20 April

Emily peered through the staircase spindles, listening to her parents rowing in the living room below, their voices drowned out by the booming hi-fi. A method her father employed to deafen Emily and her sister, Sara, from the abuse their mother hurled at him. Scarlet light stabbed through the glass front door panels. Dawn already. Red sky in morning, shepherd's warning. Her parents had argued all night, the row erupting earlier that evening, at a restaurant, ostensibly celebrating Emily's thirteenth birthday. As her mother drank more wine, the innuendoes slung at her father became less subtle, until even their waitress and the surrounding diners knew he was having an affair. Sara was away on a French exchange trip, leaving Emily alone to contend with the ensuing drama. She could have remained in bed, head buried under her pillow, until the inevitable slamming of the front door and the sound of Daddy's Jaguar roaring from the driveway, secure in the knowledge of him returning by the waking light. Yet, there had been an ominous finality about their quarrel earlier. When they returned from the restaurant, her mother graduated from wine to gin, literally her ruin, and insinuation escalated to accusation. Daddy had met someone else, and in the morning, he was leaving for good.

"You can't treat me like this. You're not going anywhere!" Her mother's scream pierced through the stereo downstairs, followed by the thump of something heavy falling. Her father's dead weight.

Emily snaps awake, clammy with sweat, adjusting to the pink gloam of the hotel room. A waft of stale vomit hits her nostrils from Jack's throw-up. As she rolls out of bed, pain stabs her coccyx. She examines the livid abrasions marking her lower back in the mirror. More disturbing are the purple bruises on her throat from Jack's chokehold. Emily circumvents his dried puke on the rug and pads over to the mini bar, selecting a bottle of mineral water. As she gulps, Emily gazes out of the window at dawn bloodying the city. *Shepherd's warning*, she thinks ominously. No time for a swim or breakfast. She needs to leave before Jack wakes with the hangover of his life.

Emily needn't worry. Jack's condition is rather graver.

34

ROSA

I ascend The Shard elevator, tugging the polyethylene boiler suit over my black linen trousers, my thoughts drifting to my children, and my husband's plans for the day. Bruce is taking Val to a fashion exhibition at the V&A, with poor Nate forced to drag along. But he'd taken Nate to the Chelsea match the previous Saturday, so it balanced out. That's Bruce, always fair. The good father. The good husband. Guilt stabs in my gut. After the exhibition and lunch, they'll pick up some meat and salad and, taking advantage of the warm weather, enjoy a barbecue in the garden this evening. I know the chances of me making it home in time: nada.

When I broke the news to Bruce earlier, he had the usual resignation in his eyes, but something else, too. Suspicion, perhaps? Even when I am telling the truth now, I feel guilty. Soon there will be no more lies, I attempt to reassure myself, but it only compounds my anxiety. Then I'll face a precipice, more daunting than the chasm yawning beneath my feet. I snap on my forensic gloves and booties, flip on the hood, position my mask and prepare to get into character. As the elevator halts at the forty-fourth floor, glimpsing my reflection, I look like a Teletubby, an incongruous costume for the stage I'm about to enter.

As the lift doors part, a Mortuary Officer wheels a gurney, escorted by DC Williams, identifiable despite his forensic hood and mask, as the only other Black officer on my team.

"Can I have a look?" I lean over the body bag on the gurney.

"Yes, ma'am," DC Williams says with a south London accent, nodding to the Mortuary Officer.

He unzips the bag, revealing the distended, purple death mask of a deceased IC1 male. In layman's terms, a white guy. His protruding eyes, bloodshot from a subconjunctival haemorrhage, are frozen with astonishment or agony. I note the thick V-shaped bruising on his neck. Ligature marks. "Let's see the rest of him?"

The Mortuary Officer unzips the entire length of the bag, exposing the deceased's naked body, a darker purple towards his feet. An athletic, gym-toned body and well endowed. Or he was. Circumcised. Jewish? Manicured fingernails. Wealthy, or gay, maybe both? No wedding ring, but the pale indent where there used to be one. No other discernible injuries, except for his testicles and upper thighs, which appear contused. The effects of the livor mortis, I wonder, or an inflicted injury?

I duck under the police tape across the doorway, and step into the palatial hotel suite. Despite the swarming forensics team, and Scenes of Crime Officers (SOCOs), it remains impressively decadent. A heady smell assails my nostrils: amyl nitrate, I recognise from my student days. Poppers.

In the bedroom, I gravitate to a glass coffee table by the window, where a SOCO is photographing drug paraphernalia. Trace lines of cocaine. A black American Express card. Definitely wealthy. A rolled twenty, and three glass phials containing the remnants of a clear liquid.

I sense the lanky presence of DS Butler, the Crime Scene Manager, before he appears. Even shrouded in forensic attire, at six foot seven, Butler is impossible to not recognise.

"Where was the body found?"

"In the wardrobe." Butler extends a gangly arm at the fitted wardrobes, being swabbed and videotaped. "Hanging from a belt, he was, bollock naked. Some sort of sex game gone awry, it would appear."

"Who found the body?"

Butler consults his crime scene log. "The maid, at eleven twenty-six. Checkout time is at eleven."

"Speaking of checking out, do we have a time of death?" I sniff one of the empty phials, but it's odourless.

"The pathologist reckons between two and four in the morning. We'll have to wait for the postmortem."

"The pathologist still around?" I ask, suspecting the answer.

"He left about ten minutes before you arrived."

DS Nicholls ambles over, nodding hello. "Ma'am."

"Do we have an ID on the deceased?"

"Jack Noble, forty-two," Nicholls says, reading from his notebook. "A divorce lawyer."

"That'll narrow the suspects down."

"You think this is suspicious, ma'am?" Nicholls asks.

"I haven't established that yet, Sergeant. Any of the neighbouring rooms hear a disturbance?"

"Nothing reported," Butler says. "The guests were partying until five, and they checked out before the body was found."

"What party?"

"Some sort of legal bash, for a city law firm."

"Not that legal, as it goes." Nicholls nods towards the goodies on the coffee table.

"Who's leading forensics?"

"That would be me," a familiar, demure voice says.

I turn to a Wahida Begum, a forensic examiner I've worked with on several investigations. "What's your initial theory, Wahida?"

"The room doesn't suggest a major disturbance, or signs of a struggle, and given the drug paraphernalia, the deceased's state of undress, the porn on the TV…"

"Porn?" I glance at Butler.

"Yeah, sorry, the maid said there was porn playing on the widescreen. She switched it off when she came in."

I turn back to Wahida. "And your early hypothesis?"

"Autoerotic asphyxiation. Textbook," Wahida says.

"I'll need a list of neighbouring guests, and anyone at the party."

"Already on it," Nicholls says.

"And CCTV."

"Bit of an issue there. The security cameras had a technical glitch last night."

"What kind of glitch?"

"Around twelve thirty, the hotel security cameras started looping footage."

"Every camera in the hotel?"

"Yep, and the exterior cameras, too. Security didn't pick up on it until it started getting light this morning. I know, weird one, right?"

"Yes." I nod, reassessing the scene. "That is weird."

35

EMILY

Emily glides through the municipal pool with the same flawless technique she's maintained for the past ninety minutes. Swimming is her solace, especially in times of psychological stress, the endorphin rush better than any pill. But today Emily's disquiet remains, last night's trauma disturbing the silt covering her long-buried memories.

As she towels off in the changing room, Emily flinches from her injured back. Mementos of her melee with Jack, evident in the purple and yellow bruising around her throat and her lower vertebrae. A small price compared to Jack's upcoming reprisal, she thinks, with a consolatory smile.

Her phone buzzes in the locker, but as she peers inside, her iPhone is motionless. The vibration must be from the burner phone in her handbag. Apprehensive, Emily checks nobody is observing and draws the Nokia from her purse. The caller ID fills her with dread. OTHELLO. Steve's codename.

"Hello?"

"Get rid of this phone," Steve says. "It's not safe. Write this number down and call me on a pay phone, quick as you can."

As Steve dictates the number, Emily ransacks her bag

for a pen and jots the digits on her wrist before the line goes dead. Satisfied the changing room is clear, she wraps the phone in her towel and smashes it under her heel, extracts the sim card from the plastic rubble and snaps it in half.

"What took you so long?" Steve's voice echoes down the phone line.

"You try finding a pay phone that actually works," Emily pants into the receiver. As she discovered, sprinting through Covent Garden, most of the remaining red phone boxes that aren't vandalised are purely ornamental. She finally found a working model outside the Nag's Head pub, ironically, and now she feels dizzy and nauseous. "Can you just tell me what the fuck this is about?"

"Emilia had a visit from the Metropolitan Police."

Emily's brain processes their codenames, recalling Emilia is Rachel.

"They informed her of her husband's death."

"Jack Noble is dead?" Emily's mind reels.

"Christ, no names."

"He can't be – that's not possible."

"Emilia just identified his body. So, yeah, he is."

"How?"

"Suicide, misadventure. The police didn't give anything conclusive. Point is, they'll pay you a visit, so you need to get your story straight. They'll have you on CCTV in the elevator, and the corridor outside your room. He came in for a wee drink and fucked off. Got it?"

"Can't I just tell the truth?"

"No!" She can hear Steve composing his tone. "You'd be

admitting to a motive. Wear a neck scarf or something to cover your bruises and just do what I say, got it?"

Emily exhales, trying to compose her own shock. "How is she doing?"

"Who, Emilia?"

"Can we dispense with the fucking codenames?"

"Stick to the protocol."

"OK. How is Emilia?"

"You can ask her yourself at the debrief after the next session."

"We're still carrying on with that?"

"Aye, we go on as normal. Especially now. Just remember: if in doubt, say nowt."

The line goes dead. As Emily steers her gaze up to the Divorce Support Centre windows above the pub, she is overcome by a portending sense that whatever calamitous momentum is propelling her now, it's just getting started.

36

ROSA
21 April

I sit at my cluttered desk, with portly CCTV analyst DC Tomlinson and DS Nicholls, ignoring Tomlinson's wafting body odour, studying the last footage of Jack Noble, alive. In The Shard elevator with the tall, auburn-haired woman.

"Update from pathology and toxicology." DCI Hughes looms over us, leafing through a manila folder. "No prizes for guessing the cause of death. Asphyxia. Although, he had enough toxins in his bloodstream to have killed him anyway. The onset of lividity, its location and colour, puts the time of death between two and four."

As Hughes plops the two documents on my desk, I flick through the toxicology report. "Recreational amounts of cocaine," I read. "But lethal levels of gamma-hydroxybutyrate."

"What's that in English?" Nicholls asks.

"GHB, the sex drug. Colourless and tasteless." I flick through the postmortem report.

"His wife stated he had a coke habit. Nothing about GBH though," Nicholls says, sipping tea from a squeaky Styrofoam cup.

"GHB." I roll my eyes back to the pathology report, sitting upright with curiosity. "His hyoid bone was fractured."

"Common in hangings," Hughes says.

"From the weight of the body falling. But in a wardrobe? And what about these contusions on his inner right thigh and testicles?" I prod the pathology diagram.

"The guy was a divorce lawyer. He probably took a kick in the balls daily; from whatever poor husband he was fleecing." Hughes's bitterness is palpable, having endured his own divorce the previous year.

"When investigating any violent death, a detective should always proceed as though it were a murder inquiry," I say.

"I don't need the Murder Investigation Manuel quoted to me, Hawkes." Hughes leans over my shoulder, peering at the CCTV image paused on screen. "Who is she?"

"No ID yet, sir, but she's potentially the last person to see the deceased alive. There's something else too." I nod to DC Tomlinson. "Play the other clip."

Later that evening, seated at the bar in the Covent Garden Hotel, the CCTV footage loops in my brain, intuition nagging me that the tall woman in the elevator is key. I sip my mojito, trying to forget the fabrication I told Bruce, that I'm meeting a Crown Prosecution Lawyer. Which is true, in part. Guilt tightens in my stomach, picturing the domestic tableau at home. Bruce's *Sexiest Dad* apron straining at his belly, glass of Rioja in hand, coaxing the kids from their rooms for Sunday dinner.

"Is this seat taken?" he asks, giving me a start. I tilt my head towards the voice, feeling the familiar fluttering in my chest. Flecks of grey highlight his short, black hair and trimmed beard. Six-two of muscle, packed into a pink button-up shirt. A younger, better-looking version of Idris Elba, he slides onto the stool beside me.

"Help yourself," I say.

"A large Glenfiddich please, no ice," he tells the barman. "Fancy one?" He smiles at me, flashing his hazel eyes.

"Pardon me?"

"Another mojito?"

"Oh, no thanks. I'm waiting for someone."

"Lucky guy." He waves a room card at the barman. "Put it in on room 304." He turns, meeting and holding my gaze. "If whoever you're meeting doesn't show, you know where I am." After draining his drink, he saunters out of the bar, looking better than any man should in tight jeans.

I awake, disorientated and dehydrated, the hotel room slowly taking shape, as does the slumbering form of Idris's doppelgänger laid beside me. Saffron street light shafts through the curtains, highlighting our crumpled clothes strewn across the floor, torn from each other's bodies the second I entered the room. Stale remnants of room service lie on a platter on the table, beside an upturned bottle of house champagne in the melted ice bucket. I reach for my iPhone on the nightstand, ignoring the missed calls and texts from Bruce, and check the time. Two in the morning. Shit. I need to get home before the kids wake up for school. I peel off the clammy sheets, scanning the detritus for my clothes. What story will I spin Bruce? My meeting overran with the CPS. Not entirely untrue. The best liars always stay close to the truth. Harder to be trapped remembering the lie, and less body-language leakage. Useful when your husband is a professor of forensic psychology. Naked, I tiptoe through the carnage, plucking a bottle of mineral water on my way to the shower, aware sparkling water isn't good for my reflux acid, but neither is champagne, or infidelity.

Gareth and I knew each other for years before we began our affair. With his role as a Crown Prosecution Service lawyer, we clashed at first, perhaps in denial of our inexorable attraction, before the inevitable acceptance. I swallow an antacid capsule with a swig of fizzy water. A paradoxical mixture, equal parts salutary and nocuous, like our affair.

"What time is it?" Gareth asks, stirring.

"Two o'clock." I lean over the bed, kissing him, relishing and lamenting our fleeting time.

"Come back to bed." His hands grasp for me.

"I can't. You need to get home, too."

"Ubi thinks I'm staying at Pete's."

"Nobody lies like a lawyer." Reluctantly, I wriggle free.

"Or a cop," he says.

I retreat to the bathroom, his words resonating.

37

EMILY
22 April

Before Emily finished her first espresso, Brenda from HR informed her of the police interviews scheduled on the twenty-eighth floor. The office was abuzz with rumours of Jack's death, varying from a sex-crazed drug overdose to an elaborate suicide, except to Emily he seemed too narcissistic to kill himself intentionally. The last person to be interviewed, Emily steps from the elevator at five thirty. She adjusts the silk scarf covering her bruised throat and strides along the hall, with Steve's instructions echoing in her head. A figure is visible in the glass boardroom, a balding, moustached man watching her through the vertical blinds before drawing them shut. She takes a composing breath before tapping her knuckles on the glass door.

"Come in," a female voice says from within. Sharp and authoritative.

Emily steps into the boardroom, adjusting her eyes to the afternoon sun. Two people sit at the Viking-sized board table, their silhouettes haloed against the window and the bleached outline of Saint Paul's Cathedral. The man with the moustache looks as beige as his suit, his thinning hair wispy as a dandelion. His colleague is austerely beautiful, with full lips, sharp cheekbones and arched brows above dark, feline eyes. With her wavy hair, restrained in a taut ponytail, and her black businesslike suit, she wouldn't look out of place with the lawyers usually sat in her seat.

"Take a seat, Emily." She waves to the chair opposite.

The position of her seat, facing the glare, is an obvious interrogation technique, but it's working. Sweat clings to the back of Emily's blouse, and the supplemental heat from her scarf isn't helping.

The female detective presses the record button on a pocket-sized digital recorder on the table between them.

"I am Detective Inspector Hawkes; this is Detective Sergeant Nicholls," she says. "We will ask you about the events on the evening of Friday the twentieth, and the early hours of Saturday the twenty-first of April, whilst you were a guest at the Shangri-la Hotel, in The Shard of London."

"OK." Emily nods, caught in the detective's panther-like stare, observing her every nuance.

"What was your relationship with Jack Noble?"

"My relationship, if you can call it that, was purely professional. I only started working at the firm a couple of weeks ago, so I barely knew him."

"And yet, you invited Mr Noble into your room?" Twisting her laptop, Rosa displays a paused CCTV image of Emily and Jack on her hotel room threshold. "That is you with Mr Noble?"

Emily's gut tightens. Despite Steve's warning, the starkness of the image unsettles her, conjuring memories of police interviews after her father's murder, and the disclosure of evidence at her mother's trial. "Yes." Emily's lips feel sticky, her mouth parched. "That's me."

"Doesn't seem professional to me, inviting an inebriated

male colleague you barely knew into your room after midnight?"

"I didn't invite him."

"Are you saying Jack Noble forced himself inside your room?"

"No, but…" Emily remembers Steve's caution. "He wanted to see the view." She winces internally at how implausibly naïve it sounds.

"The duration Mr Noble spent in your room was seventeen minutes. A long time to enjoy the view."

"He also suggested we have a drink."

"And then what happened?"

"He left."

"You're sure about that Emily, nothing else transpired?"

"What are you implying?"

"In the days leading up to the party, several of your colleagues witnessed you and the deceased interacting in a flirtatious manner."

"It was just friendly, harmless banter."

"Perhaps you considered it harmless, but Mr Noble had a reputation for being overly friendly with female employees."

"I can't comment on that. Like I said, I'm new here."

"Did anything sexual happen in your room?"

"Absolutely not."

"Not even an unwanted advance?"

"No."

"Emily, can you pull down your scarf?

"Sorry?" Emily masks her alarm.

"You appear to have a contusion hidden under your scarf. Can I see?"

"It's nothing." Emily tugs her scarf down. "There was a

kerfuffle yesterday at the homeless shelter I volunteer at."
Kerfuffle? Emily rues the word.

"We will need to corroborate that."

Shit, Emily thinks, remembering Steve's sage advice. "If in doubt, say nowt."

"Sergeant Nicholls, cue up the next CCTV clip," Rosa says, without removing her stare.

On the screen: Emily watches Jack limping from the hotel room, clutching his groin in visible pain.

"Think carefully before you answer this next question, Emily." The detective rests her elbows on the table, leaning into the question. "Would you like the opportunity to revise your statement?"

38

MALCOLM
25 April

"When is the funeral?" Malcom breaks the silence. Throughout the session, the tension has been palpable, the openness and trust gained in the proceeding weeks gone. Given the tragic news of Rachel's estranged husband, it is understandable, but Malcom senses a wariness within the group.

"When the coroner deems fit to release the body." Rachel shrugs. "It depends on the investigation."

Given Rachel's resentment for her ex, Malcolm wouldn't expect the grieving wife, but her total lack of emotion is concerning. Bizarrely, his death appears to have impacted more deeply on the others. Tal is particularly morose, and even the garrulous Ciara is barely monosyllabic.

"It's just procedure in cases of death by misadventure," Steve says, his eyes raking across the others.

"How is your daughter?" Emily avoids Steve's glare.

"Not great. Despite Jack's... shortcomings, Florence idolised him."

Emily nods. "We only get one father."

Rachel reciprocates an acknowledging nod.

"It can't be easy for you, Rachel," Malcom says. "As I

understand it, in the Jewish faith, it's important to bury the dead as quickly as possible?"

"Jack wasn't Jewish," Rachel scoffs. "He converted to Judaism to endear himself to my father, the one person on whom his infallible charms failed to work. Jack will spin in his grave, cast into eternity as a Jew." A smile gathers across her face.

Jesus, Malcolm thinks, *hell hath no fury…*

"What about his family?" Emily asks.

Rachel shakes her head. "He has a brother somewhere in South Africa. Durban, last I heard. His pregnant girlfriend and her father have turned their backs. The scandal, I suppose. So, it falls to me and Florence to bury him. His only family."

"Family is crucial in difficult times," Malcom says, annoyed at his lapse into platitude, rather than philosophical insight.

"Family is crucial," Tal imitates, rocking in his chair. "Family is crucial."

"Tal?" Malcolm asks. "Do you want to share something?"

"They are moving away." Tal groans through his mask.

"Who is moving, Tal?"

"Mehmet, my brother. Him and Simone are taking Lukas to Turkey."

"They can't do that," Calum says.

"They can, and they are. Mehmet is selling the restaurant and investing in my Uncle Emir's hotel development in Ölüdeniz."

"Tal, Calum is quite correct," Malcolm says. "They need written permission to take Lukas out of the country. From you, as his father."

The last dregs of colour seep from Tal's face. "Simone had a DNA test. I am not Lukas's father. Mehmet is." He covers his face with his hands, rocking back and forth.

As the rest of the group, Malcolm included, fall silent, Emily springs from her chair, bending on her knees to cradle Tal. He quails from her at first, before yielding to the embrace, convulsing in her arms. She whispers inaudible comfort in his ear, for what seems like several minutes, until rolling her eyes upwards, Emily meets Steve's stare with an accusatory glare.

39

CALUM

"You said what?" Steve looks furious.

"I had no choice." Emily's eyes sweep across the pub. "At that point, the truth seemed the best option."

"You did the right thing, Emily," Calum says. "Lay off the inquisition, yeah? She's been through enough."

"You think this is an inquisition, Pretty Boy? You should know better than that."

Calum falls silent.

"Should we even be here, together?" Emily asks. "What if the police are following me?"

"Do you know how underfunded the police force is these days? I doubt you're under twenty-four-hour surveillance just yet. Fuck's sake."

"Easy. Getting arsey won't help the situation, yeah?"

"Believe me, Pretty Boy, you haven't seen me arsey, yet."

One more 'Pretty Boy' crack... Calum seethes.

"Anyway, whose round is it?" Ciara dangles her empty glass.

"Yours," Calum and Steve say in unison, finally agreeing on something.

"Alright, I was only asking."

From her bag, Rachel waves two fifty-pound notes at

Ciara. "Drinks are on me. With that parasite off my back, I'm celebrating a windfall."

"You're on." Ciara wanders to the bar, smoothing down her new black bob.

"What?" Rachel asks, from their collective disbelief. "I'm not a hypocrite, so I can't pretend that every fibre of my being isn't rejoicing that the narcissistic shit is dead."

"What about your daughter?" Emily asks. "Florence adored him, didn't she?"

"She'll get over it. In the long term, Florence will see her father for the perverted degenerate he is. Was."

"And your concern for a quick burial?"

"Not for any religious purpose. Jack can rot on his slab for all I care. But Florence needs closure, so we can move on with our lives. Besides, entre nous..." Rachel lowers her tone "...the sooner we get the body back, the sooner they close the investigation, right?"

"Aye." Steve nods cautiously.

"Yes, that's not hypocritical at all." Emily shakes her head.

Before Rachel can respond, Steve cuts in. "What the hell are you defending him for, eh? After what he pulled on you? Good riddance if you ask me."

Another point Calum agrees with, glimpsing the yellow bruising on Emily's neck.

"Who's for champers?" Ciara says, returning with an ice bucket of Bollinger.

"What the fuck?" Steve trails off, fuming silently as the barman appears behind Ciara with a tray of glasses.

As she pours, Steve scowls at her, waiting for the barman to depart. "Have you lost your fucking heed?"

"Rachel said it was a celebration, and you said there's no comeback to us."

"I didn't mean to throw a fucking party."

"Well, it's opened now, so…"

Steve shakes his head. "Aye, well, let's forgo the celebratory toast, eh?"

"How long will the investigation last?" Rachel asks, sipping her Bollinger.

Steve sniffs his wine before quaffing it. "An inquest will happen in three months, and the coroner will declare it death by misadventure. End of."

"Easy for you to say. It's Emily exposed in all this," Calum says.

"They won't even call her for the inquest. She's in the clear. We all are." Steve eyeballs Ciara. "Moving forwards, though, we need to be a wee bit more careful."

"You want to carry on after this?" Emily asks.

"Too right. Especially after what those fuckers have done to Tal."

"I agree." Tal sits upright from his forlorn slump. "There must be retribution."

"Aye, lad, and there will be. Look, no plan survives contact with the enemy. Every operation has unforeseeable setbacks."

"Unforeseeable setbacks? For Christ's sake, someone is dead," Emily says, her eyes rolling toward Steve's, accusing and unyielding. "Rather conveniently."

"Yeah." Calum nods, his own doubts bubbling to the surface. "Bit of a coincidence, that."

"What the fuck are you implying?" Steve asks, the scar on his temple whitening.

"You did say he'd get what was coming to him," Calum says, recalling the icy intent in Steve's eyes that night, staring up at The Shard.

"And I was right and all," Steve says, quiet and deliberate. "But not by my hand. The degenerate fucker did that to himself. They call it autoerotic asphyxiation for a reason. As in auto. The clue is in the name."

Calum glances around for solidarity. One by one they crumble, averting their gaze from Steve. All except Emily, who doesn't blink.

"You're way out of line, Pretty Boy."

"That's it!" Calum explodes, vaulting to his feet, pulse racing.

Steve doesn't flinch, a smile curling his lip.

"Hello."

Malcolm appears like a gaudy spectre, looming over the table in luminous Lycra, clutching his cycle helmet and a glass of tomato juice.

His anger spent, Calum slinks back in his chair, unable to decide which is more jarring, Malcolm's sudden presence, or his sartorial voltage. Either way he's grateful for the intervention, not fancying his chances against Steve, who looks like his own heart rate barely skipped a beat.

"I've seen you all ensconced in here every week, so for once I thought I might join the gang." Malcolm squeezes in between Ciara and Calum. "You seemed very intense just now. What were you discussing?" His brow furrows with puzzlement at the Bollinger in the ice bucket.

Steve raises his glass in a toast. "Relationship conflict resolution."

40

ROSA
27 April

"Mystery solved." DCI Hughes rises from his desk chair, hinting that the matter is closed.

"Far from it, sir." I remain in my seat opposite, going nowhere. "It presents as many questions as answers."

My personal phone chirps in my jacket pocket. Bruce, presumably, checking when I'll be home.

"Your investigations often do." Hughes scowls like a weary bulldog. "Don't let me stop you from getting that?"

"It's only Bruce."

"Ignore those calls at your peril, and one day you'll go home to find the locks changed and your golf clubs on the front lawn."

"I'm not much of a golfer, sir."

"No, you're not." Hughes sighs. "Look, Hawkes, after what happened, why would she go anywhere near the guy? Let alone visit his room to watch his Michael Hutchence swan song."

"But with the CCTV crashing out, we can't prove if she was there or not. I'm just suggesting we get a sample of her DNA and fingerprints, to exclude her."

"Exclude her from what?

"The evidential trail points in one direction: accidental

death by autoerotic asphyxiation. And with the defendant dead, I can't see anything criminally pursuable. If anything, it demonstrates his unbalanced state of mind. His wife corroborated he was a coke head, and autoerotic asphyxiation was one of his sick party tricks."

"His estranged wife, whom he was suing for divorce, who'd left threatening messages on the dead man's phone?"

"Now his wife is the prime suspect?"

"No, sir, but what about the CCTV?"

"Forensics said it could be a technical glitch. There are always loose ends in investigations."

"There are too many on this one."

"Then I suggest you tie them up. The DSI and the senior coroner are being hounded by lawyers of a Jewish burial society, threatening a judicial review for unnecessary delays releasing the body."

"I just need a few more days."

"Absolutely not. I don't deny your capabilities as a detective, but sometimes you don't know when to quit drilling when you've struck oil." Hughes strides to the door, unhooks his jacket from the stand and tugs it on. "Finish up your report and let the coroner tie up those loose ends. Now, go home and enjoy your Saturday evening with your family."

"Yes, sir," I say, striding out of his office. Another lie. I should go home to Bruce and the kids, but Gareth called earlier, inviting me to the hotel at eight. Guilt and desire fight for supremacy in the pit of my stomach. Desire always wins.

41

EMILY

Drained from party games with her nephew and his friends, Emily retreats to the secluded end of her sister's garden for a cigarette. It is unsettling being back in Chiswick, streets away from her old house. Her old life. The proximity to Sara's house was what drew Emily and Dan to the area, but now, it reminds her of what she has lost. Shadows of Dan echo in her mind, playing with Sara's kids in this garden. Good practice for their own, she thought at the time. Then hoped, then prayed and ultimately despaired. Emily expunges the thought, tugging a pack of Marlboros from her jeans.

"Thought I'd find you here." Sara ducks under the blossom of an ornamental pear tree, carrying two sweaty bottles of Bud.

"We're all slaves to habit." Emily lights up.

"So I see." Sara frowns with theatrical disapproval, folding herself into a lawn chair, dangling a beer. "I'll swap you for one of those?"

"Deal." Emily shakes out a cigarette and takes a beer.

A passer-by could tell they are sisters, but only two years senior, Sara looks considerably older. Tall and statuesque like Emily, yet her features are not as striking. As if, as her father used to confide in Emily, Sara was the prototype to her perfected version.

"Feels like when we were kids, sneaking cigarettes behind Gramps's shed."

"I remember his lectures when he found your butt ends." Emily smiles. "You were never any good at covering your tracks. Or keeping a straight face."

"That was your fault. You kept pulling faces and making me laugh behind his back." Sara blows a plume of smoke.

Emily pulls an angelic expression. *Me?*

"You bloody did." Sara snorts beer. "And somehow I always ended up carrying the can."

"Poor Nanna and Gramps. Can't have been easy, taking on two teenage girls."

Sara nods. "I miss them."

"Me too."

"I had a letter from Mum this week." Sara studies Emily's stiffening posture.

"Not interested."

"She's up for parole next year."

"Are you deaf? I don't care."

"Em, you can't ignore this forever."

"You weren't there."

"It was a long time ago."

"For you, maybe. You're not the one with the fucking night terrors."

"I thought they'd stopped?"

"They had. Look, can you just drop it, please? It's supposed to be a party." Emily extinguishes her cigarette and flicks it over the hedge.

"You're right. Sorry. So, what do you think of Tony?"

Here we go, Emily thinks, peering around the shed at the adults congregated on the patio. "Which one's Tony?"

"The dishy blond. Tall, blue polo shirt, divorced. Lovely guy…"

Emily frowns. "Don't tell me. He likes dogs, and long walks on the beach."

"Just saying, he's on the market."

Emily spots him, chatting with two other fathers. Not bad, she must admit.

"And he's a fireman."

"Oh, that settles it then. Have him stripped, washed and brought to my shed."

"Ed could put a word in."

"I'll pass, thanks."

"Just because your marriage has ended, you don't have to throw your sex life onto the funeral pyre with it." Sara's irises, though lacking the vibrance of Emily's, still harbour their mother's fire. "You're still young and gorgeous. You should have some fun."

"Who says I'm not?"

"Really? Well go on then, dish the dirt."

"Nothing's happened yet, and I don't even know if he's into me…"

"Look at you, for God's sake. That's a given. So, who is this mystery man?"

"Just a guy I met at divorce counselling."

"I told you it would be good for you, didn't I?"

Good and bad, Emily thinks, blocking thoughts of her police interrogation.

"So, when can I meet him? You haven't even mentioned his name yet?"

Emily's gaze drifts to the lawn, watching the kids playing blind-man's-bluff. *That's me,* she thinks, *the unsighted fool, groping at the dark in someone else's game–*

"Em?" Sara's voice snaps Emily back. "Another beer?"

"Go on then, one more. Early start in the morning, prepping Sunday lunch at the shelter."

Sara grimaces, struggling from her chair. "It's great what you're doing, Em, helping those poor souls, but you need to live your own life, too."

As Sara drifts into the foliage, Emily lights another cigarette, watching as the fairy lights lining the trees ignite against the ultramarine sky. *L'heure bleue,* the French call it. The blue hour. The fleeting period before twilight succumbs to night. Not quite dark yet, but you know it's coming.

42

CHARLOTTE

A few streets away from Emily's sister's house, silhouetted in the glow of the bifold kitchen windows, Charlotte peers into the darkness, savouring a gulp of Chianti. After the usual exhausting battle royale, Ella has finally yielded to slumber. For how long, who knows. But Charlotte is grateful for small mercies nowadays. Only weeks ago, she owned the seventh most successful PR agency in London, yet now C&E Media wouldn't break into the top hundred. Like the proverbial rats on a doomed vessel, her staff are deserting her and taking with them the few remaining clients that aren't suing. A couple more months and... Charlotte banishes the thought and pours herself another glass of red, gazing outside at the cobalt light emanating from Dan's studio. An extensive steel and smoked glass construction, built to maximise natural light, whilst being spacious enough to house his enormous canvases. It cost Emily enough to purchase a small home, a debt Charlotte inherited buying her out of the house. A burdensome one now.

It wasn't just Emily's home that Charlotte had coveted. It was everything about her. Life seemed so effortless for Emily. So perfect. With her lithe figure, flawless beauty and boundless fucking talent. Staff and clients alike adored her. Especially the men, tripping over themselves and each other to do her bidding. Yes, everyone fucking loved Emily. Dan loved her. And that was too much. Because Charlotte loved Dan. Which came as a shock, as she had, to her recollection, never been in love before. Thus, all that petty envy gestating deep within Charlotte burst from its chrysalis, emerald winged, glistening and fully formed, jealousy in all its monstrous majesty. It felt liberating to finally let it out. Empowering. But in order for Charlotte to usurp her friend's perfect life, she required an equally perfect opportunity. A vulnerability to exploit. A chink in the armour of Emily and Dan's perfect marriage. And when it finally came it felt like a rapture. The joyous news that perfect Emily had a flaw. She couldn't conceive a child. Charlotte knew how desperately Dan wanted a baby, and under the weight of expectation at trying, their marriage had already begun to crack. All Charlotte had to do was apply a little more pressure to wedge them apart. Press her advantage. Provide Dan with a comforting shoulder, and bed…

Guilt nipping at her heels, Charlotte pushes the thought away and gulps her wine, drawn to the glow of Dan's studio. A nocturnal creature, Dan paints late into the night, so he fitted the studio with daylight simulation bulbs, casting it with an eerie bluish hue. She often sees his frenetic silhouette attacking his canvas, but tonight he sits at his desk, working on sketches for a prospective client. A high-end hotel chain approached his agent, scouting artworks for their hotels in the States. With twenty-four locations, it could keep Dan in work for months, so he's eager to impress. They need the money too. With buying Emily out, and the precariousness of the company, their finances are hanging by a gossamer thread. Charlotte had wanted to screw Emily's share price further, but Dan urged leniency. How she regrets allowing him to sway her now. But why had he? Insecurity twists her insides. Charlotte shakes the notion and guzzles more wine, the anaesthetic to her woes. That and food – evident in her augmented outline reflected in the bifold window. She steps closer, studying her spectral doppelgänger. The constant worry and sleepless nights have drawn dark circles under her eyes, and her face is as pallid as a geisha, but the more glaring issue is her expanded waistline. "Rubenesque" Dan had described her as the other day, but he might as well have called her an elephant. *How do I deserve this?* Charlotte sighs.

Initially, she was convinced Emily was behind the data breach, but now Charlotte is less sure. The cybercrime detective (useless as he was) asked her if she had any enemies. Obviously, Emily tops the totem pole, but over the years Charlotte has collected opponents like a spinster does cats. Plus, in her present insomniac, stress-addled state, she's no longer assured of anything. As she peers at Dan's shadowy form in his studio, Charlotte takes comfort: at least she has him and Ella. No one can take them away.

A thrumming sound makes her jump. Her phone vibrates on the kitchen counter, switched to silent for fear of waking Ella. She pads into the kitchen, checking her phone. A WhatsApp notification from a contact she doesn't recognise. The old Charlotte wouldn't entertain an unknown contact, but since the collapse of the company, her rapidly contracting staff and social circle, she needs all the new friends she can get.

It is a new thread, ominously typed in caps:
ONCE A CHEAT. ALWAYS A CHEAT.

Charlotte's gut constricts, the wine in her stomach turning bilious. She places her quivering glass on the counter and clicks on the circular profile picture on the unknown contact. It is an old painting; if she isn't mistaken, of Othello confronting Desdemona in her bed.

"What the fuck?" Charlotte peers at Dan's dark delineation in his studio, as if it were that of an intruder.

43

STEVE

"I believe you." Sue pulls his face towards hers, their fervid lips meeting.

Steve shuts his eyes, blocking the image of his wife reuniting with Nick. He sits in his car, under the anonymity of a broken streetlamp, a hundred yards from his old house, the light from his phone bathing his tortured face in an eerie glow.

"Who would do that?" Nick's voice reverberates through Steve's speaker phone.

"Steve would," Sue says, "and worse."

Steve's eyes snap open, staring at the screen.

Sue and Nick sit on the living room couch, in the ambient hue of the TV, the camera through which Steve surveils them.

"Nah, you're getting paranoid, babe." Nick kisses her forehead.

"That's how he gets you. You've no idea know how jealous and manipulative he can be, especially after his injury. They should have never let him in the police, but he hid it from them, the headaches, the rages. But I know, I lived it every day for twenty years." She tops up their wine glasses with buttery Chardonnay. Sue's favourite. "Fuck him. After the divorce, I'll sell the house and I'll back you setting up your own gym. We'll do it together."

Their voices drown in Steve's head as the pain comes, never disappointing, like a million screws twisting in his brain, tunnelling his vision and him with it, back to the foxhole in Afghanistan.

Steve placed the crosshairs in the middle of the target's head, adjusted his aim a few inches to the left, allowing for the wind, drew a breath and squeezed the trigger. The millisecond following the suppressed crack of the shot passed like an eternity, and before the round hit, the target turned in his direction and smiled.

The pain stabbing his temples wrenches Steve back into the present. With the sleeve of his hoodie, he wipes icy sweat from his face and sucks oxygen into his lungs. After several long breaths, he thumps open the glove compartment, snatching the Glenfiddich and the packet of Tramadol. He pops four pills from the foil and washes them down with whisky. As he feels the burn from the scotch, the panic ebbs and his breathing slows to normal. That fucking shrink at Hereford, and then the psychiatrist at the Met. What the fuck do they know about PTSD? He has it under control, and it doesn't take cognitive fucking therapy or anti-anxiety medication. A couple of painkillers and a swally of the hard stuff and he's good to go. Fists clenched, his forearms trembling, Steve composes himself in the only way he knows, channelling his fear into an emotion he can understand. Anger.

He glances at his phone, but the screen is blank. They must have gone to bed. Steve stares at the crack of light between his and Sue's bedroom curtains. She always had a thing about curtains – had to be quality. Like their immaculate four-bedroom, three-bathroom detached house. A monument to everything he earned serving his country. His castle. His sanctuary. When he closed that door, with Sue and the twins, the shit was held at bay. Now, an invading enemy occupies his home, his wife is a traitorous collaborator and everything he fought and sacrificed for has been stolen. As the bedroom light snaps off, Steve shuts his eyes, suppressing the images of that bastard fucking his wife. Despite the failed mission, the war isn't over. They will pay for his pain, with greater pain. All of them.

44

CIARA
28 April

Ciara awoke with a hangover, a Tinder hookup in her bed and a soupy recollection that Jim was bringing the kids back early today. Once she ejected her guest, who looked even rougher in daylight, Ciara cleaned up the evidence and hopped under a scalding shower.

As she rushes her makeup, Ciara hears the key in the door, followed by the kids' feet thumping up the stairs, to lock themselves in their bedrooms. She glances in the bedroom mirror; impressed, given her moribund state an hour ago, her outfit an homage to one of Rachel's, though, in fairness, more Primark than Prada.

Ciara sashays into the kitchen, where Jim is helping himself to the Nespresso machine, feeling a confidence she hasn't had in a long time. The impetus from viewing Jim's rows with Issy on her laptop, no doubt. And with her impending departure to Canada, Issy will soon be out of the picture. Happy days.

"Make us one of those, would ye, Jim, love?"

"Surely. I like the do." He nods to her copper-toned hair. Her natural colour. Or at least a facsimile. "I always liked you au naturel."

Ciara pats her hair. "Me too. I've decided I like being me."

"You're in a good mood." Jim pours milk into the frother.

"I had a lovely date last night with a charming guy, so, yeah, I feel grand." Ciara suppresses the image of the bridge troll who'd awakened her with the sound of his farting. "Yourself?"

"Not as good as yourself, by the sound of it, but I've got some news too."

This is it, Ciara thinks. "Oh yeah, what's that then?" she asks, masking her mushrooming schadenfreude.

"Me and Issy have been having a few troubles—"

"Yeah, I know." Off Jim's look, she catches herself. "The kids mentioned something."

"Right." Jim nods. "Anyway, with Issy off to Canada, we decided it was for the best…"

As Jim hands her the cappuccino, Ciara feels like bursting into song.

"…that I go with her."

How she maintains her forced smile, or the impulse to throw her coffee in his face, Ciara will never know.

"We decided last night."

How the fuck have I missed that? Ciara scolds herself. *Off my face drunk last night with whatever his fucking name was – that's how!*

"Isn't that great?" Jim says with a shit-eating grin.

Ciara doesn't hear him because of the blood rushing in her ears and the mantra repeating in her head: *fucking skinny bitch*.

45

EMILY
1 May

Over the music booming downstairs, Emily heard the unmistakable deadweight thud of someone falling, followed by eerie silence terminating her parents' argument. Gripped with icy dread, she crept down the stairs, already regretting her cowardice for not acting sooner. Whatever horrific visions her febrile mind constructed, nothing could prepare her for the reality. She twisted the porcelain door handle, feeling the thrumming base of the hi-fi inside. Emily stepped inside the living room, and in that instant her childhood ended.

Emily awakes with a film of cold sweat covering her forehead. She sits up and glances at her watch. Six thirty in the morning. Dawn. The scarlet light streaming through the shutters could have told her that. There is only one thing for it: she needs to swim.

As Emily towels off in the changing rooms, a buzzing sound from the locker jolts fear through her. She knows the sound before turning to it – from the replacement burner phone Steve gave her, or rather insisted she take. Satisfied the women in the changing room are distracted by their grooming rituals, Emily withdraws the Nokia from her locker.

A text message from OTHELLO. AKA, Steve.

Before clicking on the message, Emily halts, resolving to have no more part in this madness. She unfurls the towel from her hair, wraps the phone and drops it to the tiles, but raising her foot to shatter it, something prevents her. With the same fearful compulsion she'd felt stepping inside her family living room that fateful night, Emily unwraps the Nokia from the towel and clicks on the message.

46

"Wish me luck." Dan strides into the kitchen carrying his portfolio case, dressed in a sharp suit and a black turtleneck.

It's still jarring to Charlotte how handsome he looks. "You won't need it looking like that."

Charlotte spoon feeds Ella's lunch at the kitchen table. With Dan's pitch meeting for the hotel chain that afternoon, she's taken the day off. No one will miss her at the agency anyway; the place is dead. Plus, with Ella awake and crying most of the night, she feels more depleted than usual. As Dan's lips graze her cheek, she inhales his woody cologne. He used to wear it when they had their assignations. A distant memory now, like their sex life, a luxury they no longer indulge.

"Where's your meeting?" Charlotte asks, tidal thoughts of the text message battering her insecurity.

Dan avoids her gaze. "The Savoy."

He is wise to, as her Medusa stare would turn him to granite. The Savoy was a rendezvous during their affair, deliberately chosen by Charlotte to undermine a treasured memory of Emily's, when she stayed there with Dan. Part of Charlotte's scorched-earth campaign to obliterate her friend's past relationship, and upon the foundations of ground zero, build her own. A calculated strategy, rather than one motivated purely by vindictive jealousy. But if

Charlotte was honest, she knows the needle really points to somewhere in the middle.

"How long will you be?"

"As long as it takes."

As the front door slams behind him, Charlotte reassures her inner self. "Mummy is being silly," she says to Ella. "Daddy is just making an effort for his meeting."

Ella laughs and flaps her hands together. As Charlotte guides another spoonful of apricot mush into her daughter's maw, she feels a little better, until her phone beeps on the table. Timorously, she glances at the unknown WhatsApp number flashing on the screen. A cautionary voice warns her to ignore it, but she can't resist. The message contains only five words, each sending a collective chill to Charlotte's heart.

HE IS LYING TO YOU

Charlotte texts a reply: *Who is this?*

A FRIEND

To the enigmatic response, Charlotte has only one suspect. "Emily?" She taps the call symbol and presses the phone to her ear.

"The number you have dialled has not been recognised."

Charlotte stares at her phone, the automated voice echoing in her bewildered brain.

Two hours later, fidgeting on a velvet couch, Dan sips his third coffee and glances at his watch. He has stayed at the Savoy before, with Emily – and Charlotte also, he recalls with a flush of guilt, though not in rooms as extravagant as this suite. What his mysterious patron, Glenn Harrington, lacks in punctuality, he makes up for in style.

In the vacuum of uncomfortable silence, Dan meets the

gaze of his host's personal assistant. Expensively groomed and turned out, she sits at a mahogany desk opposite, peering over her laptop with an apologetic smile. His phone pulsing in his breast pocket, Dan casts his gaze out of the window, trying not to think of the constant stream of texts and missed calls from Charlotte. It's like whatever virus infiltrated the company's data has infected her entire psyche. In the last few days, she's become especially paranoid and jealous. Twice Dan has caught her fiddling with his phone, and stepping from the shower this morning, he witnessed her rifling through his pockets. It's like his last weeks with Emily, as though history were repeating itself. *Karma*, he reflects, *only what I deserve*.

Dan shakes the thought, focusing on the view over the Thames, beyond Waterloo Bridge, at the plodding rotation of the London Eye, its circumferential speed indiscernible from a distance. When Emily privately hired a carriage on the Eye for his twenty-eighth birthday, the half-hour duration of a complete rotation passed in a blur. Accompanied by a string quartet, drinking champagne as the sun slipped behind the Palace of Westminster, it was a wonderful surprise, planned with Emily's meticulous attention to detail. Back at the Savoy, ravenous for each other, they gorged on sex and room service, and afterwards sat in bed, drinking the mini bar dry, baring their souls to each other. A rare occasion Emily shucked that hard shell of hers, for the first time speaking of her father's death. As the dawn light burned in their eyes, they realised they had spent the night talking. They could afford it; they had the rest of their lives to look forward to–

"I am sorry for the delay, Mr Hunter." Harrington's PA snaps Dan from his reverie. "Would you like some more coffee?" she asks with a cut-glass accent.

"No, three's my limit. One more and I won't sleep tonight."

"I'm sure it won't be too much longer," she says, pushing a strand of brown hair off her Botoxed forehead.

By the time Charlotte's Uber halts outside the Savoy's Art Deco courtyard, she is a volcano of emotion. As she yanks the back passenger door open, it swings out with unexpected force, depositing her onto the pavement on her knees. The two top-hatted doormen rush to her aid, helping Charlotte to her feet. Ivan, the grey-haired doorman, and a younger guy she doesn't recognise, fuss around her, enquiring if she needs medical attention, hospitalisation or, judging by her appearance, institutionalisation.

"I'm fine, will you stop fussing and get out of my way."

As she attempts to bustle past, Ivan bars her path. "Are you a guest at hotel, madam?" he asks with a clipped Slavic accent.

"Ivan, for fuck's sake, it's me."

Ivan hands over her fallen purse with a bemused look on his leathery face. Charlotte was a regular at the hotel, engaging it for work functions and press junkets, but in her present state, his lack of recognition shouldn't be surprising to her. She'd charged from the house wearing scuffed trainers, sweatpants (now bloodied and torn at the knees from her tumble), an oversized T-shirt of Dan's (soiled with Ella's baby food) under his massive raincoat. Without makeup, hair pulled into a greasy ponytail, her recent weight gain, the harrowing effects of insomnia and the maniacal expression she wears complete a perfect disguise.

"Ivan, it's me. Charlotte Horsfall... sorry Hunter, I'm Charlotte Hunter now. Horsfall was my maiden name." Her babbling isn't helping her case.

"Are you a guest, madam?"

"Yes," Charlotte says, realising it is the only way she is getting in. "Now, if you don't mind. I want to go to my room."

A twenty-year veteran in the Savoy's employ, Ivan isn't convinced, but hedging his bets, he steps aside and extends his arm. "Of course, madam, please."

Charlotte shoves through the revolving doors, her grazed palms stinging and stomps towards the reception. The concierge, Pierre, bolts upright at the green marble-top desk. "Can I help you, madame?" he asks with an effete Parisian accent.

"Fucking hell, not you as well. Pierre, it's me."

"Are you a guest at the hotel, madame?"

"Christ! I've just had this with your Eastern European parrot outside."

"I do not understand, madame. Are you staying at the hotel?" Pierre peers down his gold-rimmed spectacles.

"Well, not right now... Christ, I'm Charlotte Horsfall... Fuck, Hunter, from C&E Media. I've been coming here for years."

Pierre's face flickers recognition. "Ah, yes, of course, Miss Horsfall. We haven't seen you in a while. How are you?" From his derisory expression, he's made his own assessment.

"It's Mrs Hunter now, and that's why I'm here. I'm looking for my husband."

"Ah, a guest at the hotel? What is his name?" Pierre readies his manicured fingers at the keyboard.

"Dan, Dan Hunter."

Pierre types in the name, the glow of the computer screen

reflecting in his glasses. "I am sorry, madam, but we have no guest under that name."

"He's not staying here. He had a meeting with some American CEO… fuck, what was his name? Harrington, that was it. Glenn Harrington. Try that."

"Madame, I must ask you to lower your voice."

"Just tell me where my fucking husband is."

Surrounding guests are turning to the commotion. Ivan glares through the revolving doors. With a furtive nod, Pierre gestures him over.

"Are you fucking checking, or what?"

"I'm unable to give away guests' confidential information. Now if you don't mind…"

"It's hardly confidential information, I'm his fucking wife, you cretin."

"Surely you have you own husband's telephone number, madame?"

"He's not answering his fucking phone."

"Madame, I have asked you to lower your voice. Now, I must ask you to leave."

Ivan looms behind Charlotte. "You come with me please, madam."

"I'm not fucking going anywhere until I've seen my husband."

"If you do not leave now," Pierre says, conscious of the attention of surrounding guests, "I will call the police."

"Take your fucking hands off me." Charlotte wriggles from Ivan's grasp, shepherding her to the door. "I'm fucking leaving!"

Through compact binoculars, Steve observes the melee as

the doorman corrals Charlotte along the Savoy courtyard to the corner of The Strand.

Steve sits at a table outside an Italian café across the busy Strand thoroughfare, a grin forming under his binoculars, satisfied with the plan.

As Charlotte screams into her phone, leaving another incendiary voice message for Dan, she misses Emily's taxi, turning into the courtyard.

Steve lowers the binoculars, drawing a burner phone from his leather jacket and begins texting under the table.

Rachel scans the message, slips the burner phone into her bag and sashays over to Dan. "I am sorry, Mr Hunter, but Mr Harrington has been called back to New York on urgent business."

"Oh, that's… a shame," Dan says, looking crestfallen.

Rachel empathises, before reminding herself of the hurt he inflicted upon Emily. "Indeed. But I am certain Mr Harrington will want to reconvene when he is next in London."

"Oh, OK." Dan sets his cup on the coffee table. "Perhaps I can email some of my sketches?"

"We will contact your agent. Now, if you don't mind, I have a plane to catch."

As she shakes Dan's hand at the door, Rachel can see Emily's reluctance letting go. In the tractor-beam of his sapphire eyes, she's loath to herself. Rachel's mother augured the perilous unreliability of handsome men. "Shayna Punim," she used to say in Yiddish. Roughly translated it means: "Never trust a pretty face." She whispered it when Rachel introduced her to Jack. If only she'd listened. Then again, when it comes to the heart, whoever submitted to reason?

47

EMILY

She had assumed the plan had been called off, until receiving Steve's message earlier. Throughout the taxi ride, Emily intended to confess the plot to Dan, before realising she would be culpable for the data breach. For which Charlotte would undoubtably pursue her legally. But right now, it is her very destination causing Emily the most grief. The Savoy Hotel. The last year she has consciously avoided places she and Dan visited together. Now, as the taxi pulls into the Savoy courtyard, trepidation paralyses her. Time to face her demons. Prolonged Exposure Therapy, Malcolm called it. An incremental exercise to expose and desensitise yourself to the scenarios and locations associated with your ex. Except, there's nothing gradual about this, Emily realises, stepping from the black cab onto the Savoy courtyard, memories of their weekend assailing her:

She and Dan passed through the Savoy's revolving doors, high on champagne and the simple blissful recognition of being in love. Like giggling lunatics, wandering hand in hand, through reception. The kiss that began in the elevator and continued to their room.

Ivan the doorman smiles and waves her to the entrance.

Emily smiles through gritted teeth. Was it the same hotel

room Charlotte and Dan had betrayed her in? The thought jabs her, as she pushes through the mahogany revolving doors, and Emily has the overwhelming urge to flee. As she emerges back outside the hotel, to the perturbed glance of Ivan, another latent memory hits her. Of Charlotte's reaction when Emily relayed her wonderful weekend with Dan at the Savoy. She should have seen it then, the covetous envy in her best friend's eyes.

Anger pulses through her. "You can do this," she says under her breath, turning back with renewed purpose, shoving through the doors. Emily stalks past the reception desk, halting at the entrance to the Thames Foyer restaurant. In the central birdcage, a pianist plays "Clair de Lune" for tourists dining on overpriced afternoon teas. Emily watches him play, reverie drifting her into the past, until the vibration in her handbag yanks her back. She peeks at the burner phone. A text from EMILIA, Rachel's codename:

He's coming down!

Emily's gaze darts to the elevators, girding her emotions and preparing for her role. As the doors part, and Dan steps from the green panelled elevator, she darts back through reception towards the front entrance, when she hears his voice calling out.

"Em? Emily."

Emily turns, feigning a look of surprise, as Dan appears behind her. For a moment neither speaks, standing rigid on their opposite chequered tiles, like chess pieces awaiting the next move. "What are you doing here?" they ask in tandem, laughing awkwardly.

"You first," Emily says.

"I had a meeting for a commission. At least I was supposed

to." Dan lifts his portfolio as though he requires evidence. "You?"

"Client meeting." Emily steps aside as an American family bundle through the doors, shaking out umbrellas, grumbling about the weather in Texan drawls.

"Were you just leaving?" Dan asks.

"Yes."

"I'll walk out with you."

Outside, rain lashes the pavement, so they stroll under the shelter of the hotel canopy.

"You're working again?" Dan asks.

"Yes. At a law firm in the city. Head of PR and Marketing."

"That's great, Em."

"It sounds a lot grander than it is."

"I'm just happy to hear you're... you know, getting back out there..." Dan looks away. "So, how did your meeting go?"

"Good. Brought back a few old memories, though."

Staring ahead at the traffic, he nods. "Me too."

"How about you? Did you get your commission?"

"The client didn't even show up. I suspect they've had their head turned elsewhere."

"I doubt that. But even if that's true, I'm certain it'll be their loss."

Dan turns to her, about to speak when they step from under the glass awning into the sobering rain. "Bloody typical," Dan says. "How to cap a perfect day." He lifts his portfolio case as a shield from the rain and waves her under. "Come on. We've a better chance of getting a cab on The Strand."

Emily steps under his black wing, and they splash along the waterlogged courtyard. On the corner of The Strand, as Dan flaps his arm at passing cabs, Emily watches him with a sorrow that hurts her chest. She has learned to hate him in the past year, yet in his presence, her wrath dissipates into something she dares not name. As a black cab squeals to a halt, Emily laments its arrival.

"You take this one." Dan opens the passenger door.

"No, you take it."

"Please, Em, allow me this?"

"Alright, if you insist."

"Em, before you go, there's something I need to ask you."

This is it, Emily thinks, feeling a paroxysm of guilt. *Just tell him the truth*.

"Was it you? The security data breach, I mean?"

As she opens her mouth to confess, he interrupts her.

"It doesn't matter. I couldn't blame you if it was. I'm just sorry, Em. For the way everything… turned out."

Instinctively, or simply from old habits, Emily embraces him. The only man she ever loved. She inhales his heady fragrance, not just Dan's cologne, but his very essence. *Don't let go*, a voice inside her implores. "Me too," she says, letting go.

Already feeling his loss, Emily ducks into the cab and Dan closes the door. As the taxi pulls into traffic, she glances across the street to the Italian café, where Steve sits beneath the cover of the restaurant awning, as per the plan. A few feet away, Charlotte stands rigid in the street, sodden with rain and beset with horror, having witnessed their prepared performance. At the precise time Steve's anonymous text had instructed Charlotte to be there. Masterful, Emily has to admit. She might have expected a sense of catharsis witnessing her nemesis's reprisal, yet Emily feels nothing except the hollow melancholy of regret.

48

DAN

Dan places his keys in the malachite bowl, lingering in the vestibule, agonising over how to explain his fruitless meeting to Charlotte. He won't mention bumping into Emily, obviously, but seeing her has jarred something in him. Even the emerald key bowl reminds him of her eyes. Emily bought the dish, along with most of the remaining furniture. Dan had never wanted to keep the house after the divorce. It was Charlotte's idea, and like Emily's ubiquitous presence, it haunts him still.

"Lottie, I'm back." He braces himself for the Torquemada inquisition, but wandering into the kitchen finds it deserted. In the hallway, he calls up the staircase. "Lottie?" From the silence, Dan feels relieved for his temporary reprieve.

In the kitchen, he tugs a bottle of Sancerre from the fridge, but not wishing to encourage Charlotte's recent consumption, swaps it for a milk carton. As he flicks on the kettle, he needs music to lift his mood.

"Alexa, play 'Time to Say Goodbye'." The Andrea Bocelli song that plagued his and Emily's tour of Italy. In restaurants, bars, wherever they went it seemed to follow them ad nauseam. Emily predicted that one day it would remind him of their time together. Dan drops a teabag into a mug, a sad smile forming on his lips, as the memories wash over him–

"Alexa, stop!"

Startled, Dan spins to a dishevelled figure lurking in the doorway. For a second he doesn't register it is Charlotte, drenched and unhinged as she appears.

"Jesus, Lottie, you scared the hell out of me."

"Why are you so jumpy?"

"I'm not, I just–"

"How was your meeting?"

Here we go again, he thinks. "Do you want a cup of tea?"

"Answer the fucking question."

Tired of the eggshell tiptoeing, he's ready for an argument. "Not great, if you must know. The guy didn't even show up."

"And yet you spent three hours in the Savoy Hotel?"

"I was waiting for him, but–"

"The Savoy for fuck's sake!"

"Christ, I didn't choose the venue Lottie, I–"

"Liar. You fucking liar. I saw you leave together."

"You followed me?"

"You fucking bastard."

"It's not what…" He swallows the cliche. "We just ran into each other–"

"Once a cheat, always a cheat."

"No, you've got this all twisted–"

"So, what? I'm imagining this too now, am I?"

"No, but you're not thinking straight–"

"You're not going to fucking gaslight me like you did Emily."

"Like *I* did? That's rich, even for you."

"Oh, yes, and you were just an innocent bystander?"

"Of course not. I have to live with what I've done. But not this. This is all twisted in your head."

"You're the one who is fucking twisting things–"

"Hang on…" Realisation hits him. "Where's Ella?"

"She's fine." Charlotte stiffens.

"Charlotte, where is she?"

"With Mrs Taylor. She's fine."

"The fucking octogenarian chicken lady across the street?"

"I couldn't take her with me, and there was no one else–"

"So, you left our daughter with an elderly stranger, so you could fulfil your jealous, paranoid delusions?"

"Don't you dare make this about me."

Dan storms past her, snatching his keys from the bowl. "Of course it's about you, Charlotte, everything always is."

"Where are you going?"

"For Christ's sake, to get our daughter." Through the slammed front door, Dan can hear Charlotte's wailing, even halfway across the street.

49

EMILY

Emily sits at the counter of her galley kitchen, watching on her laptop. She smiled as Dan played the Andrea Bocelli song. Evidence their life together wasn't a complete lie. But as she observes Charlotte crumple to the hallway floor a mess of snot and tears, Emily feels no vindication witnessing her pain, as deserved as it might be. At least their betrayal was driven by love, she realises, whereas her motive is born of hate. This stops now, she vows again, closing the laptop. She slips off her platinum and emerald engagement bands and places them on the counter.

"Time to say goodbye, Dan..." Emily chokes on the words.

She pinches the tears from her eyes and sweeps the rings inside a kitchen drawer. Step one complete, at least symbolically. Next, returning from the hallway, she tugs the burner phone from her bag and tosses it on a wooden chopping board. From another drawer, she takes out a tea towel and a rolling pin, wraps the phone and smashes it, determined to play no further part in this twisted game.

Oblivious to how far it already exceeded her control.

50

ISSY

Issy emerges tipsily from Soho House, the darkness and the drizzling rain surprising her. Still, with her ebullient mood, she could dance through a downpour, and it isn't just the buzz from drinks with her new cast before they fly to Canada for the shoot. More intoxicating than the alcohol is the euphoric rush of realising her dreams. A model since she was fifteen, Issy's career has been an endless cycle of rejection. Not anymore, she laughs, skipping through puddles along Dean Street. Vincent Kane, the show's leading man, suggested going to a club in Mayfair, but Issy had promised Jim she would be home by ten. Ten minutes ago, she sees checking her phone, along with eight text messages, and three missed calls. From Jim no doubt, who, since she got the part, has become insanely jealous. "Pain in the ass!"

As she marches towards to Tottenham Court Road station, Issy texts him back:

ON MY WAY!

No love, kisses or emojis. Issy feels claustrophobic and is already regretting agreeing to Jim's proposal of him going with her to Canada. Not that she'd had much choice in the matter, with him ambushing her in front of his kids. She couldn't say no then, but she can tonight, before he buys a plane ticket.

A prurient smile creeps across Issy's face, remembering what Vince had whispered to her earlier. Yes, she will tell Jim tonight. A clean break, before anyone gets hurt. Maybe he will go back home to his kids and his crazy wife, with her multicoloured hairstyles. Invigorated, Issy increases her pace along Greek Street, cutting under the arch beside Simmons bar. The ammonia stench of stale urine hits her as she enters the archway; a latrine for the homeless and inebriated, but it's a shortcut to the tube station.

As Issy rounds the corner in the gloomy alley, she glimpses a hooded figure in her path then feels a splash of liquid in her face. Before she can process, the searing agony hits, as her skin burns, bubbles and shrinks, and her vision goes black. Exothermically reacting with the rainwater, the temperature of the sulphuric acid soars to a boundless crescendo, like Issy's futile screams.

51

EMILY
2 May

On her morning commute, Emily feels a cathartic sense of release. Even the scrum of the Central Line and the malodorous builder pressed against her can't dull her sense of freedom. The thought of not seeing Calum again saddens her, but she's determined never to return to the vengeful toxicity of the group. The clammy builder turns the page of his newspaper, snapping Emily's gaze to a headline:

MODEL SUFFERS HORRIFIC BURNS IN ACID ATTACK.

Emily blinks, recognising the accompanying photograph is Issy, the shock hitting her like a fist in solar plexus. It's the same Instagram image pasted on Steve's whiteboard. Rapt with horror, she scans the article:

Former model and actor Isabel Jónsson, after a night out celebrating winning a role in hit show Swords of Destiny…

As the builder turns the page, Emily tears it from his hands.

"Oi, I'm reading that…"

Emily pores over the article as the train doors open at Liverpool Street, stumbling out with the surge.

As she emerges from the escalator onto Old Broad Street, Emily ransacks her bag before recalling that she destroyed the burner phone. "FUCK!" Her outburst draws glances from commuters. Emily doesn't care, wondering how to contact the others, and who can she trust?

Emily tears her gaze from the computer screen, staring out her office window at the Thames below, shimmering like the iridescent scales of a serpent. Unable to eat or focus, she has spent her lunch hour searching the internet for news coverage. Not on her own computer (remembering Steve's protocol), instead using her assistant Juliana's while she is out for lunch. The prolific search results shocked Emily, acid attacks seemingly a crime epidemic in London. Several featured Issy's assault, all containing the same information as this morning's *Metro* article, with one notable exception. A witness description of a man fleeing the scene: well-built, around six feet tall, wearing a dark hoodie, a Covid mask and gloves.

To the sound of footsteps, she peers over the screen as her assistant saunters from the elevators. Emily quits Google and springs to her feet, and remembering the search history, deletes it as Juliana enters, tugging off her headphones with a perturbed expression.

Emily emerges from behind the computer, waving a Biro. "Just borrowing a pen."

But this little lie is the least of Emily's concerns, realising the only way to discover the truth is to return to the group session tonight.

52

CIARA

With a serrated knife, Ciara scrapes the potato slices from a chopping board into the sizzling pan, watching as the oil swallows them, hissing and squealing. To the chime of the expected doorbell, she stiffens. "Perfect fucking timing."

Ciara wipes her hands with a tea towel and shuffles to the door, turning to check her appearance where the mirror used to be, recalling smashing it. Fingers moulding her scarlet bob, she takes a breath and with a virginal smile mastered at Catholic school opens the front door.

The man on the doorstep looks too young to flash a police warrant card. "Ciara Devaney?" he says, mispronouncing her name. "Detective Sergeant Thomas from Croydon Serious Crime."

"Sergeant? You don't look old enough. No offense, love, it's a backhanded compliment."

DS Thomas scowls like he took her literal backhand. Lowering an octave, he asks, "Can we talk inside, Mrs Devaney?"

"I was just making dinner for the kids before the sitter gets here."

"Would you prefer to come down to the station tomorrow morning?"

"Alright," Ciara huffs. "Come in."

The detective steps inside, peering up the stairs towards the booming hip-hop bass and gangster rap expletives reverberating from Steph's room.

"Steph, turn that shite down!"

DS Thomas jumps at her outburst, as does the cat, awakened at the foot of the stairs, his cerulean eyes wide with alarm. Leading the youthful detective along the hallway, Ciara leans into the living room, where Patrick sits cross-legged before the TV, shouting at his friends on a gaming headset. "Dinner will be ready soon, Paddy," she says, without a hint of response. "Might as well talk to the wall."

Ciara waves the DS Thomas into the kitchen. "I'll just check on the chips." She peers at the fries, already browning in the fat. "It's all they bloody eat. Tried rice, pasta and every imaginable way of cooking a potato. Boiled, mashed, baked, sautéed, you name it. No chance. Has to be chips. That and chicken nuggets. You wouldn't credit I worked for the Food Standards Agency, would you?"

As the detective opens his mouth to speak, Ciara says, "Grab a seat, I'll be right with you."

DS Thomas places his leather satchel on the quartz breakfast bar and climbs onto a chrome stool. As she turns the gas hob down, Ciara lights a cigarette in the flame.

"Will this take long? The sitter will here at six thirty."

"Just a few routine questions. Going somewhere nice?"

"Not exactly. Therapy group. Divorce therapy. I'm not mental or anything." Ciara attempts a serene smile, conveying the opposite.

He recoils from her exhaled smoke. "Do you mind? The secondary smoke…"

"Aye, gotcha, no problem." Ciara hops off her stool and

sashays to the open back door. *Fucking Garda*, she fumes, leaning in the doorway. "I thought all you police drank and smoked like sailors on shore leave?" she asks, shooting dragon smoke from her nostrils.

"Some still do, Mrs Devaney."

"Call me Ciara," she says, pointedly pronouncing her name.

"Right." He takes out a pen and notepad. "Ciara, I'm curious, why haven't you asked me what this is regarding?"

"I don't need a detective badge to deduce that. It's about my husband's girlfriend, right?" Ciara blows a smoke ring, floating above her head like a halo.

"The incident involving Isabella Jónsson, last night, correct. What do you know about it?"

"Only what's in the news. Shocking. Pretty girl like that. How is she doing, anyway?"

"Too early to say. They put her into an induced coma at the hospital. The acid caused third- and fourth-degree burns, and I believe surgeons are trying to save her left eye."

"You know what these doctors can do." Ciara smiles.

"If you don't mind me saying, you don't seem very upset."

"She ran off with the father of my children. So yeah, she's not top of my favourite people list."

"Fair enough. But your ex-husband described your... attitude towards Miss Jónsson as aggressively toxic–"

"He's not my ex-husband."

DS Thomas checks his notebook. "I thought–"

"We're only separated."

"In that case, how would you describe your relationship with your... husband?"

"We've had our ups and downs, sure. Who hasn't?"

"Ups and downs?" The detective scrolls through his notes.

"Which includes harassing your husband and Miss Jónsson with intimidating emails, texts and threatening phone calls."

"Just a misunderstanding."

"Your ex... sorry, your husband, alleges you trolled and cyber-bullied Miss Jónsson for months."

"Just a few comments on social media. There is no law against it."

"There is if the content is threatening."

"Well..." Ciara flicks her cigarette butt into the garden, tipping out another from her pack. "...you're the expert, I suppose."

"Where were you last night between nine thirty and ten thirty?"

"Right here, all night."

"Can anyone corroborate that?"

"Only the kids. But I need a word first. They don't know what's happened yet, and Steph, my daughter, is a wee bit taken with the girl, you know?"

"Thank you, yes, I will need to take their statements. I would also request your mobile phone for analysis?"

"Is that legal? I mean, it's not like I'm being arrested, am I?"

"Just eliminating you for our enquiries, so we can apprehend whoever did this as quickly as possible. I will get it back to you tomorrow."

Ciara stalls, trying to remember Steve's coaching.

"I can return with a warrant to seize it."

"OK. Whatever. I've got nothing to hide." From her jeans back pocket, Ciara hands him her iPhone.

"And your home computer?"

"I've got a laptop..." Ciara crafts the lie. "But I've left it at work."

"Where do you work?"

"Saint James's Park, at the Food Standards Agency, like I said."

"I'll have an officer collect it in the morning."

"But the kids use that for homework."

"We'll return it in a couple of days. I'd like to speak to the children now."

"OK, let me break the news to them first," Ciara says, shuffling into the hallway. "Keep an eye on the chips?"

53

CALUM

The mood within the group felt ominous from the start. Ciara hasn't spoken a word, and Steve seems more cantankerous than ever, if that were possible. Most disconcerting is Emily's demeanour, returning his greeting smile with a wintery stare, as if she were a stranger. Dejected, Calum zones back into Malcolm's monologue.

"Separation can trigger feelings of past loss and trauma, and only by confronting those emotions can we to move on and build successful future relationships."

What good does scratching old wounds do? Calum thinks, tonight's theme plummeting his mood. Everyone's got a past, and some people, himself included, would rather keep it there. If it wasn't for Emily, he'd have jacked this in weeks ago, and now she's giving him the cold treatment. Whatever greasy pole of wellbeing he's hauled himself up, he can feel his mojo sliding back down it. Perhaps tonight's theme has dredged up unwanted memories in Emily as well, but even before Malcolm opened his mouth, she was distant and skittish, appearing more interested in Steve. Her jade eyes fixated on him throughout the session. A fascination reciprocated by Steve, it seems to Calum, anguishing if something is going on between them.

"Steve?" Malcolm asks. "Have you ever suffered from post-traumatic stress disorder?"

Steve stiffens. "Not me, pal."

"But it is common among combat veterans?"

"Aye, I've seen it happen to too many good men to mention, but not me. I picked up the odd knock and scrape." Steve traces his finger along the white scar on his forehead. "A wee twinge now and then, but I can't complain. One of the lucky ones, I guess."

"I'm not referring to physical scars, Steve. When we spoke about our emotional family trees, you mentioned your childhood in Glasgow, and your abusive relationship with your mother."

"Mother? You can give her that title." Steve shifts in his seat. "I wouldn't."

"Well..." Malcolm removes his spectacles. "How would you describe your relationship?"

"Nice as pie when she was on the scag and the drink, then the next minute she'd beat the shite out of me for looking twice at her. When she wasn't off on one of her benders, with whatever fella was in the picture."

"Is that why you ran away at sixteen, Steve, to join the army?"

"I suppose, aye."

"Classic characteristics of ambivalent attachment." Malcolm replaces his glasses. "The insecurity and fear of rejection imposed on your childhood, manifesting in your adult relationship, through your suspicion and jealousy of your partner?"

"So, it's my fault the wife gave me the horns?"

"In part, I am afraid it is. Your jealousy and controlling behaviour, motivated by your terror of abandonment, is likely a driving factor in forcing her away."

"Fuck away with you."

"You described the army as your family. Ergo, leaving your surrogate familial relationship has compounded your feelings of betrayal and anger directed at your wife."

"What can I do about it now? I can't go back."

"None of us can, but by empathising with our former partners and forgiving them, you can let go and move forward with your life."

"Maybe I don't want to let go, eh?"

"Nelson Mandela once said, 'Resentment is like drinking poison and then hoping it will kill your enemies.'"

"What about acid?" Emily asks.

All eyes lock on her, most intently Steve's. Emily stares back at him accusingly.

"I'm not sure I follow, Emily?" Malcolm asks, echoing Calum's perplexity.

Steve throws her a death stare. "This isn't the time or the place."

"Steve, I will decide what is appropriate for discussion. This is a safe environment to express our feelings. Emily, do you want to share something?"

Emily's eyes are unswerving from Steve's. "It's not me that needs to share."

"The success of this programme is determined by trusting each other."

"Good luck with him." Emily glares at Steve.

"I was referring also to you, Emily." Malcolm slides his notebook on the coffee table. "Losing your father in your formative years would be a traumatic experience for any adolescent, but given the violent nature of his death, and the consequent loss of your mother and family unit–"

"No. Don't you dare..." Emily springs to her feet.

"Emily, I am merely correlating the triggering mechanisms of memory and trauma, coalesced not only by the separation from your husband, but with him the dream of the baby you had wanted. Your own family unit, restored."

"You have no right…" Emily looks stricken.

"Malcolm, I think you should leave it," Calum says. "Emily clearly doesn't want to talk about this."

"Calum, please, you were all warned about confronting hard truths. I know it is difficult to hear Emily, but your reluctance to deal with the past is inhibiting you from moving forwards."

"You make it sound like it's my fault that my husband ran off with my best friend. Because, what? I didn't deal with my fucking daddy issues? How fucking Freudian, from a lawyer with accreditation from some Mickey Mouse therapy course. You're not a psychiatrist, you're not even a clinical psychologist, and you're not qualified to tell me how to live my life." Emily points a shaky finger in Steve's direction. "Save your pseudo-psychoanalytical bullshit for those that need it." Snatching her bag, she charges for the door.

As the door slams, the group's attention turns back to Steve, who shrugs defensively. "What wasp got up her arse?"

"What indeed?" Malcolm asks, searching Steve's crabbed features.

"Sod this." Calum launches to his feet, chasing after Emily.

54

EMILY

Emily stomps along Floral Street. Shaking with anger and struggling to light a cigarette, she crushes it in her fist.

"Emily, wait!" She hears Calum's call from behind.

Keep walking, she tells herself, *as far away from these maniacs as possible.*

"Are you OK?" Calum asks breathlessly, catching up.

"What do you think?" Emily lights another cigarette. "No, I'm pretty fucking far from OK."

"I don't blame you. Malcolm was way out of line."

"I don't mean Malcolm. I mean the attack last night."

"What attack?" Calum looks bewildered.

"You really don't know?"

"No. What attack?"

Emily yanks her iPhone from her bag, googles the story, and hands the phone to Calum, searching his features, relieved by his visible shock.

"Jesus Christ. Oh, Jesus Christ! You don't think...?"

"It is too much of a coincidence."

"Jesus Christ, I didn't sign up for this." Calum thrusts her phone back like it's scalding.

"Me neither. We should go to the police." Emily takes a deep draw on her cigarette.

"Yeah." Calum nods, then shakes his head. "No, wait. We need to know who's involved."

"How do you propose that?"

"Simple. We ask them."

"You're out of your tiny wee minds." Steve's eyes sweep the pub. "And keep your fucking voices down."

"You expect us to believe it was just an arbitrary attack?" Calum asks.

"Believe what you want, Pretty Boy, but spraying lassies with acid is not my fucking style."

"Well, it's clearly someone's," Emily hisses. "You're even wearing a black hoodie."

"So is Tal," Steve retorts.

From grimacing at the details on his phone, Tal looks up offended. "I can assure you I had nothing to do with that."

"Half a million guys in London are wearing hoodies. It's not exactly a rarefied fashion item."

One by one, the group's focus turns on Ciara. "Don't fucking look at me either," she says, mid sip of her prosecco.

"Why not?" Emily asks. "You're the one with the motive."

"I'm fucking five foot three, the fella they're looking for is six feet tall, and he's a fella. So, shove your motive up your hole."

"I'm not saying you did it personally." Emily glares at Steve.

"Then what are you saying?" Steve asks.

Unsure, Emily backpedals. "What was it you said, Ciara? That you 'wanted to rip her skinny wee face off'."

"It was a fucking joke."

"Now you've delivered the punchline?"

"I had nothing to do with it. I swear on my kids' mortal souls."

"You don't seem too cut-up by it, though," Calum says.

"Catch yourself on. Why would I, eh? The skinny slag ruined my life. I'd like to buy the fella who did it a drink." Ciara glances at Steve.

"For the last time, it wasn't fucking me."

Ciara holds her hands up. "OK."

"Is there anything else the detective mentioned?" Steve asks. "Think hard."

"No, I've told you…" Ciara pauses, recalling. "Only… after he spoke to the kids, he did ask a lot about Jim's relationship with Issy."

"Is he capable of something like this?" Rachel asks.

"Jim's no stranger to raising his fists like, and he's a jealous one."

"Kettle calling the pot," Emily shakes her head.

"Says Mrs Brightside, here." Ciara pulls a face.

"I don't understand the reference?" Tal looks perplexed.

"Jesus, finally, Doctor Google doesn't know something." Ciara snorts. "'Mr Brightside' is a song about jealousy, by The Killers."

"Appropriately," Emily interjects.

"Enough already." Steve rubs his temples. "It all fits, don't youse see? With Issy's acting career taking off, the writing was on the wall for them and Jim knew it."

"But he was going with her to Canada," Calum says. "It doesn't add up."

"Perhaps it does." Rachel leans in. "When I spoke to Geoff Lancer, the producer of the show, there were rumours around the crew that Issy and her leading man were having a fling."

"Rumours?" Emily scoffs.

"Doesn't matter if Jim believed it. It's gotta be him. It has to." Steve twists to Ciara. "You brought your laptop?"

"Yeah." Ciara pulls it from her bag.

Steve passes the computer to Tal. "Give that a wee clean, would you, Tal lad? Make sure there's no spyware, or nothing for the forensic techies to find."

"They won't. I will ensure it." Tal nods, inserting it into his satchel.

"He's not gonna find anything about acid in your search history, is he?" Steve asks, draining his scotch.

"Is he fuck," Ciara huffs.

"And you got rid of the burner?"

"Yeah, and I snapped the sim, like you said."

"Good girl. I'll get you another one in a few days, after I've sniffed around a wee bit. See where the investigation is going. Who wants another one?" Steve raises his empty glass.

"You want to continue after this?" Emily vaults to her feet. "Well, don't think to include me. You're insane, all of you." She storms to the door.

As Emily steps into the gloomy streetlight, she tugs her cigarettes from her bag, discovering the packet empty. "Shit." As she marches across the cobbles towards Covent Garden tube station, Emily hears Calum's voice calling her name again. "There's enough weirdness right now, Calum, without you stalking me."

"Sorry. I just wanted to see if you're OK."

Emily spins round, seeing his wounded expression. "No, I'm sorry, I'm just..." She sighs. "On the edge."

"I know. What the hell have we gotten into?"

"Whatever it is, I'm out of it."

"And me."

"What are we going to do?"

"We could get a drink and talk," he says.

"Not back there?"

"No, somewhere else. Or maybe we could get some dinner?" From her perplexed expression, Calum forges on. "Look, Emily, despite everything, I've really looked forward to Thursday nights, because I know you'll be there..." Calum exhales. "I haven't done this in a while."

"Are you trying to ask me out?" Emily puts him out of his misery.

"The circumstances and the timing aren't what I'd planned, and in retrospect I wished I'd prepared a speech or something, but..."

"You really are out of practice."

"To be fair, I've always been this smooth."

"Calum, I've enjoyed... well, aspects of meeting you too... but not tonight, OK?" Calum's deflating features stir her compassion. "How about I cook dinner tomorrow night?"

"Sure," Calum says, a smile curling his lips.

Over his shoulder, Emily glimpses a hooded figure haloed in the streetlight, but before she can focus, he vanishes into the crowd.

55

TAL

In the glow of more monitor screens than an air traffic controller, Tal hunches over his desk, thrash metal pumping through his headphones, drowning out bothersome noise from the surrounding flats. He powers down Ciara's laptop and draws a mask-free breath, appreciating the air filtration system he installed in the flat. Long before the pandemic, anxious of viral infection, Tal wore a nanofiltration mask. Much to his ex-wife Simone's chagrin. *Who is laughing now?* he thinks, glaring at the time on a computer screen. Three thirty-five in the morning.

Tal isn't much of a sleeper, particularly when his intrusive thoughts are ornery, and especially now, robbed of his most precious ritual. Every evening at eight thirty, he read bedtime stories to Lukas, and in the blissful serenity with his boy, Tal's anxieties faded away. He relished being a husband and a father. All his life, bullied, rejected and marginalised, yet with Simone and Lukas, Tal felt accepted. He felt normal. If only for a while. Thoughts of Lukas makes his anguish so overwhelming; he longs for the anaesthesia of his medications. Except he stopped taking them weeks ago. Now more than ever, he needs to focus.

Consequently, like his insomnia, Tal's obsessive hoarding

has become pervasive. Evidenced all around him, in an ordered mayhem of cardboard boxes and groaning shelves stacked from floor to ceiling. Apart from a narrow gully to his desk, his living room is an amorphic mass of comics, magazines, sci-fi collectables, toys, curios and movie memorabilia. Only the wall space above the computer desk is free of his collection, reserved for his new obsession. From his eidetic memory, he has replicated the evidence board at Steve's office – surveillance images, data printouts and flow diagrams of the group's ex-partners.

Simone never tolerated his collections. A prerequisite of her moving into his penthouse apartment in Shoreditch (she demanded he rent) was that he "get rid of all your crap". Through the help of his CBT therapist and a strict regimen of prescription meds, Tal acquiesced, removing his collection into storage, and Simone deigned to move in. A smile curls his lip, recalling their lavish lifestyle together...

Reality crashes in, smile inverting, reminded of his new surroundings – a squalid low-rise flat on a Bethnal Green sink estate. All he can afford now, after being fired from the bank. Because of his medication, Tal's thought process became addled, doubting the logic of his own data. When his work suffered, so did his bonuses and consequently Simone's affections. Desperately seeking her reassurance, Tal's anxieties became insidious, checking her phone messages, emails and examining her underwear for illicit signs of sexual intercourse. He tried to convince Simone to give up her job and prevent her from leaving the apartment to avoid her meeting potential suitors. Only when Simone threatened to leave did Tal submit to the humiliation of consulting a psychotherapist. A woman, Tal seethes, fathoms beneath his intellectual superiority, whose unscientific methodology and flawed logic resulted in diagnosing his comorbidity as Othello Syndrome. A form of delusional jealousy, in which a person is obsessed with a partner's suspected infidelity, with no rationale or evidence. As it transpired, Simone's unfaithfulness invalidated the therapist's diagnosis, and vindicated Tal's suspicions all along.

"Who is laughing now?" Deafened by his blaring headphones, Tal is oblivious to the volume of his shouting. At the time of his diagnosis Simone was already pregnant, by the one person even his psychoneurotic scrutiny didn't suspect – his own brother.

"They will not be laughing soon!" Tal rocks back and forth in his chair.

It was Tal who suggested Othello to Steve as the moniker theme for their mission codename, a secret reference to his supposed Othello Syndrome. He steers his gaze across the spider's eye of computer screens, each displaying a voyeuristic portal into their exes' lives, fixating upon his personal window of enmity: his brother's restaurant.

"Don't wait up for me." Mehmet's moustached lips grazes Simone's cheek on the way to the door, to whatever card game the degenerate gambler is attending.

"Don't worry, I won't." Simone recoils. "Just try not to lose what we can't afford, yeah?"

With a fractious shrug, Mehmet slithers out the front restaurant door.

"Fucking loser." Simone thrusts the deadbolts shut, leaving her all alone. Like most weekends, they have boarded Lukas off to his grandparents, lifting the intolerable burden of parenthood. From the bar refrigerator, Simone commandeers a bottle of Chardonnay, her own nightly ritual. She pads over to the alarm security panel and keys in the code. As the activated alarm beeps, she hastens to the creaky wooden staircase to the apartment above, flicking off the main light switch and plunging the restaurant into darkness.

Tal's fingers glide across his keyboard, tapping in coding, extracting passwords and hacking security systems. He takes a sip of Coke, his index finger hovering over the keyboard, savouring the power it wields.

"They will not be laughing soon." He repeats his new mantra, and with a dismal smile, presses the enter key.

56

JIM
3 May

Jim pats his jeans pockets, remembering the police have his phone. "Shite!" He slumps on a moulded orange seat in the plastic surgery unit waiting room of the Royal Free Hospital in Hampstead. Where he's remained for the past two days, without showering, changing clothes, awaiting updates from Issy's multiple surgeries. Thirsty, he ambles to the vending machine, slots in coins and pushes the Tango button. To the clunk of the ejected can, the solitary visitor in the waiting room pops his bald head over his newspaper. Jim tilts his chin up in greeting, hopeful of conversation to break the monotony, but the man's shiny dome dips behind his rustling paper.

"Bald cunt," Jim mutters under his breath. He rolls the can on his forehead, sweaty and cool, before opening the pull-tab, inhaling the cloying citrus release of gas as the police parade into the waiting room. The boyish detective, DS Thomas, accompanied by two uniformed officers.

"Mr Devaney, please accompany us outside," DS Thomas says.

"I'm staying put. The surgeon could be out at any minute. Have youse charged her yet?"

"I think it would be better to discuss this somewhere

private." DS Thomas glances at the bald guy, peering over his *Daily Mail*.

"We'll it's here or nowhere, fella," Jim says, with a gassy belch. "Let's have it?"

"I'm afraid forensics has found incriminating searches on a laptop."

"I knew it." Jim makes a fist. "The fucking jealous cow."

"No, Mr Devaney, you don't understand. We made the discovery on your laptop."

57

EMILY

"They've arrested him, Ciara's husband?" Emily halts scrubbing a catering tray in the steel sink. "You're certain?"

Calum nods, drying an industrial-sized cooking pot with a tea towel. "According to Steve, he's in custody at Croydon police station."

"I don't trust a word Steve says." Emily's face clouds, wiping suds from her brow.

"I'm no fan of him either, but at least we're not in the frame," he says, drying the serving tray and placing it on the dish drainer.

"Maybe not directly." Emily tugs off her rubber gloves. "But our hands are hardly clean."

"But we're not responsible for what Ciara's ex did. No one could have predicted that."

"It doesn't absolve us from the fact that we started this."

"No, we didn't–"

Calum falls silent as the swing doors clatter open.

Frank, the homeless shelter manager, saunters in through the chrome kitchen doors. "Me and Ange are off now, Em. Sure you're alright finishing up?"

"Yes, Frank. See you Sunday morning."

"Before I go…" Frank hovers at the swing doors. "Dwayne

came in earlier, asking after you. I told him you weren't here."

"Thanks Frank." Emily smiles gratefully.

"Who's Dwayne?" Calum asks, drying his hands with the towel.

"Someone we helped get back on his feet," Emily says. "One of our success stories."

"Not entirely." Frank shrugs his round shoulders. "Nice to meet you though, Calum, and thanks for your help." As he pushes the steel door open, his ruddy-faced wife, Angela, appears behind it, patting down her greying blonde hair.

"Good meeting you, Frank." Calum flashes a smile. "And you, Angela."

"We'll leave you two… to it." Frank departs with a paternal nod.

Emily waits for the shelter dining room lights to go out before shaking her head. "Sorry, they're a little protective. They lost their daughter to drugs…"

"Shit, that's awful." Calum's smile slips, his tone sombre and reverent. "They're good people." He locks his ebony irises on hers. "Like you, Emily, doing all of this. It's humbling for me, and inspiring."

"It's not completely selfless. I get back more than I give."

"What's happening Sunday morning?"

"I'm prepping Sunday lunch for the homeless. You can join us if you like?"

"I'd like to, but I've got Bella this weekend."

"Saved by the Bell, eh?"

Calum's smile returns. "I've enjoyed myself tonight, but when you said you were cooking dinner, it wasn't how I pictured the evening."

"Is it better or worse than expected?"

"Surprisingly better," Calum says, leaning in close.

Emily can feel the heat from his breath as his lips meet hers. She shakes the thought of the last time she was kissed, embracing the warm flood of desire pulsating through her. As her eyelids flicker open, a hooded face at the barred window jolts her. Emily wrestles from Calum's grasp.

"I'm sorry." Calum misinterprets. "I didn't mean to–"

"I saw someone – at the window – watching us..." But as Emily points a trembling finger, the mottled glass is vacant.

Calum offers a reassuring smile. "Probably just a cat or something."

"No... it was a face. He was staring at us."

"Did you recognise him?"

"No... he was wearing a mask and hood."

"Probably just a homeless guy looking for the shelter. I wouldn't worry about it." Calum takes her in his arms. "It's not too late to get a drink somewhere?"

"Not tonight." Emily backs away "I'm sorry, I'm too... tired." Shaken up, she means.

"OK. But don't worry, everything will be fine, yeah? Trust me."

Emily nods, still far from a place where she can trust anyone.

58

SIMONE
4 May

Simone awakes, choking and sweating like she has a fever, until her eyes blink open to a wall of fire. The bedroom ceiling is a grill pan of flame, filling the room with searing heat and smoke. *Lukas*, she panics, then remembers he's staying at Mehmet's parents. She flails her hand out to wake Mehmet, but his side of the bed is empty, realising he's still out. Simone fumbles for her phone, knocking it from the nightstand, clattering to the floor, lost in the fog. She crawls out of bed, bare feet scorching on the smouldering rug. Her eyes streaming, coughing on the toxic fumes, she crouches through the smoke towards the door. As she grasps the brass handle, pain sears her palm, hot metal cauterising flesh.

Hysterical, mortal fear grips her. With every ragged breath, fumes pour into her mouth and nostrils, filling her lungs. Consciousness deserting her, she lumbers towards the window, tumbling over the bed, rolling, falling, winded on the hot-plate floorboards. Animalistic survival instinct surging, Simone lurches to her feet, clattering into the sash window, fingers groping for the latch, tugging and hammering at it. The room is hotter than an oven now, her skin blistering, hair melting as she grapples with the stubborn latch. With the last of her strength, she yanks at the unyielding sash window, sealed with decades of paint layers. Finally, it relents, sucking oxygen into the vacuum. As she inhales a lungful of air so does the backdraft, exploding the room into the inferno. Simone with it.

59

EMILY
5 May

Emily has spent her Sunday morning at the homeless shelter kitchen, peeling potatoes and using her press relations training, fielding questions about her "handsome gentleman".

"Will you be seeing Calum this afternoon?" Angela looks up from chopping carrots with a grin.

"No." *Here we go again*, Emily thinks. "He has his daughter this weekend."

"Have you met her yet?" Frank asks. "His daughter?"

"Not yet. Like I said, we're just friends."

Angela and Frank exchange dubious glances.

"You two should start a gossip column." As she plops the last potato into the pot, Emily smiles, recalling Calum's kiss. Not just the act itself, as pleasant as it was, but also what it represents. The possibility of a relationship with someone else, beyond Dan, which only weeks ago seemed unimaginable.

"Dwayne Campbell was hanging around again last night, Em," Frank says, splitting cabbages on a chopping block. "Want me to have a word?"

"It's fine Frank, I know how to handle him."

"You're too nice for your own good."

Emily's smile tightens, wishing it were true.

Angela squawks along with the radio, murdering George Michael's "Careless Whisper".

Emily washes her hands in the sink, grateful for a reprieve from the inquisition, as the song fades into a news feature.

"Dozens of homes and businesses have been evacuated on Great Titchfield Street, but the seven-pump blaze has been brought under control," the radio presenter says, before moving on to a traffic report.

"We saw the smoke coming in on the bus this morning, didn't we Ange?" Frank asks, peering at the browning chickens through the glass oven door.

"Yeah. One of those Turkish restaurants. You know what those places are like, probably a grease fire," Angela says, oblivious of her casual racism.

Turkish? Unease stirs in Emily's gut.

"Insurance job more like," Frank says with a cynical head shake. "Usually are with these restaurant fires."

Emily's stomach lurches, panic swelling inside her. "What's the name of the restaurant?"

"Some Turkish name. What was it called? Oh, it's on the tip of my tongue."

"Yusuf's?" Emily asks, praying she is wrong.

"Yeah, that's the one. Risky business, the restaurant game…"

Emily is already crashing through the swing doors, leaving Frank and Angela with perplexed glances.

60

DCI HUGHES

The heat hits DCI Hughes stepping from his car, radiating from the smouldering carcass of Yusef's. Great Titchfield Street is teeming with police, paramedics and firemen streaked with soot and sweat. He draws on his vape, exhaling into the acrid smoke, watching the mortuary van transport the body away. Hughes is proud of what he has achieved in his career, but he's wearied of it now. The tragedy, the trauma, the death. Like the smoke pervading his clothes and hair, it follows you. Still, another six months until his retirement. On to a cushy security consultancy position in the city with a fat salary and benefits. After Karen, his ex-wife, and her vulture of a lawyer stripped his carcass, he needs it. *Time for some other poor sod to take over the job*, he thinks. As a detective, and the political animal the job needs nowadays, there's no better candidate than Rosa Hawkes. But...

"Rather be on the golf course on a Sunday morning, eh, boss?" DI Pat Kruger hands him a Costa coffee cup.

"You're not wrong, Pat." Hughes sucks on his vape. Hasn't forgotten the vanilla, Hughes notes, sipping his latte. No doubt Rosa is a better detective than Pat Kruger, but there is even less uncertainty about whom Hughes will recommend for promotion. "Seen the fire investigators yet?"

Kruger shakes his coiffed head. "Waiting for them to come out."

A spectral figure emerges from the restaurant, tugging off his mask and breathing apparatus. Hughes recognises the rotund, sweaty face of a fire investigator he's worked with before, but whose name escapes him. A soot-blackened Labrador and a lanky dog handler follow. Hughes wonders how they could bear the heat and the smoke, with the building still smouldering like a dragon's lair.

Hughes nods hello, evading the awkwardness of forgotten names. "Any hypothesis yet?"

"Seat of the fire started near the ovens in the kitchen," the fire investigator says. "A waste bin jammed the fire door open, which is how it travelled up the wooden staircase to the loft space above the flat. Someone removed the batteries from the smoke detectors too. The victim didn't have a chance."

"Accidental?" Hughes asks.

"Not given the burn patterns. They used an accelerant. Dog picked up the scent straight away, but this is the real smoking gun." He waves a charred hunk of plastic.

"What is it?" Kruger asks.

Hughes licks his dry lips. "A timer."

"Spot on. A digital timer. Pretty common device. You can buy them in most DIY stores."

Hughes lets out a long sigh. "Arson."

"Hundred per cent."

"Insurance fraud?" Hughes asks.

"We need further testing, and an X-ray, but it looks like a deliberate ignition set up to look like an accident."

"OK, thanks, I'll await your report." As the fire investigator and his crew depart towards their vehicles,

Hughes reappraises the ruined restaurant. "This is now a murder scene. Any sign of the husband?"

"Not yet, boss. His phone is switched off."

At the piercing screech of car tyres, Hughes turns to the police cordon at the corner of Eastcastle Street. Amongst the throng of gawkers, a burly, moustached guy stumbles from his silver Mercedes, and ducks under the police tape before being tackled by two police officers.

"Where's my wife?" he pleads, wresting with the officers.

"Speak of the Devil." Hughes strides towards the melee, nodding for them to release him.

"Mehmet Vilmaz?"

"Yes."

"Please come with me." Taking his arm, Hughes guides Mehmet towards an ambulance.

"Where is Simone? Is she in the ambulance? Is she alright?" At the ambulance, seeing it empty, Mehmet panics. "Where is she?"

"Mr Vilmaz, perhaps it's best if you sit down inside."

"I don't wanna sit down. Please, where's my wife?"

"I am sorry to inform you, Mr Vilmaz" – *you murdering prick* – "your wife is dead."

"No." Mehmet's considerable weight sags under him.

"Pat." Hughes braces the heft as Kruger takes Mehmet's other arm. "Sit him down here." They rest Mehmet on the stoop of the ambulance.

"I wanna see my wife," he sobs.

"I don't think that's a good idea."

"I just wanna see her, please?"

"Is there anyone we can call for you?" Kruger asks.

"No." Mehmet shakes his head.

"We understand your son is staying at your parents'

house. Don't you think you should be with them?" Hughes says. "Detective Inspector Kruger will drive you there, and he will ask you a few questions on the way."

"What about my car?"

"Don't worry about that for now. Let's get you back to your family, and to your son." Hughes nods to Kruger, lifting Mehmet to his feet.

"Lukas... How can I tell him?" Mehmet sobs as they escort him to Kruger's unmarked BMW.

Pretty convincing crocodile tears, Hughes must admit. Maybe he hadn't intended on killing her? Either way, they'll push for first degree. As Hughes guides his head into the back seat, Mehmet's gaze snaps towards the police cordon. Following Mehmet's eyes, he glimpses a tall auburn-haired woman, before losing her in the gloom. Hughes watches Kruger's car pull away, trying to calibrate where he has seen her before, but as the BMW disappears into the vapour, his memory vanishes with it.

61

CALUM

As Calum drives Bella back to her mother, his usual anxiety at returning his daughter to Bex has returned with a vengeance. When he collected her yesterday morning, Bella blurted she was going to have a baby brother. But it wasn't the announcement that triggered Calum, as Bex had already dropped that ignominious bombshell. It was Bella's gleeful anticipation of her expanding family that he would play no part of. Aggravated by Bella's constant bulletins throughout the weekend, as they pull into the driveway at Bexingham Palace, his time bomb of resentment is set to explode.

"Mummy says when my daddy gets back from his business trip, we will all be a family," Bella says, for the umpteenth time.

"He's not your daddy. I'm your daddy, and he's not going on a business trip, he's going to jail, because he's a criminal." Before Calum can mitigate, Bella bolts from the car and flees towards her mother.

Atop the entrance steps, Bex halts conducting an army of removal men with furniture and cardboard boxes. So incensed, Calum hadn't noticed the three removal vans when he pulled up.

"What's the matter, baby?" Bex asks, as Bella catapults into her arms.

"Is Daddy going to jail?"

"Who said that?" Bex's eyes dart at Calum, climbing the steps.

"Other Daddy."

The words hit Calum like a donkey kick.

"No baby, he's being silly. We'll be a family again when Daddy returns from his business trip." Bex wipes Bella's tears with her T-shirt. "Go help Daddy pack your favourite toys." The moment Bella trots inside the house, Bex's demeanour twists. "What the fuck have you said?"

"It just slipped out. Anyway, don't you think she needs to know the truth?"

"She's six, for fuck's sake. And me and Matt will decide that, not you."

"Yeah, of course, I'm just 'Other Daddy'. And I can bet who gave me that title."

"I don't need your shit today, Calum. I've got enough on my plate, alright?"

"So I see." Calum glances at the removal trucks. "How are the mighty fallen?"

"Self-righteous prick! You think you are so superior, but we both know that's not true."

Calum smiles, not rising to the bait. "Where will you go?"

"Mum and Dad's." Off Calum's raised eyebrows, she adds, "It's only temporary."

"And that lot?" Calum nods at the removal vans laden with expensive furniture. "Be a squeeze, fitting that lot at your folks' bungalow."

"Most of it's up for auction," she says, unable to conceal her chagrin. "Like I said, it's temporary. I'm sorting us a flat through work."

"You're back at Manning's?"

"No. On-site sales at an apartment complex in Stratford. It's just Mondays and Saturdays… for now…"

"I thought all that was beneath you?"

"No choice, do I? Money's tight."

"Not tight enough to sell that gaudy bauble?"

Bex clasps the diamond-encrusted B at her décolletage. "Over my dead body. It was the first thing Matt bought me."

"And the last."

"Speaking of money, I'm going to need more maintenance."

"You're kidding, right? I can barely eat on what I pay you already. With Bella's school fees and everything."

"My lawyer will be in touch."

"Are you organising a seance? Last I heard, he was dead."

"There are other divorce lawyers, you know. She'll be in touch." Bex turns on her heel. Conversation over.

She? Calum winces inwardly. Even more of a ball-buster, probably. "I'll look forward to that." As she departs, Calum needs an answer to the question tormenting him since Bella's revelation. "Bex, hang on?"

"What, Calum? I'm busy."

"After everything he's put you through. You're still gonna wait for him?"

"Matt's lawyer reckons he'll only get two years."

"If he's lucky, and then what? With a criminal record and a permanent suspension from the financial sector?"

"I'm having his child." Bex clutches her washboard stomach.

"That never stopped you leaving me, did it?"

"That was different."

"Because he was rich?"

"It was never about the money, Calum." Bex waves at the house. "I don't care about any of this shit. Matt is the love of my life." A smirk twists across her face, enjoying her restoration of power. "Don't fret, Calum, you'll still be Bella's father. So long as you do what my lawyer tells you."

As he watches her disappear into the house, rage burning like a fever, his phone buzzes in his jeans. He yanks it out, reading Emily's name on the screen, shutting his eyes, swallowing his wrath before answering. "Emily, can I call you back? Now isn't the best time–"

"It's happened again," Emily says.

62

EMILY

Under the shadow of the London Eye, Emily lights her third cigarette in a row. Perched on a bench, she watches people ambling along the path and in the adventure playground, coveting their joyous weightlessness, free of the burden pressing down on her. The gigantic Ferris wheel looming above evokes memories of riding it with Dan. An oddly kinetic description for such a ponderous motion, so slow you barely notice movement. Like their gradual separation. Unable to comprehend her failure to conceive, Emily withdrew from Dan, distracting herself with work. He was hurting too, but she pushed him away – straight into the arms of Charlotte. Emily lets out a long sigh, seeing the full picture now – what psychologists call the helicopter view. Whatever wisdom is worth when it arrives too late... A wet tongue laps at her bare shins, snapping Emily from her reverie to a dewy-eyed chocolate Labrador.

"Prince, no," Calum says. "Sorry, he's been cooped up all day."

Emily strokes Prince, his fur coarse through her fingertips.

"Can I have one of those?" Calum points to her cigarette.

"I didn't know you smoked?"

"I haven't for a long time, but it seems appropriate."

"Last request..." Emily offers him the pack and a lighter. "Before we go to the police?"

"No." Calum flinches as he lights up, shaking his head furiously. "We can't do that."

"We have to, Calum–"

"You don't understand. Steve told me–"

"I don't care what he said. You know he was behind it."

"Emily, you've got it wrong. The police are questioning Tal's brother. It looks like the fire was an insurance job."

"'Looks like' is right."

"No, it's straight up, Steve's got a contact at the Met."

"I'm still going to the police."

"What will you tell them?"

"The truth."

"The truth is Tal's brother was up to his eyes in debt, so he torched the gaff for the insurance." Calum tosses his cigarette onto the path. "End of."

"With his wife in it?"

"Arson is unpredictable. It probably seemed more convincing if she was on the premises. He just didn't figure the fire would spread like it did."

"Who told you that? Steve, presumably?"

"He knows what he's talking about. He is an ex-copper."

"He seems to have it all figured out pretty fast."

"So did the police."

"Then what difference does it make if we admit what we've done?"

"The difference is, I'll lose custody of Bella..." Calum chokes up, his eyes glistening with tears. "I can't lose my daughter, Emily. I just can't."

Images wash over Emily of another playground with swings, her father lifting her into the chain metal seat, rocking her, higher and higher towards the dazzling sun...

Emily blinks away the image. "OK, no police. For now."

63

ROSA
8 May

I stride to DCI Hughes's office clutching an evidence report on a fatal stabbing, which I need his sign-off on before the suspect's seventy-two-hour detention limit expires. Through the venetian blinds, I can see Hughes ensconced at his desk with Pat Kruger, like pals at the nineteenth hole. As I rap a knuckle on the door, Hughes's brow furrows, but he waves me in.

"The pub stabbing, sir." I wave the report. "Needs sign-off for the CPS."

"One minute, we're just finishing up," Hughes says.

I wonder if that means to wait outside, but curiosity compels me to hover. Kruger doesn't even acknowledge me. Arrogant prick.

"According to the loss adjuster, Vilmaz took out additional insurance two weeks before the incident," Kruger says.

"Which he denies any knowledge of." Hughes shakes his head in disbelief.

"Yep." Kruger chuckles. "Along with his denial of the accelerant found in the boot of his car, and the internet searches on his computer for digital timers."

I edge closer, glimpsing Hughes's computer screen –

interview footage, paused on a bulky guy with an Eighties moustache. The suspect, I presume: Vilmaz.

"Keep going, Pat, he'll crack."

"Will do, boss." Kruger rises to his feet, and with an indifferent nod to me, he swaggers out.

"I could have a go at Vilmaz, sir? Maybe I can get something from him."

"Nobody can get inside a suspect's head like you can, DI Hawkes, but we don't need forensic psychology on this one. It's all tied up in a neat bundle." Hughes clicks his bony fingers. "Let's see that report."

64

MALCOLM
9 May

"Mindfulness allows us to empower our emotions, rather than them controlling us." Malcolm is shoeless, his legs crossed in a Sukhasana position. Eyes shut, he sits on a Kashmir rug at the heart of the larger therapy studio, surrounded by gongs and illuminated harmonic bowls. In the ambient glow, the others sprawl on yoga mats, circling him like a clockface.

"Close your eyes," he says soothingly, caressing the singing bowls with sonic mallets, the low-frequency chimes floating around them. "Breathe in through your nose, cleansing your inner self with calm, awareness and positivity." Malcolm inhales the perfumed air wafting from candle burners. Essential oils of sage, lavender and rosemary. His lungs filled to burst, he exhales loudly.

"Now breathe out, freeing yourself from anxiety, fear and negativity." He listens to the sounds of breathing, pleased with their communal commitment. Except for one. Steve – his attempt sounding like a petulant huff. "Try to really breathe out through your mouth."

"Talking through your hole, more like," Steve mutters.

Malcolm's eyes open, darting toward the offender. Steve was reluctant to partake from the start. And the poisonous atmosphere from last week's session has lingered, particularly between Steve and Emily. It permeates the mood, counteracting the purpose of the meditative exercise. He closes his eyes, determined to prevent the toxic energy pervading the group.

"Be mindful of mirroring other people's negative emotions. Transend them and project your own positive aura into the Universe. Remember, what we give, we get back tenfold." Malcolm sucks another lungful, releasing it with gasping exclamation.

"Close your eyes, forgive your transgressors and let go of your anger." He opens his eyes and steers his gaze around the circle. Everyone's eyes are closed.

Apart from Steve's and Emily's, locked in a staring contest.

A premonition shivers through Malcolm. As though the Cosmos itself was preparing to repay some terrible wrong.

65

EMILY

She feels Steve's glare from across the pub, boring into the back of her head.

"It's never easy transitioning careers, especially after a traumatic breakup." Malcolm takes a sip of tomato juice. "You have to find the right balance and maintain a sense of coherence."

They sit at a separate table from the usual booth, where Calum, Ciara, Rachel, Tal and Steve huddle in conference. Emily invited Malcolm, knowing it would antagonise Steve, but also, perhaps he can help.

"Everyone needs a purpose," Emily says, "but I can't lie. I miss my old job." She promised Calum not to inform the police, but surely telling Malcolm would be different. Therapists, like psychiatrists, practise a code of confidentiality. "It must have taken a lot of courage to leave a successful career like you did?"

"Courage had very little to do with it, I'm afraid. How shall I put this?" Malcolm removes his glasses, pinching the bridge of his nose. "My partners at the firm requested me to take a permanent sabbatical."

"What happened?"

"Carl, my ex, wanted to adopt. I didn't. Too focused on

my career, you see. So focused, I neglected everything else, namely Carl, so he had an affair with a colleague. A woman, of all people, who could give him what he needed."

"A baby?"

"Yes." Malcom replaces his glasses. "Anyhow, after Carl left, as a way of self-medication, I started drinking heavily, and… I wish there was another way to describe it… I began harassing him and his new wife. Then one day, the police came into my chambers and arrested me. They dropped the charges, but alas, the damage was done. A twenty-year career in criminal law…" Malcolm gestures with his fingers, poof.

"So, you set up the Divorce Support Centre?"

"Not quite. First, the drinking got worse. Until my Damascus moment when I awoke on my living room floor choking on vomit. So, you can indulge me, I know a little about anger and jealousy, and how destructive they are."

"Carl, your ex… do you still love him?"

"Lamentation for losing the emotional bond often continues following divorce, even when love turns into its antithesis, attachment remains for the estranged partner."

"Spoken like a therapist."

"You're quite right; I am being evasive." Malcolm draws a breath and releases a pensive sigh. "Yes, I still love him."

"How do you get through it?"

"Like any addict, one day at a time." Malcolm drains his juice. "What pulled me through was learning to forgive. Him first, and then myself. Ultimately, it's the only way we move on."

"I'm not sure I'm capable of that."

"Then if you can't forgive, the next best thing is acceptance." Malcolm glances at his watch. "Now, you will have to forgive me, I have a date."

"I wondered why you've abandoned the Lycra tonight." She nods approvingly at his navy suit and floral shirt. A vibrant departure from his monochrome wardrobe. "It's a better look on you." *Tell him now*, Emily thinks, *before he goes*.

"Andrew has already seen me in my full regalia. He's a fellow cycling enthusiast, you see."

"Well, if he's seen you in Lycra and stuck around, he must be a keeper."

"I suppose so," he says with a lopsided grin. "If you open yourself to the possibility, Emily, there is another life awaiting you."

Emily smiles in lieu of an answer.

"See you next week?" Malcolm asks.

"I hope so," she says, wresting with her inability to confide.

As Malcolm rises to his feet, glancing at the others, his smile slips. "Emily, is there something you want to tell me?"

Emily glances at Calum in the booth, recalling his emotional plea about losing his daughter. She opens her mouth to speak, to confess, but all that emerges is: "No."

"You have my number if you do." With a cynical tilt of his head, Malcolm departs into the throng.

"You were very cosy just now?" Steve thumps into Malcolm's vacated seat. "What were you girls gabbing about, eh?"

"None of your business."

"It is if you've been flapping your gums to that nosy fucker."

"It's all about control with you, isn't it? No wonder she–" Emily swallows the last two words – left you. Fear pierces her chest, as icy as Steve's stare.

"Don't push it, I'm warning you."

"Leave her alone." Tal surges onto wobbly legs, tumbling over a stool and collapsing on the floor.

"Fuck, he's pissed out of his heed." Steve scowls.

"Is it any wonder? His ex-wife just burned to death." Emily jumps to her feet to help Calum lift Tal back onto his seat.

"I'm glad she's dead," Tal slurs. "Who is laughing now? Who is laughing now?"

"Shut the fuck up, you eejit," Steve hisses.

"Leave him alone," Emily says. "Look what you're doing to him. He's ill, for Christ's sake, and you're manipulating him, like the rest of us, for your fucking sick game."

"No, you got it wrong. I'm trying to help the guy, and all of us."

"Us? There is no us. This stops now. It's done. Over."

"Nothing is over," Steve says, conscious of the surrounding drinkers. "Pretty Boy, give me a hand, we'll get him in a taxi."

"Yes, sir." Calum mock salutes. "We're done with taking orders from you, OK."

"Don't ever fucking do that."

Calum gets in his face. "Oh, sorry, are there snipers in the hills?"

"What did you say?"

If Calum doesn't see the twist in Steve's features, Emily does, and it terrifies her. "Calum, leave it."

"You heard me. Now fuck off and leave us alone." Calum shoves Steve back.

Viper-like, Steve twists Calum's wrist behind his back, thudding his face into the table, scattering glasses. "Never raise your hand to me again, Pretty Boy." Aware of the surrounding attention, Steve releases his grip and wrenches his denim jacket from the chair.

As he passes Emily on his way out the door, Steve leans into her face, so close she can smell the whisky on his breath and see the deathless fire behind his ice-blue eyes.

"Call Tal a cab and get the lad home, why don't you? And I'll decide when this operation is over, not you, sweetheart."

Emily watches as Steve barges out into the night, her bubbling suspicions crashing to the surface in his wake.

66

CALUM
11 May

At their last drop of the night, Calum checks his watch and suppresses a yawn. Exhaustion seeping into his bones, it feels later than midnight. At the end of Charing Cross Road, yards away from the twenty-billion-pound Crossrail terminal, the homeless congregate for soup, bread, blankets and whatever else the shelter van brings. There by the grace of God, Calum shivers, puzzling how they survive the harsh winter nights. As a boy, he assisted his father with countless charitable events, and there was a constant stream of waifs and strays at the parish house, but nothing as destitute and dispossessed as these wretches.

With her enduring smile, Emily hands out the last blanket. As the gatherers disperse, Calum can't see how she maintains the energy. Sliding the transit van doors shut, pain shoots from his wrist. "Shit!"

"You should get that X-rayed," Emily says with a concerned look.

"It's fine." Calum shrugs, pride smarting more than his wrist.

"It's not fine, Calum. None of this is fine. We should call the police."

"Right, there's my cab." Frank waves at his Uber driver. "Thanks again, Calum."

"My pleasure, Frank." Calum watches as Frank squeezes his girth into the back of a Toyota.

"Feel like a nightcap?" Emily asks with a delicate yawn.

"Like you wouldn't believe." Calum is relieved to see her showing signs of fatigue. "But will anywhere still be open? Apart from nightclubs, and my clubbing days are long behind me."

"I mean at my place." Emily smiles, climbing into the van driver's seat.

"Oh. Yeah, sure." Calum struggles to hide his excitement. "Oh, shit... No, I can't. I need to get back for Prince. We could get a drink at my place?"

"That depends if you have any decent vodka? I'm kind of fussy."

"About alcohol, or men?"

"I find the former helps with the latter."

"What you see is what you get. But I do have a bottle of Absolut in the freezer."

"Acceptable on both fronts."

As Calum jogs around to the passenger door, he notices a hooded figure lurking in a guitar shop doorway on the corner of Denmark Street. Before he can focus, the spectre steps back into the veil of shadow.

"What's up?" Emily asks as the diesel engine growls to life.

"Nothing." Calum masks his alarm with a smile. When he glances at the doorway, the figure has vanished.

67

BEX

Bex grips the balcony railings, gazing across the sun-bleached Queen Elizabeth Park at the skeletal Orbit Tower and the Olympic stadium jutting on the horizon. Faded remnants of long-forgotten glory. Like her life, she laments. "Fuck that," Bex reprimands herself. Negativity is for losers. With this view, maybe the nine hundred and fifty grand price tag isn't such a stretch. She's sold less for more, back in the day.

"How the mighty fall." Calum's words echo in her mind.

"Self-righteous prick!" She steps inside the apartment, her heels tapping the laminate flooring, echoing around the homogeneous, white-boxed interior. *I'm a fucking winner*, she reminds her inner self, admiring her outer self in the ebony-framed mirror, pouting her lips and unfastening another button on her blouse. Can't hurt, as her prospective buyer is a man. And with Matt going to prison she needs this commission. But where is he, she wonders, checking her absent Rolex, recalling they sold it along with everything else. Except for her wedding rings and her treasured B pendant, which she clutches like worry beads.

"Think positive." Bex checks the time on her phone.

Ten fifteen. "Shit. Fifteen minutes late. Better not be a no show."

The intercom buzzes in the hallway. "Speak of the fucking Devil." Bex trots to the front door, getting into her character. With a scarlet fingertip she presses the buzzer and, faux eloquent, asks, "Mr Othello?"

68

EMILY

As Emily opened the living room door, the thumping bass of The Doors' "Take it as it Comes" boomed in tempo with her racing heart. Dawn shone through the half-drawn damask curtains, casting the room in scarlet, a nightmarish hue befitting the scene. Her father was laid on the floor with a velvet cushion covering his head, asleep, drunk, or both, until Emily saw the pool of cranial blood soaking the carpet.

"Mummy, Mummy." Emily appealed to her mother, passed out on the couch, knowing from experience she was beyond rousing. Comatose from a cocktail of gin and Valium, wrapped in her fluffy pink dressing gown, soaked crimson and emanating the metallic scent of blood. The claw hammer, dropped from her mother's bloody grasp, lay on the carpet, slick with clots of her father's hair and brain matter.

Emily grappled for the telephone, tremulous fingers dialling: 9, 9, 9. "It's my daddy. My daddy is hurt. Please help."

"What service do you require?"

"Ambulance, please help."

"Is your father still breathing?"

"I don't know."

As the opening keys of "The End" faded in, Emily leaned over her father. Too afraid to lift the cushion from his face, she touched his hand, shocked by his icy chill, dropping the phone on the sodden carpet as the music drowned out the operator's questions.

With quivering hands, Emily lifted the cushion, and any hope of him being alive vanished. Her father's face was streaked with gore, his protruding eyeballs filled with blackened blood, his mouth frozen in a silent scream. She shut her eyes to block the image, but as she opened them her father's face was replaced by Dan's.

Emily jolts awake, gasping for breath as if she were drowning. Slowly she adjusts to the light shafting through the vertical slatted blinds, the alien surroundings of Calum's bedroom taking form and with it her recollection of last night. She turns, expecting to find Calum on the pillow beside her, but the bed is empty.

Blurrily, her thoughts turn to last night. Romantically out of practice, their encounter was a nervous audition. Like startled understudies, she and Calum fumbled their lines, playing their roles, desperate to please. With Calum's own lengthy abstinence, it was over before it began, leaving Emily both wanting and glad it was done. The second time, as familiarity grew with their confidence, they found their own unique rhythm. Not the all-consuming passion with Dan, but... Emily chastises herself for the comparison. Thoughts of Dan trigger the memory of her nightmare, his bloody face, usurping her father's. She shakes the image from her mind, casts off the clammy sheets and rolls out of bed.

Emily dresses in a white bathrobe hanging off a door peg, and steps into the hallway. "Calum?" With no response, she wanders through the small open-plan living room and kitchen. Calum wasn't exaggerating, his apartment is cramped indeed, and apart from an overstuffed bookcase, tan Chesterfield couch and an enormous TV, depressingly barren. "Calum?" she calls, concern creeping into her tone.

Prince arises creakily from his dog bed and lumbers towards her. Emily stoops to her knees, petting the old Labrador. "Hello there. Where's your daddy?" To the sound of a key turning in a lock, Emily follows as Prince bounds to the front door.

Calum enters, laden with the morning papers and carrier bags. "Hey boy." His smile broadens, seeing Emily. "This is a nice welcome party."

"I thought you'd done a runner."

"Not a chance." Calum grins, raising up his goodies. "I got breakfast. Hope you're hungry?"

69

ROSA

I peer over the balcony into the canyon of concrete and steel plummeting to the communal gardens. Even ten storeys up the blood is visible, staining the virginal paving stones, tainting the picture of an urban oasis promised on the billboard cresting the apartment block. The chrome balcony railing is level with my chest, making an accidental fall improbable. A puzzled head shake exacerbates my throbbing temples from another sleepless night, rendering me with a headache and a crabby mood. Val's GCSE exams are fast approaching and, after that, my intended exit point to leave Bruce and the kids for a new life with Gareth. I push the thought away, stepping back into the immaculate apartment where rangy Crime Scene Manager DS Butler, DS Nicholls and DC Husseini await. Husseini's pregnant belly strains at her forensic suit, and I try to recall if she is four or five months gone. Either way, her absence for maternity will be a loss.

"No sign of a struggle?" I ask rhetorically.

DS Butler shakes his head. "Not unless forensics turns something up."

"The railing looks safety compliant." I grip the railing, testing its sturdiness. "An accidental fall unlikely. What about the neighbours, any reports of a disturbance?"

DC Husseini shakes her head. "The building isn't ready for occupation yet, boss."

Along with Husseini's other attributes, I appreciate the nomenclature, as opposed to the archaic "ma'am", which makes me feel like a governess from a Dickens novel. "What about her appointment with Mr Othello?"

Nicholls checks his notepad. "The sales suite didn't have any further details, other than the appointment time, apartment number, client name and mobile number. From an unlisted disposal phone, which is switched off."

"Keep trying it anyway and see if we can trace the purchase."

"On it, ma'am."

"Who took the appointment booking with Mr Othello?"

"The deceased. It's weird though. She had six appointments booked that day and logged all the other clients' address and email details."

"An oversight?" Butler asks.

"She was pregnant." Nicholls shrugs off mine and Husseini's glare. "Either way, it seems the appointment may have been a no show."

"'It seems' and 'may have' shouldn't be in a detective's lexicon. On what evidence do you base that hypothesis?"

"He couldn't have got past the front desk without the concierge seeing him."

"What about the rear entrance?"

"Only if he had a staff or resident security code," Husseini says.

Frustrated, I step back onto the balcony where the others follow, cramping the tight space.

"Maybe she jumped," Butler says.

I scan the prolific deployment of CCTV cameras positioned around the gardens below.

"Let's hope the CCTV will shed some light."

"Doubtful." Butler shakes his head. "There was some kind of glitch."

"Glitch?" I snap my head around, provoking my headache. "What kind of glitch?"

70

EMILY

Calum scrambles eggs in a pan on the halogen hob. Prince hovers at his heel, hoping for scraps. Emily sits at a café-style table with room enough for only two chrome chairs, a platter of pastries, a jug of orange juice and a Sol beer bottle with a single red rose.

"You needn't have gone to all this trouble." Emily says, suppressing thoughts of the blue irises Dan used to bring her – the colour of his eyes. Prince twists to her voice and lollops over.

"It's our pleasure, isn't it, Prince?" Calum hands her a cappuccino. "Apart from Bella, you're the first guest we've had."

"I feel honoured." Emily sips her coffee, distracted by the Hieronymus Bosch print above the table, drawn to an owl-like beast. An anthropomorphic depiction of Satan, devouring souls in hell.

"I hope you like scrambled eggs with smoked salmon," Calum says, breaking her reverie.

"Is there any other kind?" Emily places a croissant on her plate. "Do you have any butter?"

"Sorry, yeah..." Calum reaches into the fridge, handing her a carton of margarine. "My hospitality skills are a little rusty."

"I might need to speak to the manager."

"That doesn't sound good."

"Let's see how breakfast goes."

A chirping on the granite counter sucks the smile from Calum's lips. Emily's too, turning to the unmistakable chimes of the Nokia ring tone. The same model of burner phone Steve gave her.

Calum stares at the screen. "Othello. Fuck, it's Steve."

"Don't answer it."

"I have to. It must be an emergency if he's calling."

"Calum, no!" Fear courses through Emily like molten lead as Calum places the phone to his ear, reading from his shock that something abhorrent has happened.

71
ROSA
12 May

"Mr Powers," the towering Family Liaison Officer says. "This is Detective Inspector Hawkes."

With a thousand-yard stare, Matt nods, his red-rimmed eyes locked on the closed hospital mortuary door.

"I know this is tough, Mr Powers," I say. "Can I call you Matthew?"

"Matt."

"Following the identification, I would like to ask you a few questions regarding your wife. Is that OK, Matt?"

"Yeah, whatever. Can I see Bex now, please?"

"Yes, of course Matt." I nod to the officer.

"Before we go through, Mr Powers," the FLO says, "I must inform you there is significant bruising to her face."

Matt winces, shutting his eyes, eliciting tears. Not the crocodile variety, either.

"Would you like a minute to collect yourself, Matt?" I ask, knowing the FLO's caution sugar-coats what awaits him.

"No."

The FLO opens the door and steps inside first, followed by Matt and me. Beneath the sheet, only Bex's left hand and head are visible, or what's left of it. Enough horror to subject anyone to. Hope of a mistaken identity flickers in his eyes, until recognition strikes him, distinguishing some peculiar feature of his wife.

"Look at her face, her beautiful face," he sobs, his entire body convulsing.

"Is this your wife, Mr Powers?" the FLO asks.

"Yes." Matt nods as the tears stream down his cheeks. "Can I hold her hand?"

The FLO glances at me for approval.

"Yes, of course."

Matt takes her manicured hand, her scarlet fingernails unscratched. "Oh God, she's so cold…"

As Matt's legs buckle under him, the FLO helps support his weight. I nod to the officer, and we lead him back the waiting room, lowering him, sobbing, into a plastic seat. "Where have her rings gone?" Matt asks.

"Get him a cup of sweet tea," I say, taking the seat beside Matt as the FLO disappears into the hallway. "The coroner will return your wife's personal items, including her rings and mobile phone, at a later date."

"And her pendant?"

What pendant? Mentally, I flick through the catalogued photographs of the deceased's personal effects. "There was no pendant at the scene. Are you sure she was wearing it?"

Matt's head snaps up, eyes burning with credence. "I'm positive. Bex never took it off."

72

CALUM
12 May

Over the scream of the kettle, the Disney Channel throbs through the wall. Under normal circumstances, Calum limits Bella's television viewing to two hours after dinner. A source of friction between him and Bex, and the moment he turned his back, she would undermine him. Still, not the worst habit she practised behind his back. Calum shakes off the thought. Today, he is glad of the TV volume, afraid of Bella hearing the conversation about to transpire. Especially having lied to his daughter that her mother is on holiday.

As he drops teabags into two mugs, Calum can feel the detective's dark, omniscient eyes probing his every nuance. His T-shirt feels clammy, his forehead gleaming with sweat and the steam from the kettle isn't helping. On such a hot day, why had he suggested making tea? Stay calm, Steve prompted him earlier, when he returned Calum's phone and laptop, wiped of spyware traces by Tal. He sucks a breath and turns to the female detective. She sits at the kitchen table, staring at the Bosch print, drawn like everyone to the grisly third panel of the tryptic, to the torture and violence. The naked, writhing souls, drowning in a blue lake of ice – the ninth circle of hell, home of the betrayers. "It looks fucking mental," was Bex's critique of the painting. From the detective's disdain, Calum fears she might have had a point.

Calum stirs in sugar for the moustached cop, and carries the mugs over, willing his hands not to shake. The female detective gestures to the vacant seat opposite, which Emily had occupied only the day before. Before…

"Can I call you Calum?" Rosa asks.

"Sure." Calum folds himself into his chair, regretting not making himself a coffee, giving his hands something to do. A steadying prop for his performance. Hardly his debut audience, Calum thinks, casting thoughts of Koh Samui from his mind. Falsely accused of his ex-girlfriend's murder, while they were backpacking on a gap year. A permanent gap as it turned out for poor Julie. *Christ, why does this shit follow me around?*

"Where were you on Saturday morning between ten and eleven?"

"I was here, at home."

"With your daughter?"

"No, she was at Bex's parents."

"Were you alone?"

Fuck. "No… I was with a friend. She stayed over."

"Does your friend have a name?"

73

EMILY

The buzz of the doorbell jolts through Emily like electricity. In contrast to her leaden limbs, plodding to the front door, her mind races, replaying her conversation with Calum yesterday afternoon at Jubilee Park.

"You'll have to corroborate my alibi," Calum said. "I'm sorry, Emily, I had no choice."

"Have you told Steve?" Emily asked.

"Not yet. I wanted to tell you first."

"Good. Don't tell him."

"We have to."

"No, we don't. It's the police we need to speak to now."

"No fucking way."

"Calum, we have to…"

"I can't let you do that."

"Let me?"

"Please Emily? I'm begging you. Bex's parents are already threatening to fight me for custody. If this comes out, I'll lose Bella for sure."

Emily gazed at the playground, where Bella rocked on a wooden chicken, remembering her own family ripped away, her grandparents thrust into the impromptu role of guardians.

"I'll lose my job. I'll lose everything. So will you."

"It's not everything, Calum," Emily said, without turning. "People have lost their lives."

"Maybe we set this in motion, but we aren't responsible... for that."

"No one was supposed to get hurt. Remember that promise we made? And look what's happened. The time for rationalising is over." Emily launched to her feet. "I'm going to the police."

"Please Emily, I'm begging you. I told Bella this morning her mother was never coming back. Please don't take her father away too."

Emily stared at Bella's solitary figure in the play area, seeing herself as a child, lost in the harrowing wilderness of anguish that no adult could bear to endure.

The sound of the doorbell snaps Emily back to the moment. She takes a sharp breath, composing herself before opening the door, shocked by the familiar face greeting her.

"Emily Hunter. What a surprise," Rosa says, looking anything but.

74

ROSA

Ten minutes after ringing the doorbell, we sit around Emily Hunter's coffee table, sipping Lapsang Souchong. After one taste, DS Nicholls wrinkles his nose and places his cup on the table beside the digital voice recorder.

"Would you prefer coffee? Or a soft drink?" Emily asks.

"That's alright," I say, before Nicholls can speak. "On the morning of Saturday, the eleventh of May, Calum Greyson claims he was with you. That you spent the night together until you left his flat at twelve noon. Is that correct?"

"Yes."

"You were together for the entire duration?"

Emily hesitates. "Apart from having a shower, yes."

"How long was your shower?"

"I don't know, five, ten minutes. I wasn't timing it." Emily reciprocates DS Nicholls's mollifying smile.

"How long have you known Calum?"

"A couple of months, I think."

"Where did you meet?"

"Is this relevant?"

"For the second time in weeks, I'm interviewing you in relation to a suspicious death. This time, a pregnant woman. I'll decide if my line of enquiry is relevant or not."

"She was... pregnant?" Emily's cool demeanour slips, her eyes gaping with shock. Or perhaps fear.

"Calum didn't tell you?" Rosa asks.

"No."

"I'll ask you again, Emily – where did you and Calum meet?"

"At a counselling group."

"Counselling for what?"

"Divorce."

Rosa places her empty cup on the table and leans into her question. "Does the name Othello mean anything to you?"

"No," Emily says, her jade gaze sliding into her tea leaves.

75

CHARLOTTE
15 May

In the boardroom of her Soho offices, Charlotte listens to her grey-gilled accountant, Roger, droning on about her grim financial situation. Hardly news to her, given the dormant offices and silent phones, and having it spelled out by this monotonous slug isn't helping her depression. "For fuck's sake, Roger, I didn't expect you to sugarcoat it, but you don't have to dip it in shit?"

"I am merely relaying the figures, Charlotte, which I'm afraid can't lie," Roger says, his bulbous eyes broadcasting his dread.

"How long do I have?" she asks, like a cancer patient awaiting her fateful prognosis.

Roger's lip wavers, fumbling a reply when Charlotte's iPhone rings on the table.

"Hold on." She thrusts a hand in his face, absently clicking on the message:

HE IS WITH HER NOW. MAKING THE BEAST WITH TWO BACKS.

IN YOUR BED. THE BED SHE HATH CONTAMINATED.

"What the fuck?" The language bemuses her, but not its meaning. Charlotte vaults to her feet, storming out of the office, leaving Roger perplexed and relieved.

Charlotte's keys swing in her front door, barging into the hallway, the heady scent of Emily's favourite perfume hitting her nostrils. Dementedly, she follows the source, her heels hammering the expensive carpet runner up the ebony staircase.

At the summit three floors above, Charlotte lumbers across the landing lulled by the distended potency of the fragrance. She bursts into the bedroom and is confronted with the sickening reality that, until now, she'd only imagined. The depleted champagne bottle and two glasses, one stained with lipstick. No doubt Emily's preferred brand and shade. Charlotte's tearful gaze falls to the ruffled bedsheets, soaked in the stench of perfume and sex. "Bitch!"

Charlotte staggers downstairs, wandering through the house, feeling Emily's ghost everywhere. The furniture, arranged with showroom precision, just as her former partner left it. From the reclaimed French oak floorboards to the high ceiling cornices, every inch designed by Emily. Even the cot in the nursery; an impulse purchase when Emily and Dan began trying for a baby. Yet without a family, it was just a beautiful facade packaging the hollowest of promises. Charlotte had fulfilled that potential, but now she feels like the intruder in her own home.

Charlotte stomps across the lawn, heels sinking into the turf, towards Dan's painting studio. Inside, he appears the picture of innocence – T-shirt flecked with paint, earbuds in blaring classical music, as he lashes acrylic on an enormous canvas, oblivious of Charlotte's presence until her shadow invades his painting.

"Christ, Lottie! You frightened the hell out of me." Dan fumbles the buds from his ears. "I didn't expect you home so early."

Charlotte reels away from his kiss. "That's why you took Ella to your parents?"

"What are you talking about? You know I need to work."

"Liar. Fucking liar. Admit it, you were with her."

"Who?"

"You know who. Emily, you fucking bastard!"

"You're being ridiculous."

"Ridiculous, am I? Then how do you explain this?" Charlotte stomps outside, back to the house.

"Jesus Christ!" Dan drops his brush on the polished concrete and jogs after her.

A minute later, as Dan catches up with her in their bedroom, Charlotte stares at the neatly made bed.

"They're gone."

"What's gone?"

"The champagne. The sheets."

"Charlotte, you're worrying me now."

"I'm not fucking imagining it. You cleaned it up, didn't you?" Charlotte snatches a pillow to her face, inhaling. "But you can't hide her scent, can you? Emily's favourite perfume."

Dan grasps the bottle from the dresser, thrusting it in her face. "You mean this? You demanded I buy it for your birthday."

Charlotte shakes her head, unable to calibrate, before recalling the text. She yanks her phone from her pocket. "What about this, then?" She scrolls through her messages, but the message has vanished from her inbox. "It's gone…"

"You need help." Dan barges past her, his voice trailing behind him. "Some of us have work to do."

As Charlotte thunders down the stairs in pursuit, she

misses a hooded figure emerging from the en suite. With a black day sack over his shoulder, the intruder descends the staircase, slipping undetected out the front door.

76

CIARA
16 May

Ciara slices potatoes into segments with the serrated knife. If the chips aren't even-sized, Paddy will throw a shit-fit. As she turns the gas down, watching the pan of boiling oil simmering, she wonders if her son is on the spectrum like Tal. She could ask Tal at the session this evening, but Steve messaged her burner phone that the operation is compromised and to stay away, destroy their burner phones, and avoid contact with each other. Instructions Ciara obeyed, but now she's eager to know why.

"How did you do it, eh?" Jim says, making her jump.

The knife clatters on the chopping board as Ciara turns, patting her hair. She needn't bother. Jim stands in the doorway, rigid, fists clenched at his sides, his blue eyes red-ringed and manic.

"Jesus, Jim, you scared the shite out of me." From his expression, Ciara regrets allowing him to keep his front door key. "You're out, then?"

"On bail, pending further enquiries." Jim edges towards her. "GPS tracker on my phone calls and messages to Issy put me back at the studio when she was…" He shuts his eyes, as if shaking away the image.

"So, you're off the hook. That's grand then, right?"

"Not exactly. The police think I had an accomplice. They think I paid someone, for fuck's sake. To do that... to Issy."

"Why would they think that?" Ciara's mouth feels dry, her lips sticking as she speaks.

"Don't play the innocent. The three grand transferred from my account to an offshore bank in Andorra ring any bells?"

"Honest-to-God, Jim, I don't know what you're on about–"

Jim wrenches Ciara's hair, twists her arm behind her back and thrusts her face towards the simmering pan of oil.

"Jim, no."

"You set me up, you fucking jealous bitch. Planting those searches on my Google history. I don't know how you did it, but you're going to fucking tell me."

"No Jim, honest, I don't know what you're on about. Stop." Ciara struggles as her face plunges towards the searing heat, needles of oil spitting and blistering her cheek. "No, Jim, please. It wasn't me. Honest-to-God!"

"Tell me." Jim shoves her closer to the molten fat.

"Alright, stop and I'll tell you who did it. Please, Jim."

"I fucking knew it!"

If she expected a reprieve, her confession has only provoked his anger. She screams, knowing the children are in their bedrooms, deafened by their headphones, and no one is coming to her aid. An inch from the oil, Ciara can smell her singed hair and scolding flesh, her vision searing to black as her eyeball cooks like a boiled egg. As she wrestles to push herself free, Ciara's fingertips slice along the serrated knife. With her last survival instinct, she fumbles for the handle, grasping it and stabbing behind her into his pressing mass.

Released from his weight, Ciara collapses to the floor. Light flickering in her right eye, she glimpses the knife, glinting in a lake of blood, spreading across the Italian marble tiles, the cost of which they had rowed over. She wonders if it's her blood, until she sees the source, pumping from Jim, slumped against the dishwasher opposite, drenching his jeans, such a bright shade of red it doesn't look real, spurting from his groin. Must have severed his femoral artery, Ciara remembers, from a work health and safety lecture. His gaze unwavering, Jim stares at her with those incredible Paul Newman eyes. His pallid lips part, as if to speak. Losing consciousness, she knows they might be the last he speaks, and the last words she hears. Ciara prays for the three she craves.

"You fucking bitch," Jim says, as her world goes black.

77

MALCOLM
17 May

Malcom sits alone, among a circle of empty chairs, iPhone pressed to his ear, waiting for Ciara's greeting message to end. "Ciara, it's Malcolm from the Divorce Support Group. I'm just checking why you have missed our meeting. I hope everything is OK? Please call me back if you can?"

He places his phone on the coffee table beside a full plate of shortbreads and checks his watch again, puzzling over their collective absence. With two more sessions remaining, why would they all cease to attend? And why are they not accepting his calls? He knows the toxic atmosphere at last week's session is the likely reason for their truancy, but what was the source of that?

With something akin to despair, he calls the last member of the group, surprised that, unlike the others, the call doesn't go through to voice mail. "Emily, it's Malcolm from the divorce support group. Emily, I can hear you breathing…"

The line goes dead.

78

RACHEL

Rachel stares at her iPhone, Malcolm's missed call throbbing on the screen. Hands shaking, she places the phone on her coffee table and sucks a steadying lungful of air. *Stay calm*, she channels her late father's counsel, *don't let emotion affect your judgement.*

Even days before hearing about Ciara's fate, Rachel knew the plan had gone awry. Gone awry? Putting it mildly. More like gone completely rogue. But when you dance with the Devil, they invariably get to pick the playlist. And now the beat is discordant, the rhythm wayward and building to some terrible crescendo. Faustian analogies aside, she should have known the perils of blindly investing in a venture without carrying out due diligence on a prospective partner first. Only once before had she failed to do so, marrying Jack. And look how that turned out.

Never trust a pretty face.

Rachel grimaces, having been played yet again. Yet she can't deny receiving a return on her investment, with a dividend to boot. Jack is gone, as agreed. Though, obviously, she will deny it, along with everything else. Or rather, her lawyers will in her absence.

She shuts her eyes, tears pricking, feeling the world

getting away from her. Rachel can almost hear the fading chords of the spectral band playing out the final number. *Keep it together*, she urges herself, having no intention of being around when the music stops.

Rachel grasps her phone, scrolling to a name she never imagined having to call.

Conrad.

An old contact of her father's. The option you choose when you're all out of options. Also known as "The Magician" due to his conjury at making people disappear. One way, or another.

Has it really come to this? Rachel ponders dismally, her manicured fingertip hovering over Conrad's name. Once she makes the call there is no way back.

Not. Ever.

Rachel opens her eyes. "You are Rachel fucking Kaufman," she reminds herself, and taps the screen.

79

ROSA
18 May

Low on blood sugar and patience, I lean against the incident room whiteboard, pasted with photographs of the Stratford apartment and Bex's bloodied corpse. A "crazy wall" it's called in Hollywood detective shows. An apt description given my present vexation. My team loll around the board table littered with coffee cups and confectionary wrappers.

"She never took it off." I prod a bitten fingernail at a holiday snap of Bex wearing a bikini and her B pendent. "Corroborated by her family, friends and colleagues: she wore the pendent everywhere."

"Maybe someone stole it. An opportunist passer-by," DS Butler says, wiping crisp crumbs off his rangy lap.

"No." I slap the crime scene images on the board. "No blood disturbance around the body. Anyone leaning over the victim would have left footprints on the flagstones. Which only leaves one option. The killer took it before she fell."

"Victim? Killer?" Hughes asks. "We haven't established a crime was committed. There was no sign of a struggle, no additional injuries other than the fall and no sign of forced entry."

"Because she let the assailant in."

"We have no evidence her appointment showed up." Hughes shakes his grizzled head.

"Estate agents get no-shows all the time," Nicholls says, preening his moustache.

"OK, but what about the CCTV?"

"You mean the lack of it." Hughes lets out a long sigh. "Any developments, Nicholls?"

Nicholls shakes his head. "Nothing sir, the cameras all stalled at eight forty-five that morning."

"Forty-five minutes before the estimated time of death. Quite a coincidence," I say.

Hughes doesn't rise to the bait. "What did the DCC say?"

"It's a bog-standard surveillance system," DC Williams says, "and because it's connected to the internet, someone could have hacked the IP address. Or a network bandwidth bottleneck could have caused it. They're running more tests, sir."

Nicholls snatches the baton. "We've also looked at local CCTV in a half-mile radius, but without a suspect or a substantial line of enquiry, we're looking for a needle in a field of haystacks."

"The witness described a six-foot male exiting the gardens around the estimated time of death," I say, hearing the frustration in my voice.

"The witness is also a known crackhead," Hughes says. "But even if this guy exists, he was wearing a hoodie and face mask."

"Another coincidence?"

"A man wearing a face mask and a hoodie in East London is hardly a Bigfoot sighting." Hughes stifles a yawn. "From the victimology, we have to consider suicide as an option."

"The deceased had no history of depression, or mental illness and she didn't leave a note," I say.

"You know most suicides don't leave a note. Her husband was bankrupt and facing prison. She lost her home, her lifestyle, her status. There were enough inciting events and life stressors to push her over the edge. If you will forgive the pun."

"She was four months pregnant."

"We know what desperate people are capable of, and maternal instinct can vary in the individual."

Was that a dig at me, I wonder, reading the crags in his face as if they were hieroglyphs. Does he know about Gareth?

Hughes drains his coffee dregs and rises to his feet. "It's Lockard's principle. A perpetrator always leaves a trace at the crime scene."

"But they did take something. A souvenir…" I prod the photo on the whiteboard. "The victim's pendant."

"At this juncture, the only plausible line of enquiry remaining to us is suicide." Hughes strides to the door.

"What about Emily Hunter?" I ask.

"Who?" Hughes turns at the door.

"The alibi of the ex-husband, and the very same witness from the Shangri-la Hotel case, who weeks later turns up in yet another suspicious death investigation."

"Coincidences happen."

I snatch an A4 printout from my files and stick it onto the board with Blu-Tack. A photograph of Emily printed off her Instagram profile. "With all due respect, sir, probability alone dictates this is a coincidence worth investigating further."

Hughes is about to retort when recognition flickers. He stalks over to the whiteboard, inspecting the enlarged photograph. "I've seen her before."

"Yes, sir." I nod wearily. "From the hotel CCTV."

"No." Hughes turns back, insight washing over him. "The arson at the Turkish restaurant on Great Titchfield Street? She was in the crowd. I knew I recognised her, and I'm positive Mehmet Vilmaz did too."

I feel the familiar stirring in my gut. "How many coincidences is that?"

Hughes concedes with a nod. "Too many."

80

EMILY
19 May

Emily wanders through the hospital car park carrying a bouquet of yellow roses, unsure if Ciara is even alive or dead. Calum's panicked phone call earlier was cryptic to say the least, and whatever news she gleaned online didn't help. As best she could work out, Ciara's husband Jim was dead, and she was on the critical list. More collateral damage from the spinning top of mayhem they have spun.

Near the hospital entrance, seeing a gauntlet of press and TV crews bustling outside, Emily slips behind a transit van. If the media posse wasn't enough, two police officers guard the doors to the main reception.

Shit! Emily realises coming here was a bad idea from the start. If anyone spots her, it will tie her to the others. Game over. Without a backward glance she flees, tossing the flowers in a waste bin. As she turns onto Haverstock Hill, her phone buzzes in her bag. Timorously, Emily draws it out, alarmed by an ominous message from an unknown sender:

YOU'RE BEING FOLLOWED

Emily maintains her course a few more paces before snapping her gaze back. Eyes narrowed against the sun, she spots a couple thirty feet behind, wearing dark suits. A young Black guy, with a visibly pregnant woman, her dark eyes shifting away. They don't fit the profile, but Emily's instincts scream they're police. With long-legged strides, she increases her pace towards Belsize Park tube station, panic and paranoia snowballing with every step.

81

ROSA

"If she brought flowers, she was visiting a patient," I say into my iPhone, leaning back on the plastic chair screwed to the concrete floor.

DC Husseini's voice emits through the phone. "Yes, but she scarpered when she saw the media circus outside."

I stare through the reinforced glass partition into an airless box that makes a police station interview room feel like a presidential suite at the Ritz. I hate the hostile claustrophobia of prisons, but Belmarsh is a purpose-built tenth circle of hell.

"Why the police and media presence?" DS Nicholls asks, seated beside me listening to my speakerphone.

"Domestic incident," Husseini says. "Husband stabbed to death and the wife on the critical list. He burned her face off in a chip pan."

"The joys of marital bliss," I say.

"That's why I stay single." Nicholls preens his feathery moustache.

"Of course it is." My eyes flick to the metallic crank of a door opening. "I'll call when we're done." I end the call as the prisoner shuffles into the secure interview room.

Mehmet Vilmaz wears grubby prison sweats and the gait

of a broken plough horse. A mountainous prison officer with a monobrow follows behind, ducking his head beneath the doorway.

"Take a seat, Mr Vilmaz," I say.

Ushered by his gigantic captor, Mehmet slumps into the chair opposite.

"Can I call you Mehmet?" I ask, bracing my nostrils to his body odour wafting through the ventilation holes in the partition.

"What's this about?" Mehmet's face carries the bruises of his stay, physically and psychologically.

"I'm Detective Inspector Hawkes, and this is Detective Sergeant Nicholls from the Major Investigation Team–"

"You got something on him?" Mehmet asks, his bloodshot eyes shining with hope.

"On who?" I ask.

"My brother. Have you checked his computer? It was him that hacked me, wasn't it? He's a whizz kid with all that shit. I'm telling you: he killed Simone…"

"We aren't here regarding that investigation, Mehmet. We're following up on another matter."

The flicker in Mehmet's eyes snuffs out. "I'm not saying anything without my lawyer."

"It might help your situation if you were to cooperate," Nicholls says.

"No fucking way. You lot twist everything."

"Mehmet, look at the picture." I slide a print of Emily from my file, pressing it against the partition. "Do you know this person?"

Recognition and confusion wash over Mehmet's face. "Yeah… What's this all about?"

82

EMILY
23 May

"I see them." Calum stares through his Ray-Bans. Across the pub beer garden, a man and woman sit in a black BMW 5 Series, their faces obscured by the sun. "Do you recognise them?"

"I can't see their faces." Emily exhales a wreath of cigarette smoke. "But I doubt they're here for a pint and a ploughman's."

"Fucking pigs." Calum sips his Guinness. "Can't even respect a funeral."

They sit on a wooden picnic table outside a gastropub, a few miles away from Bex's parents' home in rural Essex. As good a place as any for a wake. In his sunglasses and black suit and tie, Calum looks like a mobster. Appropriate attire, given their police escort. Emily wears a black Chiffon dress and burnished leather sandals she has never worn until now. There is an occasion for everything. "A time to give birth, and a time to die." The vicar's words echo in her thoughts from the service earlier, reminding her of Bex's pregnancy.

Calum lets out a sigh. "I appreciate you being here, Emily. I couldn't have got through this without you." He places a hand on hers.

"I'm here for you, and Bella." Emily shields the glare

with her palm, gazing at Bella on the swings in the sunny play area, a hefty middle-aged man pushing her as if she were porcelain.

Emily feels her grandfather's rough hand engulfing hers, as the pallbearers carried her father along the aisle.

She snaps from her reverie, feeling Calum's grip tighten, following his gaze to a glamorised middle-aged woman tottering towards them. Emily recognises the woman from her ostentatious grief at the church, and the likeness to her daughter, Bex.

"Hello Jean." Calum stiffens, letting go of Emily's hand.

"Calum, love." Jean nods, perching on the bench beside him, her feather fascinator and bleeding mascara reminding Emily of a witch doctor.

"I'm sorry for your loss," Emily says, filling the setting silence.

"Thank you, sweetheart," she replies without an acknowledging glance. As the quiet resumes, Calum and Jean focus upon Bella, the object of their commonality and discord. "I can still see Ron pushing Bex on the swings."

"Say what you have to say, Jean."

"Ron didn't mean what he said, Calum. You know what he's like."

"I thought I did, once."

"He loved you like a son."

"Until the flashier prodigal version came along."

"Neither of us were happy about that, believe me."

Mourners filter outside with their drinks, lured by the afternoon sun and nicotine.

"Please Calum, don't take our granddaughter too."

Calum releases a breath like air from a crypt. "I won't deprive you of seeing your grandchild, Jean, or Bella from seeing you. Just call off the lawyer, yeah? We'll sort something out, I promise."

Tears glisten like tangled pearls in Jean's fake eyelashes. "Thank you, son." Her carmine kiss smudges Calum's cheek. She wipes the lipstick clean with her finger, eliciting his reluctant smile, until his features twist with rage. He launches from the bench, thundering towards the swings, where Matt has usurped the role of pushing Bella.

"Calum, no!" Emily bolts after him.

"You stay the hell away from her, do you hear me?" Calum grasps the swing chains to a halt. "Bella, it's time to go home." He lifts Bella from the seat, and strides towards the car park.

"Can't I play with Matt, Daddy?" Bella asks.

"Not anymore."

"Come on, Calum. Don't be like this, son," Bex's father says.

"Stay out of it, Ron, I mean it."

As Emily arrives, Calum bundles Bella into her arms. "Take her to the car."

"Calum, no, let's just go." Emily glances at the unmarked police car.

"Just take her."

Emily takes Bella's hand, leading her across the car park, watching the BMW through the fronds of her hair. "It's OK sweetie, Daddy is just upset about Mummy."

"Never come near my daughter again, do you hear me?" Calum's voice booms behind Emily.

She folds Bella into her car seat before twisting back to the melee.

Calum's face is inches from Matt's, squaring up like rutting stags.

"You can't stop me seeing her. That's not what Bex wanted," Matt says.

"Bex isn't here though, is she?"

"And we all know why, don't we? Bex always said you were a jealous, vindictive bastard, but–"

Calum's hands grasp Matt's throat, garrotting his words, thudding him into the bonnet of a white Range Rover, setting off a wailing alarm, duetting with Jean's shrieks. Emily glances at the BMW as the driver and passenger doors swing open, but before seeing its occupants, she turns back to the fight, which is already over. Ron and several mourners drag Calum away, leaving Matt choking and spitting into the gravel.

Calum glares at the BMW as if remembering its presence. The doors pull shut, its shadowy inhabitants remaining within. As he marches away from the startled congregation, his gaze meets Emily's, startling her with its ferocity. "Sorry. That fucking guy just winds me up."

"It's been a tough day." Emily strains a pacifying smile. "Let's just get out of here."

"Yeah." Calum's smile returns. "We can stop for ice cream on the way back."

As they drive out of the car park, the BMW tailing them isn't Emily's primary concern. Nor is Calum's violent outburst, the context and emotion of which she can empathise with. Most disturbing is how placid he appears in the immediate aftermath.

83

ROSA

As I press the doorbell for the third time, the stench of urine and bleach makes me reconsider if we have the correct address. Sunlight bounces off the rust-marbled concrete, shafting through the green mesh and scaffolding infesting the exterior of the low-rise block of flats. From the signs everywhere, the council have scheduled it for renovation. A societal Elastoplast, for one of the worst estates in London.

"Not quite what I expected, boss. I thought he was some sort of IT whizz in the City?" Husseini wrinkles her nose.

"Nothing deceives like appearance," I say, as a rippled figure looms in the pebbled wire glass side panel.

"Who is there?" he asks, languid and robotic.

"Police officers. Can you open the door?"

Several bolts are unlocked within, before the door opens on a chain. A round spectacled eye, bloodshot and sunken into its socket, peers through the crack, squinting into the sunlight, a mask covering the rest of his face.

"Talbot Vilmaz?" I ask.

84

TAL

Tal stares at the photograph of Emily, conscious of his mutinous face twitching, grateful his mask covers his mouth. Steve primed him for such an inquisition, but nothing could have prepared him for the two female detectives standing in his kitchen. "No," he says, shaking his head to embellish the lie.

"You're sure you don't recognise her, Talbot?" Rosa asks.

"I prefer to be addressed as Doctor Vilmaz." He rocks on the balls of his bare feet, staring at the red linoleum tiles.

"You're a doctor?" DC Husseini exchanges a dubious glance with Rosa.

"Correct. I have a DPhil in mathematics, from Oxford University."

"Doctor Vilmaz, are you positive you don't know this woman?" Rosa asks again.

"Positive you do not know this woman?" he mimics. "I apologise. I have echolalia. When I am stressed, I repeat words and phrases."

Rosa holds the picture of Emily under his gaze. "Does this picture stress you out?"

"Stress you out." Tal shakes his head, trying to cast off his compulsivity. "No. The situation. Strangers in my home." As his Cognitive Behavioural Therapist instructed, he tries to picture something positive in his mind, but nothing manifests. He used to picture his son, Lukas, but now that makes him worse.

"It's alright," Husseini says. "Take your time."

Raven-haired, with coal black almond eyes, the pregnant detective looks Turkish. Tal recalls his father's initial disapproval of Simone. *If only I had listened and married a good clean Turkish girl...* "No." Tal shakes the thought. "I do not recognise her. Change the topic."

"OK. In that case, we won't take up any more of your time. Would you mind if I use your bathroom?" Rosa asks.

Tal stammers his objections, but she strides into the hallway. "Excuse me, that is not the bathroom..." Horrified what she might discover, he stumbles after her.

In the dingy mayhem of his living room, Tal finds the detective staring into the glow of his monitors, displaying benign flowcharts and financial data. He scans the wall above his desk, once a mosaic of incriminating evidence, now a canvas of yellowed woodchip and pinpricks. Tal exhales with relief, his sleep-deprived brain grateful for having already destroyed his damnatory montage. As instructed.

"You're better equipped than a Cyber Crime Unit," Rosa says. "You work in IT, don't you?"

"Correct. I was the top quantitative analyst at Carter and Hedges."

"And where do you work now?"

Tal flushes with anger and indignity. "Currys, on Oxford Street. I am the head of IT."

"Are you vulnerable to Covid, Doctor Vilmaz?"

"Ten nonillion viruses exist on our planet, Detective Inspector. We are all vulnerable."

"So, you always wear a mask?"

"Around other people, yes, of course. Everyone should take appropriate precaution."

Husseini steps inside the room, her shock visible, absorbing the hoarder's paradise of groaning shelves and cardboard boxes. The only light emanates from the glowing bank of computer screens displaying financial market data.

"Do you still play the stock market?" Rosa nods at the screens.

"Playing implies a game of chance, and a successful analyst applies only data, logic and intelligence."

"Any trading tips?" Rosa asks.

"Never invest unless you have superior information."

"Good advice."

85

EMILY

Calum closes the storybook, brushes the hair from Bella's sleeping face and kisses her forehead. Emily watches from the doorway, picturing her father reading to her in bed, tales of monsters slain, evil vanquished and the prince and princess's eternal bliss assured. In reality, nothing is fair, no one is whom they appear, and the abstract line between good and bad is indelibly blurred. As Calum retreats on tiptoe, Emily steps out into the hallway.

Calum pulls the bedroom door shut, his chin sinking into his chest. "I'm sorry about earlier. Today of all days I needed to be strong for Bella. I fucked up."

"Kids are resilient." Emily raises his chin with her fingertip. "Trust me, I know."

"Me too. They kicked me between foster homes until I was six. The thought of that happening to Bella…"

"That will never happen." Emily squeezes his hand.

"I wish to God I'd never set foot in the fucking divorce group." Calum's gaze locks on hers. "But I can't regret it entirely. I met you." Calum's lips caress Emily's. As she reciprocates, his kisses became more fervid.

"I should go." Emily pulls away.

"Stay." Calum nuzzles her neck with kisses.

"I've got work in the morning, and I need clothes."

"No, you don't." Calum hands roam the contours of her body, but Emily wriggles free.

"Calum, I've got a meeting first thing." A convenient excuse, Emily knows, but after his capricious behaviour earlier, she needs distance to process. "To be continued, OK?"

"OK." Calum grins, masking his wounded ego. "I'll call you a cab."

"I'm fine getting the tube."

"It's a twenty-minute walk, and it's getting dark."

"Half of the Metropolitan police force are following me, Calum. I think I'll be alright."

86

ROSA

Reclined on sweat-dampened hotel sheets, I recall my interview with Talbot Vilmaz earlier that afternoon. Analysis of his phone records hasn't yielded a connection to Emily, but his reaction had. He was obviously lying about not knowing her. I try to put the case from my mind, staring into Gareth's deep brown eyes. "How will Uberta react when you tell her you're leaving?"

"Isn't that against the rules?" Gareth's lips trace down my neck, slipping my right nipple into his mouth.

"I know..." I stroke his hair, coarse and brittle on my fingertips. "Indulge me."

"Don't I always?" Gareth rests his head between my breasts.

"Will she be jealous?"

"What's brought this on?"

"Ask a lawyer a question, and you get one back."

"OK. Yes, I suppose she would. Everyone gets jealous, right? I mean, in varying degrees."

"Freud broke jealousy into three categories." I recall my rudimentary psychology. "Normal, projected and delusional. Though even normal jealousy, he considered irrational. A competitive emotion that can cause the person to win back their partner, or exact revenge."

"Ubi isn't like that... At least, I hope not." Gareth rolls onto his elbow. "Talk about delusional jealousy, though. I've got a case right now, with a guy so jealous of his actress girlfriend, he hired someone to spray sulphuric acid in her face. And when he's charged and confronted with a mountain of evidence, he claims his ex-wife set him up. Hacked his computer, faked financial transactions, incriminating internet searches, as if she's some sort of computer wunderkind."

I sit upright, every synapse in my brain firing in unison.

"And it gets better... or worse, rather. Whilst on bail, he returns to the family home, with their two kids in the bedrooms, and burns his wife's face off in a boiling pan of cooking oil, before she stabs and kills him. It's like a fucking Greek tragedy."

"Or a Shakespearean..." I mutter, realising my eureka moment. I roll out of bed, scrambling for my clothes strewn across the hotel floor. "Which hospital is the wife in?"

Gareth looks bemused. "The Royal Free Hospital. Why?"

"Othello! That's the key."

"Rosa, what are you talking about?"

"It's all connected."

"What is? What's happening here?"

"Who's leading the investigation?" I hop into my linen trousers. "Actually, just text me the details."

"Rosa, where the hell are you going?"

I fasten my bra and lean over the bed for a parting kiss. "To work."

87

EMILY

Emily climbs the stairs to the Royal Victoria Dock Bridge, regretting declining Calum's offer of a taxi. Though the malodour is less pungent than the urine-reeking elevator, beer cans and bottles litter the concrete steps. Other than its proximity to the city, she can't see Calum's attraction to the Docklands. From Thursday evenings until Monday, its inhabitants flee their overpriced pieds-à-terre for weekend retreats in the five counties, leaving it like an abandoned set from an apocalypse movie.

Halfway along the narrow footbridge, Emily peers at the water fifty feet below, coursing like black blood, tranquil on the surface, masking the treacherous current lurking beneath. The sound of footfalls slapping the concrete behind sends a jolt of fear through her. A city worker on their way home? A police surveillance officer? Steve? Before she can compute, the footsteps quicken, getting louder and closer.

Emily rummages in her bag, tugging out her phone to call Calum, when it pings. Another message from an unknown number:

KEEP YOUR MOUTH SHUT
OR I'LL PAY A VISIT TO SYCAMORE STREET

Sycamore Street is where her sister Sara lives. Before

Emily can compute, the footsteps behind fall faster and heavier. So close she can feel the vibrations underfoot. She risks a glimpse over her shoulder and wishes she hadn't. Outlined in the drowning sun, a hooded figure bounds towards her, thirty metres away but gaining. Fight or flight? Emily chooses the former. She can't outrun anyone in her sandal heels. She stoops, pretending to fasten her sandal strap and grasps a discarded wine bottle. Adrenaline surging, she conceals the bottle and quickens her pace, listening to the footfalls, calibrating the proximity of her pursuer.

As he is almost upon her, Emily spins, wielding the bottle above her head. "Stay away from me, you fucking psycho!"

Terror freezes her pursuer in her tracks. A young woman, jogging in a sports hoodie. Before Emily can apologise, the petrified jogger sprints away, fumbling in her pocket for her phone, to call the police probably. Which is exactly what Emily should do to end this madness. Yet, recalling her chilling text, she knows that is no longer possible.

88

ROSA
24 May

As DS Thomas devours his fried breakfast, once again I'm struck by how young he looks. I struggled to find a parking space off Croydon High Street, and arriving late at the cafe, I'd discounted him as a truant sixth-form pupil.

"Have you questioned Ciara Devaney yet?" I ask, sipping from my cracked mug of instant coffee, hoping what it lacks in flavour, it makes up for in caffeine.

"Not yet. She's still in an induced coma. Best place for her, by the sounds of it." Thomas swills his food with a mouthful of dishwater tea. "What's your interest, anyway?"

"Possible connection to another investigation."

"Connected how?"

"I'm still trying to establish that. What about his claim, that his wife set him up?"

"We checked her laptop and work computer, but there was nothing to substantiate it. Likewise with her phone and her bank accounts, nothing suspicious."

"What about when you interviewed her? Any red flags?"

"She wasn't exactly cut up about her love rival's facial disfigurement. But who would be, right?" Thomas wipes ketchup from his mouth with a paper napkin. "Ironic, the same thing happening to her."

"Poetic justice," I concur with a nod. "Is there anything else you recall?"

"I interviewed the kids, who corroborated her alibi. Then her babysitter arrived, and that was about it."

"Did she mention where she was going?"

"Some sort of counselling group."

Adrenaline shoots through me, a thousand times more potent than the caffeine. "A divorce counselling group?"

"Yeah, that's right. Is that the connection?"

I'm already out of my seat and barrelling to the exit.

89

EMILY

Emily festers over the business card, as she has all morning in her office.

DI ROSALIND HAWKES
MAJOR INVESTIGATION TEAM

To make the call, she sent her assistant on a Starbucks run, but now alone with her conscience, Calum's plea not to involve the police gives her pause. But not as much as the threats to her family. Hesitantly, she stares at her iPhone when it rings. Wary of the unknown caller, Emily clicks the green button. "Who is this?"

"Who is this?" he echoes.

"Tal? Why are you calling?"

"Don't worry, it is an encrypted line." Tal's panic is audible, like he's hyperventilating.

"I don't care about that, Tal. What's wrong?"

"What's wrong? What's wrong?"

"Tal, tell me what's happened."

"Detectives came to my flat, asking questions."

"What about?"

"About the fire. About you. She knows, Emily, she knows."

Emily's eyes slide to the business card. "Detective Hawkes?"

"I didn't tell her anything, I promise. I followed Steve's protocol."

"Don't listen to Steve anymore, Tal. He's not to be trusted, do you hear me?"

"This wasn't part of the plan. Why can't people stick to the plan."

"Tal? Tal?" Emily asks the dead line.

90

ROSA

I'm prodding the Divorce Support Centre buzzer when the door opens and a short, wiry man emerges wearing neon Lycra, carrying a cycle helmet.

Five minutes later, I return to the pub booth with our drinks, placing a tomato juice on the table beside Malcolm's cycle helmet. The pub is half empty, with drinkers mainly congregated outside, imbibing the last dregs of sunlight.

"Thank you, Inspector." Malcolm sips his tomato juice. "Now, what, may I ask, is this is about?"

I taste my diet Coke, wishing it had rum in it. "A divorce counselling group your clinic runs."

"I'm afraid you will have to be more specific," he says stiffly. "We have dozens of classes and several counsellors."

"This group includes Talbot Vilmaz, Calum Greyson and Emily Hunter, but I think you already know that."

"This is about Ciara Devaney?"

"Why do you think that?"

"I saw it on the news. That is what you're investigating?"

I flip open my notebook. "I need the names of the rest of the group."

"Under law, that would violate confidentiality."

"Not if there is a risk of harm."

"But Ciara is in no state to harm anyone else?"

"This isn't just about Ciara. In the past two months, three people connected to your counselling group have died in suspicious circumstances. Notwithstanding Ciara's husband, and his mutilated girlfriend."

"Oh my God." Malcolm's constricting Adam's apple betrays his fear.

"I need those names."

"I need to seek advice from my professional association before breaching confidentially."

"You can seek guidance from the Dalai Lama, but I'll get them either way. Also, if the sessions are recorded, I want them too."

"They're backed up on the cloud, but again, they're confidential."

"I'll be back in the morning with a seizure warrant anyway, but if you try to stonewall me, more people could die."

Malcolm gives a relenting nod. "Come to the office in the morning, I'll give you everything you require, but right now, I'm late for an appointment." He rises to his feet.

"Just tell me this. Does Othello have any significance?"

"I sometimes use it as an analogy in my sessions. As a cautionary tale, you know, about the perils of jealousy and vengeful obsession. Why do you ask?"

"Do you consider anyone in the group capable of violent retribution against their ex-partners?"

"They used to meet here in the pub after our sessions. At this very table. I didn't give it much thought, at first. Clients often form bonds with other members, though there was something clandestine about their meetings. I popped in for a drink one evening to join them and they stopped talking, like I'd interrupted their plans. But I can't believe they would engage in this…"

"People with no history of violence can see red when it comes to jealousy. The perpetrator in this case might display characteristics of an antisocial personality disorder, or even psychosis. Does anyone in the group fit that description?"

"Perhaps…" Malcolm's eyes mist over. "But Inspector, this isn't the place. Can we reconvene in the morning?" He glances at his watch and rises. "I really must go."

"What time does your office open?"

"Nine o'clock."

"See you in the morning, then. Nine sharp." I drain my Coke as Malcom straps on his cycle helmet and slips into the throng.

91

MALCOLM

Malcolm cycles through the heavy traffic along Mansion House Street, blaming himself for not seeing the warning signs and acting on his intuition. He had reservations taking on the client from the start. A disruptive, inflammatory influence throughout the process, but he never thought it would come to this. Whatever the aetiology, at least now Malcolm can help by informing the detective of his suspicions.

At the traffic lights at Bank Junction, he focuses on the positives of his imminent dinner date at Andrew's favourite vegan restaurant. Vegan cuisine is an oxymoron to Malcolm, but as he espouses to his clients, successful relationships are based on compromise and placing value on your partner's interests and desires. At a figurative crossroads in his own relationship, Malcolm decides he will invite Andrew to join him on his cycling holiday in Majorca. No more prevaricating. As events have shown, life is too short. Yes, he'll ask him tonight.

As the traffic lights flash to green, Malcolm pedals into the junction towards Threadneedle Street, not seeing the sky-blue Peugeot e-208 shunting into his rear wheel, but feeling its impact, cannoning him into oncoming traffic.

In the millisecond before the twenty-six-tonne tipper truck hits him, Malcolm's final thought fills him with agony. That he'll never see his face again. Not Andrew, he realises defeatedly, but his ex, Carl.

92

CALUM

Calum presses the buzzer for Emily's apartment, struggling to assemble an agreeable facade. The five-hour round trip to his sister in Leicester has left him weary and testy. It went as well as predicted, turning up on her doorstep unannounced with his daughter and dog in tow, but at least Bella is safely away from the madness.

"Come up." Emily's voice cackles through the intercom, followed by the click of the door lock.

As Calum steps inside her flat, the aroma of garlic perks him up, not having eaten since breakfast.

"In the kitchen," Emily calls, stirring sauce in a frying pan. She wipes stray hair from her face, greeting him with a smile. "Are you OK?"

"Yeah, sorry I'm late, traffic was a nightmare." Calum adopts a smile. "Bank Junction was gridlocked."

"I heard on the radio. Another poor cyclist killed." Emily blows on the wooden spoon, tasting her sauce.

"Jesus, they're dropping like lemmings."

"Dinner will only take a few minutes. Just waiting for the pasta." She dips spaghetti into a large pot of boiling water on the halogen hob. "There's wine in the fridge, or beer if you prefer?"

Calum curses, having intended to pick up a bottle on the way. "Wine is good. I'll get it." He scans the galley kitchen for the fridge.

"The large cabinet." Emily nods at it. "It's integrated."

"Right." Calum opens the refrigerator, perplexed by several options. "Any preference?" he asks, wishing he read that wine book collecting dust on his bookshelf.

"The Verdicchio will pair nicely," Emily says, over the blender crunching roasted breadcrumbs.

Calum scans the labels, sliding out the bottle.

"Corkscrew is in the top drawer," she adds, as if reading his mind.

Opening the drawer, Calum takes out a waiter's corkscrew, noting the well-thumbed inscription: FIRENZE. Florence, he translates, recalling Emily's Italian travel tales with her ex, jealousy needling him.

"Glasses are in the cabinet behind you."

Calum snaps from his reverie, skewering the cork. "Smells amazing. What's for dinner?"

"Linguine alle Acciughe."

"Spaghetti with anchovies."

"You speak Italiano?"

"*Un po.*" Calum smiles, gesturing with his forefinger and thumb. "Bits I picked up from Latin, mostly."

"You read Latin? At school, or university?"

If she is impressed or surprised, Calum isn't sure. "Not exactly. From my dad. He was in the clergy."

"Your father is a vicar?"

"A pastor. At least he was, he died last year."

"I'm sorry."

"Don't be. We didn't speak for years. He was proper Old Testament, all fire and brimstone. Not a fan of TV. Or music, or video games, or any kind of fun, basically. Apart from books, that is. The right sort of books, of course. Consequentially, I read a lot as a kid."

"So, your passion for literature, is that why you wanted to teach English?"

"It was more like a forced contrition than a cultivated passion, but yeah, I guess so. Plus, I lacked the concentration span for pretty much everything else."

"What stopped you from teaching?"

"Bex, in a word. There's no money in teaching… at least, not enough to keep her satisfied…"

"It was never about the money." Bex's words echo in his mind. "Matt is the love of my life."

Calum shakes the thought, as the cork pops out. "Which is why I got into recruitment. 'What shall a man give in exchange for his soul?'"

"You can always go back into teaching."

Eager to change the subject, Calum scoops a spoonful of sauce into his mouth. "Sorry, I haven't eaten since breakfast and I'm starving. This is delicious, by the way."

"Good, I'm glad you like it. Acciughe is an acquired taste."

Calum pours the amber wine into two glasses. "They sound a lot better in Italian."

"Most things do." Emily clinks his glass. "Salute."

"I feel honoured that you're cooking just for me. Not the other five thousand."

"You're just the first to arrive."

Calum smiles, quaffing his wine, allowing himself to relax.

"Was Bella OK staying with your sister?"

His smile hardens. "She was, yeah. Though my sister took a little more persuading. I mean, she adores Bella, and Bella gets on great with her kids, but convincing her to take on an eighty-pound Labrador with questionable toilet training was a harder sell."

"Are you and your sister close?" Emily tops up their wine.

"Not as much as I'd like. We only reconnected a year ago."

"Is she younger or older than you?"

"Younger."

"Your parents adopted her after you?"

"It's complicated." Calum stiffens. "My adoptive parents couldn't have kids. At least, they weren't supposed to. Then, out of the blue, Mum got pregnant, and after my sister appeared like a gift from the divine, I became the poor relation. Wasn't her fault, but... anyway, enough of the past, let's try to enjoy the evening, yeah?"

Emily's expression clouds. "Calum, I invited you over so we can talk."

"That doesn't sound good." His mind reels back to Bex's Dear John speech.

"With or without you, I'm going to the police tomorrow."

"No, Emily, you can't do that."

"That psycho is out there, meting out his warped justice in our name. And I'm positive Tal is involved somehow."

"Look, we're all feeling a little paranoid, but–"

"Don't tell me I'm paranoid after everything that's happened."

"OK, I'm sorry. But there's more to consider than our own consequences if we go to the police. What about the threats to your sister's family?"

"The police will protect them."

"From Steve? Apart from being an ex-copper, he was in the SAS. A trained killer. Have you considered that?"

"I can't sleep for thinking about it. If anything happened to Sara or the children…" Emily's voice cracks.

"I know." Calum exhales, shutting his eyes, picturing his goodbye hug with Bella earlier. "It's so fucked up." The thought pierces him, what if that was his last? With him in prison, Bex's parents will take custody.

"We have to, Calum. It's the only way."

"I'm not losing my daughter."

"You don't know that will happen, Calum."

"Easy for you to say, isn't it? You can't even have kids…" Calum flinches, regretting his words. "Sorry, I only meant you don't have kids, so you–"

"Get out." Emily's eyes ignite like green embers.

"Emily, I'm sorry–"

"Get out!"

93

ROSA
25 May

When I parked behind the police car outside the Divorce Support Centre, I knew immediately this corkscrew of a case had taken another twist.

A glance through the reception door confirms my fears. Two luridly garbed traffic officers interview a receptionist along with three colleagues. From their harrowed expressions, I sense Malcolm Lindsay won't be keeping our appointment.

The tall officer barely looks out of adolescence. "Excuse me, madam–"

I wave my warrant card, silencing him. "DI Hawkes, MIT. Can I have a word, Constable?" I nod to the door.

With a glance at his stocky partner, he follows me out onto the stairwell. His youthful face, raw with acne, reminds me of DS Thomas, and I wonder if the Met are recruiting officers from kindergarten now. "I take it my nine o'clock appointment with Malcolm Lindsay isn't happening?"

"No, ma'am. He was killed in an RTC on Bank Junction yesterday at nineteen hundred hours."

Just after I'd met him, I realise. "A hit and run?"

"Yes, ma'am. The casualty was hit by a tipper truck, but

witnesses reported an initial collision with a blue Peugeot. The driver failed to stop at the scene."

Fuck! I should have pushed Malcolm harder last night when I had the chance.

"Sorry ma'am, can I ask if your appointment was professional, or personal?"

"Part of an ongoing inquiry," I say, wondering why the insinuation offends me. "Any ID on the driver?"

"Not yet, but a traffic cam picked up the vehicle reg. We're waiting on the DVLA."

I'm shocked, given the enigmatic history of the case so far. I note the force number on his epaulettes and tug a business card from my linen jacket pocket. "Call me when you get the registration, and I mean the very second, Constable." As I start down the stairs, the burly officer peers around the reception door.

"DVLA came back."

"What's the name?" I ask, surging back up the staircase.

The stout officer flips his notebook open. "Talbot Vilmaz, flat 133–"

"Thank you, Constable. I know where he lives."

Ninety minutes later I sit in the Putney incident room with the team, listening to the speakerphone at the centre of the board table.

"Armed Response are in position." Operational Support Group leader Sergeant Osman's baritone booms from the speaker. "We're two minutes from the address."

"Be careful on entry," I say. "The suspect is to be considered extremely dangerous."

"We've got everything. Full body armour, tasers,

firearms around the corner and a negotiator if we need it."

"Stay on the radio, Osman," Hughes says, "and let me know when the suspect is apprehended."

Hughes turns to me. "What do we have on the rest of this Othello Club?"

"Running background checks now," I say, already regretting the shorthand moniker I'd coined for them.

"And the status on the therapy session recordings?"

"There's at least a dozen hours of video, sir."

"Get more ears on it, I want transcripts yesterday."

I nod, though my team are already stretched. "We should pull them all in for questioning."

"Let's get Vilmaz into custody first and see what he has to say for himself."

"We're outside the address, about to gain entry," Osman's voice crackles, refocusing our attention.

A thunderous crash erupts. The battering ram, splintering wood and glass. "Police. Stay where you are." A cacophony of voices and thudding boots, followed by an ear-shattering bang. Some sort of tactical flash grenade, I think initially, but this is the OSG, not the special forces.

"What was that?" Husseini's gaping eyes meet mine.

"An explosion." I listen to the panicked sounds of mayhem.

"Osman, are you there?" Hughes's tone betrays his concern.

"I'm here." Osman coughs. "An explosive device was detonated on the property. I've pulled my team out. The bomb squad and fire brigade are on the way."

"Are your men alright?"

"All accounted for. A few cuts and bruises, but nothing serious."

"Any evidence of anyone being there?" I ask.

"No persons from what we saw, but it's impossible to confirm. The place is a death trap. There's junk everywhere and the living room is a fireball."

94

EMILY

On her lunch break, she steps into the elevator at 20 Fenchurch Street. An early meeting at a Soho design agency consumed her morning and diverted Emily from her task. She'd intended calling Detective Hawkes first thing, once again prevaricating, but now the time for rationalising is over. She draws her phone out of her handbag and the detective's business card, takes a calming breath and dials the number.

As the call tone rings, her attention is captured by the digital screen playing a silent news report of fire crews fighting a blaze at a grim apartment block covered in scaffolding. The breaking news at the bottom of the screen flashes unconfirmed reports of a bomb on the Cranbrook Estate in Bethnal Green. The address feels familiar, but before she can compute, his face appears on screen, a photograph taken years before, less gaunt, without his beard and unkempt hair, but without doubt Tal. Emily reels with shock, staring at his visage before it snaps to the next news feature.

"DI Hawkes," Rosa answers. "Who is this?"

Panicked, Emily cancels the call.

95

RACHEL

"Florence, you need to hurry, sweetie." Rachel attempts to sound calm, waiting at the foot of her grand staircase, still reeling from seeing the news reports of Tal's explosive demise. Thank God she had made the "getaway" call days before. Getaway? But what other word is there for fugitives on the lamb. How had it come to this? Fucking Jack, that's how.

Their suitcases await in a van in the driveway. A fraction of Rachel's treasured clothes, but with the eighteen million transferred to her Venezuelan bank account, she can buy a new wardrobe, to go with their new life.

Conrad, a simian hulk sporting a black suit, lurks at the front door. "Madam, we need go now," he says, with a guttural Armenian timbre.

"Florence!" Rachel abandons her pretence of calm.

Florence thumps down the staircase wearing pink rabbit-eared headphones, clutching her violin case and armfuls of cuddly toys. "God, I can't believe you're making me leave all my stuff."

"I'll buy you all new stuff when we get there."

"Where are we going, anyway?"

"I've told you, on a lovely long holiday."

"What about school?"

"You'll go to a new school."

"I like my school."

"You will like your new school."

"Where is this school?"

Somewhere without an extradition treaty, Rachel thinks, ushering Florence out. "Far away from here." At the door Rachel turns, taking a mournful glance of her beautiful Holland Park mansion, lamenting how, even from the grave, Jack is still fucking up their lives.

96

ROSA

As the paramedics wheel the gurney into the car park, along with the ravenous news crews, the entire local community has assembled at the police cordon, vying for a glimpse of the body bag. The fire is extinguished, but like the crowd, the stink of diesel and smoke is less inclined to disperse.

In the epicentre, circled by police vehicles and fire engines, I watch as they load the body into the ambulance. Suspect? Victim? Like everything else with this investigation, it's yet to be determined.

"Any thoughts on the media strategy, sir?" I ask. "With Yilmaz's ethnicity, the press is already assuming a terrorist connection."

"Let them invent their own narrative, for now." Hughes exhales a plume of smoke from a vape the size of an oboe. "Until we get DNA and dental, we don't even know it's Vilmaz yet."

"Any status on the other suspects?"

"They can't stay hidden for long." Hughes looks away, sheepish.

He should be. We should have arrested them all in one swoop. With perfect timing, Pat Kruger swaggers towards us, setting off an alarm in my head: what the fuck is he doing here?

"I asked him to come," Hughes says, reading my expression. "Pat is on the Great Titchfield Street fire, so it makes sense to have him on board. Besides, this investigation is too big for one team."

"Sir, with all due respect–"

"Hawkes, I've made my decision."

Three blackened firefighters and an arson dog emerge from the stairwell.

"The fire investigators." Hughes strides across the car park, no doubt glad of the distraction.

Kruger and I catch up as Hughes greets the grime-streaked investigators. "DI Hawkes, this is Sam Helms. You already know DI Kruger."

"I asked Sam to attend," Kruger says smugly. "He did the report on the Vilmaz restaurant fire."

Helms tugs off his respirator mask, revealing his sweaty porcine features.

"Any similarity between the two?" I ask, bottling my fury.

"Same SCR digital timer, and a similar mixture of petrol and diesel. Only this time they used a lot more accelerant, which caused the explosion."

"What about the computer hard drives?" I ask. "Will they be salvageable for forensics?"

Helms shakes his head. "The seat of the fire was where the victim sat at his desk. Unlikely any data could have survived."

I feel my phone vibrate in my jacket. More perfect timing. *Bruce or Gareth?* I assume, stepping away for privacy. But tugging my phone out, it's the same unknown number from earlier. "Who is this?"

"Emily Hunter."

I tap Hughes on the arm. "Sir, it's her," I say, muting the speaker with my hand. "Emily Hunter."

"We want to turn ourselves in," Emily says.

"Who do you mean, 'we'?"

"Calum Greyson and I. We want to cooperate."

"Where are you?"

"Behind you, at the barriers."

I spin on my heel, staring into the crowd, spotting her immediately. Tall and imperious, russet hair gleaming in the evanescent sun, her gaze meeting mine with conviction. Calum is beside her, shoulders stooped, presenting a more submissive countenance. "She's here, sir, over by the Bow Brook Road entrance, with Calum Greyson."

Hughes squints into the sunlight. "Arrest them, but away from the press."

"With pleasure, sir. But what am I arresting them for?"

"For starters, conspiracy to commit murder."

97

EMILY
26 May

"Do you know where Rachel Kaufman is?" Rosa asks, seated across the interview table beside DI Kruger.

"No idea." Emily expels a sharp breath. "Why would I?"

"I thought you were friends?"

"I hardly knew her. Or any of them," Emily realises, Calum included.

"Try to think," Kruger cuts in. "Perhaps Rachel said something that might help us track her whereabouts?"

What is it with these two, Emily thinks, *wrangling to lead the interview*. "I've already told you everything I know, repeatedly."

"I'm new to this investigation." Kruger flashes his perfect white teeth. "Indulge me."

"I'd prefer it if you played catch-up on your own time. In the last twenty-four hours I've barely slept, I'm wearing a paper suit, I haven't had a cigarette and we're going around in circles."

Rosa rests her elbows on the table, leaning closer. "I'm sorry for the inconvenience, Emily, but you're here because of your involvement in a multiple murder inquiry."

Emily stares up at the yellow strip lights, waiting for her ire to pass.

"I spoke to your former business partner, Emily." Rosa smiles. "Do you know what she said about you?"

"I'm assuming it's not adulatory."

"She said you are a manipulative, callous, ruthless, vindictive bitch."

"Callous and ruthless? Charlotte's vocabulary is as redundant as her veracity. It's also a perfect description of herself."

"'Vindictive' is a perfect word to describe you, Emily. That is why you are here, because you and your friends wanted revenge?"

Emily sighs. "For a little justice, maybe. Violence was never my intention–"

"Justice? Do you know how many women I've seen murdered by jealous boyfriends and coercive ex-husbands in the name of justice?"

"I'm not like that."

"No one ever is, until they sit where you are."

Emily falls silent, recalling Steve's wisdom. "If in doubt…"

Kruger scans his concealed clip folder. "According to your statement, after your telephone conversation with Talbot Vilmaz on the twenty-fourth of May, you feared he was unstable and potentially dangerous?"

"Yes, but… I never thought him capable of…" Emily trails off, blocking the thought.

"Then why didn't you alert the police sooner? If you had, both Tal and Malcolm Lindsay would still be alive."

Emily reels. "Malcolm is dead?"

"You didn't know?" Rosa snorts.

"How?" Emily covers her quivering mouth.

Kruger offers her his burgundy pocket square. "Traffic collision at Bank Junction. A hit and run. Talbot Yilmaz's car was identified fleeing the scene."

Emily takes it, daubing her eyes, trying to calibrate. "You're right, I should have contacted you earlier. I will have to live with that…" She chokes on a sob, shutting her eyes. "But he threatened my family."

"For the purpose of the recording," Kruger says, "the 'he' you are you referring to is Steve Fallon?"

"Yes. Or at least I thought it was. Now, I don't know…"

"Do you believe Talbot Vilmaz made the threats to your family?" Rosa asks.

"If he could kill Malcolm, maybe… I don't know."

"I think you know a lot more about these murders than you are letting on, Emily."

"I know nothing about any murders."

"That's not entirely true, is it?" Rosa leans back, smiling like a chess master gifted her next move. "You've had formative and very personal experience of murder, haven't you, Emily?"

"I won't discuss that."

"The childhood trauma of discovering your father, bludgeoned to death by your mother, must have had a profound psychological effect on you?"

Emily can feel the quickening of her breath, her heart a premonitory drum announcing her onsetting panic. No. She wills herself. No more the victim. "I don't know what you are implying, but like I've told you, I have nothing to hide."

"In my experience, Emily, everyone has something to hide." Rosa's eyes flick to her left hand.

Emily glimpses it, sensing vulnerability. "You glanced at your wedding ring when you said that, Inspector. What are you hiding?" From Rosa's flummoxed expression, Emily knows she's tapped a nerve.

"I was looking at my watch." Rosa recovers her repose. "Need I remind you of the expedient nature of this investigation? Or the severity of the charges, Miss Hunter."

Miss Hunter now, Emily notes. "I wasn't aware I had been charged. Or have you changed your position?"

"Unless you change yours, and tell us what really happened, I will charge you with conspiracy to commit murder and perverting the course of justice. I can promise you that."

"I've had no part in conspiring to murder anyone." Emily meets her gaze and holds it. "And I'm not saying another word until I speak to my lawyer."

98

CALUM
27 May

Calum feels like a Rottweiler's rag doll. He wants to scream his innocence and deny his guilt, but on the advice of his solicitor, repeats his feeble mantra. "No comment."

"Your alibi depends on your co-defendant, Calum," Kruger says, "and during the other incidents, you can't account for your whereabouts?"

"No comment."

Rosa leans forward, her dark eyes boring into him. "Did you murder, or conspire to murder, your ex-wife, Rebecca Powers?"

Calum glares at his doughy solicitor.

"My advice remains the same."

Exasperated, Calum shakes his head. "No comment."

"Calum," Kruger cuts in, "is there anything you are not telling us, that could help our investigation?"

"And help yourself," Rosa adds, "because you're not denying any of it."

"He also hasn't admitted it," his solicitor finally chirps up.

"This isn't the first time you've been questioned in a murder inquiry, is it Calum?" she asks.

"No comment."

"Only you weren't called Calum then, were you?"

"No comment."

"You went by the name of Marc Williams."

"No comment."

Rosa peers into her thick folder. "The same Marc Williams, arrested in 2008 by Thai police and detained in Koh Samui on suspicion of murdering your former girlfriend, Julie Watson, and Timothy Morelli, an American student, whom she'd entered a sexual relationship with, after breaking up with you?"

"Until they caught the guy who did it." Calum ignores his solicitor's glances.

"The illegal Burmese vagrant," Rosa continues, "denied legal counsel and tortured into confession."

"His DNA matched semen taken from Julie's body!"

"Up to the moment of his execution, he admitted to robbing the bodies and having sex with Julie's corpse, but not murdering them."

"They exonerated me for Christ's sake!"

"You still changed your identity when you returned to the UK. Not the act of an innocent man?"

"Because the press wouldn't leave me alone." He spins to his counsel. "Do I have to take this?"

"I must remind you of my advice."

"Jesus Christ!"

"In the days prior to her death, Julie's parents alleged you were harassing her."

"No comment."

"Did you murder your ex-girlfriend and her boyfriend, Calum, like you murdered your ex-wife and her unborn child?"

Calum surges from his seat.

His solicitor places a restraining hand on his shoulder. "I

must protest if your line of enquiry continues to be reliant upon speculation, conjecture and the word of a convicted, necrophile rapist and murderer. Whereas my client is of good character and has no prior convictions."

"Your client has previous convictions for assault and breaking and entering."

"As a juvenile."

Rosa leans into Calum's face. "You might have pulled that trick with the Thai authorities, Calum or Marc or whatever your name is, but you won't get away with it here."

Calum hammers his fists into the table and leaps to his feet. "This is bullshit. I was innocent then, and I am now."

"Sit down Calum." She vaults upright, squaring up to him across the table. "This isn't the place to demonstrate that temper of yours."

"Or yours, Inspector." The solicitor looks shocked by the escalation. "If you continue in this oppressive manner, anything said in this interview will be inadmissible."

"I don't have any further questions, for now." Rosa locks eyes with Calum. "But I am obliged to advise you that a court or jury may draw an inference from your refusal to give a proper account. Are you sure there's nothing you'd like to add?"

"No comment."

99

STEVE
28 May

Could have run when I had the chance, Steve thinks, sipping piss-tasting coffee from a Styrofoam cup. But he'd have to stay hidden, never see the girls again, and Sue and that fucker would win. So, when an armed response unit raided his Hertfordshire office, he'd gone quietly. As Steve was expecting them, any trace of evidence had already been disposed of. Cops rarely catch criminals these days, anyway. Technology does the work for them. CCTV, ANPR, mobile phones and the fucking 'Hercule Poirot' of them all, DNA. None of which, Steve is confident, they have. Gary, his raw-boned solicitor, jots notes at the interview table with a Montblanc. Which Steve probably paid for when Gary represented him on his assault charge.

To the sound of the door handle twisting, Gary stops scribbling, sitting upright. "Here we go. Are you sure you won't reconsider?"

"No, pal. I've got this." Steve sips his watery coffee as Hawkes and the new guy, Kruger, swagger into the interview room, taking their bolted-down seats.

Kruger presses the green record button. "We are in interview room three. This interview is being recorded on a secure digital hard drive. The date is the twenty-eighth of May. The time is five fifty-three pm."

Steve rolls his eyes; *I know the drill*.

"I'm Detective Inspector Patrick Kruger, and I'm with Detective Inspector Rosa Hawkes."

Two DIs conducting the same interview? Steve notes. *They must be feeling the heat.*

"This must be strange for you, Steve?" Rosa places her files on the table like a torturer's implements of affliction. "Sat on the wrong side of an interview table."

"Not as strange as two DIs conducting the same interview. Which one of youse wasn't considered competent enough to lead the investigation?"

Rosa stiffens. "Perhaps it's not strange at all, given your previous conviction?"

"It's you." Steve cackles.

"Can't be easy, dismissed from the force like that?" she retorts.

"Can't say I miss the hours, the pay, the politics…" Steve winks at her. "Or the shite coffee." He drains the dregs with a wince. "Especially the coffee."

"The first truthful thing you've said." Her lips twitch into a half smile.

"Och, you'll hurt my feelings." Steve crosses his tattooed arms.

"You don't like having your feelings hurt do you, Steve?"

"Do you?"

"No. But when your feelings get hurt, you like to hurt back. Like the assault on your wife and her new partner?"

"I didn't mean to…" Steve sucks a lungful of stale air. "She got between me and him, was all. Collateral damage."

Rosa's smile vanishes. "You broke her cheekbone, in what witnesses described as a psychotic rage, and you consider that collateral damage?"

Easy, Steve calms himself, channelling his SAS enemy interrogation schooling. Which was a fucking cakewalk, compared to the real thing. He glances at the welted scars on his hands – mementos of interrogation, Baghdad style. A power drill through his hands, but all he gave up was the big four: name, rank, serial number and age.

"I recall justice being served in that regard. I was tried and convicted, and rightly so."

"Justice is a big thing with you, isn't it, Steve?" Rosa asks. "That and revenge?"

"No. Forgive and forget, me."

"Why do you have those very words written in Gaelic on your arms?" She points with her Biro to the ink on his biceps. "Motive, right there in black and white."

"I've also got a Rangers tattoo on my arse. No crime in that unless you're a Celtic fan."

"Some might consider your suspended sentence as you getting off lightly," Kruger says. "For an offence normally resulting in a two-year custodial sentence. It helps to have friends in the right places?"

"I can't comment on that."

"Of course, confidential information." Kruger flicks through his file. "Like your military record, at least the parts that aren't redacted."

"Again, I can't comment."

"Your record in the force was a lot more edifying." Her smile makes it all the way this time, flicking open one of her files.

"I'm glad my professionalism is a source of enlightenment for youse. I reckon you guys need it."

"Particularly the police psychologist's report, whom your DSI referred you to for psychological risk management, after you threatened to break every bone in his body."

"The guy's a dick."

"So physical violence is your solution for anyone who falls into that category?"

"Not anymore. Born again pacifist, me."

"The psychometric report suggests you displayed clinical symptoms of PTSD, and multiple traits of narcissistic and borderline personality disorders." She pulls a document from her folder. "It's quite a list, so I'll skip through the extracts. A pronounced lack of empathy. Exhibits reckless behaviour, thriving on risk at the expense of others' safety. Displays a pathological externalisation of blame. Is self-righteous, yet judgemental of others. Egocentrism. Interpersonal dominance. Excessive sense of self... Ah, this is interesting." Her ebony irises meet his. "Chameleon-like charm to manipulate others in pursuit of his self-serving ambition. The manipulation, I get. Not so much the charm."

"Because it's a load of fucking psychobabble!"

"An antagonistic propensity for aggression and violence, engaging in vengeful behaviour. And hypersensitivity to being slighted or offended. We'll take that one as read."

Steve cocks his head and smiles. "Touché."

"The police psychiatrist recommended your suspension from duty whilst you received a full psychiatric assessment, including the Triarchic Psychopathy Measure, which in layman's terms is a test for psychopathy."

"Don't make me laugh. A third-rate police shrink? If she was any good, she wouldn't be working for the Met."

"Yet only weeks later you were suspended for violent assault. An astute diagnosis for a third-rate shrink."

"Anyone can have a bad day."

"A bad day? You put two people in hospital. One of them was your ex-wife."

"Aye, well, finding out she's fucking a–" Steve stumbles for the right word.

"A what, Steve?" she pounces. "What were you going to say?"

"Another guy... I was gonna say another guy."

"Does it bother you that your wife's partner is Black?"

"Don't start on that shite. Black, White, brown, makes no difference to me. I've served alongside them all."

"Yet, you were charged with racially aggravated common assault."

"That was bullshit."

"Witnesses stated, as you beat Nicholas Kamara senseless outside the Montcalm Hotel, you called him a Black bastard."

"If I did, I didn't mean it... A heat of the moment thing."

"The subconscious has a way of manifesting our true feelings."

Steve looks away, the shame stinging. He hadn't meant to say that. Never thought himself capable. "Where I grew up, prejudice was part of the curriculum. But believe you me, I'm not proud of it."

"It bothers you though, doesn't it?"

"That he's Black? No. That he's fucking my wife? Aye, too right it does."

"So, you took the law into your own hands and exacted violent revenge on them, didn't you? Just like you planned with Talbot Vilmaz and the other conspirators on your Operation Othello?"

"Whatever Tal was up to, he acted alone."

"Othello is a character who murdered his wife for her suspected infidelity. He was a soldier too."

"Are we starting a wee book club now? Cuz I vote for Harry Potter next time."

"Interesting you picked Othello as your codename?"

"He's just a character from a story. Like the one you're concocting now."

"Was that your big finale? Murdering your ex-wife?"

"She's still my wife."

"Pardon?"

"She's not my ex. We're still married."

"It's important to point out that distinction, yet you're not denying your intention to murder your wife?"

"If that was my intention, she'd be dead."

"Married people fall out of love with their partners all the time. They meet someone else and move on with their lives. Don't you think people deserve a second chance at happiness?"

"When does anyone get what they deserve? I've seen guys get their legs blown off by IEDs. Wives widowed. Children fatherless. You think they got what they deserved?"

"I think you gave Jack Noble, Isabella Jónsson, Simone Vilmaz and Rebecca Powers what you thought they deserved. And then murdered Talbot Vilmaz to incriminate him."

"Back to the storytelling, eh? I think you missed your vocation. You'd make a better writer than a detective, because without inculpatory evidence, a story is all you got."

"Your ex-wife..." Rosa draws her eyebrows together, stare hardening. "Sorry, *your wife*, told me an interesting story."

"Aye, Sue can spin a wee tale." Steve smiles, masking his apprehension.

"A year after you married, Sue admitted to having an affair." Rosa pauses for effect, or what effect it has on him. "Whilst you were on tour she met Peter Caine, a young soldier serving with the nearby Monmouthshire Royal Engineers."

Another pause. The oldest interrogation trick in the book. Silence. Steve holds his inscrutable expression and continues his breathing. That he can control. Not the sweat beading at his temples, or the blinding pain between them.

"You found out about the affair didn't you, Steve?"

"Aye, so what? I'm not the first guy to have his old lady put the horns on him."

"How did you discover your wife's infidelity?" She twists the blade.

"I can't remember. It was twenty years ago."

"You found out because of the hidden cameras and recording devices concealed around your property."

"For security reasons. In my line of work, you pick up enemies along the way. IRA, Al-Qaeda. It pays to take precautions with those lads."

"Yes, but you fitted those cameras without the knowledge or consent of your wife?"

"Lots of things she can't know. Part of the job."

"Part of your job in late 2001 was fighting in Afghanistan."

"I can't answer that question. Classified." Steve tastes the heat and dust in his mouth.

"In November 2001, whilst stationed in the Helmand Province, an unidentified sniper shot and killed Peter Caine. The same period you were based there."

Steve placed the crosshairs in the middle of the target's head and steadied his breathing. He allowed for the wind, adjusted his aim a few inches to the left, drew a breath and squeezed the trigger.

"They attributed the assassination to a Taliban sniper, but your wife claims during one of your night terrors, you alluded to being responsible."

Before the round hit, the target appeared to turn and look back at Steve.

"Is that true? Did you murder your wife's former lover, Steve? You're not denying it?"

"Fucking right I deny it. Sue would say anything to get me out of her way, so she and that fucker can play happy families with my kids." Steve wipes his clammy forehead with the back of his hand, focusing through the pain boring into his brain. "What is this? You've got no evidence, so you're fabricating offences from the past now. Need I remind youse, your seventy-two hours are almost up. So, charge me or let me be on my way."

A smile formed on Peter Caine's lips, and as he spoke–

Pain shoots through Steve's brain, forcing him to grip his temples.

"Are you alright?" Her voice is distant through the cacophony of his agony.

"Aye, a wee headache is all. Can I get a glass of water?" Steve's vision returns, the pain subsiding as he takes five-second breaths.

Rosa nods to Kruger, who rises to his feet and exits the room.

Gary shuts his notebook. "I would like to take a break now, so I can consult with my client. But as we have arrived at the question, can I assume a decision has or is being made?"

"As soon as we know the outcome, you will be informed. But whether we decide to charge him or not, your client is not being released. First thing in the morning, he'll be in front of a judge for breaching the conditions of his suspended sentence and transferred to prison."

Steve masks his vitriol with a chuckle.

"I doubt you'll find it amusing when you're in prison, Steve. The laughs tend to be scarce for ex-coppers on the inside."

"I've got out of worse situations."

"Not this time." She reciprocates his smile.

We'll see, Steve thinks. Patience is an integral part of military planning. He's never failed to see a mission through to its upmost conclusion, and he won't start now. With every instinct he possesses, Steve knows this isn't over yet.

100

ROSA

"He's right." Hughes rubs his bloodshot eyes. "Without inculpatory evidence we have to release them." He leans on a desk before a huge digital screen split into six, each paused on an image of a suspect – Rachel, Ciara, Tal, Calum, Steve and Emily.

I sit in the front row along with two dozen officers crowding the incident room. "We can't just let them walk."

"Without corroborating witnesses, or anything forensically substantive, we have no option," Hughes says.

"Sir, I disagree. If we–"

"If you'll let me finish, Hawkes. Even if Talbot Vilmaz was alive to charge him, the evidence is questionable. Despite the similar MOs to the fires, any proof of his involvement in his ex-wife's death, or hacking his brother's computer, burned with him on his ruined hard drives."

"Conveniently for some."

"Not for our investigation." Hughes's face looks more haggard than usual. His breath reeks of stale coffee, mingling with the collective body odour from the team, mine included, having worked double shifts without a shower. It is nothing compared to the stench of defeat permeating the room. "With Ciara Devaney still on life support, the weight of evidence remains on her deceased ex-husband, James Devaney, for the acid attack on his girlfriend, Isabella Jónsson. There is no doubt these individuals' vengeful efforts caused a domino effect of violence and destruction and incited the actions of a delusional and psychotic individual, Talbot Vilmaz, who then took his own life."

"Are you quoting your forthcoming press release, sir?" I snap, regretting my tone, if not the sentiment.

"It's part of my responsibility, as some day you may or may not discover."

The veiled threat is not lost on me, or the sneer on Pat Kruger's lips, but right now, Hughes can shove the promotion up his arse. "Surely you don't believe Vilmaz acted alone?"

"It doesn't matter what you or I believe. We're nowhere near the threshold of proof required for prosecuting the others. What we can substantiate was that Talbot Vilmaz was driving the vehicle that caused the death of the therapist, Malcolm Lindsay."

"We can't prove it was him driving the Peugeot. All the CCTV shows is a face mask, hoodie and sunglasses."

"I don't understand you, Hawkes. Now you're questioning the only inculpatory evidence we have and undermining your own argument."

"I'm just illustrating that Steve Fallon could have been the driver."

"To support your hypothesis..." Kruger sniggers. "He murdered Vilmaz and fabricated it as suicide?"

"What about the autopsy report, and the cuts to his wrists? He was probably dead before the fire started."

"He set the fire with a timer device. Whether he burned up or cut his wrists, he topped himself." Hughes's impatience rises with his tone.

"His face mask was fused to his mouth by the fire, which meant he was wearing it when he died."

"He was paranoid about pathogens and never took the bloody thing off."

"Exactly, but he only wore it around other people, which proves he wasn't alone. Someone was there when he was killed."

"I can't predicate an investigation on conjecture."

"The toxicology report states he was sedated."

"Dutch courage?" Kruger shrugs.

Hughes nods in concurrence, or thanks.

"And that's not conjecture?" I fume. Fucking brown-noser, Kruger.

"You said it yourself, his bathroom medicine cabinet was a pharmacy," Kruger retorts. "Not to mention his history of mental illness."

"He was autistic, for Christ's sake, and he had OCD, but no history of violence."

"He made up for lost time," Nicholls mutters, garnering titters of laughter.

"His former psychologist said he suffered from delusional jealousy," Kruger continues, relentless.

"Othello Syndrome," Hughes tags in. "The genesis for their mission codename, and another indicator that Vilmaz was the orchestrator. He fits the profile. Socially deficient, obsessive compulsive, fastidious and extremely intelligent."

"You watched the counselling recordings. They all fit the profile of a jealous murderer. What about Greyson's ex-girlfriend in Thailand? Quite a coincidence?"

Hughes blows out a sigh. "Her killer was tried and convicted."

"Or Steve Fallon's wife's statement that he murdered her previous lover?" Husseini adds.

"Again, unsubstantiated," Hughes says.

"His psychology report was substantiated." I can hear my exasperation. "His PTSD and his risk assessment was off the scale."

"Trauma resulting from his long, decorated military career, serving his country. Besides, show me a copper that doesn't have PTSD? Two in five now, apparently." Hughes's tone softens. "I'm just being devil's advocate, Hawkes. Even if the CPS agreed to prosecute, you know how it would play in court."

"Steve Fallon is behind this, I know it." I vault to my feet, jabbing a finger at Fallon's image on the screen. "An ex-cop who knows the system. Ex-SAS, trained in surveillance and assassination. The only question is how involved the others are."

"Without trace evidence, speculation won't help us meet the Crown Prosecution's charging standards."

"Four people are dead, almost certainly murdered, another maimed for life and we're just letting them walk?"

"We can still charge them with the lesser offences."

"For what? Illegal surveillance, phone tapping, data protection and privacy laws? Which we all know is a massively grey area, legally."

"Maybe we can push the CPS for coercive behaviour, even harassment with threat of violence. At least they will get their day in a crown court."

"Rachel Kaufman won't."

"Let's see what Interpol come back with."

"Interpol?" I scoff. "They couldn't find their arse with both hands. And besides, even if we could get Lady Lucan into a courtroom with the rest, you know they'll get suspended sentences at most."

"I'm no happier than you are, releasing potentially dangerous individuals back into society. But with what resources we have, we'll monitor them."

"What about the others?"

"What others?"

"The other exes and their new partners?"

"You mean issuing Osman Warnings?"

"Not just that. They will need protection."

"Talbot Vilmaz is dead, and Steve Fallon will be locked up for breaching his suspended sentence. I can't see the immediate threat."

"He'll be out in three months."

"Then we will deal with that then. For now, the line we take is that we're investigating the deceased, Talbot Vilmaz, for the murder of his ex-wife and his therapist, Malcolm Lindsay. The others are helping us with our enquiries. Any whiff of Othello Club conspiracy stories and I will hold some people in this room accountable. Is that understood?"

I shut my eyes, listening to the obedient round of "Yes, sir" from the team.

"Go home and get some R&R. Especially you, Hawkes. We did all we could." Hughes slips out of the room with Kruger at his heel. Off to help tailor the press strategy, no doubt.

Husseini lifts her bulk from the chair. "You OK, boss?"

"Hunky fucking dory!" I shut my eyes, regretting my misdirected anger. "Sorry, Yasmin, I didn't mean to snap."

Husseini smiles forgiveness, or sympathy. "Hughes was right about one thing, boss. You should go home."

Home? I glance at Husseini's swollen belly, recalling my own pregnancies, when everything was uncomplicated, my path lucid. Where will my home be soon?

"Goodnight," Husseini says on her way out. I barely register her voice.

"All we could?" Hughes's words taunt me as I gaze at Steve Fallon's pixilated visage on the screen, those icy blue eyes staring back. Psychopaths, unlike most people, are undaunted by uninterrupted eye contact. A predator's stare, it's called. The expression of someone who's got away with murder.

101

EMILY
5 September

Emily powers through her lane at the municipal pool, focused on her goal. Head and spine relaxed, her hips and shoulders rotating in perfect unison, and legs straight with a slight bend at the knee, maximising the efficiency of her kick, propelling her through the water. Like her father taught her. Their thing they always did together, every Saturday morning. So impressed with Emily's ability, he encouraged her to swim the Channel. She trained for hours at the school pool and lay in freezing cold baths so her body could acclimatise to Atlantic temperature. But Emily never got to brace the challenge. Consumed with his affair with that woman, her father's interest waned and shortly after he was dead. Ever since, swimming has been Emily's sanctuary. A place where she can commune with his memory, close her mind off and escape harsh reality. With Steve's impending release from prison tomorrow, she needs it.

Only when her fingertips touch the tiles does Emily turn to her challenger, half a length behind, thrashing like a hydrophobic cat. As Calum slogs through the water towards her, she recalls swimming with Dan in Capri – the day he proposed. Emily pushes the memory away, reprimanding her weakness.

"Jesus, it's like racing a dolphin." Calum's voice echoes around the empty pool. A Thursday evening, they have the place to themselves. "Or actually, more like a shark, because you definitely hustled me."

"A bet is a bet."

"Fair play. Dinner is on me. But in return, you don't fancy teaching me a few strokes?"

"I honestly wouldn't know where to begin."

"Lost cause, eh?" Calum drapes his arms around her.

"Not entirely." Emily's lips meet his, tasting chlorine. "Everyone deserves a second chance."

Dusk drenches Covent Garden's teeming streets in scarlet and gold. Emily and Calum sit outside a bar on the corner of Seven Dials, watching tourists and theatregoers squeezing out the last press of summer. A few weeks ago, such a public appearance would have been unimaginable given their media attention. DCI Hughes's plan of starving the press only fed its insatiable appetite, and following their initial court appearance, 'The Othello Club' went platinum. They were front page news for weeks after Tal's explosive suicide, with a constant stream of stories emerging of their histories. Some true, some not so. At least Emily hoped.

The uninitiated would hide from the scrutiny, but Emily knows the best communications strategy is getting in front of the story and controlling the narrative. Crisis and reputation management are not her speciality, but from her erstwhile partner, Charlotte, she learned from the queen of media spin. Emily marshalled a team of techies, journalists, bloggers and influencers to transform the media perception of The Othello Club from villains to victims. It cost a small fortune, depleting Emily's savings and remortgaging the flat, but the dividends of propaganda are already evident. The press revelled in the salacious details of their cheating ex-partners, depicting them as deserving of their fate. Tal's vindictive crusade took centre stage, with Emily and the others recast as unwitting pawns in his game. The world authority on Othello Syndrome was wheeled out on everything from the *News at Ten* to *Loose Women*, and features appeared in publications as diverse as *Psychology Today* to a quiz in *Cosmopolitan*. Inevitably, as the weeks ebbed away, interest began to wane and the press cycle moved on.

"Can we get the bill, please?" Emily asks a rangy waiter passing with a tray of empty glasses. He scrutinises her face, trying to recollect where he's seen her before.

"Do you want to go somewhere else for another?" Calum asks. With Bella staying at his sister's for the weekend, he appears eager to seize the opportunity.

"I just want to go home," Emily says, feeling drained.

"Cool with me."

"Sorry, I'd rather be alone tonight." Seeing his drooping features, she adds, "Early start... for work."

"Yeah, sure." Calum shrugs, rigging up a smile.

But Emily can see through it, his bruised ego rippling under the surface. Her mention of work probably hasn't helped, with all the pre-trial publicity costing Calum his job. For Emily it's had the opposite effect, her old clients flocking back, rallying support. No doubt motivated by titillation and gossip, but either way she has more PR work now than she can handle. "I'll see you Saturday though, at my sister's?"

"If you're sure she's OK with that?"

"Of course. She's looking forward to meeting you," Emily lies.

"I'll get this." Calum reaches for his wallet as the beanstalk waiter looms with a card reader.

"You paid for dinner." Emily hands the waiter her credit card. With him losing his job and legal bills stacking up from Bex's parents' custody action over Bella, she's conscious of his perilous finances. *Maybe Sara has a point*, she thinks, *I sure can pick them*. As the waiter reads her name on the card, recognition dawns across his gaunt face. Emily watches him disappear inside to inform his colleagues. "Time to go."

"I wondered what it would be like to become famous," Calum says.

"I think you mean infamous." Emily rises to her feet.

"What's the difference?"

"You're right, nowadays it is a distinction without difference."

"Let me walk you home at least."

"It's OK, I'll get this cab." Emily waves as a black cab pulls up at the roundabout, its orange lamp illuminated.

As Calum opens the taxi door, Emily kisses his lips. "See you tomorrow night." She slides into the back seat. "Bloomsbury Square, please."

"Try not to worry about tomorrow," Calum says, verbalising the subject they've been avoiding all evening. "He won't do anything, you know. The police will be all over him."

"I know." She smiles, hearing the doubt in her voice.

102

STEVE
6 September

Forty-five minutes after his release from Pentonville prison, Steve has already shaken off his police tail. He clocked them before he climbed into his oldest friend Spoons' eighty-grand Mercedes. In the back seat he changes out of his grey joggers and sweatshirt, pulling on a pair of black cargo pants, a black T-shirt and hoodie. In place of his prison issue Velcro plimsolls, Steve tugs on a pair of lightweight hiking boots. He tips his belongings from a plastic bag. The police kept his clothes and mobile for forensics, leaving only his tactical watch, wallet and wedding ring. He peers at the black rucksack on the seat beside him. His grab bag, which Spoons retrieved from Steve's secret lockup on an industrial estate in Harlow. Passports, travelling cash, a new burner phone and charger, toiletries, spare socks, T-shirts, underwear, torch, first aid kit and a steel fighting knife. From the bottom of the bag, Steve draws out a compact Glock 19 with a holster, which he straps to his ankle under his cargos.

"Need anything else?" Spoons asks in a clipped South London accent. "I mean it mate, anything you need, I'm there."

He means it too, Steve knows. They passed selection

together and fought side-by-side until Steve left the regiment. But Spoons is a family man now, with too much to lose. Whereas Steve only has his mission.

"No, pal." Steve twists the wedding band over his knuckle. "Got all I need."

103
ROSA

Under a gibbous moon, I loll on a garden steamer chair listening to the white noise of neighbours' laughter and music drifting from Clapham High Street. The tepid evening air brings a sense of portending grief, faint but undeniable, the first putrefying breaths of autumn. Despite the heat from the stone fire pit, the thought of Steve Fallon on the loose chills me to the core. I take a warming sip of Rioja, but the unease lingers, as it has these past three months. The thumbed paperback of *Othello* on the glass table, pored over in search of clues, yielded nothing more than a grudging reminiscence of my adolescent frustration for Shakespeare's antiquated text. As did the spread of textbooks requisitioned from Bruce's study – authorities on criminology and psychopathy. Or antisocial personality disorder, as it's now clinically referred. Even psychopathic killers get a politically correct nomenclature these days. It evokes memories of my psychology studies at university, a lifetime away now. In a couple of years, my daughter Val will finish her own A-levels and depart for college herself. The thought twists my gut, knowing by then I'll be gone too. My deadline for leaving Bruce has already twice expired: after Francesca's GCSE exams, then following her results, so I negotiated a new exit date with Gareth, allowing Valerie to settle into sixth form studies, in two weeks' time. Two weeks until I walk away from everything. My home, my husband and my children. For what – some impulsive notion of romantic love that might soon dwindle into the sanguine, sexless marriage I share with Bruce?

I dispel the notion and return to my other compulsion: the digital video recordings of the Divorce Support Group. I replace the headphones in my ears, take another swallow of wine and tap the red play button on my phone, watching The Othello Club in session.

"It is a common reaction during a difficult breakup to indulge in revenge fantasies, but they are seldom helpful in moving forwards," Malcolm says.

"They certainly make me feel better." Steve chuckles, without humour.

"Of course, it can feel cathartic, venting feelings of resentment and jealousy. So, for the purpose of this exercise, let's indulge our revenge fantasies. Rachel, let's start with you?"

I have watched this part many times, but still, the hairs on my nape tingle.

Rachel taps her Bulgari necklace. "How would I get back at Jack?"

Malcolm nods. "What would your vengeance be? It's just an exercise, Rachel, to expunge all that rage. Just let it out."

"Alright." Rachel considers her response, before her eyes light up with inspiration. "I would have the bastard strung up and displayed to the world as the parasitic degenerate he truly is."

"Thank you for sharing, Rachel. Ciara, your turn?"

"I'd like to rip the skinny tart's pretty wee face off, so I would."

I turn up the volume.

Tal's eyes glimmer with mischief. "I would see their world consumed in flames while they watched it burn around them."

I can see Steve smiling, the cogs turning in his mind. The genesis of his plan forming.

"Your turn, Calum." Malcolm cleans his glasses with a cloth.

"I'd like to see how long Bex would stick around if Matt lost all his money and privilege. Then I'd watch her fall from that big ivory tower of hers."

These aren't fantasies, they're the blueprint for a sociopathic murderer. Rachel's ex, Jack, strung up in that hotel wardrobe. Ciara's ex's girlfriend, Issy, her face ripped away by sulphuric acid. Tal's ex-wife, Simone, burned alive. The incidents even follow the same chronological order of the session recording.

"Steve..." Malcolm's voice attunes my attention. "Your turn."

Steve grips the armrests of his chair. "I'd teach them what it feels like to have your heart torn out of your chest."

Glass clinks on the table, making me jump. Bruce sloshes wine into his glass, slumping into the chair opposite. I tug my headphones off, placing them on the table beside the copy of *Othello*.

"A little light reading?" His face is flushed, eyes glazed and watery. Normally the paragon of self-control, Bruce appears to be drunk.

"Something like that," I say. "Kids in bed?"

"I told them they can read for half an hour."

"You wish. They'll be on their phones watching YouTube or TikTok the second you closed the bedroom door."

"We live in hope?"

"I'll say goodnight in a minute, but I want your opinion on something first. Unless you've had too much of that?" I nod to his glass.

"I haven't felt this lucid in a long time," he slurs. In this light, Bruce looks older than his fifty-three years. The glow from the fire pit isn't helping, pronouncing the bags under his eyes. His hair, already greying when I met him, is white now. He sits upright, belly straining his polo shirt as he thumbs his old textbooks. "I did my second-year thesis on Cleckley's *Mask of Sanity*. Takes me back," he says, draining his glass and refilling it. "What's all this anyhow, a trip down amnesia lane?"

"Just work."

"Obviously." Bruce scoffs. From my look, he smiles it off. "OK, I'm all yours, as ever."

"Is it possible for a psychopath to be diagnosed with PTSD?"

"Comorbidity of antisocial personality disorder and post-traumatic stress? I don't recall any specific research." Bruce tilts his head, a ponderous habit of his. Sadness pulses through me. "PTSD is an anxiety-based disorder, and given their relative impunity to negative emotions such as fear, for someone with antisocial personality disorder, I would say it's unlikely."

I frown, recalibrating.

"Not the answer you were hoping for?"

I shake my head.

"Is it possible your subject could fake symptoms of PTSD?" Bruce asks. "It's not uncommon among the military or the police, seeking compensatory benefits, or medical discharge perhaps."

"Maybe." I nod, unconvinced. "But by that rationale, given a psychopath's resistance to negative emotion and their lack of empathy, what would be the motivator for homicidal jealousy?"

Bruce rolls his eyes. "You know I don't like that pop psychology term. 'Psychopath' isn't a recognised a clinical diagnosis."

"I'm not one of your students, Bruce, can you just answer the question?"

"Might as well be, it's all my students talk about." Bruce gulps his wine, wiping the dribble with the back of his hand. "This bloody Othello Club of yours."

"It's not like I coined the title, Bruce." Though, in fact, I had leaked it to the press. No way I'd let that cabal waltz into the sunset with anonymity.

"The title is a misnomer anyway. Irrational and false beliefs that their partner could be unfaithful characterise Othello Syndrome. Whereas all the partners in question were adulterers."

"The media picked up on the Othello Syndrome, but they're called The Othello Club because of their codenames, taken from characters in the play. And calling them adulterers? For fuck's sake, that's the same Victorian hypocrisy the tabloids are preaching."

"What would you prefer I called them?"

"Victims."

"Either way, you caught the bloody guy, and now he's dead. Why can't you let it go?"

"You sound like Hughes."

"He has a point."

"Vilmaz wasn't behind this. Not alone, anyway. It's extremely rare for people with high-functioning autism to commit violent crimes."

"Any wounded prey can strike back, Rosa."

"Yes, but you don't become a serial murderer overnight, Bruce, you taught me that. There would be a history of violence. Talbot Vilmaz has none."

"None you know of. The clever offenders cover their tracks."

"Can we get back to the question?"

"The motivator for jealousy in a subject with antisocial personality disorder? That's like asking if they can fall in love."

"Can they?

"A highly socialised covert one can. At least on face value."

"You mean by affecting normal behaviour?"

"If they are clever enough, and obviously self-aware." Bruce sloshes his wine glass at the books on the table. "Just like in Cleckley's *Mask*, they can be so adept at the deception, some start believing the lie themselves."

"I get the benefits of fitting in with social norms, but not the pathological jealousy. Could an abusive childhood or past trauma be the trigger?"

"Of course, abuse and or trauma are all characteristic, and individuals with anxious attachment styles are more predisposed to disproportionate jealousy. Also, psychopaths, to use the popularism, perceive interpersonal relationships differently. Adoration from others feeds their excessive self-esteem and narcissism, so the subsequent withdrawal of that infatuation, or worse, infidelity by their partner could be a catastrophic psychological trigger. They're also master manipulators, coercive and competitive by nature, so they wouldn't appreciate being outplayed. Christ help their partner if they did."

"Could someone like that fool a trained psychologist or psychiatrist?"

"Depends on the therapist, but there would be signs if they pushed the subject. You would glimpse that godlike egotism, whether it's defiance, arrogance or domination." Bruce's words choke with emotion. "It's evident in the eyes." He hauls himself to his feet, his eyes glistening with tears. "But even the best of us can be fooled."

"Bruce, what's wrong?" I ask, already suspecting the answer.

"You think your job gives you some sort of singular insight into the pathology of human emotion, Rosa? Yet, you have no concept of the pain you inflict, do you? Or maybe you just don't fucking care?"

The implication hits me like a fist to the solar plexus. He knows. I open my mouth to speak, to deny, to confess, but all that emerges is, "How long have you known?"

"For a while… though I didn't want to believe the signs… not of you…" Bruce pinches the tears from his eyes. "Until I received this." From his cargo shorts, he tugs out a folded white envelope and tosses it on the table.

"What is it?"

"You'll see."

From the envelope, I draw out several loose sheets of paper folded into quarters. Unfolding them in the firelight, I'm stunned. The first page reveals a photograph captured with a telephoto lens, of Gareth and me on the steps at the Inner London Crown Court, taken months ago, I recollect, in March or April? Underneath is a caption, in gothic type:

LOOK TO YOUR WIFE, OBSERVE HER WELL.

A quotation from *Othello*, I recognise. From him, Steve Fallon.

"All I've ever done is love you, Rosa. You were my fucking soulmate… my entire world. How could you do this?" Bruce stumbles to the house.

"Bruce, who gave you this?"

"A courier. What does matter?"

"Of course it matters. It's from the killer!"

He spins at the patio doors, his expression a mask of contempt. "Do you want to know how to catch a psychopath, Rosa? Look in the bloody mirror."

As he disappears inside, I open the next sheet. A photograph of me and Gareth emerging from the Covent Garden Hotel, arm in arm, in a palpable postcoital haze. The caption reads:

AND SEE HOW HE PRIZES THE FOOLISH WOMAN, YOUR WIFE,
SHE GAVE IT TO HIM, AND HE HATH GIVEN IT TO HIS WHORE.

With trepidation, I unfold the last photograph in the flickering firelight. An image of Gareth and me sat in my car, engaged in a passionate kiss. A stolen moment, in both senses, captured earlier today, I recognise with horror and rage, realising Fallon has had me under surveillance. Does he have eyes on me now? My eyes pinball in all directions. He could be anywhere or have hidden a camera watching me. I snatch my phone to call in a counter-surveillance team to sweep the place, but before dialling, my eyes fall on the final caption, compelled to read the chilling words aloud.

"'Arise, black vengeance, from the hollow hell. Yield up, O love, thy crown and hearted throne, to tyrannous hate.'"

104

EMILY
7 September

When Emily went for her morning swim, it was dark. Now, strolling through the iron gates into Bloomsbury Square, sunlight streams through the trees, dappling the paving stones. In the park's heart she sits at an empty bench, sipping her latte and taking crumbly bites of pain au chocolat, feeling her blood sugar replenishing. On top of her swim, she'd worked a six-hour shift at the shelter last night. The least she could do, given Frank and Angela's support, rallying in her defence and eulogising her to the press. She didn't intend exploiting publicity from the charity, but with her trial weeks away the media optics don't hurt. Watching two pigeons squabble over her pastry crumbs, she knows from painful experience only the ruthless come out on top. Emily drains her coffee dregs, wishing she had a cigarette. Given the turmoil, it seems a bizarre time to quit smoking, but it felt symbolic of her determination not to be governed by past addiction. To distract herself from the craving, she surveys the park, empty except for a stylish couple ambling along the path pushing a stroller. It could be her and Dan, she laments, a parallel universe playing in her mind before the couple disappear through the gates. Loss jabs at her insides, as ferocious as the day he left, leaving her wondering if the pain will ever diminish, let alone end.

One day at a time, she recalls Malcolm's wisdom, meandering along the path towards her flat. As Emily approaches the gates she freezes, stunned by the figure lurking on the steps of her Georgian apartment building. Her appearance looks haggard, but undeniably it's Charlotte. Conscious of breaching her restraining order, Emily doesn't budge. Yet it is Charlotte visiting her, blocking the entry to her threshold, so Emily breaks the deadlock, striding across the road, halting at the stoop. Despite Charlotte's vantage on the steps, with Emily's elevated stature they remain on eye level, weighing each other up like wary strangers. Charlotte's appearance is jarring. Her skin sallow, eyes puffy and bloodshot. Emily almost pities her old friend.

"Hello, Lottie."

"I'm not here on a fucking social call. Where is he?"

"Who?"

"You know damn well who. He's up in your fucking flat, isn't he?"

"No one is in my flat."

"You fucking lying bitch. His mum said he was on a trip to New York."

"You're looking for Dan?"

"Who the fuck else?"

"Have you called him?"

"He's not answering his phone. He wanted his precious time apart."

"Have you two… fallen out?"

"Don't play the fucking innocent, where is he?"

"He's not here."

"Fucking bullshit."

"His mum and I didn't always see eye to eye, but I don't think she'd lie, not even for Dan."

"New York? Fuck off. It's the same lie he fed you. This is all part of your scheme, isn't it? You won't be happy until you've taken everything from me?"

Just like you did to me, Emily wants to yell, but bites her lip, tasting briny blood. "No," she says, as realisation hits her. "Lottie, where is Ella?"

"Like you don't know."

"Lottie, I promise you, I don't. Where is your daughter?"

"With Dan's fucking parents. Apparently, I'm unfit to look after my daughter now." Charlotte sobs, her body convulsing. Emily reaches out, folding her oldest friend into her arms. "It's all turned to shit, Em. Everything."

"It'll be OK. Everything will be back to normal soon, you'll see. Come inside and I'll make some tea."

"No, no, no." Charlotte wrestles from Emily's grasp. "This is all your fault. You did this to me."

"I know, and I'm so sorry, Lottie."

"Don't you fucking 'Lottie' me, and you can drop the fucking Mother Teresa act you're spinning. It's just camouflage to hide the cold, manipulative bitch you really are. Even if you don't go to prison, my lawyer is preparing a civil case which will squeeze you drier than that withered husk you call a uterus." Charlotte flinches, afraid she might have stepped too far.

Months ago, Emily would have ripped her throat out. Instead, she takes a breath and channels Malcolm's final guidance. "I can never forgive you for what you did, but I have learned to accept it. By reconciling my resentment and anger, I've let go of my grievance. If only you could do the same?"

"Let go? You're fucking joking. I'm going to bleed you for every drop, and when I'm done, you'll be out on the street with your homeless friends."

"Lottie, please believe me, it doesn't have to end this way."

"No! You believe me, this is not over yet."

As Emily watches Charlotte stalking away, she has the foreboding sense her old partner is right.

105

NICK & SUE

In the ancient woodland of Hatfield Forest, Nick Kamara enjoys the seclusion of his morning run. In an hour, the trail will teem with dog walkers and fellow joggers, impeding his run time. To check his progress, he glances at his smart watch (a birthday present from Sue). Fifty seconds behind his goal. In training for the Iron Man Triathlon, every second counts. He switches up the volume, booming rap through his headphones, pounding along the elevated wooden path. Ahead, Nick detects a shape emerging from the gloom. Sue's warning of her crazy ex-husband flashes to mind. But as the unseen predator takes form, it's just a fallow deer and her two younglings, before scampering into the darkness.

"Pussy," Nick scolds himself.

He loves living out here in the fresh air, nature at his doorstep. A long way from his old estate in Brixton. Although that had its own share of wildlife too, he smiles. Distracted, Nick doesn't see the hooded figure step from behind the broad Scots pine. Until it's too late. The hammer blow to his chest ruptures the air from his lungs. His legs stumble on for several yards before his muscles fail. He collapses on the mossy wooden slats, coughing blood. An émigré from Sierra Leone raised on the streets of Brixton, yet it's here in bucolic suburbia that Nick finds himself on the wrong end of a blade. It must be Steve, he realises, Sue's ex. Panic surges now, not from his fear of dying, but of never seeing Sue again.

Someone grips his ankles, dragging him through the undergrowth face down, choking on foliage and blood.

His attacker flips him over. Nick's vision is bleary. The hooded figure looms above, face veiled in shadow. He opens his mouth to beg for mercy, only frothing blood as the knife rips into his chest.

Sue examines her reflection in a changing room mirror at John Lewis. Skinny jeans are out, the girls assured her, and flares are in. She can hear the twins outside, nagging her to hurry so they can go TGI Fridays. A cheeky splurge of fat and sugar will be a welcome relief from Nick's health food regime. Guilt jabs at her, thinking of the culinary cheat she is about to indulge in, but glancing at the lingerie in the shopping bag on the bench, she will make it up to Nick tonight.

Her phone pings on the bench. She grins, opening the message from Nick:

I WILL WEAR MY HEART UPON MY SLEEVE FOR DAWS TO PECK AT.

Cryptic, but cute, she thinks, as another message pings from Nick with a photograph attached. Her eyes focus and pull on the image, unable to compute the full pictorial horror.

A jagged incision splits Nick's chest from sternum to diaphragm. Placed on his left shoulder, glistening with blood, is his severed heart.

106

EMILY

Through the thicket, Emily can see him edging towards her hiding place. She holds her breath, listening to his footfalls on the grass, his shadow falling across her.

"Found you!" he shouts.

Ollie, her golden-haired nephew, stares at her with laughing eyes, his dimpled cheeks flushed pink.

"You're too good at this game." Emily stretches her hand up. "Can you help me up?" Oliver tugs his aunt to her feet. "You're so strong. Give me a hug." She scoops him into her arms, spinning him in the sunshine.

"Me too?" Eve says, racing from behind a rhododendron bush.

Emily places Oliver on his feet and whisks her four-year-old niece into the air.

"OK you two, put your auntie down." Sara clutches a sweaty bottle of Heineken in each hand. "Go help Daddy light the pizza oven."

With a squeeze Emily releases Eve, watching them scamper to Ed on the patio, lighting his chrome monstrosity. She brushes grass from her white linen dress, admonishing herself for envying her sister.

Sara waves the beers. "Our turn to hide."

Behind the shed, Sara liberates a crumpled packet of Marlboro Golds from under a terracotta planter.

"What would your patients think if they saw you?" Emily folds herself into a plastic garden chair. "Hardly the paragon of public health."

"Is anyone more sanctimonious than an ex-smoker?" Sara lights her cigarette, flopping into the lawn chair beside Emily.

"An ex-business partner and best friend, apparently."

"Charlotte always was a duplicitous cow."

Emily nods, coveting Sara's cigarette.

"So, are Charlotte and Dan separated?" Sara shoots a wreath of smoke.

"So it would appear."

"How do you feel about that?"

"I'm past all that." Emily shrugs her lithe shoulders. "I'm with Calum now."

Sara rolls her eyes heavenward.

"I saw that."

"Em, I'm glad you're moving on with your life, but as recent events demonstrate, relationships with obsessive personalities are like introducing Sid and Nancy to a bag of smack and a flick-knife."

"I am not obsessive." Emily catches herself, masking her anger with a smile. "And couldn't you think of a more contemporary couple to reference?"

"Kate Moss and Pete Doherty aren't as dramatic. Or tragic."

"Or contemporary."

"You're evading the point, Em. I know you, remember?"

"At least I'm moving on."

"If you want my advice, and your lawyer's, you should keep away until after the trial."

"You mean like a trial separation?"

Sara tilts her head.

"He's a good guy, Sara. You should see him with his daughter."

"That's what they said about Ted Bundy."

Now it's Emily's turn, giving her the look.

"OK." Sara holds her hands up. "What time is he coming?"

"Eight-ish. Please, Sara, just give him a chance?"

"I'll be polite. But what's with your predisposition to flawed men?"

"Oh, please."

"You were the same about Dad, idealising his memory like he was a saint. Then Dan."

"What a ridiculous comparison."

"Apart from them both being narcissists who cheated on their wives."

"Come off it, Sara, you adored Dan. As I recall, you couldn't take your bloody eyes off him!"

"So, you're beyond all that?"

"Oh, just give me one of those, Sigmund Fraud." Emily snatches the cigarettes and lighter from the step. "It's not like flicking off a light switch, you know."

"I'm your big sister. It's my job to worry about you."

"I know, and speaking of looking out for me…" Emily respires on her cigarette. "…remember to bring cigarettes when you visit. They're like currency in prison."

"Don't be so bloody dramatic. Your solicitor said a custodial sentence is unlikely."

"Whatever the price, I'm prepared to pay it." Emily jets a plume of smoke. "I've made another decision, too. I'm going to visit Mum in prison."

"What brought this on?"

"Something I learned from our therapist at the group…" Emily trails off, thinking of poor Malcolm.

"Perhaps some good will come of it still."

Emily smiles, disguising her apprehension.

107
ROSA

"What time was the body reported?" I ask, peering at the glowing forensics tent in the forest clearing, casting a shadow play of the pathologist performing his morbid tasks inside. It conjures a scene from a Grimm's fairy tale. But, I suspect, not half as grim as what awaits me within.

"Sixteen hundred hours," DCI Metcalf says. The Hertfordshire detective, like Hughes and myself, wears a forensic boiler suit, gloves and booties, Metcalf's straining at his belly. "His partner confirmed he went running at six in the morning as usual, although his runs could vary from an hour to three."

"He lay here for hours until the dog walker found him." Hughes blows a plume of vape smoke up into the trees. "Poor bastard."

I'm unsure if he's referring to the victim or the dog walker, both qualifying for sympathy. At the perimeter cordon, a legion of reporters and news crews skirmish with police officers, for a glimpse of tabloid titillation.

Metcalf scowls. "They were here before us, bloody ghouls. It's already all over the internet, too."

"Has the pathologist indicated a time of death?" Hughes asks.

Metcalf shakes his jowly face. "He hasn't come out yet."

"Let's ask him then." I stride towards the tent along the mossy wooden slatted path.

"Prepare yourself," Metcalf warns. "It's not pretty."

I've seen worse, I think, ducking inside the forensics tent, but whatever awful picture I imagined is a teddy bears' picnic compared to the horror awaiting me. Nick is splayed in the undergrowth like a slaughtered animal, gutted from sternum to stomach, baring a yawning chasm of blood, pink intestines and yellowed bone. His heart balances on his right pectoral, still glistening with gore. The stench of dead meat and rotten foliage hits me, but I fight the urge to retch.

Hunched over the body, the pathologist squints up at me, mole-like through his bifocals, knees cracking as he rises.

"Time of death?" Hughes asks, his face ashen.

"Given the advanced state of rigor mortis, I would say between eight to twelve hours."

"We can be more accurate than that," I say, crouching over the ruined corpse.

"Determining a time of death is an estimate. Unless the deceased died with a doctor present and a stopwatch." Without looking, I can hear the sneer from his tone.

"Or even better, a smart watch?" I prod a gloved finger at the watch on Nick's wrist. "It should tell us the precise moment his heart stopped beating."

The pathologist's smirk withers.

"What can you tell us about the knife?" I ask.

"A seven- or eight-inch blade, serrated on one side."

"Like a special forces knife?"

"Possibly. Something lethal enough to cut through the breast plate."

With a nod, I duck outside the tent, grateful to be out of there. Not as relieved as Metcalf, rubbing his eyes as if scrubbing the image from his retinas.

"We can rule out accidental death on this one, sir."

"Yes, he's changed his MO." Hughes rummages for his vape. "Maybe he's in a hurry to finish his vendetta."

As Hughes's glassy eyes finally meet mine, he gives me a little nod. Part apology, part acknowledgement that I was right. But for once, I wish to God I wasn't.

"You think this is your guy?" Metcalf asks.

"Without a doubt." Hughes exhales a waft of vanilla smoke.

"We thought it was drug related. Gang on gang, you know." Sheepish, Metcalf avoids my look. "When we ran a check on the victim's ID, he had a drugs offence."

And because he was Black.

"Or voodoo, you know, like some sort of ritual killing?" Metcalf digs himself deeper.

"It was, in a way." Steve Fallon's session recording echoes in my head. *I'd make them know what it feels, to have your heart torn out of your chest.* I think of the tattoo on his bicep, of a dagger piercing a bleeding heart, and the Celtic word for vengeance across it.

Metcalf glances at the forensics tent. "Texting a photo like that to the victim's partner. And that poem – like a twisted valentine card."

"It's from *Othello*. 'I will wear my heart upon my sleeve for daws to peck at.'" The following line from the play flashes to mind. 'I am not who I am.' Its significance resonating…

"What kind of lunatic does that?" Metcalf asks.

"A jealous one." Hughes pockets his vape.

"Where is Fallon's ex-wife now?" I ask.

"At her home address. The FLOs are with her," Metcalf says.

"She'll need more protection than Family Liaison Officers."

Hughes unzips his boiler suit, digging out his phone. "I'll call an armed response unit and get her and the kids to a safe house."

"The others, too. Dan and Charlotte Hunter?" I tug my phone out.

Hughes prods a number into his phone, covering the receiver with his hand. "I want Calum Greyson and Emily Hunter back in custody."

"On what charge?" I ask, listening to my dial tone.

"Tell them it's for their own safety."

I nod, speaking into my phone. "Emily?"

108

CHARLOTTE

Charlotte searches for a second bottle from the refrigerator, feeling the chill on her wet hair. Her relaxing bubble bath after her confrontation with Emily hasn't had the desired effect. The wine isn't helping either, but she grasps the second bottle of Sancerre regardless. Her phone thrums on the kitchen table. She twists with anticipation, hoping it's Dan finally returning her calls, clinking the bottle on the marble counter and snatching the phone.

"Fuck!" she says, disappointed it's not Dan, and spooked by the unknown caller. Curious and drunk, she clicks the message:

AND SWEET REVENGE GROWS HARSH

"What the fuck?"

Emily, she thinks, as her phone rings. Another unknown caller. This time she lets it go to answerphone, slips the phone in her dressing gown pocket and returns to the wine.

"Thinks she can play mind games with me?" As she fumbles with the corkscrew, a cobalt light snaps on in Dan's painting studio. He must be back, she realises jubilantly.

Charlotte swings the bifold doors open and tramps barefoot across the sprinkled grass, her anger at Dan subsiding with every dewy step. As she tugs open the glass door, linseed oil assails her nostrils, bitter like decay. She squints, adjusting her eyes to the blue strip lights. It bounces off the vast canvases, zigzagging the studio like a maze, dissecting the floor with heavy shadow. Dan's latest commissions are decadent, vivid oil colours of copulating nudes, a paradox of abstract innocence and graphic indecency.

"Dan?" She shuffles across the chilly polished concrete, the word hanging in the air. Despite the lack of response, Charlotte can feel someone's presence.

"Dan?" she calls, her reconciliatory mood waning. "Stop fucking about, Dan. I'm not in the mood."

Her frustration at boiling point, she peers behind the canvases until only one remains. An imposing canvas, eight feet high, blank, save for a spectral outline sketched in charcoal. Light dazzles from its vacant surface, forcing Charlotte to shield her eyes, blindsiding her as a hooded figure lunges from behind the canvas, swinging the claw hammer.

109

EMILY

Emily bites her pizza, avoiding dribbling onto her white linen dress. As the pergola lights ignite against the ultramarine sky, she checks at her watch and lets out a sigh. Almost nine. Given Calum's lateness, she resolves he isn't coming.

"Em?" Sara glides from the house, waving a phone. "You left your phone in the bathroom. You've got seven missed calls."

Calum apologising, Emily thinks. "Thanks." She wipes her fingers on a paper napkin, shocked seeing DI Hawkes's caller name flashing again. Masticated dough churns in her gut. Her plate falls to the grass.

"Emily?" Rosa asks when Emily finally answers.

"What's happened?" Emily launches from her seat, stalking away from her sister's earshot.

"We've tracked your phone to 58 Sycamore Street, Chiswick. Can you confirm that is your present location?"

"Yes. I'm at my sister's house. Has something happened?"

"Do you know the whereabouts of Calum Greyson?"

"Calum? What's happened? Is he alright?"

"His phone is switched off. I thought he might be with you?"

"He's supposed to be, but he's late." Emily asks breathlessly, broadcasting her panic: "Has something happened to him?"

"Not as far as I'm aware. This is just a precautionary measure. If he calls, tell him to call me."

"Tell me what's happening?"

"Just stay where you are. Officers will be with you directly."

"Can't you just tell me? Please?" The call disconnects.

"Emily? What is it?" Trepidation is etched into Sara's face.

Emily tries to focus, scrolling news feeds on her phone, searching for imagined atrocities Steve has committed. The unease she felt all day manifests, recalling Charlotte's inability to contact Dan. What if he's hurt Dan? Or worse? Emily's fear peaks, flicking across a news headline:

MAN'S HEART CUT OUT IN WOODLAND ATTACK

Febrile with terror, she scans the story for salient facts, praying not to see Dan's name:

The victim, NICOLAS KAMARA, 30, a fitness trainer from Brixton…

Relief floods Emily, that it's not Dan, but Steve's wife's lover, Nick.

…the killer texted his partner a grisly picture of the victim's severed heart, along with a chilling passage from Shakespeare's play, Othello*: 'I will wear my heart upon my sleeve, for daws to peck at.'*

Guilt stabs Emily for feeling relieved that the victim isn't Dan, but some other poor… "Oh, God." She realises, if Steve has continued working through his warped murder list, exacting revenge on their exes, the next victim could be… "Dan!"

"Has something happened to Dan?" Sara looks stricken with panic.

Emily presses the phone to her ear, listening to an eternal dial tone.

"Emily? What's happened to Dan?"

"I don't know, Sara, shut up."

"Em?" Dan's voice asks.

"Thank God." Emily exhales.

"Em? I'm about to go into a meeting. Why are you calling?"

"Where are you?"

"My agent's office in Tribeca."

"You are in New York?"

"Yes. Is everything alright?"

"Yes, sorry Dan, I must have misdialled you. Go to your meeting." Emily ends the call with jubilant relief, but it's fleeting. If Dan is safely in New York, that only leaves... "Charlotte."

"Emily, for God's sake. Tell me what is going on?"

Sara's appeals spiral after Emily as she barrels through the back gate and scurries up the gravel driveway. Emily's old house is a few streets away, but her sandals skid across the pavement. She halts her run, unbuckling the straps, kicks them off and sprints barefooted.

Two minutes later, Emily halts breathlessly outside the familiar brick-walled gates of the house she once shared with Dan. Except for the wisteria's inexorable advance up to the roof, the three-storey Georgian detached looks unchanged, as though the elapsed eighteen months had been a bad dream. A picture of suburban harmony, yet as she steps towards the front door something feels wrong. The same trepidation she felt twenty years ago, before opening her parents' living room door.

Emily presses the brass doorbell, listening for footsteps or life within, finding neither. She rings the bell again, peering through the small window panel, but the smoked glass yields only a bleary vision of normality. Charlotte blocked her number eighteen months ago, and the landline is ex-directory, so calling isn't an option. She cups her hands, peeking through the shutter slats into the living room, glimpsing no one and nothing out of order.

"Lottie?"

Emily hammers the double glazing with her palms. Maybe she isn't at home, she tells herself, pacing to the back gate. Sidestepping the waste bins along the path, she attempts to rationalise her fears. Everything is as it should be. Nothing unusual. Until stepping into the back garden, her dread returns unbound, seeing a blood drop on the slate flagstone. A metre away, another scarlet droplet, then another, part of a trail leading into the house.

As Emily steps through the bifold doors into her old kitchen, it feels familiar and alien. She follows the splatter across the ebony floorboards when it dawns on her: Steve might still be here. Mortally afraid, she scans the kitchen for a weapon, drawn to the steel block of chef's knives. A wedding present from a client, she recalls, drawing out an eight-inch razor-sharp blade. With the cook's knife gripped before her, Emily follows the gory trail into the hallway, where it continues up the staircase, staining the carpet runner.

"Lottie?" Emily ascends the staircase listening for life, hearing only her own creaking footfalls and pounding heartbeat. She follows the gory trail up to the third floor, until it disappears underneath the closed door of her old master bedroom. As she reaches for the doorknob it glistens with blood, evoking visions of her father's corpse waiting beyond the living room door. With a fortifying breath, Emily twists the cold porcelain knob, and steps inside, once again unprepared for what awaits.

Charlotte lies on the bed in an ivory towelling robe, her face covered with a pillow. For a moment, Emily hopes she is asleep, but experience has taught her otherwise. Unlike her father's moribund skin, Charlotte's exposed legs and arms retain their fleshy vitality. Emily stumbles to the bedside, praying she might still be alive. Charlotte's hand still feels tepid, giving her hope, but as Emily lifts the pillow, it departs.

Charlotte's mouth gapes open in a petrified scream, her pale blue eyes protruded with fear. A gash glistens on her temple, but Emily knows this isn't the cause of death. He suffocated her, just as Othello murdered Desdemona. Great rolling sobs escape her now, racking though her body. After despising this woman and wishing her dead, Emily no longer sees the face of her nemesis, but of her oldest friend.

"Oh Lottie," she sobs. "I'm sorry." As she stumbles backwards, Emily freezes with horror. On the wall above the bedpost a message is scrawled in blood:

STRANGLE HER IN HER BED, THE BED SHE HATH CONTAMINATED

Emily flees her old bedroom, staggering down the stairs, a mess of snot and tears, torturous images morphing between her father's death mask and Charlotte's. At the foot of the stairs, she falls into the front door with a clatter, realising the cook's knife remains in her grasp. With trembling fingers, she fumbles the lock and chain free, and stumbles outside into the path of a shadowy figure. *Steve!* She panics, wielding the knife at him.

"Emily, no," he says, not in Steve's Glaswegian tones, but Calum's Midlands lilt. "Jesus Christ, it's me."

"Calum?" Emily snaps from her daze.

"Your sister told me you flew over here like a bat out of hell. Emily, what's happened?"

"Charlotte is dead," Emily says, as if doubting her own words.

"No…" Calum shakes his head. "Jesus Christ, no…"

"Yes. He's murdered her too…"

Calum catches Emily as she falls into his arms. As he lowers her, sitting on the stoop, the knife slips from her grasp, clattering on the block paving.

"Emily?" Calum's eyes broadcast his fear. "Why do you have a knife?"

"I thought Steve might still be in the house."

"How did she die?" Calum's eyes flick to the discarded knife, and Emily's bloody fingers.

"Suffocated with a pillow, like in *Othello*."

"Oh, Jesus Christ. He's out of his fucking mind."

Emily fumbles in her dress pocket for her phone.

"Emily, what are you doing?"

"Calling the police."

"Wait." He snatches the phone. "No."

"Calum, we have to call them."

"What if this is part of Steve's plan? Setting you up for the fall. Or both of us? Fuck that. When the police show up, we can't be anywhere near this."

Calum's words resonate, triggering memories of Charlotte's bloody corpse under the pillow, and the similarities to her father's murder. It can't be coincidence, she realises. Steve is setting her up.

"But we still have to call the police, we don't have any choice."

"Yes, we do. We need to disappear. Somewhere the police

and that fucking maniac can't find us, at least until they've got him locked up."

"The police can protect us."

"No, they can't, and we can't trust them either. Steve was one of them, remember? With his cronies in the Met, he'll know their every move."

"But where can we go that they, or he, won't find us?"

"I know somewhere, trust me."

As Calum takes Emily's wrist, she holds firm.

"I'm not forcing you to do anything, Emily." He relinquishes his grip. "Stay and take your chances or come with me. But if you're coming, we have to go now."

110

CALUM
8 September

Baseball cap tipped over his brow, Calum strolls back across the petrol station forecourt to the silver BMW 5 Series parked at the pumps. The beamer is Tony's – a neighbour from his apartment building, working in Dubai. Along with watering Tony's plants in his flat, Calum recruited Tony for the cushy Dubai job, so he owes him a favour. Three hundred grand a year, tax free. Lucky sod. Calum would have applied for it himself, but no amount of money could lure him away from Bella. Of course, there were also the stringent background checks, which would have proved tricky to hurdle. A car door slams, snapping him back. Just a weary father returning to his family SUV, distributing snacks and drinks, but the image provokes Calum's envy, separated from his own daughter.

As Calum slides into the plush leather driver's seat, Emily's expression announces her distress.

"We're being followed."

"Where?" Calum's eyes rake the forecourt.

"The black Range Rover, over there."

He follows her gaze, squinting at the empty parking bay.

"It's gone." Emily peers into the darkness. "It was right there."

Calum exhales, realising he was holding his breath.

"When you're exhausted and traumatised, the mind plays tricks."

"I saw it, Calum. I'm telling you."

"OK, but it's gone now, yeah?"

Emily nods, unconvinced.

"Try not to worry. No one knows about this car, or where we're going." As he presses the start button and the engine purrs to life, Prince rouses in the back seat, before closing his eyes. His sister agreed to accommodate Bella, but after Prince fouled her new carpet last time, she drew the line. "We'll be there in a couple of hours." Calum steers out of the petrol station. "Try to get some sleep."

"I know what I saw."

Calum's mind spirals back to stopping by Emily's flat to pick up some travelling clothes. Despite his protests, shoeless and mascara-streaked, Emily had convinced him. What if her flat was being watched by police? Or worse, Steve? Calum shakes the thought.

"If the police had tracked us, we'd already be in custody," he says, as much to calm his own runaway imagination.

"It's not the police that scare me."

"Why would Steve come after us?" he asks, merging onto the A11. "What did we ever do to make his shit list?"

"What did Tal?"

"Trust me, where we're going, no one will find us." But in the rear mirror, his reassuring smile slips.

111

EMILY

Dawn bleeds into the Norfolk marshlands, drenching it in crimson light like a Martian landscape. Emily stares through the passenger window, wishing they were on some remote planet, far from Steve's psychotic reach.

"The best sunrises in the world here." Calum breaks the silence. "Amazing, isn't it?"

Emily nods, recalling dawn on the Amalfi coast, aware of the unfair comparison. As they pass a dilapidated windmill pump, its broken blades stabbing the bloodied sky, she realises it's the first building they've seen for miles. Then, in the distance, another construction slowly reveals itself from the misty reeds.

"There she is…" Calum steers the car along a bumpy dirt track. "Milton Cottage."

'Cottage' seems euphemistic to Emily as they approach the ramshackle house.

"It's comfy inside," he says, as if reading her thoughts.

Emily hopes so, assessing the Tudor-style cottage perched on the grassy bank of the River Thurne. Abandoned to the elements, Emily suspects a powerful gust of wind might blow it in.

Calum turns off the engine. "It's not *Homes and Gardens* yet, but it has potential."

"That it does," Emily agrees, stepping out into the long dewy grass.

Prince lumbers out onto his haunches, stretching creaking joints before trotting down a balding grass slope towards a rickety jetty. Emily follows, careful not to slip down the muddy bank. Not the idyl she'd pictured from Calum's halcyon description, but it is remote.

"Like I said," Calum says, as if on cue, "no one knows about this place. Not even my sister. Even Bex's lawyer and his forensic accountants never knew of its existence. We're at least a mile from the nearest house, and the low bridge further up the river prevents larger hire craft and keeps the water traffic to a minimum. We're about as off-grid as you can get."

She steps onto the jetty, testing its stability, before peering into the water. The last blush of dawn shimmers on the surface like a golden oil slick, buoying her spirit at the prospect of swimming. Perhaps Calum is right, this place could provide the sanctuary they need. Until Steve is caught. And at least Emily knows Sara and the kids will be safer under police protection. The last thing she did before dumping her phone was to send a warning text to her sister. Either way, the further Emily stays away from her family, the safer they will be.

"Come on, let's get you inside." Calum's voice yanks her from her thoughts. "I'll make some coffee."

As they climb the slope to the house, Emily inspects a shabby wooden garage. Above the paint-blistered double doors, an inscription is carved. "Sons of Zebedee?" she reads.

"My dad…" Calum rolls his eyes, as if it were an adequate explanation.

"I'm guessing he wasn't a *Magic Roundabout* enthusiast?"

"They were the fishermen Jesus met on the Sea of Galilee.

Dad's two favourite things in the world were fishing and preaching the word. At least, his version of it."

Emily peers through a crack in the door, her eyes adjusting to the darkness.

"You don't want to go in there, trust me, it's filthy and full of spiders."

"What's in there?" Emily squints in the darkness, making out the rickety contours of a wooden boat in similar disrepair to the cottage. "You have a boat?"

"Not one that's seaworthy, yet. I'm renovating Dad's old dinghy."

"God." Emily grimaces from a malodour. "What's that smell?"

"It's also the tackle shed, where you gut and clean the fish." Calum grins. "You do like fish?"

"Eating them, yes. Not so much the catching part."

"That is something we will have to remedy."

"I can't wait."

"Come on, I'll give you a tour of the cottage." Calum rummages in his pocket for the keys.

"What about the bags? I need a change of clothes and a bath." Emily glances at her bloodstained white linen dress.

"We'll need to burn that."

Emily opens her mouth to protest.

"It's DNA evidence."

"It was a present…" Off Calum's grimace, Emily doesn't add it was from Dan.

"Go inside. I'll get the bags." Calum unlocks the door, gesturing her inside like a matador. "Welcome to Milton Cottage." Prince brushes past her legs, bundling through the door. "Prince can show you in," he says, striding down the slope to the car.

Despite the fumes of mildew and dust festooning every surface, the interior offers a more homely environment than the exterior promised. Two shabby Chesterfield couches encroach on an oak coffee table and a stone fireplace, surrounded by bookshelves. Emily draws the faded velour curtains, revealing French doors overlooking a decrepit deck over the river. A wooden staircase leads upstairs to the bedrooms and a bathroom, she hopes, with an actual bath. Mounted above the hearth, an elongated fish gapes at her with needle-sharp teeth.

"That's a pike," Calum says, clutching their bags. "A thirty-pounder."

"Impressive." Emily feigns appreciation. "Where's the TV?"

"Dad wouldn't have them in the house. I've been meaning to get one, but I don't know… seems sacrilegious somehow."

"So, there's no broadband?"

"Afraid not, and the mobile signal is spotty at best." Calum frowns at the French doors. "You shouldn't open those curtains. The sunlight bleaches the books."

"Sorry, I didn't realise." Emily starts to the windows.

"No, leave it. It's fine." Calum smiles. "Brightens the place up."

Emily is relieved to see a dusty telephone on a mahogany sideboard. "At least there's a landline?"

Calum shakes his head. "I had it disconnected. Who uses a landline these days?"

"People without cellular connectivity." A moot point anyway, Emily remembers, having disposed of their phones before leaving London.

"It's not like we can use the phone anyhow, and there's

no digital footprint that can lead... anyone to us. Like I said, we're off the grid."

"How will we know if they catch him?"

"There's a transistor radio."

"Great, all mod cons. Please tell me there's a bath?"

"That I can do." Calum places the bags on the scraped coffee table and disappears into the small kitchen, like a parody of the Fifties with Bakelite fittings and Formica counters. "I'll put the immersion on. Takes about an hour to heat, though." He reappears at the doorway with an impish grin. "I'm sure we will find some way to occupy our time."

"Yes, fishing." Emily smiles. "And reading." She gestures at the library of books surrounding them. "Quite a collection? And old? They look like first editions?"

"Some of them are. Another legacy from my dad." He clinks a copper kettle on the gas hob.

"You OK with powdered milk in your coffee?"

"Black is fine." Emily slumps into the Chesterfield facing the French doors. Closing her eyes, she can hear the morning call of water birds and clanging pipes as the boiler awakens. *At least there's hot water*, she thinks. When did she last sleep or shower? Twenty-four hours at least. With that realisation, bone-deep exhaustion hits. As sure as the tide, sleep will immerse her soon. Emily welcomes the chance of escape. Her eyelids flickering, she stares across the river. *Red sky in morning*, she recalls as the somniferous darkness drags her into its depths.

112

ROSA

Bea's coffee remains untouched on her pristine quartz kitchen island. With her pallid skin and strawberry blonde hair, she might be Calum's sister, but not by blood.

"Me and Marc... sorry, still can't get used to it. I've always known him as Marc. Me and Calum only reconnected last year." Bea has a soft Midlands lilt.

"Yet you have still taken on his child in his... absence." I nod to the sounds of children's laughter from the living room.

"Couldn't say no, could I?"

"Why the disconnect between you and your brother?"

"Marc, sorry... Calum isn't my actual brother. Not biologically, anyway. He's adopted."

No shit. "Were you adopted too?"

"No. My parents thought they couldn't have children, then I came along."

"Lucky for them. Not so much for Calum, though. A cuckoo in the nest."

"My parents divorced anyway, a couple of years later. I went with my mum. Calum stayed with... him."

Him. I note the disdain. "Why did your parents split?"

"He wasn't my real father."

"Your mother had a sexual relationship with another man?"

"Yes, with my real dad. I was the lucky one, I suppose, growing up in a loving household, but poor Calum..."

"You're not a fan of Calum's adoptive father?"

"You could say that. He's dead now. Good riddance. He was horrible. Religious nutcase, you know, and super strict, like. I can still remember him going off on one, taking off his belt..."

"He beat you?"

"Not me. Mum protected me..."

"But not Calum?" Disconcertion stirs in my gut.

Bea's gaze slides to her latte, blowing it before sipping. I'm about to press her when my phone rings. "Excuse me," I say, recognising the incident room number. "I need to take this."

I step onto the wet decking, wishing I'd brought my umbrella and my coffee. Caffeine and adrenaline – the only things keeping me vertical. "Any news on Fallon?"

"Not yet." Hughes's voice reverberates through the incident room speakerphone.

"Shit!" On the assumption Steve has access to his old network, we leaked false information in the corridors of the Met on the whereabouts of his ex-wife and children, hoping to smoke him out.

"He knows our game too well," Hughes says.

"What about the media appeal?"

"Sightings from Land's End to John O'Groats," Husseini says, "but nothing substantial yet."

"He's trained to be a ghost," Hughes growls. "He's probably on the Continent, or even further by now."

"No, he's not done yet." I take partial shelter under

a grapevine-covered pergola. "But with his intelligence network, we have to assume anything we know, he does."

"Which is precisely nothing." I can hear the snigger in Kruger's voice.

I bite back my temper. "Do we have anything on Calum Greyson's vehicle?"

"It's not his own car," Kruger says. "Emily Hunter's sister said he arrived at her barbecue in a silver-coloured vehicle. A BMW or a Mercedes."

"OK, let's retrieve CCTV in a mile radius of Greyson's Docklands flat, and the victim, Charlotte Hunter's Chiswick address. Council, business, domestic, the lot. We need a registration number."

"That could take days," Kruger groans.

"Then get your team on it, sharpish," Hughes says.

"Yes, sir."

I hear the scrape of Kruger's chair and the swish of the incident room door shutting. *Prick.* My first smile for days.

"How are you getting on with Calum Greyson's sister in Leicester?" Hughes asks.

"She swears she has no clue to his whereabouts, and he hasn't contacted her since he dropped his daughter off on Thursday. Her phone and comms are being monitored. She checks out."

"There's something you need to be aware of, Hawkes..." Hughes pauses for gravitas. "I spoke with Steve Fallon's former commanding officer at Hereford. Apparently among his many talents, targeted killing was his speciality."

"Assassination?"

"There's more. In late two thousand, Fallon took some shrapnel in the head from an IED, which he never recovered from, psychologically."

"Frontal lobe trauma could account for his personality disorder."

"When he came back from his last tour of Afghanistan, his condition declined sharply."

"Because he'd just murdered his wife's lover."

"Either way, Fallon became so unstable, if he hadn't left the regiment, they would have medically discharged him."

"Just like the police psychologist's report."

"His old CO also gave me a warning: that Fallon will never stop until he's achieved his mission or eliminated his target. Rosa, if you get close to this guy, don't you try to arrest him with your stick and CS spray. Call in armed response, do you understand?"

"Copy that, sir." As I pocket my work phone, my personal mobile vibrates in my pocket. A message from Gareth:

R U OK? MISS U, LUV, G

I hoped it was from Bruce, having not seen or spoken to him since his revelation in the garden the other night. The contempt on his face and his tone haunts me as I stare at my estranged reflection in the kitchen. "Do you want to know how to catch a psychopath, Rosa? Look in the bloody mirror."

113

EMILY

Emily places her hands on the cushion. As she removes it, the bloodied face is not her father's. It's Charlotte's, her bulging eyes filled with blood and accusation.

Her lips crack open, as if to speak–

Emily awakes, fighting for breath, unable to move or calibrate her whereabouts. Slowly Calum's cottage takes form, dissipating her panic. She struggles to sit upright on the couch, trapped under a quilted blanket Calum must have draped across her after she passed out. Emily glances at her watch. Six fifty in the evening. She's slept for over twelve hours. Her mouth feels parched and it's difficult to swallow. Emily cups the chipped mug from the mahogany coffee table and slurps coffee, cold and watery, but she drains it to the bitter grains. "Calum?" she calls out, her words lost to the perpetual drum-roll of rain rattling the leaded windows.

Prince wakes from slumber before the dying hearth, stretches creakily and pads over to her. "Where's your daddy?" She strokes his velvety ears. Prince repays her with a wet lick across her cheek. Emily places the mug on the table, finding a note next to it from Calum:

Gone for supplies. Back soon.

As Emily heaves herself upright, the blanket slips off, exposing she is wearing only underwear. She shivers, chilled by the cold, and her inability to recollect undressing. Calum must have undressed her, the realisation striking her as intrusive and disturbing, until recalling her bloodstained dress. She glances at the embers in the fire. Calum has burned it, no doubt. Emily lets out a forlorn sigh. That was one of her favourite dresses. Another memory of Dan, condemned to ash. He bought it when he was visiting his New York agent. Or, the thought stabs her, he said he did. Whatever, it's not like she'd ever wear it again. Even if it was dry-cleaned, Charlotte's bloodstains would be indelible. Emily shakes the thought, rubbing the blood back into her arms, considering rekindling the fire before remembering her desire for a bath.

Emily carries her holdall up the creaky staircase, following the smell of mildew to the bathroom. Twelve hours since Calum switched the boiler on, as the murky water sludges out Emily isn't optimistic, but soon the water runs clear and hot. Within minutes steam drips off the whitewashed wainscot.

In the rush at her flat, Emily forgot to pack her wash bag. She searches the porthole mirror cabinet for foam bath, or shampoo, but its contents, like the bathroom's nautical theme, are all masculine. An antique shaving foam can, a bottle of Old Spice, a half-toothless comb, cutthroat razor and a bar of Pears soap. Emily elects the soap and, from no instinct other than survival, the razor, which she drops onto her jeans, folded on a wicker cabinet.

About to wipe the steamed mirror, she halts, recalling that, in movies, sweeping the steamed glass reveals the killer behind. "Get a grip," she chastises herself, squeaking her hand over the patinated mirror. Her reflection, though not as terrifying, is still jarring. Her skin is pale and drawn, and as her grumbling belly announces, she hasn't eaten since yesterday. If Calum doesn't return with supplies soon, he might discover his trophy fish above the fireplace in a frying pan.

She dips a toe into the salutary warmth before climbing into the chipped enamel tub, her body melting into its amniotic warmth. Her formative memory of her father is him teaching her to swim. In the water, she feels closer to him somehow, connected to his spirit, surrounded by his love and protection. Safe. But Emily knows better than anyone, nothing good lasts.

114

CALUM

Calum remembered the convenience store from the first time he visited the cottage, after Bex left him for Matt, when he stocked up on supplies, live bait and enough booze to comatose a herd of rhinos. Because of the latter, he'd done little fishing those two weeks. But through his hazy recollection he recalled the lone village store had no security cameras.

The shopkeeper, a mummified geezer with missing teeth, packs his groceries into plastic bags, along with a cheap Nokia phone. On the counter, spread out in stacked newspapers, are fugitive-style images of Emily, Steve and himself. Calum's is a photo from his work website profile, taken years ago, without his beard. He struggles to recognise himself, but it's the front-page headlines on the counter that really set his heart racing:

OTHELLO CLUB STRIKES AGAIN!
MURDER PROBE FOR BROKEN HEARTS KILLERS!
SAS KILLER ON RAMPAGE!

Steve is still out there, he realises. *Shit!* Emily wanted him to buy newspapers, but there's no chance he's setting that distress flare off. As he hands over cash, the shopkeeper squints through his thick glasses. From myopia, Calum hopes, or good old-fashioned bigotry, as minorities tend to stick out round here.

"Cheers." Calum attempts a Norfolk accent.

The old man nods. "Keep yew a troshin."

Calum strides into the rain, vaguely translating that as bumpkin for "goodbye". Bottles clinking in his shopping bags, he can feel the old man's gaze following him to the car.

Miles from the store, Calum parked on a grass verge along the roadside. He tries to compose his addled thoughts, but the rain pummelling the car roof isn't helping his concentration. The torn Nokia phone packaging lies discarded on the passenger seat. He plugs the charger cable into the dashboard USB, connects the phone and switches the power on. The screen ignites his febrile features as he calculates the risk versus reward. Like a junkie, knowing he's kidding himself, Calum dials the number and presses the phone to his ear.

"Bea, there's no time for that. Please, just put Bella on." A lump forms in his throat as he listens to his daughter's footfalls.

"Daddy?"

Her voice wrongfoots him, unprepared for the wave of emotion.

"Daddy, is that you?"

"Hello, sweetheart."

115

ROSA

"We've got a lead," Hughes says.

I snap from a troubled dream, slumped over my desk, clutching the battered paperback of *Othello*. I sit upright, wiping imagined drool from my mouth.

DCI Hughes looms into focus, unshaven, unkempt and as depleted as I feel. I glance at my watch, alarmed it's almost eight o'clock. "Christ, I've been out for hours. You should have woken me, sir."

"You were out for the count."

"Shakespeare has that effect on me."

Hughes surveys the thumbed York and Spark Notes on *Othello*. "Your research of any use?"

"Only as a cure for insomnia. What's the lead?"

"Calum Grayson's sister received a call from an unlisted phone, which activated a cell tower in the Norfolk Broads. And we've had intelligence of a man matching his description, driving a silver BMW. The owner of a village shop in Limpenhoe identified him. Where Greyson purchased a burner phone, a few miles away from where the call was triangulated."

I lumber to my feet. "Have you tried calling the number?"

"It's switched off. Or destroyed." Kruger leans in the doorway.

"What about Steve Fallon?"

"The incident room received a call earlier today. An unconfirmed sighting in a petrol station in Thurnton, Norfolk. A thirty-minute drive from where Calum Greyson made his call."

I snatch my copy of *Othello*. "What are we waiting for?"

"The cars are already outside. You may be right, Hawkes," Hughes says. "Looks like Fallon has unfinished business after all."

116

EMILY

Emily stands in the hearth's glow, dressed and wet hair slicked into a ponytail. Prince lies at her feet, basking in the warmth. Spooked by a crashing sound outside, she creeps over to the rattling window, seeing nothing but the impenetrable dark only found in the remotest countryside. Just a casualty of the wind, a fallen slate or something, she hopes, glancing at her watch and seeing it's past eight o'clock.

"Where the hell is he?"

In need of distraction, she wanders to the mahogany writing bureau, tugging the veneer roll top, but it is locked. The drawers also, except the bottom one, rammed with utilities bills. Emily notes the addressee's name, Abraham Williams, wondering why Calum doesn't share his father's surname, until recalling he changed it after the media frenzy surrounding his ex-girlfriend's murder.

Emily turns to the shelves, heaving with non-fiction books, ranging from fishing to ecclesiastical texts. The opposite wall is reserved for leatherbound novels – classics by Austen, Chaucer, Dickens and Shakespeare – all alphabetised. She studies the antique spines, drawn to an early edition of *Paradise Lost* by John Milton, illustrated by

William Blake. Dan's favourite artist, and the inspiration for his own painting style. Emily slides the tome from the shelf, blowing off the dust, thumbing the pages, illustrated with Blake's surrealist style, drawn from the imagination. His inner eye, as Dan described it.

One illustration draws her attention: *The Temptation of Eve*. The snake-like serpent, coiled around Eve's nakedness, feeding her the fateful apple whilst the cuckolded Adam turns away, oblivious of his wife's betrayal. Emily reads the caption underneath:

So saying, her rash hand in evil hour. Forth-reaching to the fruit, she plucked, she eat.

Typical, Emily thinks, a patriarchal theology demonising a woman for her sexuality. She lays the book on the coffee table, drawn to the complete works of Shakespeare. Her fingertip runs across the oxblood leather spines, tracing the gold lettered titles: *The Merry Wives of Windsor*, *A Midsummer Night's Dream*, *Much Ado About Nothing*, until arriving at *Othello*. Hardly surprising to find it amongst a comprehensive collection, yet Emily feels uneasy by its presence. As she slides out the leather spine, car headlights slice through the curtains. Emily thrusts it back on the shelf, knowing it's probably Calum returning. But what if it's the police? Or, fear blooms in her chest, Steve?

117

ROSA

As our cars screech on the rain-slick forecourt, I glower at the press and TV crew vans lined up like vultures over carrion.

"How did they get here first?" DS Nichols asks from the driver's seat beside me.

"Tipped off by the public," Hughes says, from the back seat. "Parasites."

I unshackle my seat belt. "Might as well have put the blues and twos on." The moment I step into the lashing rain, the press crews surge from their vehicles.

"We'll handle them," Hughes says. "You're back in charge of this investigation, Hawkes."

As I march across the petrol station forecourt, I can hear Hughes ordering Kruger's team to keep the press at bay, bringing a smile to my lips.

Minutes later, Nicholls, Husseini and I huddle behind the sales counter, peering at CCTV footage on a laptop screen. "No sound?" I ask.

Abdul, the petrol station manager, shakes his head. "Just pictures. I'm not made of money, you know."

"Play it again, please?"

Abdul obliges.

A bulky figure wearing a hoodie stalks up to the counter carrying a ten-litre petrol canister. Beneath the shadow of his hood, a thick beard is visible, streaked with white.

"Check out the beard." Nicholls jabs a finger at the screen. "Like Fallon's."

"And half the male population," Husseini says.

"She's right, not enough to confirm identification."

"I saw him in the face." Abdul prods the screen. "Clear as day. It was him; I'm telling you."

I peer at the grainy footage, watching as the hooded customer hands Abdul cash. "Pause it. There, look at his hand." All eyes affix on the pixilated frame. The hooded man has scar tissue in the centre of his hand. "Steve Fallon has the same scars." I meet Husseini's excited gaze. "We have a positive ID."

Abdul beams like he's won a competition. "What am I telling you?"

"You're certain you didn't see the vehicle he was driving?"

"He must have parked at the bays. I only recognised him later, from the news." Abdul points to a miniature TV set on the counter.

"Your CCTV cameras don't have eyes on the parking bays?"

Abdul shakes his head.

"We could review surrounding CCTV?" Nichols suggests.

"We don't have time, but I'll get the local Bobbies on it. Get a copy of the footage." I stride towards the exit.

"Wait?" Abdul asks. "Isn't there a reward?"

"I'd say you've already had it." I glare towards the press vans. "Wouldn't you?"

Abdul's smile slips. As I suspected, it was him who'd tipped off the press.

I stride towards the car inhaling petrol fumes, troubled

by what Steve Fallon intends with a ten-litre can of it. Presumably so he could refill the tank away from CCTV recording his vehicle and registration number. But I can't shift the thought of a more explosive motive, and the final fiery act of his hellish masterpiece.

118

EMILY

Emily peeks around the curtains, blinded by the headlights, unable to determine the figure in the driver's seat. Thunder cracks like a gunshot, compounding her pulsating fear. The car door swings open, the driver's hiking boots sinking into mud. Emily's brain rewinds, attempting to recall Calum's footwear, but she was asleep when he left. The driver turns towards the house, locking on Emily's gaze, his features shadowed by a baseball cap, revealing nothing but his dark beard.

Steve! She panics until lightning flashes, illuminating Calum's dripping face. Relief courses through her as Calum sloshes to the tackle shed, hauling open the barn doors in a tug-of-war against the wind. After securing the doors with cinderblocks, he steers the BMW into the large shed; the headlights raking across the interior, flashing its innards. The butler's sink she glimpsed earlier, fishing rods hanging on the walls, dusty shelves filled with junk and a decrepit dinghy. Calum kills the engine, plunging the shed into darkness.

When he emerges laden with shopping bags, Emily's relief turns to anticipation. Apart from her rabid hunger, she is desperate for a cigarette. She greets him at the front door as Calum trudges into the porch, stamping his soaking boots on the welcome mat.

"What took you so long?" Emily asks.

"I took the scenic route back to be safe." He hefts the shopping bags through to the kitchenette, placing them on the Formica table, the clink of bottles reassuring the promise of alcohol. "Sorry, I didn't mean to worry you."

"I forgive everything if you got the cigarettes?"

Calum tugs three packets of Marlboro Golds from a bag. "Ta-da!"

"Thank Christ." Emily grasps them, unwrapping the cellophane. "You're a lifesaver."

"I'm pretty sure it's the opposite." Calum dries his face with a tea towel. "Every one of those takes ten minutes off your life."

"Under the circumstances, I'll risk it." Emily lights her smoke with a box of kitchen matches. "Did you get the newspapers?"

"Shit. I knew there was something."

"Calum? We're in the dark here."

"You know what the press is like. It'll all be lies and fake news, anyway."

"Maybe you're right." Emily knows you don't sell newspapers by reporting the truth.

"I glimpsed a few headlines and trust me, you don't want to know."

"They haven't caught him yet?"

"They will. No one can stay hidden forever."

Emily smiles, letting the irony pass.

"I'll get the rest of the stuff from the car."

"Let me help." She starts for the door.

"No, I'll go. I'm already soaked, and it's getting evil out there. A storm is on the way."

Emily watches Calum disappear into the tempest, his forecast resonating ominously.

119

ROSA
9 September

I splash water in my face, staring at my exhausted reflection in the bathroom mirror, where I've stepped out from our temporary incident room at Norfolk police station.

"Do you want to know how to catch a psychopath, Rosa?" Bruce's words echo in my head. "Look in the bloody mirror."

I know Bruce was just hurt and lashing out. Psychopaths have no sense of guilt. My tormented conscience absolves me of that charge at least. But it reminds me that, when probing Steve Fallon for racist abuse on his wife's lover, I glimpsed in his wintery eyes something akin to shame. Then there's his PTSD. An unlikely disorder for psychopathy, given their immunity to anxiety. Unless he was faking it, like Bruce suggested, to mitigate his suspension from the force? Or presenting a benign diagnosis to mask a malignant identity?

"He's changed his MO." I recall Hughes's words, tabulating my doubts. After exonerating himself so meticulously, why would Steve Fallon point the finger at himself now?

I pat my face with a paper towel, reminded of a quote from *Othello*, haunting me for days: "I am not what I am."

"You OK, boss?"

I jump at Husseini's reflection in the mirror, wondering how long she's been there. "I didn't hear you come in."

"Are you alright?"

"Yes. Just... it's been a long day." I smile at Husseini's swollen belly. "You shouldn't still be on your feet, Yasmin. Go back to the hotel and get some sleep. For both your sakes."

"The DCI called everyone back. There's been a development."

"On Steve Fallon?"

Husseini shakes her head. "No, boss. It's not about him."

120

EMILY

Slumped on a couch in the dying hearth light, Emily rests her head on Calum's shoulder. Her hunger sated on steak, baked potato and cheesecake, she feels replenished and lulled into a sense of normality. She stifles a yawn, glancing at her watch, shocked it's so late. Or rather, so early. "Calum, it's nearly morning." She strains upright, sipping her coffee.

"Jesus, where did that go." Calum's words slur. Due in part to exhaustion, but mainly from the amount of Malbec he consumed over dinner.

She can't blame him. Right now, oblivion is an alluring mindset. "We should go up."

"One for the road." Calum hunches forwards, pouring himself another large brandy.

His third, Emily notes, reaching for her cigarettes on the coffee table. "Is that a good idea?"

"Let those without sin…" He frowns as she lights up.

"I just mean if we've got an early start, teaching me to fish?"

"I'll make you a daughter of Zebedee yet."

"That's if the weather settles down."

"Bad weather fronts are the best time to fish. Something about the barometric pressure makes the fish bite like crazy."

Emily smiles, doubting his hangover will have blown over by the morning.

Calum pours himself another glass. "Sure you don't want a drop in your coffee?"

"I know my limit, thanks."

If Calum took the hint he discounts it, draining half the glass and slumping back onto the wheezing Chesterfield. Curled up at his feet, Prince's eyes flicker before returning to slumber.

Emily waves her cigarette at the bookshelves. "Your dad must have really loved books?"

"More than he did me."

"I'm sure that's not true."

Calum scoffs. "Lord help you if he found you touching them." As he reaches for the brandy bottle on the coffee table again, his eyes flick to *Paradise Lost*, the page still open on Blake's illustration of Eve's temptation. "He'd spin in his grave, seeing the spine cracked open like that."

"Sorry, I didn't think…" Emily reaches to close the book.

"No, leave it. Fuck him."

"At least he gave you your passion for literature."

"What's the point of a passion if you don't live it? It just rots inside you, like another broken promise."

"You can always go back into teaching."

"That ship has sailed." Calum sighs. "After all the sacrifices I made for her, it was never about money. Bex told me that herself, before…" He curbs himself, draining his brandy. "I just wasn't good enough." He glowers at Blake's depiction of Eve. The serpent thrusting the apple into her mouth. "They all bit into that apple. Mum, Julie, Bex…" His tone sours with his expression. "Didn't taste so sweet in the end, though. They fucking choked on it."

Julie was Calum's ex-girlfriend, murdered in Thailand. The coincidence forms a disquieting lump in Emily's throat.

'"The heart is deceitful above all things."' Calum snorts. "The old man was right."

"Not everyone is like that, Calum." Emily drops her cigarette hissing into her red wine and heaves herself upright. She learned from her mother how to read the barometric signs of a bad drinker. "Let's call it a night."

"Bollocks, the night is still young," Calum slurs.

"It's nearly daylight." Emily offers her hand. "Come on, let's get some sleep."

"OK." He takes her hand, but as Emily pulls away, he holds firm. "Something's been bothering me..."

"Whatever it is, it can keep until the morning."

"No, it can't." Calum's grip tightens. "Why were you so desperate to keep that dress?"

Emily winces, her hand crushing in his grasp. "Calum, you're hurting me."

"Just answer the question!"

Emily yanks free. Calum's face is so contorted with rage, she barely recognises him.

"It was because he bought it for you, wasn't it?"

That's why he stripped me of the dress, Emily realises. *Not just to eliminate DNA evidence, but because of his jealousy.* "Just because I'm sentimental, doesn't mean–"

"I fucking knew it! The wonderful fucking Dan. After what he did to you?" Spittle forms in the corners of his mouth. "You still love him, don't you? Admit it!"

"No." The lie catches in her throat. "I admit I don't want any harm to come to him. No more than you would have Bex?"

"'Who commits adultery has no sense; whoever does so destroys himself.'"

"What is that supposed to mean?"

"It means they lit the fuse themselves."

"Calum, you don't mean that?" Emily stares at him, imploring a retraction, but he doesn't yield. As he reaches for the brandy, she snatches the bottle. "You've had enough."

"I'll decide when I've had enough." As he lunges for the bottle, he tips Emily's wine glass over the book, blood red Malbec and ash bleeding into the inks. "Christ! Look what you've done." He daubs at the stain with his shirt tail. "He'll fucking kill me."

"Who the are you taking about, Calum? Your dead father?"

"No." Calum shakes his head. "Course not, I just…"

"For God's sake, Calum, you're drunk, and you haven't slept for two days. You need to go to bed."

"Sorry… I don't know what came over me. It's just… speaking to Bella hit me harder than I thought, you know?"

"You spoke to your daughter?"

"No." He shakes his head. "I meant not speaking to her is doing my head in. Don't listen to me, I'm just pissed. You're right, I need to sleep."

Emily's mind reels, puzzling how he called, and who could have traced it? But a more ominous question afflicts her now, fearing the answer to which resides in the bookcase.

Calum stumbles to the staircase. "You coming?"

"I'll just put the dishes in the sink." Emily holds her amiable, humouring expression, watching him ascend the creaky stairs until he disappears. She listens to the floorboards straining under his weight and the groan of the bedsprings as he collapses on it. When the only audible sounds are the storm outside, she tiptoes to the bookcase to address her creeping incertitude.

Unlike the other tomes, the *Othello* spine is free of dust, recently handled. Emily takes a deep breath and draws out the book. As she opens it the crippling weight of realisation falls upon her.

121

ROSA

I scurry into the makeshift incident room, which despite the hour feels charged with energy. Though tousled and dishevelled, the team is alert with adrenaline, and the long dormant fire in Hughes's eyes has rekindled. He nods at Kruger, perched on the board table beside his laptop.

"From CCTV near the Chiswick home of Charlotte Hunter," Kruger says, "we got the registration on the silver BMW driven by Calum Greyson."

"You've run it through the DVLA?"

Kruger tilts his head like an irritated puppy. "The registered owner is Anthony Daniels. He lives at the same apartment block as Greyson, though currently he's working in Dubai."

"Let's use the press to our advantage, putting out an appeal for the car," I say.

Hughes nods. "Let the vultures provide a useful service for once. But there's more. Go on, Pat."

Kruger spins his laptop around on the desk and hits play.

Grainy footage of a silver BMW emerging from a basement garage.

"The CCTV harvested outside Calum Grayson's residence on the morning of his ex-wife's death captured the same vehicle, timecoded at nine twenty and returning at ten fifty.

The pathologist's estimated time of death, and an ample window of opportunity."

"Have you checked if this neighbour, Anthony Daniels, was in the country?"

Hughes grins. "Daniels was in Dubai."

"Besides," Kruger continues, "we have an ID from the CCTV." Kruger taps the mouse, pausing the image as it merges into traffic. Visible through the windshield, pixilated and hazy, is Calum.

"It's him."

Hughes's eyes meet mine. "His alibi was bogus."

"Which puts him back in the frame."

"And Emily Hunter too. She lied about his alibi."

"Unless he manipulated her, like the others." I recall a phrase from *Othello*, voicing it out loud. "'That thinks men honest that but seem to be so, and will as tenderly be led by the nose, as asses are.'" From the bewildered looks, I add. "It's a quote from *Othello*. A soliloquy Iago delivers at the end of Act One."

Hughes, Kruger and the team look mystified.

"It means Iago intends to manipulate Othello, exploiting his jealousy, leading him like a donkey to exact his own twisted agenda. Shit." I peer at the still image of Calum on the screen, gripping the steering wheel, his expression full of intent. Bunched around his neck, the folds of a dark cowl. "Look at what he's wearing."

Husseini's eyes widen with realisation. "A dark hoodie."

"Why didn't I see it sooner?"

"See what?" Hughes leans into the screen, bemused.

"Not on the screen." I tug the battered *Othello* paperback from my jacket pocket. "The play. The fucking play! It's been bothering me for days, but I couldn't put my finger on it."

"I like suspense as much as anyone, Rosa, but is there a point coming?"

"'I am not what I am.' Iago says it near the start of the play."

Hughes frowns. "And?"

"Othello isn't the real villain. Yes, he's a jealous, controlling and misogynistic prick." I glance at Kruger. "But he only becomes violent after being manipulated by Iago. A psychopath if ever there was one."

"Remind me," Hughes asks, "what was Calum Greyson's codename?"

An icy chill shivers through me as I say his name. "Iago."

122

EMILY

The hair on Emily's nape bristles, her eyes wide with recognition, gaping at the book. Scratchy red ink highlights and underlines passages of text, scrawled in ballpoint pen, piercing the pages.

"Arise, black vengeance, from the hollow hell. Yield up, O love, thy crown and hearted throne to tyrannous hate."

Emily riffles to another page, defiled in blood-red ink.

"I will wear my heart upon my sleeve for daws to peck at."

Images of Nick's woodland slaying flash in Emily's mind. His severed heart, still beating, steaming in the morning chill. Fear ratchets up inside as she searches for the inevitable passage. Then, turning the page, there it is, marked in red, as indelible as her nightmares.

"Strangle her in her bed, even the bed she hath contaminated."

The same passage scrawled in blood above Charlotte's suffocated corpse. The full, terrible force of understanding falls on Emily now. She clamps a hand to her mouth, fighting the urge to scream. The book slips from her numbed fingers, thudding to the floor. She staggers backwards, her stomach churning, grasping a hand to her mouth to stop herself from vomiting. On her knees in the ebbing glow of the hearth, she coughs and retches, reappraising events in her head. A terrifying, uncut version, too horrific to process.

"They lit the fuse." Calum's words echo in her mind.

"No." Emily sobs. "You did, you sick fuck…" Memories swirl, transposed through her altered prism of perspective.

The morning of Bex's death, awaking groggy and dehydrated, Emily attributed her hangover to exhaustion from the night shift at the homeless shelter and the couple of vodkas before bed. But what if her disequilibrium was caused by Calum slipping sedatives into her drink? Incapacitating her so he could murder his ex-wife, and have Emily provide him an alibi. She recalls those fateful words, months before, arguing over their codenames.

"An eye for an eye. A heart for a heart," Calum said in the pub. Drunken bravado, it seemed at the time, but now Emily replays it differently. As if he was deadly serious, intent on punishing the sinful for their adulterous betrayals.

Survival instinct kicking in, she realises the peril of her isolation, miles from anywhere, trapped with an apparently murderous sociopath. *Car keys*, she thinks, her eyes flicking to his jacket on the coat stand. She creeps across the floorboards to the front door, lifting Calum's leather jacket silently and rifling his pockets. A wallet, sunglasses, no keys, but from his inside breast pocket she pulls out a cheap Nokia phone. A burner, Calum must have used to call his daughter earlier. With it, she can call the police. Emily remembers DI Hawkes's business card in her purse. She unhooks her bag from the coat stand and fumbles in the purse, drawing out the business card.

With Calum's jacket to smother the sound, Emily powers

up the phone, but as the screen lights up, her stomach plummets, seeing zero bars. She needs to get to somewhere with reception. Further up the road, hadn't Calum said? Worse, the battery has no power. Of course it doesn't, she realises, it's a new phone. But if he called his daughter earlier, the charger must be in the car. "Fuck." Panic rises in her throat, typing in the mobile number from the business card, hoping a text message will minimise the phone's power exertion.

I am Emily Hunter. Calum Greyson is the killer. He's here with me now. Please send help. My location is…

Emily possesses only the vaguest sense of her location, until recalling Calum's father's utility bills, which will have the postal address. She scurries across the living room, conscious of every floorboard creaking underfoot. Quietly slipping a bill from the bureau drawer, she texts the address and postcode, before pressing send. Emily stares at the screen, her eyes glistening with hope, but the reception bars remain on zero, the text undelivered. "Fuck."

She needs to find those car keys, but the only place they can be is Calum's jeans pocket. Emily peers up the dark staircase. There's no way she is going up there without a weapon. *The razor*, she remembers. From her back pocket, Emily tugs out the cutthroat, extends the blade and climbs the arthritic staircase into the inky void.

On the landing, fumbling along the walls, her fingers touch a Bakelite switch. Afraid the light will awaken Calum, she stumbles onward through the dark. Her eyes adjusting to the amorphous blackness, she makes out the ajar bedroom door. Even over the battering wind and rain rattling the windows, Emily can hear Calum's snoring within. She peers through the door crack, drawn to the phosphorescent light of the bedside clock, its glow giving her a sense of the room's topography. As she steps inside, a floorboard squeals. Emily flinches, peering at the black mass of the bed, but Calum remains still. She can barely discern the outline of his body, splayed on his front, his head twisted to the side.

Emily creeps towards the bed, the floorboards awakening with every step, as if pleading for her retreat. At the bedside, she studies Calum's features for any glimmer of consciousness. Satisfied he is dead to the world, she slides her fingers into his back pockets, finding them empty. To check his front pockets, Emily places the razor on the bed. Levering her hands under Calum's hips and shoulder, she heaves him onto his back. He moans softly. Emily snatches the razor, fear leaping into her throat, but Calum drifts back into his soporific coma. Releasing the air trapped in her lungs, she checks his pockets. But to her dismay, no fucking keys.

Fighting her rising panic, Emily looms over Calum, watching the rise and fall of his chest, whiffing his alcohol breath, hot and sweet. She stares at his slumbering, peaceful face, juxtaposing the external beauty with what lies underneath. A mask disguising a monster?

Emily can feel her grip tightening around the extended razor. His exposed throat, jugular pulsating. One slash and it will all end. Justice, final and absolute. *After everything – Jack, Issy, Simone, Bex, Nick, Malcolm and Tal – who could blame me? It would be like self-defence. Me or him.* Emily raises the blade, waiting for her trebling hand to steady, ready to plunge it into his throat–

A dog barks. Emily spins to the door. Prince's eyes glow in the dark as he howls furiously. A light snaps on, the bedside lamp arching the garish green paisley wallpaper.

"Emily?" Calum says, his bloodshot, bleary eyes snapping

focus seeing the razor. "What the fuck?" He grabs her wrist. She wrestles his grasp, but he's too strong, her wrist burning, skin tearing, bone crushing, about to snap.

The razor clatters to the floor. Emily yanks her hand free and barrels to the door, past Prince's growling protests, her moccasins thumping down the stairs three at a time.

Fingers fumbling, Emily twists the front door latch, hearing Calum's footfalls pounding the floorboards above. On the side table is an aluminium flashlight. Useful in the pitch dark outside, she snatches it and flees into the night.

123

CALUM

Calum stumbles through his alcohol fugue, unsure if what just happened was real or if he has awoken from a nightmare. But seeing the glinting steel on the hardwood floor, he is confronted by the sobering evidence. The cutthroat razor. "What the fuck?" Calum gasps, recalling the intent in Emily's eyes.

He snatches the razor, his fuddled brain reaching the only rational conclusion. Adrenaline coursing through him, Calum launches across the landing, hammering down the staircase.

In the dying firelight, Calum's eyes rake the empty living room. "Emily?" Silence confirms his fears. She's gone. The familiar pain twists in Calum's gut, of yet another betrayal. Like every woman in his life. He glances at the opened drawers on the bureau and the ransacked kitchen. What was she looking for?

Prince barks at the front door, steering Calum's gaze outside. "Car keys," he realises out loud.

As he charges to the front door, Calum's shin clips the coffee table. He yelps in pain, rubbing his leg, seeing the oxblood leather book and the glint of gold lettering. *Othello*. He crouches to the book, leafing through the pages until he sees the red ink, highlighting the text. "Oh, shit."

The book thuds to the floor, his stupor cleaved by sobering realisation. But she won't get far. His eyes drop to the vermilion pair of wading boots by the door.

Calum tilts a boot upside down, a smile forming as the BMW fob drops to the rug. *Not without a key. On foot, miles from a neighbouring house or the nearest town. Unless*, the thought shudders through him, *she called someone*. Calum tugs his leather jacket from the stand, rifling the empty pockets. The burner phone is gone. "Oh, Jesus."

Emily only needs to reach the road to pick up a mobile signal. Christ knows what she'll tell the police. As he thrusts his arms into his jacket, Calum's panic dissipates, seeing a glow emanating from the crack in the tackle shed doors. "Bitch!"

124

EMILY

The torch slices through the darkness, glimpsing the tackle shed interior. A tin of rusty fishhooks on a dusty counter, cobwebbed shelving filled with fishing gear, the decrepit wooden dinghy on concrete blocks and the silver BMW. Emily grasps the door handle, relieved as it opens, arching the sapphire beam across the dashboard compartments but finding no key fob. She pops the glove compartment and reaches inside, her eyes widening with hope, feeling cold metal and the jangling of chain. "Please?" As she yanks it into the glare, her optimism vanishes. The chain is gold, attached to a jewel-encrusted pendant, with rubies spelling the letter B. B for Bex. Of course, she remembers. The pendant Calum's ex-wife was wearing when she died. Which Emily knows only her killer could possess.

"Emily, what the fuck's going on?"

She feels the lurch in her heart before spinning to his sound, catching Calum's tortured face in torchlight.

Fuck! Emily had bargained on the key being in the car, but now she's trapped herself.

"You won't get far without this." Calum dangles the car fob. Clutched in his other hand is the razor.

Emily tries to swallow her fear, but her voice is shrill with it. "You stay away from me."

Calum glares at the pendant. "Where did you get that?" As he lunges for it, Emily crawls over the passenger seat. He grabs at her ankles, but Emily kicks his face. "Fuck." He recoils, clutching his jaw.

Emily fumbles with the door handle, tumbling out, her forehead hitting the dank concrete. Dazed, she flounders for the torch, but it's lost in the car. She can hear Calum's footsteps scurrying towards her. Emily thrusts herself onto her feet, staggering in the vague direction of the counter she glimpsed earlier. Calum lumbers after her, but she reaches it a millisecond before him, snatching the tin of fishhooks, hurling it in his face. He wails in pain, the razor clattering to the floor.

"You bitch." He gropes at a fishhook impaled in his eyelid, tugging it out, blood gushing down his cheek. "Fucking bitch!"

Emily scans the gloom, locating where the sound of the blade fell. She grasps it, spearing it before her, along with the pendant, warding him off like a vampire. "Keep the fuck away from me, I'm warning you."

"Fucking give me that." Calum launches at her.

Whether he means the razor or the pendant, Emily isn't relinquishing either. Her wrists searing from his grip, she thrusts a knee at his groin, but he blocks it with his thigh. This isn't the public schoolboy tussle she had with Jack Noble, she realises, as his right fist hammers into her mouth, followed by his left connecting with her cheek, snapping her head back.

Stunned, Emily staggers back, the razor and pendant slipping from her grasp. Her blood tastes coppery, and she can feel the burn of her lip already swelling.

"Emily?" Calum sounds apologetic, but Emily is already stumbling towards the door, crashing her shoulder into it, bolting into the darkness. "Emily, wait."

She skids across the sodden grass, hearing his footfalls behind her, the strobe of Calum's torchlight illuminating the jetty ahead, until feeling the hard wooden planks under foot.

"Emily, there's nowhere to go."

You're wrong about that, Emily resolves, kicking off her moccasins. The jetty falls away from her feet, plunging into the bracing chill of the river. Like a sea of needles, so much colder than she'd imagined. She emerges gasping, feeling for the directional flow of the current, following its tidal gravity, swimming hard and fast, merging into the centre of the river. Her left shoulder throbs from impacting on the shed door and the numbing cold would debilitate a seal, but Emily is adroit at negating pain, and with each masterful stroke Calum's demented cries grow fainter. With his inferior swimming ability, he'll never catch her. In a mile or so there'll be a house where she can call for help. Emily has swum much further distances and with far less motivation.

As she settles into a rhythm, Emily hears a fearful sound. The splutter of an outboard engine starting up. She risks a backward glance, seeing a light bobbing in the water, approaching fast.

His dad's boat. He told her it wasn't seaworthy, yet now it's powering towards her. Emily swims for the riverbank, but the dinghy cuts across her path, its wake submerging her. She fights for breath, grappling the side of the boat when Calum yanks her wrist. For a moment Emily thinks he's assisting her, until seeing the intent in his eyes, and the iron-tipped boat hook held at his side.

"I won't let you drag me down with you…" Calum releases her wrist and grips the long boat hook with both hands. "Into the icy lake of hell, with the betrayers."

"Calum, please, don't do this," Emily pleads, gagging on water.

"You've given me no choice. I can't risk losing Bella. Not again." A smile twists his features. "What was it Iago said? 'This is the night that either makes me, or undoes me.'" Calum swings the boat hook over his head.

"No!" Emily ducks beneath the water, the blinding thud cracking the top of her skull. Mercifully, the pain is as fleeting as her consciousness, sinking into the darkness, resting on the silty bed.

The charter boat slows as they approach three rock formations towering over the Capri coastline. The central stack has a natural arch, wide enough for small vessels to pass, unto which a queue of tourist boats congregates.

"I Faraglioni, they're called." Dan says, as their boat joins the queue. "The middle one is Faraglione di Mezzo. Also known as the Arch of Love. Legend has it that if you kiss underneath it, your love will last forever."

As their turn comes, passing under the rock, the air cools, prickling the hair on Emily's nape. As she leans in for the kiss, Dan is on one knee, tugging a small Tiffany box from his shorts, revealing an engagement ring. It sparkles, reflecting the aquamarine water, but it can't compare to the luminous light in his eyes.

125

STEVE

"Fuck!" Steve yanks up his night-vision goggles as Emily vanishes into the black water. He drops from the tree branch, his observation post these last hours, and sprints towards the jetty, Glock drawn and safety off.

Calum spins to the thunder of Steve's boots on the jetty, but he isn't allowed the time to protest his fate. Steve fires two rounds into Calum's chest, catapulting him from the dinghy into the water with a dull splash.

In a heartbeat, Steve drops his Glock, wrenches out of his jacket, kicks his boots off, and dives into the river, swimming towards where Emily sank, gulping air into his lungs and plunging into the intractable darkness. He crawls in every direction, groping at the mucilaginous riverbed but, barring slithering fish and dank vegetation, finds no sign of life.

A minute later, his lungs burning, Steve can feel his brain functions failing. On the cusp of losing consciousness, he kicks upwards, bursting to the surface, gulping oxygen, before submerging again. He should have known it was Calum all along, but hell-bent on his mission, he couldn't see it. It wouldn't have happened back the day, before that IED scrambled his brain... Steve's fingertips feel flesh! Cold to the touch, but human skin. A wrist? Or an ankle? A wrist!

He gropes along her arm until, touching hair, then her neck, wrestling Emily into a rescue position, kicking to the surface.

From the shallows he cradles her lifeless body up the muddy bank, before laying her on the wet grass under a crooked elm. Steve sucks oxygen into his lungs, covers his mouth on Emily's, giving her two short pumps of air, watching for her chest to rise. He presses his hands on her chest and compresses, counting to thirty. With no sign of life, he increases his tempo, pounding his fists into her chest. "Come on, Em, fight. Fucking fight."

After several minutes, Steve rolls off her onto his back, shutting his eyes. The familiar nausea churns his gut, heart racing, breathing ragged. His mind wrenches back to the foxhole in Helmand Province.

Steve steadies his breathing and places the crosshairs in the middle of the target's head. Peter Caine, Sue's young lover. He allows for the wind, adjusting his aim a few inches to the left, draws a breath and squeezes the trigger. Before the round hits, the target appears to turn and look back at him. A smile forms on Peter Caine's lips, and as he speaks…

Concrete dust peppers the air above Caine's head, the round impacting in the bunker wall behind him. As Caine falls to his belly for cover, a cacophony of shouting and return fire ensues.

Steve snaps back. To the reality that he never killed Peter Caine. The poor bastard bought it anyway two weeks later, catching a real Taliban sniper bullet. Steve hadn't pulled the trigger, but he nearly had, and that haunts him still. He wipes the tears from his eyes, sits up and stares across the river. Towards the east, wisps of pink sunlight slither across the Norfolk Broads. As ever at dawn, Steve thinks of his mother–

A choking sound snaps Steve from his reverie. Emily spews water, coughing and gasping. Astonished, Steve rolls her onto her side as Emily dry heaves into the grass. "You're alright Em, get it all out."

His fingers trace her scalp, feeling for a head wound. The top of her head is slick with oily blood, a flap of skin exposed under his fingertips. Emily winces. A good sign, Steve recognises, of consciousness. "Can you hear me, Em?"

"Yes."

"How do you feel?"

"I've felt better."

"Aye, I'm sure you have. Do you feel disorientated, lethargic or confused?"

"All the above."

"That's OK, Em, I'm gonna sit you up?" Emily moans but doesn't move. Steve lifts her into a sitting position, resting her against the tree trunk. "You've had a bonny crack to your nut, Em. I'll need to get a dressing on it, but I can't see for shite. I need to get my kit from the car."

"Calum?" Emily's eyes gape with fear.

"He's gone."

"Where?"

"Somewhere he can't hurt you or anyone else. Hold on, Em, I'll be right back." Steve scrambles into the darkness to where he discarded his torch, kicking it underfoot. He grasps it, switching the beam on. Having located his Glock, he sprints barefooted to the outline of the Range Rover on the verge above. From the passenger seat he snatches his backpack and charges back down the slope.

On his knees, torch clamped in his teeth, Steve examines Emily's scalp, clotted with blood and an angry two-inch gash. "Och, it's nothing." He masks the lie with a breezy tone. "A few wee stitches is all."

"You're not a talented liar."

"Not as gifted as some, that's for sure. Close your eyes, I'm gonna clean your wound." He twists the cap off his water canister and pours the contents over her scalp, making her wince. "You need a hospital," he says, gently wiping the blood from her eyes and face with gauze. As Steve compresses a field dressing on her wound, Emily moans. "I know it hurts, Em, but the pain is a good thing."

"I can't see how."

"The more it hurts, the more it tells me you're conscious." Steve wraps a bandage under her chin, tight enough to stem the blood, but not obstructing the trachea. Emily's eyelids flutter and shut. "You need to stay awake, even if you feel drowsy, OK?"

Emily opens her eyes, shivering. "I doubt I'll ever sleep again."

As Steve drapes his jacket over her shoulders, Emily grasps it across her chest. Anger surges through him, studying her battered face in the pink dawn glow. The sight of her swollen cheek and cut lip makes him regret slotting Calum. Too quick and easy. "He did a number on you. The fucker."

"On us all."

"Aye. That's on me. I knew he was a wrong 'un the moment I clapped eyes on him. I should have known…"

"We all should." Emily places her hand on his, unfurling his fist. They stare at the sunrise burnishing the river.

"My ma used to say sunrises were nature's way of reminding us we can always start again, no matter what."

"Beautiful." A smile forms on her swollen lips.

Steve is uncertain if she is endorsing his mother's counsel

or the view. Either way, best not to mention his mother's failure to follow her own philosophy. Steve was just a kid when he found her withered corpse in a puddle of piss and vomit, overdosed on smack. For some, starting again isn't an option. "Are you fit to get up, Em?" Steve rises to his feet.

"As I'll ever be." Emily holds up her hand.

As Steve grips it, he hears the chopper blades whipping the air. The sound of a National Police Air Service helicopter. He releases her hand, drawing the Glock from his waistband as the Xenon searchlight rakes across the water, trapping them in its beam.

"This is the police," the voice says, reverberating from the loudspeaker. "Drop the weapon and lie face down."

Steve listens to the screech of vehicles pulling up on the ridge, doors opening, boots on the ground as the armed response unit take up their positions. He can see the look of relief falling from Emily's face, seeing his own expression.

"Steve, what are you doing? Get down."

"Whatever happens, Em, stay down."

126

EMILY

"Steve, please, do what they say?"

The text message she sent on Calum's burner phone must have delivered to Detective Hawkes. Now Emily wishes it hadn't.

"Always knew the muzzle flash would be the last thing I'd see." Steve nods. "Come a lot later than I reckoned."

"Steve, please? Think of your children."

"After this, Sue will never let me near the girls again. Not in this life. Besides, they'll be better off without me."

"No, Steve, your girls need their father. Trust me."

Steve's expression softens. He's wavering, Emily can sense it.

"Drop the weapon and lie face down," the metallic voice booms, from the blinding glare of the helicopter searchlights.

"You can start again."

Steve gazes at the fading efflorescent dawn light and smiles. "It's too late."

"It's never too late. Like your mother said, you can always start again, no matter what."

"You can, Em, but not me. Malcolm was right, forgiveness is the only way." The words choke in his mouth. "Trouble is, I can't forgive myself. All of this is on me."

"This is your final warning. Put the weapon down, now."

Flat on her stomach, Emily watches, horrified, as Steve raises his pistol. "Steve no." She vaults to her feet as gunshots cackle, scything Steve into the river. Before she can scream, a searing pain hits Emily like a sledgehammer, ripping her into oblivion.

127

ROSA
20 September

D-Day. I perch on a bar stool in the Covent Garden Hotel, as I have countless times before, waiting for Gareth. Only this time it's different. This time, two suitcases rest at my feet. This time, I am leaving everything I hold dear. My home, my husband, my children, my life. What kind of person abandons their family for their own gratification? The question I've been asking myself these last months. Now I have the answer. Someone too cowardly to tell my family I'm leaving. I planned to last night at dinner. Prepared a speech and rehearsed it, but when the moment came, I couldn't bear to witness the pain on their faces.

Instead, I left a note on the kitchen table for Bruce to discover when he brings them home from school. I shut my eyes tight, the shame coursing through me like a flu-ache. As painful as it is to admit, I know the kids will be better off with Bruce. Less disruption staying with him in the family home, and with his relaxed hours at the university, better suited to parenthood than my all-consuming career. Especially now DCI Hughes has recommended me for promotion to his job when he retires early next year. Bruce was always the better parent, better partner, better person… I choke back a sob, dabbing my eyes with a bar napkin. I just hope they can forgive me…

I fill my lungs full of air, letting it out slowly, and as I often do now, I think of The Othello Club. Especially their dead partners. People just like me, trading their spouses, their families, their lives, their very souls, in exchange for happiness. Did they feel the anguish that I'm feeling, hurting the people they loved the most? In the end, they paid a price far greater than mine, but it brings me no comfort–

"Is this seat taken?" Gareth makes me jump. His familiar swaggering line, delivered with aplomb today.

"Yes." But, climbing off my stool, I realise. "Sorry... I can't do this anymore." I grip my suitcases and stride to the door, the tears already streaming my mascara.

As I duck into the taxi on Monmouth Street, Gareth calls my name, his footsteps scuffing the tarmac in pursuit. What kind of person?

Not me.

128

EMILY
21 September

"You have a visitor," the nurse says. From her smile, it isn't another police visit.

"My sister?"

The nurse has already gone, the sound of her shoes tapping along the hallway. As Emily struggles to sit up in bed, pain pierces her right shoulder, bandaged in a sling. A few inches lower, her surgeon said, the bullet would have passed through her heart. Lucky, he called her. Not a word she'd use to describe herself. Her facial wounds have faded to faint yellow bruises, but her shoulder pain is a constant reminder of her luck.

She feels nauseous again. The painkillers are wearing off. She could ask for a stronger prescription, but they would fuddle her brain, and with Detective Hawkes's constant interrogations, Emily needs clarity. Rosa, as she now knows her, has attended her bedside every day, spending many hours poring over Emily's story, compiling a chronological narrative of events and building psychological profiles of the Othello Club members who cannot speak for themselves. The dead appear in her waking thoughts like apparitions: Jack, Simone, Bex, Malcolm, Tal, Nick, Charlotte, Calum and Steve. In her sleep, she dreams of drowning, their bloated corpses writhing around her, grasping, pulling her into the depths. At the point of asphyxiation, a hand reaches for her, before she awakes, gasping for breath. Her saviour changes, altering between Steve, her father and Dan. Sometimes she sees Malcolm – the only innocent person in all this.

To the sound of the door handle opening, Emily brushes the matted strands of hair from her face and assembles a smile to greet Sara, but as her visitor steps inside, it falls from her face.

"Hello Em," Dan says, clutching a bouquet of blue irises.

Emily opens her mouth to speak, but no sound emerges. She must be dreaming, if not for the pain jabbing her shoulder. "Dan? What are you doing here?"

"I've been asking myself the same question." Dan shuffles to her bedside, his eyes red from lack of sleep, or crying, or both. "I just… with everything… I needed to see you." He wipes a tear with a shirt sleeve.

"It's alright." Emily chokes on her words. "I'm happy you did." Her own tears welling now.

"I got you these." Dan rests the flowers on her bedside table. "I know you like them."

"That was thoughtful. Thank you."

Dan nods in response, slouching on the bed, head bowed, sobbing silently. Emily tries to hug him, but her sling and the pain in her shoulder won't allow it. Instead, she rests her head on his chest, feeling his warm reverberations.

"I'm so sorry, Em… For all of it."

Emily unshackles herself painfully from the sling and folds her arms around him, combing his black hair between her fingertips. "It's not your fault, Dan." She pulls from the embrace, raising his bearded chin until their eyes meet. "It's mine."

"No." He shakes his head. "None of this would've happened if we hadn't... if I hadn't..." Dan's eyes glisten with tears. "Oh God, Em, can you ever forgive me?"

129

ROSA
17 December

The public gallery erupts with approval, most audibly from Ciara Devaney's family from Cork, and Emily Hunter's sister, Sara. As the judge calls for order, I stare at the Perspex-encased dock. Ciara is so overwhelmed, a custody officer supports her from collapse. Even behind the prosthetic mask and scarlet wig covering half her mutilated face, her relief is palpable. Who can blame her? From facing five years in prison, to a two-year suspended sentence for harassment, data protection and privacy law offences. Just as I predicted.

Emily maintains the same stoic expression she has throughout the four-day trial. Dressed in an expensive grey woollen suit, she wears the sling from her gunshot injury like an ambassadorial sash. A theatrical prop, no doubt, to elicit sympathy. *Bravo, girl*. I shake my head, still smarting from the judge's summing up. Not only did he advocate leniency for the defendants, given their physical and psychological scars, but he also criticised the police for a litany of failures leading to the shooting of Emily Hunter and the wrongful death of Stephen Fallon.

Given their generous sentences, it's a matter of time before their other surviving accomplice, Rachel Kaufman, slinks back from hiding. Rachel's lawyer has already reached out to the Home Office and the CPS, probing the judicial response for her surrender. But even if she does return to face trial, I doubt we'll ever learn the depth of Rachel's true involvement. The unsuspecting financier of the operation, as the defence suggested, or a darker, more pivotal role?

I turn towards the instructing solicitors' bench, seeking Gareth, speaking with the Crown Prosecution barrister. When he turns in my direction, Gareth tilts his head and smiles vaguely, a gesture of sympathy or embarrassment. As I smile back, he's already turned away. Sadness pulses through me.

At the foot of the steps outside the Inner London Crown Court, snowflakes flutter on the chilly breeze. I inhale the bracing cold into my lungs, lingering unfettered amongst the swarming reporters and television crews. They have no interest in me. Their only concern is the beautiful protagonist of the story, Emily, for whom they await her climactic exit from the court.

As Gareth steps through the doors my heart lurches, watching him merge into the throng. Accompanied by another prosecutor, he doesn't see me. He wouldn't stop if he had. We no longer talk outside of the job. The urge to shout after him is overwhelming as he strolls through the main gates, returning to his life that I won't be part of. I heard from a mutual friend that Gareth's wife is pregnant and they're giving their marriage another go. I love my children as only a mother can understand, but there isn't a moment I haven't regretted making another choice that day.

Love is brutal. My own words to Emily Hunter all those months ago. They goad me now, watching her stride from court to an encore of publicity, without justice for the victims, who had the courage I lacked. Emily crests the court steps with her ferrety solicitor, a flurry of snow announcing her arrival like confetti cast upon the victor.

"My client will make a brief statement." Her solicitor sounds as rodent-like as his visage. "And then I hope you will all respect her privacy in this difficult time."

Emily cranes her neck down to the jostling microphones. "Firstly, I want to extend my sympathy to the families of the victims. When I set out on this regretful journey, I never intended physical harm to anyone, and could have never anticipated the abhorrent actions of Talbot Vilmaz and Calum Greyson…" Emily shudders to a halt, as if choking on emotion. "Be that as it may, anger and jealousy consumed me. My counsellor, Malcolm Lindsay…" her eyes brim with tears "…turned me from that road and made me realise the antidote to betrayal isn't revenge, it's forgiveness. I intend to spend the rest of my life helping others steer from that destructive path, in the sincere hope that someday I can earn my own forgiveness. That is all I have to say."

The barrage of questions intensifies as Emily's solicitor leads her through the gauntlet down the court steps. Head aloft, in her four-inch heels, with those broad swimmer's shoulders, she towers above the haranguing troupe pursuing her to the car park.

A black BMW pulls up, the driver stepping out in a black suit, tall and obscenely handsome. A chauffeur, I assume, until recognition strikes me: it's Dan Hunter, Emily's ex-husband. His lips glance her cheek, before opening the passenger door. Inside, an auburn-haired little girl strapped to her child seat exchanges a wave with Emily. A gesture a mother and daughter might share.

"Mummy," the infant calls out to Emily. Her real mother's archenemy.

Realisation hits me, sucking the air from my lungs.

Emily's voice echoes from the therapy session recordings. "I just want my life back."

The revelation rocks me on my heels, only the jostling crowd keeping me upright. What if they weren't the regretful words of a victim, but a villain's statement of intent?

Emily stoops, folding her tall frame into the back seat, twisting her head owl-like, locking eyes with me, her green irises gleaming, malevolent and imperious. A predator's stare.

Bruce's words echo in my head. "Eventually you would glimpse that godlike egotism. Whether it's defiance, arrogance, or domination… it's usually evident in the eyes."

My mind gathers speed, recalling my own words. "You don't just become a serial murderer overnight, Bruce, you taught me that. There would be a pattern. A history of violence." The fragmented puzzle pieces mesh in my brain.

When I read the old case files of her father's murder, something about the evidence bothered me. The distraught thirteen-year-old Emily covered in blood when the police and paramedics arrived. She stated the blood came from hugging her father's corpse, but the bloodstain analysis report was contradictory. Her mother confessed, but she was blacked out on gin and Valium. An easy patsy to pin a murder on. Besides, what mother wouldn't take the fall for her child? What if Emily killed her father, as a reprisal for leaving her to be with his mistress? Since childhood, camouflaging her psychopathy by fabricating symptoms of trauma, faking emotion, empathy, even love.

Did Emily return to Jack Noble's hotel room, slip GHB into his drinks and watch... no, assist his autoerotic asphyxiation, tightening the ligature, robbing his brain of oxygen and his life?

With her height and broad shoulders, a sweatsuit bulking under her clothes, shrouded by the hoodie and Covid mask, Emily could pass for the man the witnesses described, fleeing the scene after squirting the acid in Isabella Jonsson's face.

Had she manipulated Tal from the start, exploiting his computer genius to doctor the CCTV and wipe her digital footprint? The morning after the restaurant fire, when DCI Hughes saw Emily in the crowd, was she reconnoitring the crime scene?

What if Calum didn't use Emily as his alibi, but the other way around? Whilst he shopped for breakfast, she made Mr Othello's appointment herself. As Bex gave her the tour, Emily shoved her off the balcony, baby and all.

When Malcolm suspected her psychopathy, she recruited Tal to eliminate him. Later, at Tal's flat, she slipped him a sedative, slit his wrists and torched the evidence.

With Steve's recognisance, knowing Nick Kamara's daily running routine, did Emily lie in wait for him in the forest? Her jade eyes the last he saw, as piercing and deadly as the blade splitting open his chest.

Was it Emily hidden in Dan's studio, stunning Charlotte with the hammer (the weapon of choice in her father's murder), then suffocating her with a pillow? Another mocking reference to the titular avenger.

Did Emily plant Bex's pendant at Calum's father's place, along with the survival knife that killed Nick, and the trove of incriminating items hidden in the tackle shed? Serial murderers often keep mementos from their victims, but all the same, it felt like an orgy of evidence. When Emily discovered the leather tome of *Othello* in Calum's father's bookshelves, it must have seemed too perfect. While Calum was out getting supplies, she could have easily scrawled the damning passages into the book. Especially convenient as Calum's fingerprints and DNA were already riddled throughout the pages. All she had to do was eliminate Calum and let him take the fall posthumously, but he awoke, thwarting her plan to murder him. When Calum discovered the vandalised book, he realised her game, and rather than risking his own culpability informing the police, attempted to handle her himself.

Luminous shock strikes me. I've been outplayed from the start. Manipulated like the rest. Without the surviving members of The Othello Club, I have constructed most of this story from Emily's version of events, her insight helping me to build psychological profiles of the others. "I am not what I am." Iago's words chill me to the core. Was Emily the real Iago, all along? A Machiavellian psychopath, spinning a labyrinthian fabrication to mask her vengeful master plan?

But already I can feel my hypothesis unravelling in its outlandish complexity. Emily had solid alibis for at least two of the murders. Unless... she had another accomplice? Some other patsy, beguiled like Tal, by her nefarious charms. But who? Over the clicking paparazzi cameras and the blood thrumming in my ears, I scour my memory: a friend, colleague, someone from the homeless shelter?

Through the passenger window, as the car peels away, Emily's irises glimmer, fathomless and impossibly green.

*"Oh, beware, my lord, of jealousy!
It is the green-eyed monster which doth mock
the meat it feeds on."*
             WILLIAM SHAKESPEARE, *OTHELLO*

Acknowledgements

Eternal thanks to Samantha Brace, my incredible agent, for betting on a newbie and championing me all the way to publication. A huge thank you to the wonderfully talented people at Peters Fraser and Dunlop, especially Rosie Gurtovoy and Ava Moore.

To my amazing editor Gemma Creffield, for your intuition, passion, and patience. And to Dan Hanks and Dan Coxon for your edits. Caroline Lambe, April Northall and the entire team at Datura, thank you for helping make my dream a reality.

To Jessica Connell, and everyone at Gaumont and Paramount+, for your enthusiasm and vision in bringing the book to the screen.

Thanks to Gary Lawrenson, criminal lawyer extraordinaire, for your legal and procedural insight, and for putting me inside a police interview room (figuratively speaking, thankfully).

My enormous gratitude to the divorcees who shared their candid stories with courage, humility, and humour. To all the lost and broken-hearted: hope awaits you beyond the crossroads ahead. Just beware of choosing the wrong path.

Last, but in no way least, a special thanks to my readers. I hope you will join me again next time.

About the Author

J.D. Pennington is an award-winning creative director and copywriter with over twenty years of experience in film and television advertising, creating campaigns for major studios and leading independents.

A native of Merseyside, he lives in Hertfordshire, United Kingdom with his wife, two children and a mischievous Patterjack terrier. *The Othello Club* is his first novel.

The Othello Club has been developed and adapted for television by Gaumont for Paramount+.

@j.dpennington 📷
www.jdpennington.com